MEN TOO RUGGED TO BE HARNESSED,
WOMEN TOO SPIRITED TO BE TAMED—
THESE ARE THE INTREPID AUSTRALIANS,
FULL OF FIGHT AND FIRE, FILLED WITH
AMBITIONS AND DREAMS

TOLO MASON—Young, large in size and spirit, his dream from childhood was to explore the arid red heart of Australia and learn the ancient lore of the native peoples . . . even if it meant facing risks few white men had survived.

JAVA GORDON MASON—A child of the new Australia, vivacious, daring, she was willing to follow her young husband to the back-of-beyond . . . to face men's lust, and hardships that no white woman had ever dared.

GANBA—Deadly and cunning, this outcast Aborigine hid his brutal desires behind a smile . . . luring the unwise, like the Masons, where they could be prey to unspeakable horror.

MATTHEW VAN BUREN—Stalwart and brave, this Aussie lieutenant saw only the joy of building a future with his wife, Kit Streeter. He was blind to the seduction that could entrap, enslave, and destroy Kit and him both.

GUINEVERE—Sensual, dangerously beautiful, this Eurasian princess was willing to escape the colonial outpost that had become her prison and the husband who had failed to give her the luxury she desired.

Other books in THE AUSTRALIANS series
by William Stuart Long

THE IMPERIALISTS

William Stuart Long

A DELL BOOK

 Created by the producers of
White Indian, The First Americans,
and **The Holts: An American Dynasty,**

Book Creations Inc., Canaan, NY • Lyle Kenyon Engel, Founder

Published by
Dell Publishing
a division of
Bantam Doubleday Dell
Publishing Group, Inc.
666 Fifth Avenue
New York, New York 10103

Produced by Book Creations, Inc.
Chairman of the Board: Marla Ray Engel

ISBN: 0-440-20648-0

Printed in the United States of America

Published simultaneously in Canada

June 1990

10 9 8 7 6 5 4 3 2 1

OPM

What's Australia? A big, thirsty, hungry wilderness, with one or two cities for convenience of foreign speculators, populated mostly by mongrel sheep and partly by fools.
—*Henry Lawson, Australian poet and storyteller*

One who would travel this country for pleasure would go to hell for a pastime.   —*R. T. Maurice, Australian geographer*

Australian History does not read like history, but like the most beautiful lies. It is full of surprises, and adventures, and incongruities, and contradictions, and incredibilities; but they all happened.   —*Mark Twain, an American tourist*

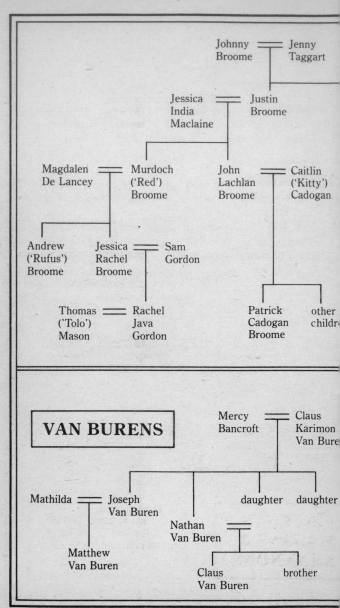

Johnny Broome ══ Jenny Taggart

Jessica India Maclaine ══ Justin Broome

Magdalen De Lancey ══ Murdoch ('Red') Broome

John Lachlan Broome ══ Caitlin ('Kitty') Cadogan

Andrew ('Rufus') Broome

Jessica Rachel Broome ══ Sam Gordon

Thomas ('Tolo') Mason ══ Rachel Java Gordon

Patrick Cadogan Broome   other childr[en]

VAN BURENS

Mercy Bancroft ══ Claus Karimon Van Bure[n]

Mathilda ══ Joseph Van Buren

daughter   daughter

Nathan Van Buren ══

Matthew Van Buren

Claus Van Buren   brother

© BOOK CREATIONS INC. 1989

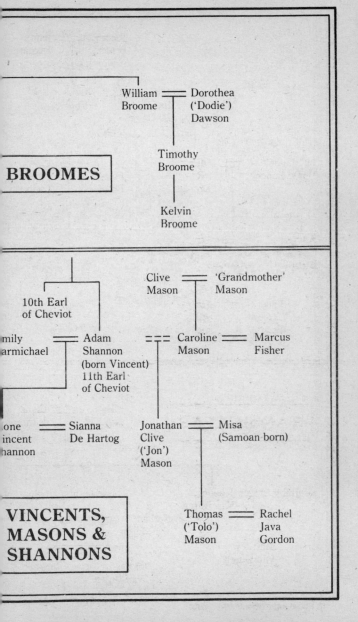

William Broome === Dorothea ('Dodie') Dawson

BROOMES

Timothy Broome

Kelvin Broome

Clive Mason === 'Grandmother' Mason

10th Earl of Cheviot

...mily ...armichael === Adam Shannon (born Vincent) 11th Earl of Cheviot

=== Caroline Mason === Marcus Fisher

...one ...incent ...hannon === Sianna De Hartog

Jonathan Clive ('Jon') Mason === Misa (Samoan born)

VINCENTS, MASONS & SHANNONS

Thomas ('Tolo') Mason === Rachel Java Gordon

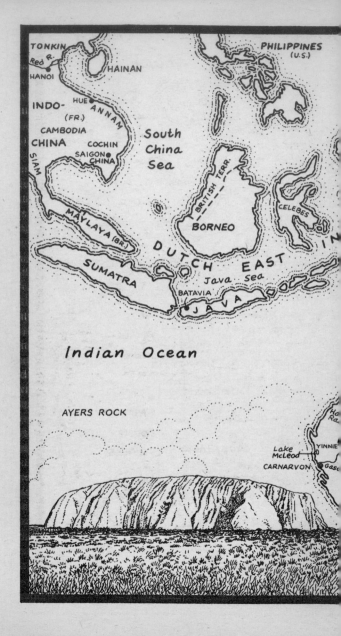

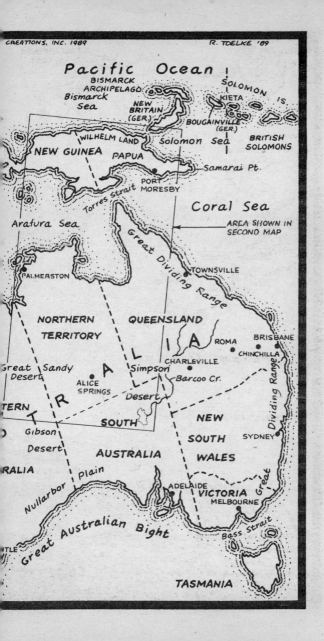

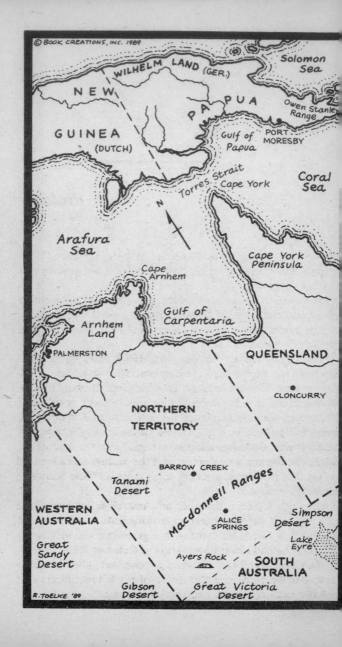

Prologue

"IF YOU ASK me, sir," said Lieutenant James Camber, "there are some parts of the British Empire that I'd just as soon give back to the natives."

Captain Andrew Broome, Royal Navy, turned to his junior officer and chuckled. "I think you have a point there, James, though I doubt the Colonial Office would see it your way, or the British people either."

Standing at the rail of his ship, HMS *Durable*, Captain Broome took in the scene before him. The vessel lay at anchor in Port William Inlet on East Falkland Island. Onshore the few clapboard houses of the town of Stanley overlooked the harbor, their roofs painted in gay colors, as if to offset the drab, chill landscape of this outpost of the British Empire. For the first time since *Durable* had steamed into the area of the Falklands, the sun was shining, and the captain was surprised to find that there was, after all, *some* color on these islands in the South Atlantic.

Although Captain Broome, an Australian by birth, had been baptized Andrew, his most striking feature—the rust-red hair inherited from his father—had given him the nicknames by which he had always been known, Rufus or Rufe. Indeed, he could not recall the last time anyone had called him Andrew, and he suspected that some of his fellow officers and men did not even know his true given name.

On deck he was a tall, formidable figure, bulky and snug i
his winter blues and cold-weather gear. His greatcoat colla
was turned up, and he stood with his hands in his pockets, hi
visored cap pulled low over his eyes. Even in the summertim
it could be chill in the latitudes beyond fifty degrees south.

"It takes a sailor to appreciate the extent of the empire
doesn't it, James?" Rufe commented.

"That it does, sir," the lieutenant answered.

"As for me," Rufe went on, "I'll be glad when this voyag
is over and we've reached home port in Sydney. D'you knov
that in my thirty-odd years in the navy I've barely set foot in
my native land? My family are mostly in Sydney now, and
haven't seen some of them more than half a dozen times in al
those years. It'll be good to be back there."

"I can imagine it will be, sir," the lieutenant replied. Then
seeing a hint of motion at the coaling station on the Stanle;
wharves, he lifted his binoculars. "Signal, sir. They're ready
for us."

"Very well," Rufe said. "Make preparations to get unde
way, Lieutenant."

The *Durable* was a Havoc-class torpedo-boat destroyer, al
though most Royal Navy men referred to her and her clas
simply as destroyers. She was 180 feet long, displaced 320
tons, and mounted three 6-pounders and a 12-pounder, in
addition to her three 18-inch torpedo tubes. She had been
built to serve defensively against enemy torpedo boats and
offensively as a torpedo boat to attack larger ships. Why a war
vessel was assigned to duty in these cold and largely empty
South Atlantic waters would have been a mystery to her cap
tain and her crew, except that wherever the British Empire
was, there, too, was the Royal Navy.

The empire in the Falklands was evidenced by the Union
Jack flying over the coaling station in Stanley. The empire
extended even farther south, across the Drake Passage to the
South Shetland Islands just above the Antarctic Circle and—
at least in claims—beyond that to Antarctica itself, to the

storm-driven snows and the eternal ice of the southernmost continent.

After taking on a full load of coal, *Durable* was covered with black dust. The crew, grumbling as all sailors do, turned out to spit-shine the ship, seeking out all the tiny places on deck tainted by coal dust.

The weather closed in with fog so thick that one could not see the brightly painted roofs of Stanley. Finally, when visibility permitted, Rufe took *Durable* out into the open sea. The Antarctic summer was coming, and Rufe's orders were to use the days of almost unending light to explore the seas around the icy continent. He set a course for the South Orkneys, sighting Coronation Island on a glowering day that threatened storm. Past the Orkneys he gave the order to steer due south, into that part of Antarctic waters known as the Weddell Sea.

Durable had not been designed for the comfort of the men who lived in her. The wind whistled through the open bridge, bringing with it the scent of the ice cap, and the officers' and the crew's quarters were inadequately heated. The ship pitched and tossed as around her the seas towered up, dwarfing her. When she was in the trough of a wave, her stacks were lower than the crest. The wind was holding at about force seven; on land such a gale would sway whole trees, but it was not unusual at sea, particularly in these latitudes.

As the icy swells grew in size, the seas reaching ninety feet, *Durable*'s passage became a carnival ride. She was quartering the swells, and that angle of attack gave her all of the motions that a floating body can achieve: up, twist, twist again, and level out momentarily, then dive, twist, and thunder down into the trough, with the cold spray driving all the way back past the forward gun turrets.

"Rather a spectacular show," Rufe Broome commented. Although he was all navy and had been since the age of four-teen, Rufe had an easy way with his junior officers, so long as they did not try to take advantage of his amiability.

"I'm quite sure there's a misunderstanding somewhere," James Camber replied. It was his watch, but the captain was on the bridge with him, both officers bundled into their cold-weather gear. "Are you sure our orders aren't to sail straight for the Coral Sea?"

Rufe laughed. "Too bad you're not the senior officer. If you were, I'd pretend ignorance and let you interpret our orders in just that way." Rufe would have liked nothing better than to have been able to sail straight to those balmy waters off Australia's northeastern shore.

The *Durable*'s job in the frigid Weddell Sea was to take weather observations and investigate the conditions of the ice packs. Afterward she was to proceed westward through the Drake Passage, sailing as close to Antarctica as weather permitted until she reached the Ross Sea and the Ross Ice Shelf —a frozen mass almost the size of France.

Down here at the bottom of the world a relatively short journey took a ship quickly across many degrees of longitude; accordingly, the run from the Weddell Sea to the Ross Sea would bring *Durable* from a point south of South America to a corresponding point southeast of Australia and New Zealand. After the tortuous haul past the Antarctic coast, Rufe would at least have the consolation of being nearer to home.

The exploration of high latitudes was a priority in naval circles, and other ships were doing the same as Rufe's. The fact that *Durable* had not been built for pushing through ice packs seemed not to have troubled the Admiralty. Fortunately, Rufe's orders were hedged with the words *if possible,* an escape clause that he would not hesitate to use if he needed it. He would turn back the first time the ice threatened, because if *Durable* were caught in the pack, her metal sides would be crushed much more easily than those of the specially constructed wooden ships used for Antarctic and Arctic explorations.

The men assigned to take the weather observations were doing their jobs efficiently. Sooner or later, when *Durable*'s readings in the Weddell Sea were compared with records she would make in the Ross Sea as well as simultaneous readings on other ships, scientists would have a more detailed understanding of the climate on various sides of the icy continent.

In the next half hour the wind swung a quarter of the way around the compass and peaked at force ten—whole gale. Now the huge swells hissed with white on the top, and they were closer together. *Durable* bucked and twisted, dived and wet herself back to the stern with frigid salt spray that, as the gale continued, began to freeze on the deck, riggings, and superstructures. Rufe gave orders to put the storm on her stern, steaming northeastward. It would have been more comfortable bracing the storm bow on, but that way lay the Palmer Peninsula and the offshore ice packs.

The sky was clear, and visibility was unimpaired. The wind blew out of some huge polar disturbance, and by morning the ship was badly iced, weighed down with tons of it. Rufe turned out the crew with axes to begin chipping away the increasingly dangerous burden.

The whole gale blew on unabated; on land such howling winds would have uprooted trees. The waves lifted *Durable*'s stern, swept under her, and let her fall backward off their crests. The men chipping ice had to be rotated often to prevent frostbite. Conditions underfoot were hazardous, for the decks were made perilous by the slick ice; men moved with difficulty, leaning on the wind, huge sheets of ice flying as they chipped at it with the axes.

The wonder of it was that the accident did not happen sooner. Suddenly an ax slipped off ice, then glanced with force into the knee of a seaman. Blood spurted from an opened artery as the man fell, moaning with fright, his hands clutching at his leg.

James Camber saw the incident from the bridge and raced down to the deck. Sailors tried to stanch the flow of blood, and a medical corpsman was arriving just as Camber reached the spot and began to shoo the sailors away. The corpsman tightened a tourniquet on the outside of the injured man's clothing and ordered that he be carried to the infirmary. Camber followed.

Once in the infirmary Camber had to swallow hard to keep from losing his breakfast while the corpsman bared the leg. The ax had severed the sailor's kneecap and cartilage, leaving the lower leg dangling by a thin strip of flesh and the tough tendons at the bend of the knee.

"There's work for a surgeon," the corpsman said.

"Not likely," Camber said.

The injured sailor was comatose.

"He'll pack it in if that leg isn't taken off and the bleeding stopped," the corpsman said. "There'll be a doctor at the whaling station on South Georgia."

"I'll speak with the captain," Camber said.

Hearing the report, Rufe Broome checked the charts and did some calculations. *Durable* was more than fifteen hundred miles from South Georgia and caught in the midst of an Antarctic storm. With his second-in-command, Lieutenant Camber, on the bridge, Rufe went below.

The injured man was awake but dazed with the morphine that the corpsman had given him. "How are you, son?" Rufe asked him.

"Doc says I'm going to lose my leg," the sailor said weakly.

"That's a fact," Rufe said. "There's a bit more to it, though. Are you man enough to face some hard truths?"

"Ain't got no choice, have I, sir?"

"Not much choice," Rufe confirmed. "The nearest sawbones is on South Georgia. One choice is to turn north and run for South Georgia, rolling in the troughs all the way and maybe, in the time it takes us to get there, having you bleed to death."

The man shook his head in negation.

"The other choice is for me and the doc, here, to cut through what little remains of that leg and tie off the arteries while we ride out this storm, and then head for South Georgia to have the doctor there neaten up what we've done." He put his hand on boy's shoulder. "I think you can see what we have to do."

The boy nodded grimly.

The nervous corpsman gathered tools and readied the ether. Rufe, dressed in a medical smock, hands and arms scrubbed thoroughly, surveyed the damaged leg as the corpsman administered the ether.

The tendons of the sailor's legs were surprisingly tough, requiring a lot of force before they were severed. Rufe worked with the corpsman as he located and tied off the main artery. Pressure slowed the bleeding from other veins, and when at last there was nothing more than a slow ooze into the bandages, Rufe wrapped the severed lower leg in a sheet, washed himself, and went back to the bridge.

Over the next few hours the ship came north gradually as the storm abated somewhat, but the rolls were still severe. The seaman's leg was buried at sea but without ceremony.

The South Georgia whaling station was a bleak, severe place made odoriferous by the rendering of whale fat and the dumping of refuse into the bay, where thousands of seabirds squabbled over the bits and pieces. The doctor in residence smelled of rum, but his hands were steady when he examined the seaman's stump.

"I wouldn't call it a neat job," the doctor said. He looked up at Rufe and smiled. "But you quite obviously saved the boy's life, Captain. And I've seen worse cutting by licensed doctors."

With the corpsman's help the doctor put the seaman to sleep again and trimmed up the stump, pulling skin down from the leg to suture over part of the raw flesh. The seaman was left on South Georgia in the whaling company infirmary to be under the doctor's care. *Durable* steamed southwest.

The detour to South Georgia Island had used up some of the time for exploring Antarctic waters. Rather than return to the Weddell Sea, *Durable* proceeded directly through the Drake Passage toward the Ross Sea, crossing the invisible line that marked the Antarctic Circle and circumnavigating a good portion of the globe as she made an arc past 150 degrees west longitude.

They entered the Ross Sea in weather so clear that the sky was a deep blue, unlike any sky that Rufe had ever seen. A distant soaring seabird gleamed like a white jewel in the brilliant sun, and the waves that rolled easily under the ship were as free of coloration as a chunk of freshwater ice. *Durable* made her cautious way through a field of free ice, passing bergs that were as large as a cathedral. The air was cold but intoxicatingly pure.

The gleam of snow-covered ice was on the horizon when, gradually, the sea began to turn to slush, and floes of shattered pack ice caused frequent changes of course. A shoal of penguins stitched its way past the ship, the trim little swimmers surfacing and diving, heading for the distant gleam of whiteness. A drifting floe banged *Durable*'s port bow with a force that made Rufe wary.

"Well, Lieutenant," he said to Camber, "it seems to me that this is as far as ice conditions permit."

"I came to that conclusion yesterday, sir," Camber said.

"Sort of anticlimactic, though," Rufe said. "Since we're this near, I'd like to see the ice shelf. Maybe just to say I've been that close to Antarctica."

"Let's pretend we got close enough to see the ice shelf and I swear that I'll never tell anyone you're prevaricating, sir."

Rufe sighed. He gave orders to bring *Durable* about. As if to prove that his decision to end the penetration of the outlying ice field had been correct, the skies darkened with fearful swiftness, bringing night in the middle of the Antarctic day. As the waves built, freezing rain coated the ship with an icy shroud. The slush through which the ship had been pushing began to freeze into a thin, hard crust of ice. Rufe ordered half speed ahead, and *Durable* breasted the waves, smashing her bow into them challengingly until, two days later, she emerged from the darkness of the storm into diminishing seas where there were merely sixty-foot smooth-topped swells.

Rufe took *Durable* just to the west of Macquarie Island southwest of New Zealand, bypassed Tasmania to the east, and in a climate more to his liking brought her slowly into her new port at Sydney Harbor. He had come home.

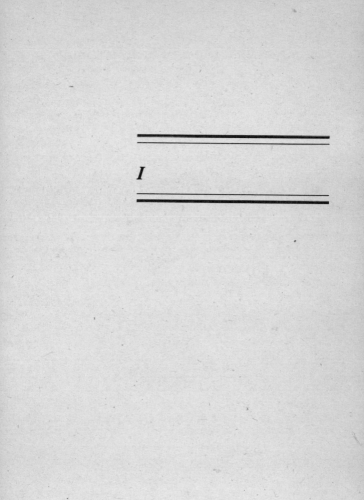

I

Chapter I
Western Australia

FOR THE THIRD straight season, drought held the land of the-snake-as-big-as-a-hill-walking-about in a red haze of heat, hunger, and thirst. The small tribal unit of the Baadu of Warrdarrgana, wandering far from the home given to them in the long-ago time of the Dreaming, suffered great privation. If it had not been for Ganba, they would have starved.

Still, the Baadu hated Ganba as much as they respected or feared him.

For a Baadu, Ganba was a hairy man, his features large and impressive. From his prominent fleshy nose and heavy-browed eyes, his forehead swept back in an almost flat plane to a shock of hair that was heavily greased and formed a pointed mass at the back of his head. His facial hair was stiff and dark, and his broad chest bore the sweeping scars of ceremony.

The old ones said that Ganba was large because as a boy, during another time of drought and hunger, he had been given his baby sisters to eat one by one, their fat being spread on his skin as protection against the burning sun. Ganba had accordingly grown faster than the other boys his own age, and he had been initiated into manhood with older youths who, in spite of their years, lacked his size and strength.

The flesh of Ganba's baby sisters had not only made him

broad and fat but given him a permanent taste for human meat.

No one in his tribe knew exactly what had formed Ganba's attitudes toward his fellowman, but it was said that he had never met a man, woman, or child that he liked. He had hated his natural mother, his various tribal mothers, and his older sisters and brothers as well. He would gladly have eaten them all, but that would have been impossible, for they were older and stronger than he. However, as soon as he had grown big enough, he regularly beat his mother and any other female who dared challenge his wants or needs. Once he blinded a young girl by throwing pebbles into her eyes, and he seemed proud of the deed.

For these reasons, when the time came for Ganba's initiation, the men who threw him into the air during the *wawarning* dropped him several times instead of catching him, and the blows they struck him were not merely ceremonial, as they were with the other boys. Ganba was furious but forgot his rage when it came time for the drinking of blood. All Baadu were blood drinkers, but few of them relished human blood as much as did Ganba.

After surviving the initiation ceremony, Ganba became, as he matured into manhood, a wearer of "murderer's slippers" —the ceremonial anklets, without soles, that were worn by those appointed to carry out tribal executions. He thus became a stalker of human game. He was also—in that time of direst hunger—the chief supplier of food for the small, displaced unit of Baadu.

Finally, as the sun continued to bake the land and no clouds formed in promise of breaking the drought, Ganba made two decisions. First, he would leave the land of the-snake-as-big-as-a-hill-walking-about, and second, he would not travel alone. Selecting a young, plump, hardworking woman, he told her family—he would not deign to ask—that she would be his wife. The bride price he offered was the food that he would supply.

Bildana, the young girl, was terrified, for she was not sure

whether Ganba wanted her as a bedmate or as a meal. She
wanted to run away and was prevented from doing so only by
her greater fear of unseen things in the bush—beasts and spirits that were even more terrifying than the possibility that she,
like several of Ganba's former wives, might end up in his cook
fires.

Unwilling to flee, Bildana appealed to her *kommuru,* her
mother's brother. "The killing of wives must be stopped," she
pleaded. "While it is true that women who wantonly give
themselves to any man may, by custom, be eaten in times of
hunger, Ganba's wives were chaste, and Ganba broke tribal
law when he killed them."

The *kommuru* nodded.

Ceremony was a vital part of the Baadu's life, as it had been
since the Dreamtime, when men walked the earth as kangaroo and barramundi and wallaroo. In this year of unrelenting
drought four young men were preparing for marriage along
with Ganba. During one phase of the drawn-out festival
Bildana's *kommuru* tried to kill Ganba.

The five men to be married were lined up facing the *kommurus* of Bildana and the other wives-to-be. The older men
held in their hands the livers of unfortunate members of another tribal group who had been slaughtered by Baadu hunt-
ers and thus had unwillingly joined the festivities. The young
men preparing for marriage had to catch pieces of raw liver in
their mouths as they were tossed by the *kommurus;* the
youths were forbidden to touch the slippery chunks of meat
with either hands or teeth. It was not an event to be taken
lightly, for if a man-to-be-married touched the liver with his
hands, or if he was observed using his teeth, or if he vomited
up the raw and bloody pieces, then he, too, would die and
become a part of the wedding feast.

Bildana's *kommuru* gradually increased the size of the
pieces of liver that he tossed into the gaping mouth of the man
who wanted his favorite niece. He was fervently trying to
force Ganba to miss, or to hit the meat with his hands or
teeth, or to gag and reject the larger and larger pieces.

To Ganba's left came a strangled cry. A young man, made frail by sickness and the long drought, bent at the waist and coughed up bloody bits of liver. From the darkness beyond the blazing fires a woman cried out in sorrow as a tribal elder struck the blow that was ordained by ancient ceremony. The frail young man would never know the pleasures of having a wife.

Ganba laughed and opened his big mouth to catch a still larger piece of liver tossed by Bildana's *kommuru*. He let the slick meat glide past his teeth and tongue, then swallowed convulsively. The fresh blood in the liver almost satisfied his thirst.

"Now you have failed, old man," Ganba mocked. The *kommuru* angrily hurled one last piece of liver, and Ganba swallowed it greedily, burped contentedly, and leered at the cringing Bildana. "But this one"—with one dusty foot he lifted the lifeless body of the frail young man who had died— "this one will not make much of a meal."

Bildana's wedding night was painful but mercifully brief. Ganba used her fiercely and then kicked her disdainfully away from him. She cowered as closely as she dared on the other side of the fire, shivering in the chill of the night. In the deathly quiet of early morning she rolled naked into the still-warm ashes of the fire and slept.

When Bildana learned her husband's intentions for her, she almost would have preferred to be eaten right away. Ganba planned a long walkabout to the west, all the way toward the swollen and blistering sun to the sea. For Bildana a march so far into the unknown with Ganba seemed a fate beyond enduring, and she was weeping and moaning as, laden with sun-dried human flesh, she followed her master into the sunbaked never-never.

At the last moment a few of the Baadu chose to join Ganba in his trek. Ganba sneered at them, taunting them and asking them how they intended to live during the crossing of the desert, for he had only enough food for himself and his wife.

"If these people come," he confided to Bildana, "they will be food we do not have to carry, food we do not have to hunt!" His wide mouth split in a satisfied grin that showed his rotting rear teeth.

Bildana shivered. She almost warned the fools who had chosen to accompany her husband that they were no more than a walking feast for him, but in the end she feared Ganba too much to betray him.

Soon the food that Bildana carried was gone. Hungry, fearful that she might be the first to satisfy Ganba's appetite, Bildana found herself rejoicing when one of the other women who had come with the group fell into a rocky crevasse. The woman lay there moaning, red blood spurting from both legs where jagged ends of broken bones had torn her flesh. Ganba scrambled down into the crevasse, swiftly dispatched the screaming woman, and began to butcher her on the spot, for to lift her bodily from the deep crevasse would have been difficult. Then he began to pass up the various pieces.

The woman's husband had made no protest, for he had quickly seen the necessity of Ganba's deed. Actually, it was merciful, for the injured woman would have died a painful, lingering death had not Ganba's ax ended her suffering. Now, at least, she would face the spirits of the Dreaming with the credit of having helped her fellows in a time of need by providing several days' worth of life-giving food.

Ganba's little group reached the hills near the sea and a white man's town built on a river. No further members of the band had been lost or killed, for as the group neared the coast, Ganba's spear had found targets in the form of kangaroos.

Now Ganba stood looking down at the town that the white men called Perth. There was movement in the streets, and in the harbor a small ship left a trail of black smoke as it made its way seaward.

"These whites," Bildana asked, "are they fierce?"

Ganba growled. As a young man he had encountered occasional groups of white men in the outback. He had watched as they brought down their meat with firearms, the magic smoke reaching out from the muzzles of their long black sticks and felling kangaroos at a distance many times greater than the strongest man's spear throw. He had hated the white men then, for he knew that they were intruders. But he had also coveted their weapons.

On one occasion he had seen a white man give another a shooting stick in exchange for round pieces of metal. An elder of his tribe explained to him about the white man's money, and again Ganba felt greed.

Now, as he looked down on Perth, he felt confident. "The white man will not harm us," he told Bildana. "We will go there and be among our own kind." He was pointing toward an outlying district of dilapidated dwellings called humpies, poor houses constructed of all sorts of discarded white man's material.

When he led his companions into the shantytown, Ganba found that the people who lived there were representative of several tribal groupings. Various dialects were spoken, with a sort of fractured English being the accepted way for one tribesman to communicate with another of different dialect.

Ganba did not know, nor would he have cared, that the original coastal Aborigines had long since succumbed to the white man's weapons and diseases and that the present inhabitants of the humpy town were, like himself, outsiders who had drifted in from the arid interior. Nor did Ganba know that Western Australia, as the white man called Ganba's native lands, was now part of a unified continent-wide nation, the Commonwealth of Australia. Ganba knew only two things: He wanted to get his hands on the white man's goods, and in order to do so, he would be obliged either to earn the white man's money or to steal it. Stealing lay more within Ganba's talents, but he knew ways of earning money, too.

Ganba ousted a weaker man and his family from a poorly built house, and by a combination of bullying, cheating, and stealing, he managed to scrounge enough food so that the group was adequately fed and Bildana's buttocks remained attractively plump. That was desirable, since Ganba had plans for her.

Going down to the waterfront, Ganba watched the comings and goings of ships until a Japanese pearling boat docked and chattering little men scurried ashore. The brown-skinned men were met by a grim, grizzled, fierce-looking Abo man with a plump-bottomed girl at his side, a girl who, they were told, was for hire.

For as long as the Japanese ship was in port, Ganba lived well. But then the Japanese vessel left, and subsequent ships brought only white men, most of whom had no taste for Aboriginal girls. Eventually white constables caught and punished Ganba for stealing, and when he was released from the white man's jail, there was no food in the humpy. He ached for a real meal of half-roasted human flesh; but the white man's law ruled Perth, and he dared not risk that sort of hunt.

It was at that juncture in his life, when he was almost ready to give up and go back into the never-never, that he heard of the young white man who was looking for a guide into the interior.

Chapter II

THE AGENT IN Perth representing the interests of Misa Mason and the far-flung Mason business holdings was Robert Endicott, barrister, businessman, and family man. Endicott hated Austrialia—particularly Western Australia—with a passion that he vowed would last forever, if the good Lord granted him eternal sentience. A well-built middle-aged man, he affected a neatly trimmed goatee separated from side whiskers by an area of almost unnaturally pale English skin, and he went about the town dressed—or so said the fair dinkum I-am-very-damned-definitely-Australian types—like a London whoremaster.

Endicott was worried.

When the son of the woman who had inherited Jon Mason's business empire appeared suddenly in the outer office, accompanied by his young bride, the agent was caught off guard. The Mason business in Perth consisted largely of routine shipping, day-to-day necessities coming in and raw materials and foodstuffs going out; the traffic constituted but a small part of the Mason trading enterprises. But Jon's widow had acquired a reputation for ruthless efficiency, for after taking over her husband's business, Misa Mason had purged it of corrupt employees and had dismissed a few of the independent agents as well. Endicott himself was scrupulously honest in his dealings, but since his law practice in Perth was not all that remunerative, the generous fees that he charged for the work of handling the Mason ships made up an important part of his income. Mrs. Mason, living at a safe distance across the continent in Sydney, had never questioned those charges, but perhaps that was about to change.

As Endicott nervously watched Thomas Mason come through his door, he was impressed at once with the youth's most obvious feature—his size. Young Mason had taken his height and bulk from his mother's Samoan forebears, and he towered over the older man. His broad shoulders, though well fitted with an expensive business suit, seemed ready to burst through the cloth, and they seemed almost menacing to Endicott, who at five feet eight inches and 150 pounds was the average size for a man of his generation.

Endicott eyed the youth appraisingly. Under a shock of jet black hair Thomas Mason's face was well formed, the skin only slightly darker than that of any white man who had spent most of his time in the bush. His nose was narrow—very English, like his father's—and his eyes were dark brown. The young man stood easily, his natural poise an overt expression of his self-confidence.

It was a full thirty seconds before Endicott turned his attention to the young girl clinging to Thomas's arm, her head coming only to his shoulder, and when he did so, he was taken aback by her radiant beauty. He had to clear his throat awkwardly before he could stammer a greeting.

Red-haired Java Gordon Mason was only eighteen, but she possessed the radiance and poise of a happily married matron. The recent voyage around Australia from Sydney had browned her face, in spite of her care to protect herself from the sun, but the tan was becoming. She wore a sensible traveling gown of dark blue, and the hand that clung to her husband's arm was delicate, the fingers long and the nails well manicured.

She fixed her eyes on Endicott as if taking the measure of the man and then, evidently satisfied with what she saw, lifted her face to her husband, whom she addressed as Tolo. The look in her eyes made the older man uncomfortable. It was like that with some young couples: At odd moments they seemed to exude an aura of sexual energy, a disquieting passion that might rouse envy and covetousness in younger men but that in Endicott's case caused only a smile of empathy followed swiftly by a hint of sadness. That youthful flame, he thought, would all too soon consume itself of its own intensity.

"Ah, Mr. Mason," Endicott said, stepping around to the front of his desk to shake the young man's hand. "It is a great honor and pleasure to have you visit us." He cleared his throat again. "I had a communiqué from your mother only last month." He took a deep breath. "Or was it the month before?"

"We're not here on Mason business," Tolo replied.

Endicott sighed with relief that Mason would not be prying into his books, but then he was puzzled. Perth was not noted as being a health spa or a holiday spot. "How may I be of assistance?" he asked finally.

"Our intention is to travel into the interior," Tolo replied flatly. "I want to study the Aborigines."

" 'Strewth," Endicott said. "You can't be serious!"

"Quite serious," Java confirmed.

"I might want to draw on cash reserves in your accounts for the purchase of equipment," Tolo added.

Endicott merely nodded. He suspected that the son of the extraordinary woman who handled the Mason business affairs knew absolutely nothing about the murderous bush that crowded Perth against the sea, but it was not his place to begin the young man's education. "You will need a guide," he said.

"Yes. Have you anyone in mind?" Tolo asked.

"As a matter of fact, yes," Endicott said. "His name is Terry Forrest. I should guess that he knows more about the outback than any man alive." His face flushed. It seemed almost indelicate to refer to survival when it seemed likely to him that Thomas Mason, in spite of his size, would probably die if he insisted on traveling into the interior. It would be a shame, he thought, if the young fool took his pretty wife with him to shrivel in the heat and to die of thirst and starvation. But he was the Mason agent in Perth, and the son of the owner had asked a service of him. He would provide.

Tolo and Java had arrived in Perth only a day earlier, the ship having made port in Fremantle's spacious harbor in the early, sunny hours of a day in May, giving them plenty of time to make the twelve-mile journey by launch up the Swan River to Perth Water, the broad bay that fronted the city.

Now that the adventure was under way, Tolo had lingering doubts. After the long, quiet, blissful months that he and Java had spent on the Mason homeplace, a time when he did not have to share Java with anyone, he could almost resent the presence of other people. Java, however, was thriving on it. She had enjoyed the trip around the southern coast of Australia. She knew the names and the life histories of the officers and most of the crew on board the Mason Line ship. She loved meeting new people and looked forward to their arrival in Perth. She, more than Tolo, had been responsible for their leaving the cattle station, for she had been eager to get on with the expedition to Western Australia.

It was, in fact, not their first visit to Perth. Nearly two years earlier, when Java was not yet seventeen, they had eloped, causing a family crisis in the Sydney home of Java's parents, Sam and Jessica Gordon. The elopement had been impulsive, but Tolo had carried it out wisely—bringing his bride to Perth, beyond the reach of the laws of the state of New South Wales, in case the Gordons should seek to have the marriage annulled because Java was a minor.

Tolo had considered taking his bride directly to the old Mason station outside Melbourne. There they would also be outside the Gordons' legal reach, but Sam could, if so minded, follow the couple to the station to retrieve his daughter. No, Tolo reasoned, it was better by far to take Java as far away as possible, to an unknown place.

As it happened, Sam and Jessica took no steps either to pursue Java or to counter the marriage. Instead, Sam advised his distraught wife to resign herself to having her daughter wed; Tolo, after all, was not a bad sort. He had the look of success about him; indeed, he had already proven himself an able land purchaser and would most likely be a good provider and a loving husband.

These sentiments were included in a letter that Sam posted to Java in care of the Mason Shipping Company, having no other address for her. The letter finally caught up to her in Perth, and reassured by its contents, she and Tolo decided to go back to the Mason station outside Melbourne—the home where Tolo, as a boy, had first heard the wondrous tales of the Aboriginal Dreamtime.

In the next few months Java learned to love the station almost as much as her husband did. More letters went back to Sydney, always answered by Sam, the replies full of expressions of his love—and Jessica's, too, though Jessica herself did not write. Java noticed that omission, and it pained her; she longed to see her mother, both her parents, in fact, believing that she would never entirely make her peace with them until she saw them face-to-face. And she longed, too, to see her grandmother, Jessica's mother, Magdalen, whose letters, though less frequent, were both loving and full of commonsensical advice on married life. But somehow the months slipped by, the young couple being absorbed in their happiness and the routines of the busy station. Tolo proved himself to be a capable young manager, never too proud to learn the finer points of running a large spread from the old hands who had served his family for many years.

Tolo wrote to his mother, Misa Mason, now permanently residing in Sydney. She had been startled at first by the elopement but then was happy for her son, praying that his life's course should not be difficult because of the sudden step he had taken. As a full-blooded Samoan she had encountered her own share of prejudice among white Australians, and in her mind racial considerations had no place in matters of the heart—or in any other matter either. In these liberal leanings she was encouraged by her friend and business partner, Bina Tyrell. Together the two women toasted the young couple in absentia in a celebratory dinner at Bina's fashionable restaurant, an event that Misa described to Tolo in a letter, adding that she hoped to do the same again with him and his bride present whenever they felt ready to return to Sydney.

After more months of blissful residence at Tolo's old home, Java began to grow restless. She was eager to travel, and she also thought that if Tolo was going to study the Aborigines, as he claimed he wished to do, he should not put it off any longer. The station, in the hands of its experienced employees and overseer, could run itself. So she nudged her husband to take their second trip to Western Australia.

Arriving in Perth, they found the accommodations no better this time than on their earlier honeymoon journey. Although Tolo could well afford to pamper himself and his wife, money could not buy luxury when it did not exist. The hotel was barely adequate, but at least the room was clean, and it had a wonderfully soft double bed, which Tolo and Java put to excellent use.

After calling on Robert Endicott, they had to wait a few days until their prospective guide could be located and a meeting arranged. Tolo and Java used this time to revisit many of Perth's sites, which on their first trip they had only half seen through the hazy glow of honeymoon happiness. Tolo, voracious reader though he was, found his literary appetite matched by his wife's, so both were by now well versed in Perth's history. Walking its streets, they examined the three-story Tudor-style gateway of the headquarters of the Enrolled Pensioner Forces, the soldier-settlers who had founded Perth. The archway and the clock tower of the city hall, built by convict labor, were splendid examples of intricate Flemish bond brickwork. Near the town stood King's Park, an area of natural bush set aside years earlier so that children could, a

thousand years hence, see what the bush had been like when
the first settlers arrived.

The parklands and the town itself lay along the lower
reaches of the Swan River. At Perth Water, where the Swan
River widened to over half a mile, they saw a myriad of small
sailing craft and barges as well as the steamships that ferried
passengers down to the port at Fremantle.

It seemed a pleasant place, Perth, the temperature quite
comfortable as Java and Tolo strolled through the often narrow streets, observing the people, who were a mixture of
roughly dressed outdoor types and neatly cravatted businessmen. But then, one morning, as they were walking toward the
outskirts of town, the scene changed abruptly. Stopping, they
looked down a slight slope at a jumble of makeshift huts, the
humpies belonging to Perth's Aboriginal inhabitants.

The dilapidated buildings were arranged in no discernible
pattern. Most were nothing more than ragged pieces of canvas
over bush timber frames; only a few of the sturdier dwellings
had corrugated iron roofs. All of them, Tolo reckoned, had
nothing more than dirt floors.

The scene was one of unbelievable chaos and poverty.
Blackfellows moved about among the buildings or lounged
half dressed in whatever bit of shade could be found. Naked
potbellied children played in the midst of the incredible filth
of rank bones splintered to remove the marrow, rotting garbage, and the offal of man and beast.

For a long time neither Tolo nor Java spoke. Then Tolo
took Java's arm and turned her to walk away, to put the
humpy town behind them, to hide it safely from sight behind
the neatly kept homes of Australia's white masters. It was
Tolo who finally broke the silence.

"These people come to the cities because they've had a taste
of what our so-called civilization has to offer—alcohol and
tobacco mainly. They want other material things we have, but
they don't have the knowledge or skills for earning the money
to buy them. So they're reduced to eating the leftovers from

our refuse cans and wearing our cast-off clothes. And they die of diseases as mild as measles."

Java would have been forced to admit that her interest in the original peoples of her continent was not as fervid as her husband's. She could pity them, of course, and decry their lot, but she could not altogether fathom Tolo's fascination with them. What was it about the man she loved that made gaining knowledge about this unfortunate race of people so important?

It could only be his own mixed blood, she had concluded long before she saw the humpy town on the outskirts of Perth. He had told her that he was no longer bothered by insults against people of brown or black skin. But she knew his temper, and God help the man who made a racial slur against Samoans in Tolo's presence, particularly if it touched upon his mother, full-blooded Samoan that she was.

Java's love for Tolo had begun, she knew, in sympathy, for she was mature enough to understand her own weaknesses. His struggle against the color barrier had touched her from the start. She had been reared in a house where open discussions on every subject were the rule, and she had heard both sides of the race question. She had listened to the writer Henry Lawson, one of the most vocal and visible advocates for a White Australia, who believed the Aborigines were a dying race, and good riddance to them. And she had also heard from some religious leaders the often febrile arguments in favor of human equality. She considered herself liberal in her own racial attitudes. After all, had it not been for an old man of dark brown skin—a near savage who lived in a hut in the highlands of Java—she herself might not be alive. The man had rescued her mother when Jessica, pregnant with Java, had nearly been killed in the eruption of Krakatoa and the tidal waves that followed. With the help of the women of his village, the old man had nursed Jessica back to health and seen to the safe delivery of her baby.

So Java could be interested in Aboriginal lore, but that did not necessarily mean that left to her own devices, she would have gone to any great effort to hear the tales of the Dreaming from the lips of a descendant of one of Australia's first inhabitants. True, she found some of their myths touchingly amusing in their naiveté and simplicity, but some of the stories struck her as repetitious and lacking in imagination.

Nevertheless, Java was ready and willing to follow Tolo into the far never-never simply because he was her husband, the man she loved, and she would help him in his chosen calling. She did not doubt for a second that he would accomplish his avowed goal of making a thorough study of Aboriginal life and putting his findings into print. And because she had been a part of Australia's intellectual awakening in the 1890s, she did not question the value of knowledge for its own sake. Though she could not bring herself to apply the word *culture* to the blackfellows' way of life, she believed that Tolo's desire to record their myths and legends, their chants and customs, was laudable; his research would be a gift to the future. When the native Australians had died out completely, scholars could go to the book that Tolo would write to study the quaint beliefs and customs of an extinct race. And extinct they soon would be, she suspected, for one look at the humpy town had persuaded her that the Aborigines could not survive in the modern world. The theories of Darwin seemed to be at work: The fittest for modern life—the whites—would live, while the blackfellows would perish.

Her thoughts had thus grown somber by the time they returned to their hotel, where they were due to meet with the guide whom Endicott had recommended. Pausing in the lobby, Tolo pulled out his watch and wound it as he checked the time. "Want a bit of tea before this fellow Forrest arrives?"

"That would be lovely," she agreed. The idea of something so civilized as tea, after they had seen the humpies, was heaven to her.

The hotel dining room was not crowded. The prenoon customers were mostly male, and all eyes were drawn to Java by her assertive stride and proud stance, the beauty of her face and hair. Some took a second look at the bronzed face of the big man who escorted her. One man leaned forward, whispering, to his companion, but he let his eyes fall away when Tolo stared directly at him.

Terry Forrest arrived before they had finished their first cup. From the moment he entered the large room Java knew that he was the man they had arranged to meet. Tall and sandy tan, he paused to speak to the headwaiter, then crossed the room with an easy gait, removing his wide-brimmed bush hat to reveal curly, short-cut hair. His eyebrows had the look of having been permanently bleached by the desert sun, and under blond lashes his eyes were the ice blue of the waters she and Tolo had traversed in the Bass Strait.

"G'day, mate," Forrest said as he reached the table. As Tolo rose to take his hand, Forrest grinned widely at him. "Well, ain't you the stud horse. Ain't often I have to look up to see a man's eyes."

"How do you do, Mr. Forrest," Tolo replied. "Won't you sit down?"

"Pleasure," Forrest said, but first he bowed to Java. "And this is Mrs. Mason?"

"My wife," Tolo confirmed.

Tolo waited to sit down until Forrest had taken a chair and then tossed his hat carelessly onto the seat of the fourth, unoccupied chair at the table. Forrest's eyes were on Java, making a frank appraisal. His broad grin made it evident that he liked what he saw.

"So you want to go walkabout in the land of drought and disappointment," Forrest said. "At least, that's what Endicott told me."

"Yes, that's right," Tolo replied. "My intention is to study the nomadic Aborigines in the wild."

Forrest looked up at the ceiling and remained silent.

"Mr. Endicott said that you know the deserts as well as any man," Tolo said.

"As well as any whitefellow," Forrest said. "Know 'em well enough to stay out of 'em."

"I would be willing to pay you well, Mr. Forrest, if you could bring yourself to guide us into the Nullarbor."

"That's the last place you want to go if you're hunting Abos," Forrest replied. "Nothing there but saltbush and bluebush and Jeedarra."

"Jeedarra," Tolo said, "the mighty, magic snake that eats men."

Forrest squinted his eyes and looked closely at Tolo. "That's right, mate. The blackfellow might chase a kanga a few miles into the Nullarbor, but he'll bloody well get his arse out of there before the sun sets, 'cause if he's caught there after dark, Jeedarra gets him or he's sucked down a blow-hole."

Java spoke for the first time, and Forrest's eyes watched her lips, a musing smile on his face. "I'm familiar with the mighty magic snake," she said, "but I haven't heard of—what did you call it?—a blowhole."

"You find 'em miles and miles from the coast," Forrest said. "Whole Nullarbor Plain is riddled with caves and under-ground passages. Some of 'em are directly connected to un-derwater caves on the coast, so that the movement of the water might make a strong wind blow out of one hole to hell and gone in the middle of the Nullarbor and suck the hot air of the plain down into another hole. Some of them make a sound like thunder."

"Where would we find nomadic Aborigines, then, if not in the Nullarbor?" Tolo asked.

Forrest sighed and ran his sun-browned hand through his kinky sandy hair. "Let me tell you, mate," he said. "I came over here expecting to find a Sydney poofter out looking for a thrill in the wild, wild outback. Maybe even an Abo hunter. We still get a few of those, city blokes who think that the blackfellow's a relic, an obstacle to be removed from the path of white progress, you know?"

"You don't mean you . . . *hunt* them?" Java asked, her voice rising.

"Oh, no. That's against the law of our united Australia,

nissy. 'Course, now and again some of us have been known to *mprove* a few Abos."

"Improve?" Java said in a shaky tone.

"Improve them off the face of the earth," Forrest said. "Shoot 'em. We're a little, ah, old-fashioned out here. Still go by the original motto of the early settlers, you see: If it moves, shoot it; if it doesn't move, cut it down."

"Tolo," Java said, her face flushed in shock, "I don't think Mr. Forrest is quite the man we need."

But Tolo merely squeezed her hand under the table and winked at her.

"As I was saying," Forrest said, "you're not at all what I expected. You don't want to go Abo hunting, and you're not after gold?"

"No," Tolo said. "We want to travel with the Aborigines, study their way of life, their myths, their customs."

"I'm afraid, mate, you'll have to do it without me." Forrest reached for his hat. "Mind you, it's no affair of mine, but were you, I'd go talk to a few of the tame blackfellows in humpy own. For a bottle of booze or a few coins you'll find a dozen Aboriginal males who have legitimate claims to being men of high degree—that's what they call their wise ones. They'll talk and chant your ears off."

"Thanks for the suggestion," Tolo said. "But we've already seen those people. We'd be better off getting our information from people who haven't been tainted by contact with the white man."

Forrest looked into Java's eyes. "And you're going out here with him?"

"Yes, of course," she said quickly.

Forrest shook his head. "They'll make meat food of you," he said, leaning toward her and lowering his voice. "They won't rape you. That's not their style. Their primary aim is to stay alive in one of the most hostile areas inhabited by man, and they won't waste time using your body carnally. No, they'll butcher you as if you were a pig. They'll extract the fat from your kidneys and rub it onto their skin for the smell and to keep the skin from baking in the sun."

"That's enough, Mr. Forrest!" Tolo interposed.

"Yes, I suppose it is," Forrest said, rising. "But the humanity in me forces me to make one last statement, Mr. Mason. You're a bloody fool if you go out there and start looking for wild boongs, and a double fool if you take this lovely sheil with you. If the boongs don't have you for dinner, the desert will kill you. It's killed better men, even if they weren't as big as you." He was holding up one hand as if asking for peace as Tolo jerked himself up out of his chair.

"Thank you, Mr. Forrest," Tolo said, his voice rising.

"Another final word."

"You seem to have no end of them," Tolo countered.

"If you must go looking for wild boongs, the Gibson is the place for you to go. Starting, maybe, from Carnarvon."

"That's five hundred miles up the coast," Tolo said, interested in spite of his irritation.

"That'll save you a lot of walking," Forrest said, turning away.

"Mr. Forrest," Java said. He turned. "Won't you please reconsider my husband's offer to take you on as a guide?"

Forrest walked back to the table, hat in hand, and looked down. "Change of heart, eh?" he asked, smiling. "Well, darlin', let me tell you, I have considered it."

"I'm sorry you're not interested," she answered.

He sat down again, put both elbows on the table, leaned toward her. "The Gibson Desert is named for Alfred Gibson, and as you probably know, they don't usually name places after a bloke until he's dead. Gibson is. Not so long ago he died trying to cross that desert. Believe me, it's four hundred miles of hell. There's nothing there but rock and sand and heat and a few sprigs of spinifex grass. Just as soon as you leave Carnarvon, you're in the Gibson, and then there's nothing between you and Ayers Rock, in the Northern Territory. I mean nothing."

"That's the great rock that's sacred to the Aborigines?" Java asked.

"That's right, Mrs. Mason. It's huge, over a thousand feet high. You can see it for miles around."

"Have you crossed the Gibson?" Tolo asked.

"I have."

"Mr. Forrest, I won't be robbed, but I'm not averse to paying any fair price you want to name, if you'll accompany us," Tolo offered.

"As I told your missus," Forrest said, "I *have* considered it. To tell the truth, I am very tempted. Let's say I did go along with you and we made it, say, two hundred miles into the never-never and found you some wild boongs and they had you for dinner. That would leave just me and the little sheila, right?"

"Do you make it a practice to insult people?" Java asked, seeing Tolo tense and trying to head off a confrontation.

"Only hardheaded half-breeds," Forrest said.

Forrest was fast, but the blazing speed of the young man, now on his feet, surprised even the seasoned bushman. He had a protective hand only halfway up before Tolo's fist connected with the side of his jaw.

Forrest went down heavily. The action had been so swift that hardly anyone had noticed, and then a waiter, making little sounds of distress, was hovering over the motionless body of the big bushman.

"Get some help," Tolo said, "and carry Mr. Forrest into the lounge. Perhaps you might call a doctor."

The waiter started to scurry away. "And," Tolo called after him, "please send someone immediately to take our luncheon order."

Java watched, wide-eyed, as two waiters struggled with Forrest's inert bulk. Tolo winked at her. "I think your first instinct was right," he said, smiling. "He's not our man."

In the lounge a doctor was bending over Terry Forrest, waving smelling salts under his nose and lifting one eyelid to check the pupil. Forrest groaned and began to stir, and in a few minutes he was sitting up. He looked toward the arched door leading to the dining room and started to stand, but he sat back down weakly as his head went aswirl. When he was at last able to stand and walk, he reentered the dining room.

Tolo and Java were eating kanga tail soup. Tolo put down his spoon and prepared himself as he saw Forrest approach.

"Mate," Forrest said, "last time I was hit that hard was by the kick of a mule. I didn't know you'd be quite so sensitive about, ah, your breeding?"

"If that's an apology, I accept," Tolo said, his voice low and even.

"Oh, it isn't," Forrest said. "Not for one bloody second. It was simply an admission that you've got quite a punch." He grinned down at Tolo. "It almost makes me want to go up to Carnarvon with you, because once we were in the desert, we'd have ample opportunity to see whose arse is the blackest, as they say. But that would be sort of like going to hell to punish the body for shivering in the cold, wouldn't it? No. If you by some chance survive, maybe we'll run into each other again, eh, mate?"

"It's possible," Tolo said.

"So," Forrest said. "As Ned Kelly said when they put the noose around his neck, such is life."

Tolo watched the tall, tanned man walk away. "Too bad," he said. "I think he'd be a good one to have with us."

"I think all he has is flashness," Java said.

He grinned. "Picking up a bit of the Strine talk, are we, mate?"

Two days later, on the curb outside his hotel, Tolo met the Aborigine who had requested a meeting with him. The man, who called himself Ganba, would, of course, not be allowed in the lobby.

"Sir, you want guide to never-never?"

Tolo saw a typical blackfellow, perhaps a bit taller than

most, thicker in the chest and more powerful in the arms and legs.

"I will need blackfellows for porters," Tolo said.

Ganba looked puzzled.

"Blackfellow carry," Tolo said, making the motion of putting a load onto his back.

"This blackfella not carry," Ganba said, insulted and drawing himself up to stand rigidly. "This Ganba"—he thumped himself on his bare, ritually scarred chest—"Ganba is guide. Best bloody guide you find."

"I see," Tolo said. "Then you know the Gibson?"

"Know what whitefella call Gibson," Ganba said. "Know all the way to the great-red-sacred-rock."

Tolo had made a few more futile attempts to find a suitable white guide into the Gibson Desert, and he was about ready to move his base up the coast to the little northwestern town of Carnarvon. "Your name is Ganba?"

Ganba nodded.

"Ganba, I look for blackfellows live in bush."

"I find. Know all blackfellas in Gibson."

Tolo talked with the Aborigine for a few minutes more. Tolo knew very little about the desert himself, although he had traveled the bush in drought-ridden New South Whales. He tried unsuccessfully to think of questions to ask Ganba, to verify the fellow's statement that he knew the Gibson well. He was seriously considering taking a chance on the man. He could take him to Carnarvon. Perhaps there would be a white guide there, and if not, he would at least have Ganba.

"I'll think about what you've said," Tolo said finally. "How can I see you again?"

"You not see me, I see you," Ganba said.

"Tomorrow, then," Tolo told him.

In their room Tolo discussed the situation with Java. "The problem is we know nothing about this Ganba," he said, "and there's no way that I can see to verify his claim to know the territory."

"Do we have much choice?" Java asked.

Tolo grinned. He had learned from experience that his wife had a way of cutting through to the essence of a matter when he himself tended to be indecisive. "No choice at all," he agreed. "I'll go over to Endicott's office and arrange for a small vessel. I don't think we'll want to wait for a coastal steamer. We should go now, so we can do our desert traveling in the winter months, not in the heat of spring or summer."

It seemed advisable to outfit the expedition in Perth, for Carnarvon was only a small town. For three days they busily organized supplies, loading the equipment and preserved foods onto the small steamer that Endicott had found for them. They tried desperately to make Ganba and the Aborigines he had brought with him understand that if they would only help load the gear, the expedition could get under way faster. In the end Ganba persuaded his people to work, while he himself acted as longshoreman's boss, screaming imprecations at Bildana and the others if they slowed their steps.

Once the vessel was under way and into the Indian Ocean, Ganba and his people slept on the deck, quickly turning it into a seagoing imitation of the cluttered humpy town at Perth. Ganba had selected, in addition to himself and Bildana, three young couples, all of whom were fed up with life in the humpy town. The women of the group were surprisingly plump. Unbeknownst to Tolo or Java, Ganba had brought them just in case the huge amount of food purchased by the white man was spoiled or lost.

Terry Forrest told himself that he had not intentionally made his way to the small docks on the shore of Perth Water to get another glimpse of Tolo Mason's little sheila, but he was there. Standing with one booted foot cocked up on a low bulkhead, he watched the gang of boongs settle in on the open deck of the small coastal steamer. Java Mason appeared on deck in the same blue traveling dress she had worn the first day he saw her, and she was rather spectacular with her red hair partially loose, blowing in the breeze. Tolo Mason was in shirtsleeves. Seeing the size of his biceps, Terry could understand how the lad had been able to coldcock him with one blow. It would be interesting indeed to have a go with this Mason boy in some lonely place.

Terry shrugged, turned to walk away, halted, then turned back. As the ship moved away from the dock, he saw Java leaning on the rail, one hand rising gracefully to push back her windblown hair.

"Ah, little darlin'," Terry murmured. "What does the half-breed have—other than money—to lure you off with him on his fool's errand?"

He walked quickly to a seaman's pub, ordered a dark, tall one, and looked around belligerently. If anyone present doubted that Terry Forrest was no city poofter, he would welcome the opportunity to have a little exercise, but his size and his glowering face discouraged anything but furtive, wondering looks from the men in the pub. Terry, drinking his beer, tried to picture Java's face. He could recall her body in detail, the flare of hip, the thrust of breast, but her face was just a blur of perfection.

Ah, God, he said to himself, *don't waste that juicy little one. Don't dry her out and leave her for the scavengers on some hardpan desert or let her be meat food for the boongs.*

It was a waste. Truly, it was a bloody waste.

MAGDALEN BROOME, SLIM and regal in black, her silver hair flawlessly in place in the large top-heavy mass that was the fashion, squeezed her sister-in-law's arm as the minister looked across the open grave and nodded at the widow. Magdalen heard Kitty Broome stifle a sob as she bent, closed her white-gloved hand around a handful of the soil of Australia, and straightened to toss the dirt atop her husband's coffin. The sound was muffled, like light rain.

It was a beautiful autumn day on the outskirts of Sydney. Some said, "It's a nice day for a funeral." Others said, "It seems so incongruous, having a funeral on such a lovely day." All around the cemetery horse-drawn vehicles and a few motorcars waited as the exceptionally large crowd gathered around the open grave to lay to rest John Lachlan Broome, known universally as Johnny even into the ninth decade of his life.

Because Johnny had been one of Australia's leading newspaper publishers, men and women of prominence were present, among them Alfred Deakin, premier of the Commonwealth of Australia. Deakin had spoken a few words.

"Although there were times when those of us in public service were stung by Johnny Broome's skill with the English language, we read his daily comments faithfully as a way of keeping up with the feelings and aspirations of Australia—of the laborers, of the men who work in the bush, and of the small businessmen in our cities. When Johnny Broome took an editorial stand, he was uncompromising, and he was usually proven to be right in the long run. I'm sure that when future historians chart the course of the nation during the last decades of the nineteenth century and the beginning of the twentieth, they will record that the editorial voice of John Lachlan Broome was one of the decisive influences in molding our united Australia. Johnny, old friend, we will miss your daily outpourings of wisdom, and we will miss *you*, sorely."

Kitty Broome, her children at her side, dried her tears, thankful for the veil that hid her reddened eyes. She accepted the condolences of the premier and many others before she was free to walk toward Sam Gordon's gleaming Daimler, with Magdalen's support.

Magdalen, having survived the loss of her own husband— Johnny Broome's brother, Red—was the strong shoulder upon which Kitty had been leaning from the moment she learned that Johnny had collapsed in his office, to be pronounced dead upon the arrival of a doctor.

Magdalen's son, Rufe Broome, immaculate in his dress uniform, opened the door of the Daimler and helped his mother and his aunt Kitty into the car. He had missed his father's funeral thirteen years ago, having been at the time on Her Majesty's naval business in the Atlantic. But with his ship attached to the Australian squadron and presently at anchor in Sydney Harbor, he was able to attend his uncle's burial, following which it was his melancholy duty to escort his two weeping relatives to the house on the hill, the place that had been his home until he had left to follow in his father's footsteps and join the navy.

In the back seat of the car Magdalen turned to Kitty. "You can cry now, darling," she said.

As if permission were all that she had been awaiting, Kitty Broome let the hard, frantic sobs take her as she clung to her sister-in-law. Magdalen, weeping in sympathy, patted Kitty's shoulder tenderly.

When the Daimler shifted into a lower gear to climb the slope to what many still called the Broome house, Magdalen said, "All right, Kitty, dear. Time to pull ourselves together, isn't it?"

Magdalen escorted Kitty upstairs to her own spacious, airy bedroom, the windows of which looked out over the harbor. "Rest awhile," Magdalen said. "I'll come and help you freshen up for dinner."

"Please," Kitty said, "I couldn't eat a bite and—"

"None of that now," Magdalen said with mock severity. "Being alone might seem to you to be the greatest luxury at this very moment, but you're quite wrong." She smiled. "If you sleep, I'll waken you in plenty of time."

Amazing woman, Rufe thought as he stood at the foot of the stairs just before dinner, watching his mother make her way down toward him. Her face was wrinkled, and the body was becoming a bit frail; but her mind was sharper than that of most young people, and her energy and wide range of interests were twin sources of awe to him.

Because Rufe's naval career had taken him away at an early age, his family had not seen him mature, acquiring the dignified bearing that marked him now. They had seen him on rare occasions, of course, and they had become resigned to his long absences. As Australians they stoically accepted the tyranny of distance, for despite modern advances and the growing dominance of the steamship, Australia remained far from the mother country and most other centers of imperial civilization. Even within Australia one was limited by distances, for it was a big land—a continent for a nation and a nation for a continent. Rufe's niece Java, for example, might as well have been on the moon as to have been in Western Australia when Johnny died. Even if she could have been contacted, her great-uncle would have been weeks in the grave before she could have arrived in Sydney.

Since distance and duty had kept Rufe from sharing crucial moments of joy and sadness in the family, occasions such as his sister's marriage and his father's death, his homecoming this year had been a poignant one. Over the years his visits to the old house in Sydney had been so few that each one stood out vividly in his memory. Mainly he remembered his father's house as a microcosm of Australian thought. Although his fellow officers had long since stopped thinking of him as a mere "colonial," he still took pride in being Australian, and he was pleased to find that the Broome house, now owned by his sister's husband, the Scotsman Sam Gordon, was still a gathering place for influential and powerful people.

So, although much had transpired—his promotion to captain, the deaths of his father and his uncle, Australian federation—many things still possessed a reassuring sameness. It was now Jessica Broome Gordon who sat in the place of the lady of the house opposite Sam Gordon, but Magdalen was either at Sam's right or in a seat of her own choosing, next to a guest who interested her. It pleased Rufe to see that his mother was treated with great respect, and it amused him to find that her opinions were as biased in favor of all things Australian—and as adamantly voiced—as had been the statements of his father.

New faces were at the table these days, to replace those who had passed on or those who were current victims of the tyranny of distance that was always a fact of life in Australia. Politicians came and went with the fashions. A ship's captain would fill the chair to Sam's left, and the talk would be saltily nostalgic for Sam, who had once been master of the finest clipper of them all, the *Cutty Sark*.

Sometimes business affairs were discussed, but usually the conversation was more diverse, ranging from lofty dreamings about Australia's brilliant future to controversial opinions that were often startling and potentially offensive.

On this particular night in the autumn of 1902, the evening of Johnny's funeral, the conversation was suitably quiet at first. As Magdalen had insisted, Kitty had come down to dinner, and the guests—some close friends as well as immediate family—spoke in hushed tones about inconsequential topics, out of deference for what they assumed were the widow's feelings. Rufe noted that the atmosphere seemed subdued to the point of being oppressive and unnatural, even for a postfuneral supper. He knew from his own experience and what his mother had told him that conversations around the Broome-Gordon table were generally far more lively and contentious, even outrageous at times, so the gloom tonight seemed exceptional.

Finally Kitty, evidently also sensing that the mood was an unnatural one, took steps to break it.

"Please," she said in a firm voice, "I'm so glad you could all be with me this afternoon, for I know how much you all loved and respected Johnny. But for his sake, and mine, don't let's put a damper on the conversation. Why, if he were here, I suspect he'd be saying something provocative just to startle people and keep things moving!"

Magdalen reached over and put a hand on Kitty's. "You know, dear, I think you're right."

With that the conversation lightened, and the discussions intensified, the volume growing until finally a rather surprising series of statements issued from a woman whose poise, good looks, and overt confidence caught the attention of everyone at the table.

"Present company excluded," said Bina Tyrell with a sly little smile, "the Australian male at the beginning of this new century shows a certain lack of charm."

Rufe, who had been listening to his sister, Jessica, speak about Java and Tolo, far off in the west, turned his attention to the nightclub owner. Bina Tyrell was a petite woman, with a touch of Ireland on her tongue and black Irish beauty in her hair and eyes. She looked, well, fan-bloody-tastic.

"As a rule," Bina went on, "the Aussie male is boring in his frank bigotry. His opinions are hopelessly one-sided, and he is, most often, quite brutal. . . ."

Beside Bina another lady who looked to Rufe even more fan-bloody-tastic laughed a little uneasily, hiding her soft, full lips behind her hand. Rufe's eyes had returned to her often during the evening. She was the widow of a very rich man, Jon Mason, and, he had been informed by his mother, quite a sharp businesswoman in her own right.

"He enjoys fighting even more than shooting at things, and drinking most of all," Bina was saying.

"Really, Bina," said Misa Mason. She glanced in Kitty's direction. "I know Kitty said Johnny relished strong opinions, but there's a time and a place—"

"No, that's all right," Kitty broke in. "Please go on, Bina."

"Well, you hear much about this great, masculine, Australian thing called mateship." She mimicked the Strine accent in the pronunciation of the word. "The fair dinkum man is mate to all—except, of course, if you'll pardon the expressions, to wops, wogs, poms, coons, boongs, niggers, rice-eyes, kikes, chinks, eyeties, nips, frogs, krauts, poofters, slopes, wankers." She paused a moment and looked at Rufe with a sly wink. "And, of course, except to sheilas, chicks, and birds."

Jessica Gordon's voice held just a bit of irritation as she spoke. "Are you saying, Bina, that for a woman to accomplish anything in our society she has to be a man-hater?"

"May I answer that?" Misa asked, silencing Bina momentarily with a hand on her arm. "Actually, Bina has had a more difficult road than I, for my husband had built quite a good business position before he died. So when I encountered the typical Australian attitude toward women, I had a bit of leverage in the form of Mason money. Bina, on the other hand, had nothing. She left a hardscrabble little sheep station in the bush with only a wagon, two broken-down horses, and a few items of clothing. Then, too, I had my son, Tolo, at the time I first began to extend Mason interests into the field of banking. Bina had only herself."

"So good of you to come to my defense, dear Misa," Bina said, "though it's hardly necessary. I've had my share of fights with . . . certain specimens of Australian manhood." Bina was smiling, but her tone was dark.

"Still," Misa answered, "I don't think one could call you a man-hater, Bina."

"Certainly not. Blokes have their uses," Bina said archly.

Jessica stiffened, but Magdalen led the others in laughter at Bina's innuendo.

"Bina simply knows," Misa added, "as do all women who function in public life, that in order to claim their God-given rights women have to fight a bit harder than men."

"One proof of that, I'm afraid," Magdalen offered, "is the difficulty we're having convincing you masculine brutes that we're responsible enough to have the vote."

Rufe had been watching Misa Mason closely. At first his interest in the Samoan woman had been curiosity. He knew that there was a bit of a strain between his sister and Misa because Jessica was still having difficulty accepting the fact that her one chick, Java, had flown away with Misa's son. Rufe suspected that deep down his sister was something of a bigot, that the thing that bothered her most was the fact that her new son-in-law was half Kanaka.

As a career navy man Rufe had encountered his share of people with black, brown, tan, and yellow skins, those races that the British lumped together as "wogs." He was free of prejudice against other races, but he had never really had close associations with them. He had never gone native. To be sure, he had been tempted, especially when he had spent months in the South Seas as a young man, touching frequently on the French-controlled islands. But a subtle, unspoken stigma attached itself to officers who succumbed to the temptations of brown flesh, and from the beginning Rufe had sought to avoid this, putting his naval career first. He did not pass judgment on fellow officers who fraternized with the lasses of Polynesia and Asia, nor would he have preached his own abstinence to anyone else. Nevertheless, the fact remained that he had been promoted over the heads of men senior to him, and while he could not prove that his habits had anything to do with this, he had continued to confine his amorous pursuits to a very few discreet encounters with ladies of his own race.

As his interest in Misa Mason grew beyond mere curiosity, he came to realize that he had not seen anything half so beautiful in all of his years, in all of the far places to which various ships had taken him; nor had he seen anything that he wanted more, not even the first time he had set eyes on a clipper ship dressed in a full suit of sails. Having never been in love, he was unfamiliar with the urge to be closer to a woman, and he rather resented Misa's intrusion into his thoughts.

The swirl of conversation had shifted away from the two attractive widows. Magdalen was seated next to a new chum, the second son of a minor member of the English peerage who had come to Australia to seek his fortune and had ended up working as a tyro reporter on Johnny Broome's newspaper. They were discussing Australia.

"The first thing that one must remember," Magdalen told him, "is that Australia is a state of mind. In fact, Australia was imagined long before it was discovered. In the fourth century B.C., Theopompus, a Greek poet, wrote about a land far from the known world, a land with green meadows and pastures, with big and mighty beasts. Greek mapmakers actually put Theopompus' imaginary continent on their maps, saying that it was needed to balance out the continents of the north. They called Theopompus' continent the Antipodes."

"Where creatures walk upside down," the young reporter said.

"Literally, 'against the feet,' " Magdalen explained. "The Romans called Theopompus' continent Terra Australis Incognita."

"What a place we live in," the reporter said. "Conceived in the mind of a fourth-century Greek, named by the Romans, and—if you listen to those who've been ruined by drought—forgotten by God."

Magdalen smiled, "Well, you know what they say. All Australia needs in order to be a Garden of Eden is water. But you can say the same thing about hell, can't you?"

* * *

On Sam Gordon's right, Kelvin Broome sat next to Kitty. Kelvin, not long back from the African wars, had spoken hardly at all during the evening, not even joining in the discussion of the Australian male. What few remarks he made he addressed to Kitty.

She, too, had listened in silence throughout the evening as the conversation, carried on over the occasional clink of silver on china, shifted and turned. Probably because she herself had encouraged the conversation to take a lighter turn, no one had said much about Johnny or seen fit to dwell on the achievements of his long life. Perhaps people feared that mentioning his name would only cause Kitty pain. Whatever the case, she was by now beginning to mind the fact that people did not even mention him—as if the most important man in her life had never existed.

Her voice was strong as she filled one of those odd silences that come now and again in any group conversation. "Sam," she said, speaking to her host, "now that Johnny's no longer here, I have decided to recommend that Kelvin be made managing editor of the newspaper."

She saw Kelvin's face flush with pleasure, and she was glad. Johnny would have wanted the job to go to him, she knew, for he had said as much before he died, during those days when Kelvin was in South Africa, sending back first-rate reports on the nasty war between the British Empire and the Boers.

Kelvin was, to be sure, only a distant cousin of the deceased, but none of Johnny and Kitty's own children had shown any interest in following in their father's footsteps. The youngest, Patrick, a few months older than Java Gordon Mason, was currently at the Anglican university college in Melbourne, and the others were already established in lives of their own.

"I don't think you could make a better choice, Kitty," Sam said. He turned his gaze on Kelvin. "Well, Mr. Editor, what's it to be?"

"Give me a chance to get my feet on the ground before I

start making editorial policy," Kelvin said with a laugh. "After all, I've been out of the country for most of the past two years. I think I know more about South Africa than I do my own native country, at least at this moment."

"Well, then, tell us your views of the war," Sam Gordon said.

"I'm sure I have more views than you want to hear—certainly more than would be appropriate for this evening." Kelvin put down his fork and looked reflective. "But since you ask, I will say it was bloody awful for the participants. I'll never forget Spion Kop, for instance. That was a foolish charge up a useless hill, ordered by a British general for no good reason, and nothing came of it except slaughter."

"They say that the Boers are good fighters," Sam commented.

"Indeed so," Kelvin agreed, warming to his subject. "In fact, in the early part of the war, before British troops were landed in force, the Boers might have swept throughout all of South Africa, capturing the ports at Cape Town and Durban and preventing the British from landing. But as it was, their leaders bungled things and allowed their armies to become bogged down in useless sieges at Ladysmith and elsewhere. That gave the British time to pour an army into South Africa that outnumbered the entire Boer population—men, women, and children. It was inevitable that imperial forces would eventually triumph in the field."

"But the war went on for so long," said Magdalen. "It was awful to read the reports."

"The Boers are a stubborn people," Kelvin said. "When they couldn't win in set battles, the Boer commanders—Generals Koos De La Rey and Christiaan De Wet in particular—took to the hills and led their men in hit-and-run strikes against us. For the longest time those commandos evaded our best efforts to hunt them down, and they might still be holding out if the British hadn't begun burning Boer farms and interning civilians in camps so they couldn't grow food or aid their fighting men."

"Lord Kitchener's infamous concentration camp policy," Magdalen snorted. "We heard a lot about that. From all reports conditions in those camps were appalling."

"I'm afraid you're right. The camps were crowded and filthy, and there was never enough food or medical supplies. A lot of innocent people died, more than were killed in combat, according to reports. It's a sad fact, but this is the first war—in modern times, at least—to make a soldier's family active participants, with women and children being punished and killed along with the soldiers."

"Correspondents also ran risks," Sam said. "Let's not forget that."

"Well, thank God *you're* back safely," Kitty put in. "I need you at the paper. Besides, you deserve a change of pace. You'll have a chance to take a good look at Australia for a change. There's lots to talk about on the domestic front, you know."

"I daresay there is," Kelvin replied, smiling and looking relieved to be leaving the topic of war. He nodded in the direction of Misa Mason and Bina Tyrell. "For example, I think the Terrific Threesome"—that name had been applied to Bina, Misa, and Magdalen Broome—"will be pleased to know that this editor, for one, favors women's suffrage."

"Hear, hear," Bina exclaimed.

"And what will be the editor's attitude toward the mother country in the future, sir?" asked the young reporter seated beside Magdalen.

"We are, of course, still bound to England," Kelvin answered. "Our war service has cemented that tie, though there are a lot of Australian soldiers who'd rather not fight under British officers in the next war. But we have trade ties to consider. Blood ties, too. And let's not forget that we owe the mother country not a small amount of money. In addition, the British Isles will continue to be, I'd guess, our chief source of new immigrants."

"Will you, then, support labor's position that the chief plank of any program should be a White Australia, with no compromise allowed?" This question came from Magdalen.

Only she would have dared raise the subject of race in that household, with Misa Mason present.

"Please, Mrs. Broome," Kelvin said, holding up both hands. "I've only just been told that I'm to be the editor. Give me a little time to enjoy it before I have to put my head on the block."

Sam Gordon spoke up. "Perhaps, Kelvin, you can tell the British, diplomatically, of course, that Australia is all grown up now, that we no longer need to have our noses wiped on the royal apron."

Rufus Broome laughed.

"You know what I'm talking about, don't you, Rufe?" Sam asked.

"It's true, I fear," Rufe said. "The British attitude toward Australia and Australians is still that of a haughty adult looking down his nose at a petulant child. I've been in the navy so long that they forget sometimes that I'm Australian. I was told by one of my superiors that the only way to see to it that the colonials—meaning Australians—don't go off half cocked is to see to it that they never get their hands on a capital ship. What that means is this: The Royal Navy intends to keep the Australian squadron firmly under the control of British senior officers."

"Even if we build the ships, eh?" Sam asked.

Kelvin said, "From their standpoint that's merely our duty to the mother country and our sovereign. Just as it was our duty to send men to South Africa to fight under pommy officers."

Magdalen rose. "These men will get violent soon, ladies," she said. "Let's leave them to their cigars and politics."

Magdalen was helping Kitty prepare for bed. The house had emptied. Sam and Jessica were closed away in their own bedroom at the other end of the hall.

"Don't let me keep you," Kitty said. "You must be tired."

"No, no," Magdalen said. "A bit like an unwound watch, perhaps, but still ticking."

"You've saved my life, taking me in like this," Kitty said. "But now I think it's time I begin to stand on my own two feet. I'll go back to the house tomorrow. God only knows what state it's going to be in, with only the servants there."

"You know, darling Kitty, that you're welcome to stay here as long as you like."

"Yes, I know," Kitty said, patting Magdalen's hand.

"It's nice having you, as a matter of fact," Magdalen said. "The house seems so empty these days."

"Java," Kitty said.

Magdalen nodded. "I can easily forgive her for marrying against the wishes of her mother. What I can't forgive is her total desertion." She sighed. "Oh, I don't really mean that. She and Tolo must have felt they were justified, and indeed, perhaps they were. Jessica would have tried to annul the marriage if Sam had let her. But I miss her so—and now they're off in Western Australia again."

"Tolo will take good care of her. He's a fine boy."

"Yes," Magdalen said. "That's it. He's a boy."

Kitty went into the bath and a few moments later came out in her nightgown. Magdalen was still sitting at the dressing table.

"Magdalen, do you ever stop missing Red?" Kitty asked, her voice going hoarse before she finished.

"Never," Magdalen said. "But you will find that you can learn to bear the emptiness, here." She pressed her breast. "Whenever you need me, come to me. Activity. That's the secret. We'll stick together. We'll go to Bina's every night and drink too much wine."

Kitty laughed. "My stomach couldn't take it."

Magdalen rose. "Can you sleep?"

"I think so."

"If not, and you want to talk—"

"Oh, I'll be all right."

Magdalen paused at the door. "I hope you enjoyed the evening. Bina's a bit strong, but she's always like that."

"Oh, I didn't mind that at all. It was a lovely evening," Kitty said.

"I wish that Adam and Emily could have been here," Magdalen said.

"I'm sure that he would not have missed"—she paused, swallowed, then managed to get on with it—"would have been here for Johnny's funeral had it been at all possible."

"Yes," Magdalen said. Adam Shannon, born Vincent, was now the eleventh Earl of Cheviot. He and Emily had gone to South Africa to see their son, Slone, and then on to England to handle affairs that had arisen when Adam's older brother had died unexpectedly, leaving him with not only the title but a country estate to look after. "It's rather lonely being the sole surviving member of the old guard, except when you are here and there are two of us." She sighed.

"They'll be home soon, I suspect," Kitty said. "Knowing Adam, I wouldn't put it past him to hand over the title to Slone and go back to Brisbane."

"I don't think he can do that, at least not till he dies," Magdalen replied. "Odd world, isn't it? Suddenly our old friend is an earl, and young Slone is a viscount." She mused for a few moments. "And Tolo is the grandson of an earl."

"I suspect that in the minds of some, having noble blood doesn't make up for his brown skin," Kitty said.

"An odd world, indeed," Magdalen repeated.

Chapter IV

South Africa

THROUGHOUT THE TWO and a half years of the Boer War, which Kelvin Broome had been covering for the Broome paper, members of the Australian forces fighting in South Africa had, as a matter of policy, been rotated home after one year's service. Lieutenant Matthew Van Buren had had little trouble circumventing the policy after his first year, volunteering to stay on with the Queensland Mounted Infantry; but at the end of his second year, with the war winding down, he had been forced to pull a few strings in order to stay on in the Cape Colony.

As the date assigned for his rotation drew nearer, Matt became panicky, for his reasons for wanting to remain in South Africa now were much more compelling than they had been previously. After the first year Matt had wanted to stay simply because the job he had come to South Africa to help accomplish was not finished. But after his second year not even the most optimistic Boer supporter could hope for victory. In spite of the stubbornness of De La Rey and De Wet and their commandos in the High Veld, it was obvious to all that the end was very near. The task allotted to the British soldiers—and to the troops from the various colonies of the empire—was nearly done.

But by this time Matt was in love, and that passion obscured all else. Before his love for Kit Streeter, the desire to see his home in Queensland, the wish to see his mother and to a lesser extent his father faded into the background. Home? He could have no home without Kit.

For some time Matt had been attached to the staff of Colonel Roland Streeter, his assignment being to ease the integration of incoming units of Australian and Canadian volunteers into the huge British armies in the field.

Matt felt that he had been quite lucky, for of all the hundreds of assignments that could have been given him, only duty in Streeter's offices provided him with the one thing that he desired most: to get a look at Kit Streeter now and then, to have the odd chance to speak with her, to let her know, gently but persistently, that he was determined to make her his own.

Matt had met Kit Streeter on an occasion that had been a happy one for him and for Adam and Emily Shannon: the return of the Shannons' son, Slone, to Cape Town after a period in which he had been listed as killed in action. The introduction had been quick, just a passing formality as Colonel Roland Streeter showed routine courtesy to Matt as a junior officer and personal friend of Slone's. At that time Kit had been informally engaged to Slone, and she had just lived through her mother's painful, extended, and terminal illness. On that first occasion Matt had found himself with the most beautiful girl he had ever seen, but the situation had not been, to say the least, optimum. Kit had fainted dead away upon seeing Slone Shannon again, for Slone turned up with a pretty blond girl at his side and proudly introduced her as Sianna De Hartog Shannon—his wife.

Now the war was almost over, and preparations were under way for all Australian units to be sent home. Matt would be among the last to go, but unless he wanted to take his leave of the army in South Africa and thus be free to choose his own traveling time, it was a good bet that he would be leaving Cape Town before the start of the South African winter. He began to intensify his courtship.

* * *

In a short period of time Kit Streeter had suffered two highly emotional catastrophes. After the loss of her first love, Slone Shannon, in a way that maximized the shock and exposed her to public curiosity, she had endured the death of her mother following a lingering illness. By this time she was simply worn down.

So at first, when yet another young Australian officer began to let it be known that he wanted to spend time with her, Kit resisted. It had been the fact that Slone was Australian that had engendered her father's early disapproval of him. Streeter's stunning about-face and acceptance of Slone—when it was learned the young man had fallen heir to an earldom—had not eased Kit's bitterness and fatigue. It had come at the same time she was witnessing the mental and physical deterioration of her mother, inexorable and irreversible unto death.

The humiliation of seeing Slone with someone else was thus a single chapter in a book of sorrows, but it was, for Kit, the most memorable chapter. She burned with the shame of having fallen unconscious when she saw Slone accompanied by his new wife, a pretty little dumpling of a Boer girl, all blond and pink and smiling. The mere sight of Matt reminded her of that fiasco, for it was Matt Van Buren who had caught her as she fainted and fell.

Oddly enough, it was Matt's reference to that particular episode that made the first dent on Kit's cold indifference toward him. After weeks of speaking to her politely when she visited the military offices to see her father, after he had eaten the customary meal in the home of his commanding officer and then extended several very polite and proper invitations to Kit, Matt—obviously desperate—had boldly mentioned the incident.

"I don't quite understand it, Miss Streeter," he said to her one day after she had declined yet another of his invitations to dinner. "The first time I met you, you literally fell into my arms."

Kit flushed, and then she saw the wry humor of it. "I suppose, Lieutenant Van Buren, since I led you on so shamelessly by falling into your arms, as you put it, that I should have dinner with you. It will give me adequate time to explain to you that I am not desirous of forming new relationships or entanglements."

"I consider that fair warning," Matt countered. "No worries."

Kit Streeter's complexion was of the sort that had become legend among some few fortunate English girls. So perfect, so creamy was her skin that it seemed incredible, nothing less than a miracle, that the pale, rosy look had survived the African sun. Matt was not the first to note that her hair held all the startling red glory of an autumn sunset, and her huge green eyes had the power to stun any male within twenty feet of her glance. Her girlish slimness made her look almost frail to Matt, but when, during an evening of dining and dancing, he took her into his arms for a waltz, he felt all the youthful strength in her very feminine body. Exuberant energy seemed to radiate from her.

She was in blue on that first night, as she was again on the night that she first allowed his kiss. In blue she was as English as Boadicea spirited into modern times, as gay as Queen Mab at play, as beautiful as Venus abirthing. To Matt she was all things, all women collected into one slim-waisted, long-legged, soft-armed bundle of wonder. His passion, his feeling of total awe and disbelief that such beauty and tenderness could be his by dint of a kiss must have been transmitted to Kit, for she was suddenly breathless. She broke the kiss to stare at him, her green eyes wide and startled. In that instant, with the heat of his kiss on her lips, all that had gone before became prelude.

"Matt?" she whispered, as if in fear.

"I'm sorry. Did I hurt you?" He had, in his eagerness, been quite forceful in his kiss.

"No, no." Now she was truly fearful, and for a moment she tried to pull away but did not persist when his hands tightened on her arms. She began to wonder if she had merely imagined the tumult that his kiss had generated in her. To her everlasting surprise—she would remember the moment all her life—she heard herself whisper, "Again?"

"Yes," he answered.

"Gor and blimey," she said softly, the second kiss having made her even more breathless. Her first Australian had announced blithely that he was going to marry her not five minutes after she'd first met him. Her second Australian had not been so precipitous, but the final result was the same, except that her feelings were sweetly stronger, pleasingly deeper in conviction. In that moment, during that second kiss, she gave herself heart and soul to Matt Van Buren.

Only once during their rather brief courtship did they discuss her long, ultimately fruitless relationship with Slone Shannon, and it was she who brought up the subject.

"I must have been fated to marry an Australian," she said.

Matt, of course, was aware that she had had a long-standing agreement with Slone. He and Slone had shared some of the best and worst moments of the war. It had been Matt who had shouldered the unpleasant duty of telling Slone's father and mother that Slone was dead. But he never once had the feeling that he was taking Slone's leavings as Kit, little by little, was able to admit to herself—and then to Matt—that she had fallen in love with another colonial. So when she said that fate must have intended her to marry an Australian, he was silent.

"You've never asked me about Slone," she said.

"No."

"Wonderful luck, his becoming a peer."

"Jolly for him," Matt said, then: "No, really. I'm very pleased for him." He kissed her lightly. "Tough luck on you, girl."

She pulled away, and for a moment he feared that he had said the wrong thing.

"I mean, after all, Slone's a fine-looking fellow. Me, I'm just a bushranger."

"Hush," she said. Her smile was radiant. "Actually, it was bad luck only for my father. Poor dad. Lost his chance to have his daughter be a countess."

"Speaking of your father . . ."

"Yes, I guess it's time we spoke of him," Kit said. "Matt, he was very much against my marrying Slonc. Even before my mother became ill, he was against it, and then, when she began to become affected by—that awful thing that grew in her head, he used her illness and her need for constant care as an excuse to have me postpone even thinking of getting married."

"So I have your father to thank for saving you for me," Matt said.

"I suppose so," she said seriously.

"Slone's a gentleman, even if he is Australian." Matt grinned. "If your engagement had been announced, old Slone wouldn't have gone back on his word. So I say nice things in my prayers about your father and about Sianna De Hartog."

"You're not going to ask me if I was in love with Slone?" she asked.

"Were you?"

"I'm going to say yes," she said, "but then I'm going to qualify it. Yes, I was in love. I'd never met anyone so brash, so impetuous, so . . . pushy."

"That's an Aussie for you."

"I won't use the excuse that I was young. In fact, I don't think I need an excuse. But I *was* young, and it was a young love." She took his hand. "Matt, it was as if I were being taught a lesson in how to love. It was almost like a drill, a practice, so that I could perfect the emotions of loving a man in time to meet you."

A wave of tenderness swept over him. His eyes were moist. He held her wordlessly.

"Now I've confessed all," she said.

"Not quite all."

"Oh, he kissed me a couple of times."

"A couple?"

"That's all. I'll bet you've kissed a lot of girls."

He laughed. "Not really."

"Liar. You kiss too well not to have practiced."

"I told you, I'm an old bushranger. I practiced kissing on my horse."

"Ugh!"

"Big, soft lips. She was quite accomplished. Good teacher."

She elbowed him in the stomach. He grunted and then, laughing, lifted her face to his.

When Kit told her father that she was going to marry Matt Van Buren, the scene developed much as she had expected it would.

"My God, Kit, not another bloody colonial!" Streeter's face had gone blotchy red. "I know, my dear girl, that you have reached an age where you're burning to marry and can't control your urges, but—"

·"Don't be insulting and crude, Father," Kit said harshly.

Never in her twenty-two years had his daughter spoken to him in such a tone. For a moment he was speechless.

Kit took advantage of his silence. "You will *not*—ever again —prevent me from seizing my own happiness," she said quietly.

Streeter's voice was calm. He had regained control. "Actually, aren't you letting your emotions run away with you? Your mother's death. The, ah, unfortunate incident with the Shannon fellow—"

She had been sickened and shamed by the way her father had toadied to the Shannons when he learned that Slone was heir to an earldom, toasting the union he had earlier opposed. She knew, too, how sorely disappointed he had been when Slone had returned to Cape Town married to a Boer girl. She had not, to this moment, rubbed salt in the old wounds, but now her anger boiled over.

"That Shannon fellow? Do you mean Slone Shannon, the

viscount, son of the Earl of Cheviot? The man you would not let me marry because he was a colonial?"

"Really, Kit," Streeter said. "This Van Buren fellow—"

"Who is a colonial. Who is not a viscount."

"He's the first man to come along since your, ah, disappointment with Shannon. You're too wise to take the first offer, to marry on the rebound."

"Actually, Father," she said, smiling sweetly, but with her eyes blazing with anger, "if I had any doubt that I loved Matt, your opposition to him would dispel it. Your record of counseling me in romance is not, to say the least, outstanding." Then, seeing the hangdog look on her father's face, she went to him and took his arm.

"Be happy for me?"

She was shocked to see him lift his arm, wipe a tear from his cheek with the back of his hand.

"I'll try, kitten," he said. "It just hit me quite hard, that's all, to think that you're going off to Australia after all."

"I know," she said. "But it isn't the end of the world. You'll be retiring soon, and there are all sorts of opportunities in Australia. Talk with Matt. What is it? Two years, three? And then you can come and stay with us, and Matt will help you get established in some enterprise that will be quite profitable, quite gentlemanly, and you'll be there to bounce your grandchildren on your knee."

He managed a smile. "Well, that's the price we pay, I suppose, when we don't pull our own chestnuts out of the fire but call on the colonies for help."

"You're incorrigible," she said, standing on tiptoe to kiss him on the cheek.

So it was that the formal request for the lady's hand was made by a red-faced young Australian officer standing at attention. The request was acknowledged and granted with some grace by the older officer. Then, with a sigh of relief from everyone, the three of them stood around a splendid mahogany table and toasted the engagement with cape smoke, a good but fiery local brandy.

Kit took only a sip. Streeter and Matt tossed off their drafts and held out their glasses, silently demanding that Kit refill them. Soon, while Kit made trips back and forth to the kitchen to see that the cook was getting on with dinner, the potent brandy engendered a relaxation of the tension between the two men. Streeter was talking easily, telling Matt all about Kit's respectable but not spectacular forebears. Matt listened with interest. Anything that touched on Kit was of value to him. Streeter was still talking when Kit maneuvered them to the dinner table.

The food was excellent, the wine adequate. Kit spoke of her mother, telling how the two of them had consoled each other when Streeter was away.

"At least," Streeter said, "you won't have that problem now. Thank God this lad has enough sense not to be career army. Now that the Boers are about licked, you have to consider how slow advancement is during peacetime."

"Well, it's the army's loss and my gain," Kit said. "But all in all, it wasn't really such a bad life for Mother, was it?" She smiled. "It seemed to me, Father, after I passed the innocence of childhood and became a more impartial observer of life, that your frequent absences made the reunions that much fonder."

Streeter flushed and chuckled, remembering, and then his face darkened, the realization of his loss a sudden stabbing pain.

Matt, celebrating the completion of a difficult chore with perhaps too generous a quantity of cape smoke, did not notice Streeter's change of mood. "I'm afraid, Kit, that my family tree won't ever be as complete as the Streeters'. I've often regretted not having talked more with Grandfather Van Buren while he was alive. I saw him a few times before I was about twelve years old. But I was more interested then in my horses than in my lineage. All I know is that Claus Van Buren was the unwanted son—" He paused and made a face. "If you can imagine a more descriptive word, use it in silence. The son of a Dutch trader and a Javanese woman—"

Matt did not notice that Roland Streeter's face went pale.

"He began life as a lowly servant and became one of the richest and best-liked men in New Zealand. He extended his business holdings into Australia and into far countries through his ships. He took my grandmother with him most of the time. She was American, and again, I know nothing of her lineage. I guess people didn't have time for genealogy in early Australia. Everyone was there for a new start, and I suppose that forgetting the long list of ancestors that seems to give pride to the Englishman was a part of wiping clean the slate of the past."

Matt had never told Kit about his grandfather Van Buren because they'd always been busy with other things, getting to know each other, experimenting to see why each new kiss seemed to provide a deeper thrill than the last one. And Matt was from Australia, where there were no titles, where a man's worth was measured by his abilities, by his fists, by his courage in the constant battle against contrary elements, and not by his ancestors. He did not see the slight surprise on Kit's face, followed by an anxious glance at her father.

"We were all very proud of the old boy," he went on expansively. "He fought against some pretty tough odds and held the world to a standstill. He even won a few rounds."

Streeter's voice was icy. "Do I understand you to say that your paternal grandfather was half Asiatic?"

"Javanese," Matt said. "Actually, they're a unique, industrious people. My father says that Claus Van Buren's willingness to work hard came from his Javanese—"

"And am I to sit here in silence when my first grandchild might revert to the brown skin of the savage?" Streeter asked in a dead, small voice.

"Father, please," Kit begged.

Streeter rose, towering over the seated couple. Kit reached

for Matt's hand, the pressure of her fingers urging him to be silent.

"I was willing to keep my mouth shut and pray that you were not wasting yourself on a colonial," Streeter said. "I was willing to try to forget that you were going to leave English civilization and journey to a country founded by the dregs of British society, by whores and thieves and murderers. But now I am told that my daughter is to marry a mixed-breed."

Matt jerked his hand away from Kit and stood to face the colonel, blood rising to his face. Reason told him to hold his tongue, to leave quietly and give Kit the choice of coming with him or staying. But thoughts were flashing through his mind like lightning, and he recalled that Slone had done something of that sort, had walked away after giving Kit the same choice. She had chosen her family—not surprisingly, considering the state of her mother's health at the time. So Matt knew that it would not be in his best interest to give Kit an ultimatum now.

For a moment he held Streeter's angry stare, and then he shrugged and turned to Kit. "I'm sorry I haven't told you before about my grandfather."

"No worries, mate," Kit said, biting off the words angrily, using the Strine pronunciation. Those words and the look in her eyes told Matt all that he wanted to know.

"Sir," he said, "I will try to understand your concern, even if I can't understand your reasoning, that I am tainted by my grandfather's Javanese blood. In all honesty it's something to which we Van Burens never give a thought. My grandfather was a pioneer in a bloody tough part of the world, and I'm proud to bear his name. I hope that you will come to understand that pride."

"I will not be called upon to understand anything!" Streeter blustered. "Must I ask you to leave, Lieutenant?"

"I wouldn't do that, Father" Kit said, rising to stand and face him.

"You stay out of this, Kit," Streeter said.

"Not bloody likely," Kit said, her green eyes flaring. "I

ve Matt, Father, and I'm going to marry him. I pray that
u can find the manhood to ask his forgiveness for the things
u've said tonight, but if not—"

"You will go against my wishes totally?"

"If it comes to that," she said evenly. She took Matt's hand.
Ve're leaving now," she said. "When you see me again, we'll
married."

Streeter's eyes blazed. "Lieutenant," he said, "I want you
the office early tomorrow morning. You will find that or-
rs are awaiting you."

"Father, if you do that, if you send him away—"

"Fortunately, the army has not given over its running to
rebrained young girls," Streeter said. "And you, Lieuten-
t, are still in the army and attached to my command."

"I will be there," Matt said coldly. "And at that time I will
nd you a letter resigning my commission."

"Be that as it may," Streeter said, "you are and you will be
morrow morning an officer under my command."

Kit pulled Matt out of the room, then handed him her coat
that he could hold it for her. Outside, they walked away
om the Streeter house arm in arm, each lost in personal
oughts, each waiting for the other to speak. Overhead the
oon swam in a clear, star-fired sky.

"Kit, if it makes a difference to you—" Matt began at last,
s voice low and soft.

"You bloody bastard," she hissed.

He started and looked down at her.

"To think that it would," she said. "I wouldn't care if you
ld me that your grandfather was a bloody Zulu."

He laughed as he squeezed her to him.

"Your quarters—could we sneak in without waking that
d dragon who rents you the room?"

"I imagine we could."

"All right."

He stopped, turned her, bent to kiss her lips softly. "Why,
it?"

"He's going to send you north. He'll try to put you in the

thick of what fighting is left. I suppose, knowing you, th
you'll obey orders. But dammit, Matt, if you let my father k
you this way—"

"God, I should hope not."

"I will kill you myself," she continued with some lack
logic. "Now I want you to take me to that room of yours.

"Tell me why," he said.

"Because you're going to do your bloody bushranger be
to give me a baby," she said. "If father cuts orders for you
ship out tomorrow, we won't have time to get married. V
can't accomplish that tonight, but we can become as one. V
can become man and wife in fact and in the eyes of God, a
then you, being an Australian gentleman, won't dare dese
me."

"Ah, Kit," he said.

"I'm bloody serious," she said.

He shivered at the thought of having her, of knowing t
heats and softnesses of her.

As it happened, they had no difficulty getting into his roo
without awakening his landlady. As usual the old woman ha
turned down his bed, and a dying fire was still glowing in t
fireplace. Matt stoked it, adding a bit of coal, and short
afterward heaven came to earth for intermittent intervals th
saw the full moon climb the sky, then begin its long desce
and go pale with the dawn before they rose, still sleeples
dressed, and went out into the new day.

"I wonder if I did as you ordered," he whispered, his li
brushing her ears, causing her to shiver.

"Hmm?" she inquired.

"You ordered me to give you a baby. If I didn't, it was n
from lack of trying."

"You were quite valiant," she said.

"If I failed, you'll forgive me, won't you?"

"I suppose," she said.

"Because if I did fail, then we get to try again," he said, an
he felt a faint and unexpected resurgence of need at the ve
thought of such a happenstance.

She left him, at his insistence, outside army headquarters. He found a lavatory and freshened himself as best he could. Then, finding a vacant desk with pen and paper, he wrote out a letter resigning his commission, stuffed it into an envelope, and put it in his pocket.

Five minutes later he was standing tall in front of Roland Streeter. An odor of brandy wafted across the desk into his face. Streeter's eyes were bloodshot, his jowls heavy with unshaven beard.

"Sir, Lieutenant Matthew Van Buren reporting as ordered, sir."

"Stand at ease, Lieutenant," Streeter said. "This office has been requested to make a survey of concentration camps in the northern Cape Colony, in the Orange Free State, and in the Transvaal. I consider you to be the logical choice to conduct this survey, Lieutenant Van Buren. You will leave as quickly as you can pack your duffel. You will take as much time as is required to visit each of the camps, to survey the state of medical and food supplies, medical and army personnel, and the health of the detainees."

"Yes, sir," Matt said.

"That is all," Streeter said, giving him a set of handwritten orders.

Matt took them, then reached into his pocket for his envelope. "I think you know what this is, sir," he said, handing it to the colonel.

Streeter stared at the envelope without opening it. "Yes. It will be processed through the usual channels."

"Thank you, sir." Matt clicked his heels, did an about-face, and marched to the door. There he turned. "She's still going to marry me, Colonel," he said. "And I still extend my hand to you, sir, as the father of my wife-to-be."

Streeter's face was impassive. "I had guessed that, Lieutenant, by the fact that my daughter did not return to her home last night. But then, such licentious behavior is not surprising—is it?—when one realizes that she's come under the influence of a mixed-blood colonial."

*   *   *

Before he saw it, Matt smelled the camp. The sandy tra
he was following ran alongside a muddy stream, a small trib
tary of the Vaal River; the waters reeked of human waste.

The wind was in his face, and the stench from the car
was at first indistinguishable from a smell that he had come
know too well during the years of war, the all-pervasive ran
ness of decaying human flesh. Then, as he rode slowly up
rise, topped it, and saw below him in a valley alongside t
stream the extent of hovels and tents, he was able to ident
the sources of different odors from amid the overall stenc
Vomit. Open slit-trench latrines. Masses of unwashed, over
crowded bodies. A hint of carrion, but no bodies in view, or
shrouded, child-sized canvas bags lying in a row in a barr
cemetery, where a dozen soldiers in various states of undre
worked lethargically to dig holes in the ground to match t
size of the canvas bags.

It was easy to see that discipline at the camp was lax. I
was greeted at the gate by a slovenly soldier in a dirty ur
form, who smelled as if he had not bathed for weeks. I
admitted Matt past the gate with a show of total unintere:

Directed to the camp supervisor's tent, Matt found it sep
rated from the maze of hovels, lean-tos, and other tents by
littered area that might once have shown a growth of gra
There another soldier, only slightly more tidy, told Matt th
Captain Fortesque was at the main medical tent, to which
pointed.

At the open flaps of the big tent that served the camp as
hospital and dispensary, other smells prevailed: strong disi
fectants, the never-to-be-forgotten rankness of a gangreno
wound, and chicken soup.

Chicken soup.

The patients on cots were at their meal. The soup was bei
served in standard-issue metal cups, and only a few of t
women and children had spoons. Most of them were tilti
the cups eagerly, slurping the lukewarm liquid with obvio
hunger.

Matt saw an officer in a white smock and made his way
toward him between the rows of cots. As he passed, lank-
haired Boer women with blank eyes stared at him dully, while
one bright-eyed little girl with a bandage on her leg examined
him curiously.

"Captain Fortesque?"

The medic was bending over a woman whose leg had been
shattered by a pom-pom shell. He was using a method of
treatment about which Matt had heard but which he had
never seen. The smell, combined with what he saw, caused
his stomach to heave. The doctor had loosed dozens of mag-
gots onto the dead and dying tissue surrounding the woman's
wound, and the larvae were doing their assigned task, eating
with a diligence that forced Matt to look away.

"What the hell do you want?" Fortesque demanded. "Can't
you see I'm busy?" But he straightened, put his hands to his
back, and stretched with a groan. "I'm sure you're not going
to tell me that you're a doctor, one of the replacements I've
been screaming for."

"No, sir. I'm from army headquarters, Cape Town. Inspection tour for Colonel Streeter, Kitchener's staff."

"Ballocks," the doctor said. He was a small, sharp-faced
man with a beard that had grown bushy from lack of care. He
smelled of disinfectant and other unpleasant, unidentifiable
things. There was a fresh spot of blood on his white blouse. "I
don't suppose headquarters has even received my request for
medical personnel?"

"I don't know, sir," Matt said. "I'm here to assess the
status of your supply system—"

"Nonexistent!" Fortesque snapped. "We had a shipment of
half-rotted chickens last week. I'm trying to feed five thousand women and children with rations for five hundred. I'm
trying to keep people alive, in a tent, when they should be
under intensive care in a city hospital. Damn it all, Lieutenant, people are dying here every day. There are more casualties in this camp alone every day than are occurring on the
so-called fields of battle. Well, you're bloody well standing on

the field of battle now, and the combatants are here." He
waved his arm. "Women. Children of all ages. They're fighting hunger, typhus, the fevers, and infections that attack the
most minute scratch. They don't have adequate clothing. The
nights are cold, the people are weak, and when they get
chilled, they come down with lung congestion, dysentery, you
name it."

"You're supposed to be supplied out of army field headquarters in Kimberley. Part of my assignment is to find out
why the camps haven't been getting enough food and medical
supplies. Do you have any opinion along those lines?"

"They bloody well don't care," Fortesque retorted. "Last
time I went down there I was told not to worry about the
Boer baby makers. Good God, man, it's as if the women and
children are our enemies, not the commandos, not De Wet
and De La Rey up in the High Veld."

"I'm going to do what I can to help," Matt said.

"Fine, fine. Now, if you don't mind, I've got enough patients for five physicians and precious little with which to
treat them. Make yourself at home. Have some chicken soup.
If you put enough hot pepper in it, you can cover up the fact
that it's made from spoiled meat. But no problem. We boil it
long enough to make it edible without being fatal. Worst that
can happen is a case of the soldier's disease."

"If you don't mind, I'll pass on the soup," Matt replied.
"I'll have a look around the camp."

He saw a woman who looked very much the way Slone
Shannon's wife, Sianna, might have looked if she had been
twenty years older and had been living in squalid conditions
for months, washing clothing in an iron pot over a wood fire.
A younger woman sat in the dirt, leaning her back against the
wall of a shanty, a potbellied infant sucking on one of her
stringy, shrunken breasts. It was, Matt knew, totally unlike a
usually modest Boer woman to expose her breast, even when
nursing an infant.

"When are we to go home?" the older woman asked.

"Soon," he said. "When the war is over."

"We'll be dead before then," the younger woman said wearily.

"Perhaps you had better double your guard, British," the woman at the washpot spoke up. "Aren't you afraid that we're going to attack and overwhelm you?"

There was little privacy at the slit-trench latrines. Makeshift screens failed to hide the dozens of women and children who squatted there, faces showing pain as their bodies were racked by dysentery.

From one dirt-roofed lean-to came a scream of agony. Startled, Matt ducked his head and peered in. He saw an incredible sight, the almost bald head of a child in the process of being born, the baby's shoulders stuck in the wet, unbelievably stretched vaginal cavity of an emaciated young woman. And even as he looked, a woman skillfully twisted the baby, freed one shoulder, pulled, and quickly lifted the infant by its heels to spank its bloody, wet bottom. The wail of a newborn child seemed almost obscenely out of place in the squalor and misery of the camp. Matt fled, hurrying his tour of inspection.

Before word came that at long last the final Boer holdouts had surrendered, that the war was over, Matt had visited a half dozen other camps. The story was the same in each of them. Women and children, the old, invalided ex-soldiers—all were crowded together under incredibly unsanitary conditions. Death was an everyday experience in the concentration camps.

"You see your own daughter die," a woman told him, "and there's nothing anyone can do. The doctors try, but there aren't enough of them. They don't have the proper medicines. My daughter stepped on a rusty nail down by the latrines. Her foot cankered. She died of lockjaw. Did you ever see anyone die of lockjaw, Lieutenant?"

"No," Matt admitted.

"Pray God that you never have to."

* * *

After an all-night train ride Matt was back in Cape Town.
He went to his lodgings, where he found a reminder of the
magic night he'd spent there with Kit: a scarf that she had left
behind. He had been away for weeks, but the scarf still held a
hint of her perfume.

He reported to Colonel Streeter just before noon, delivering
his written summation of his observations and recommendations.

"Give it to me in brief," Streeter said.

"Sir, my urgent recommendation is a crash effort to get
medical men and supplies to the concentration camps at all
costs. Food and medicines first. Then clothing. And then I
have recommended that the population of the camps be dispersed back into the civilian economy as quickly as possible,
since it is beyond our ability to provide care or even decent
sanitation for the thousands of people there."

"Our first priority, Lieutenant, is to bring our armies in
from the field and to ship them home. It's costing the crown a
bloody fortune every day to keep so many men here."

"The priority, Colonel, is humanity," Matt said.

"I will read your report," Streeter said.

Matt left the office with the sick feeling that his report, with
its urgent recommendations, would be filed and forgotten.
Then God only knew how long it would take for the army to
get around to supplying the camps while their occupants were
being dispersed back to the countryside. If all of the people in
the camps were turned loose at once, more people would die,
for many of them would be returning to burned homes and
ruined farmlands. That, he had decided in advance, he could
not abide without making some effort to remedy the situation.
He had made copies of his report.

Just before lunch Matt managed to catch the senior civilian
representative of the Australian diplomatic offices in Cape
Town. The diplomat scanned the report.

"Rather a hot potato, Van Buren," he said. "I think we
should let the Brits handle it, don't you?"

"I think, sir, that the people back home have a right to know how this war was conducted, just what kind of war they sent their sons and husbands to fight. And if you don't see to it that that happens, I have other copies. I feel that some Australian newsman would be happy to publish this paper, or at least the gist of it."

"Well, Lieutenant, if you want to foul your own nest . . ."

Foul the nest he did, but he didn't consider it *his* nest. It was a British nest, and as he had suspected, the Australian newsmen, with no war action to report, were happy to jump on the collective British back in criticism of the concentration camp policy.

And then he went to see Kit. She was wearing a faded housedress. Her autumn hair was covered by an old blue cloth, and in cleaning the house, she had gotten dirt on her hands and a smudge on her left cheek. She was the most beautiful charwoman Matt had ever seen.

He was called to Streeter's office the next day. Streeter was wearing the star of a brigadier general.

"Congratulations, sir," Matt said, saluting.

"You are very goddamned lucky that this paper arrived this morning—" Streeter said, handing a one-page document to Matt. It was Matt's release from his commission.

"Thank you, sir," Matt replied.

"—because otherwise I'd have you up before a court-martial," Streeter finished.

"Then I am lucky that it has come," Matt retorted coldly.

"What you did was despicable," Streeter said. "Did you not consider, even for a moment, that depriving the Boer commando of home comfort, food, and supplies—by burning his farms and interning those who would have fed him—has saved British lives?"

"Not as many, I fear, as were lost in the camps," Matt said.

"You have tried to discredit my country in the eyes of the world," Streeter went on. "Your hateful actions in blowing things out of proportion with the press detract from the well-earned glory of those men who fought bravely against a determined and able enemy. I hope, Van Buren, that someday you will understand the harm you have done, and I pray that God will see to the punishment that I am now unable to mete out to you."

"Is that all?" Matt said.

"Get out of my sight."

"I'll be leaving for Australia in two or three days," Matt said. "I've seen Kit. She has secured the necessary papers. For her sake, will you attend your daughter's wedding?"

"I have no daughter," Streeter said.

Because he was traveling with his wife, Matt Van Buren did not return to Australia as he had come out to Africa, aboard a troopship. He took a first-class cabin on a Mason Line reefer ship that reserved a portion of one deck for passengers. Kit and he settled in to enjoy their honeymoon.

General Roland Streeter had not attended the small wedding in Cape Town, nor had he been at the docks to see Kit off to her new country.

"No worries, mate," she had said, trying to sound gay, but there were tears in her eyes, and it became Matt's pleasantly extended duty to kiss them away after the ship had left the dock, making its way out of Table Bay and onto the long swells of the Indian Ocean.

The passenger cabins had been full when the ship landed at Cape Town, outbound from London, but most of the passengers had disembarked in South Africa. Matt and Kit were two of the three passengers who ate at the captain's table, the third being an affable Englishman dressed impeccably in whites, his black cravat in perfect form, his hair neatly trimmed, his gray eyes echoing the smile on his lips. Introducing himself as Trevor Gorel, he said he would be changing ships in Sydney and traveling on to New Guinea.

"It's the land of opportunity," Trev Gorel commented, speaking of the island to the north of Australia. "There's gold there and timber that a million men couldn't cut in a million years. There's copra and land for growing coffee and tea."

"And natives who eat people," Kit said.

"Oh, that," Trev said, waving a hand dismissively. "They only eat each other, you know. No large animals on New Guinea. The natives have to get protein from somewhere."

Although Matt and Kit spent lots of time alone together—after all, Matt still had his assignment, for there had been no signs to suggest that Kit was going to have a baby—there was a lot of time aboard ship, and some of it was spent in the salon with Trev.

"I like him, don't you?" Kit asked after one pleasant evening during which Trev had waxed poetic about the opportunities to be found in New Guinea.

"Pleasant chap for a pom," Matt said.

"You're married to a pom, mate," she said, punching him in the belly.

"You're working up a wicked chop with that elbow," he said. "A few inches lower, and you'd have a soprano for a husband."

"I would never do damage to the family jewels."

"Crude," he teased.

"I'm an army brat, after all. You knew it when you hounded me into marrying you."

"Arf, arf," he said, nuzzling her in intimate places.

Chapter V

IN THE CROWN colony of Natal, South Africa, a tall, weather-bronzed Boer stood on the stoop of his solidly built house and watched a fringed surrey roll smoothly up the approach lane behind two perfectly matched bays. Beside him his sister, Anna De Hartog, was all asmile as she returned the eager wave of a graceful feminine arm extended from the seat of the surrey.

Two and a half years of war had not touched Dirk De Hartog too unkindly. There was silver at his temples, his neatly trimmed beard was a salt-and-pepper mix, and his sun-tanned skin showed permanent lines of sun squint. But his eyes were clear and hard, and he was still strong and fit for the work of running his farm, situated on the outskirts of Pietermaritzburg, Natal's capital city.

Anna gasped. "Look at her, Dirk. Would you just look at her!" she exclaimed as her daughter was helped down from the surrey by a tall, slim man in the uniform of the Queensland Mounted Infantry.

"Marriage agrees with her, Anna," Dirk commented. "She is looking more and more like you."

Anna was running down the steps. Sianna De Hartog Shannon met her at the bottom step, and the two women threw themselves into each other's arms with happy cries. Dirk side-stepped them, extended a hand to Slone Shannon. "Welcome, Captain," he said.

Slone Shannon had arrived in South Africa shortly after the outbreak of war, shipping down from Egypt, where he had been one of "Kitchener's boys," a select group of engineers who had pushed a railroad through the deserts of Egypt and the Sudan. It had always been his intention to be a career military man, but the death of a member of the British peerage in England and a chance encounter with a blue-eyed Boer girl in the South African High Veld had combined to make him reconsider his plans for his life.

His uncle's death, making Slone's father Earl of Cheviot and Slone heir to the title, would not by itself have been reason for Slone to consider leaving the army. On the contrary, the military had many officers of noble rank, men whose titles had ensured their rapid advancement. But the new responsibility of his title, coupled with his marriage to Sianna De Hartog, had spawned restless thoughts in Slone's mind, thoughts that were confirmed as he observed Herbert Kitchener's conduct of the war in its final stages. A niggling sense of shame had begun to build in Slone's consciousness.

Slone's promotion to captain had come shortly after he had appeared in Cape Town to be reunited with his father and mother, who had come to South Africa to inform their son of the family's sudden and unexpected rise to the peerage. The reunion was a particularly joyous one because it served to correct army records that had reported Slone killed in action at the Battle of Zilikiat's Nek. It was also, quite incidentally, the memorable occasion on which Kit Streeter had fainted into Matt Van Buren's arms upon seeing Slone accompanied by his new Boer bride.

Slone had been cynically unsure whether his captaincy had come as the result of his war record or because his father, General Adam Shannon, was now also the Earl of Cheviot. But he had accepted the promotion, and he had not objected when he had been given leave in order to take his new bride on a visit to England and the estates that would one day be his. They had left his father and mother in England to return to South Africa to attend to the details of Slone's leaving the army and also to spend the remaining portion of his leave and perhaps even longer with Sianna's family in the spacious old house in Natal.

The tearful reunion of mother and daughter moved up the stairs and into the house. Servants ran to carry in the young couple's luggage. Dirk pulled Slone aside onto the comfortable seating area of the porch and poured gin and quinine water into tall glasses. He lifted his glass, his eyes quite serious. "To peace," he said.

"Amen," Slone said.

Peace had come to the South African colonies at 11:00 P.M. on May 16, 1902. The Boers had fought bravely, but as Dirk De Hartog had often told those who wanted to continue the hopeless fight, it had gone on too long. By the time the last holdouts, Koos De La Rey and the elusive Christiaan De Wet, had sent their ragged commandos home and Louis Botha had joined Jan Smuts at the peace conference at Pretoria, too many had died, civilians as well as soldiers.

"Koos De La Rey didn't sit at the conference table," Slone commented after a satisfying sip of the rather potent drink that Dirk had made for him.

"He wouldn't," Dirk said. "And only pressure from Louis Botha and Jan Smuts got De Wet there."

During a silence Slone looked out over the fields and orchards of the De Hartog farm. He had spent a pleasant period of time there, recuperating from his wounds and falling wonderfully in love with his nurse, the blond and smiling daughter of the house. He almost wished that he could stay in Natal forever.

"Well, you chaps taught the British generals some lessons," Slone said. "The tactics developed by your man De La Rey will change the face of warfare forever."

Dirk sighed. There *had* been a certain magnificence about it, at least at first. If only men like De La Rey and De Wet had been in charge of policy, they'd have swept across South Africa to the sea like the scourge of God. But cautious leaders had restrained the troops instead of unleashing them to go on the attack. The last-ditch commando struggle—after the Boer capitals of Bloemfontein and Pretoria had fallen to the British —had had its own kind of glory, but in the end had it been worth it?

"It was, I fear, all for the worse," Dirk concluded sadly.

"It was for the British, certainly," Slone said. "Down in Cape Town they're beginning to add up the total cost, and so far the estimate is twenty-two thousand British dead as opposed to fewer than seven thousand Boer dead. The Boers proved that a small, mobile force of men, living off the land, can run rings around conventional forces and impose casualties in multiples of their own losses."

"But we must not count only the fighting dead," Dirk said. "How many thousands have died in Kitchener's concentration camps?"

Slone made a face. "Let's not saddle old Kitchener with all of the responsibility for the camps," he said. "Remember that his predecessor, Lord Roberts, started the policy of cutting off support for the commandos by burning farms and interning the women and children."

Dirk shrugged. "Does it matter which leader started it? If I were British, I wouldn't be a proud man today."

Slone nodded. "Some of our own people agree with you and have said as much in print. Just as he was resigning his commission, my comrade-in-arms Matt Van Buren stirred up a hornet's nest simply by releasing to the press a blistering eyewitness view of the worst of the camps."

"I'm glad that good men on both sides hold enlightened views," Dirk replied. He sighed again. "But, my friend, the question is, Will we learn from all this? Or will history repeat itself in future wars?" He rose and began to refill the two glasses. "I would guess that public opinion might have something to do with that. Tell me, what do people in *your* country think of the outcome of the war?"

"As a matter of fact, sir," Slone said, "I've been a little

surprised at some of the opinions published in the press. Friends have been sending me news clippings right along. I think the Brisbane *Worker* expressed the feeling of Australian radical labor leaders when it said that it was galling to see the innocent people on both sides suffer while the warmongers reveled in their ill-gotten gains. The *Worker* said that Australia had been nothing more than a cat's-paw for greedy gold stealers. The Sydney *Bulletin* said that all Britons descended from Moses would be richer than before."

Dirk laughed. "And we Boers have been accused of being bigoted against peoples other than our own."

"The Melbourne *Tocsin* is afraid that our boys who fought in South Africa have been totally militarized, brutalized, as the editors put it. They cite a case in Fremantle where fifteen soldiers raped a fifteen-year-old girl, one man for each year of the girl's life."

"Terrible," Dirk said.

"The editors of the *Tocsin* seem to be alarmists," Slone said. "From one brutal act by a group of drunken soldiers they postulate that the societies of all the civilized nations—Australia, Europe, America, and the British nations of Africa— are living on the slope of a volcano with a terrible explosion imminent."

"And what do you think?" Dirk asked.

"You saw the pom-poms and Maxims in action."

Dirk nodded grimly. As a matter of fact, he had struck one of the first blows of the war, and he had been shocked by the devastation wrought by his own Maxim machine guns against a British train.

"If, as some think, the next war involves the highly developed nations of Europe—"

"Frightening to think of it," Dirk said. "No man should ever again have to advance into the muzzles of pom-poms and Maxims."

"But they will."

"In all probability," Dirk said. "Do you really think that Australian public opinion is totally against the war?"

"No, not really. The extreme opinions come from publica-
tions that lean heavily toward socialism or from those who,
before the death of the old queen, referred to the British world
as Victoria's nigger empire. I'm told that men who returned
from the war were greeted as heroes and that riotous celebra-
tions were held in the major cities. But there'll be a lot of
thinking and talking about it. After all, the British Empire
spent about two hundred fifty million pounds on the war. The
Bulletin, which is not really a rabble-rousing newspaper, said
that all that was accomplished by the war was a monstrous
pyramid of skulls and the taking of two Dutch islands in the
middle of the Dark Continent."

Slone reached into his tunic for a wallet, from which he
removed a newspaper clipping. "This one I saved, because it
was written by a friend of mine, Kelvin Broome. He was here
during the worst of it. He, too, says that the gold of the Rand
was at the bottom of the British response to the Boer uprising.
Kel isn't a rabble-rouser either; but he isn't too happy about
Australians dying under the command of British officers who
often obtain their rank not by experience but because they
hold a title, and like Matt Van Buren, he speaks out quite
strongly against the concentration camp and farm-burning
policies. I saved the clipping primarily because of this."

He held the paper up to the fading evening light and read in
a low, even voice. *"It remains to be seen whether the majority
of Australians will remain true to the motto 'For the Empire,
right or wrong.' Australia sent 16,175 officers and men to fight
in South Africa. Five hundred eighteen of them will not be
coming home, 251 of them having been killed in action, 267 of
them dying of disease."*

"I'm surprised that the casualty list is so small," Dirk said.

Slone grinned. "Well, we had some rather rugged dinkum
diggers over here." He sobered. "No, actually, we just were
damned lucky. At first the British would point to a fortified
position and say"—he minced his words and went through
the motions of dipping snuff—"'I say, you insignificant
colonials, would you mind terribly dying a little while you

take yon hill? Please simply ignore the wily Boer's cannon and machine guns.' "

Dirk laughed.

"Then the pommy officers came to realize that the Queensland Mounted Infantry was of more value scouting the field than assaulting rocky hills, where the Boer was entrenched with his Maxims and pom-poms. In the field, and on a good horse, I think the Australian came close to being a match for the Boer commando."

"I'll grant you that," Dirk said.

"So the Boer republics have recognized the sovereignty of Edward the Seventh and have accepted payment from the British of three million pounds for the farms that were burned and destroyed, and the gold mines of the Rand are producing again," Slone said. He cast a questioning look at Dirk. "Will the Boer be able to live with this status?"

Dirk nodded grimly. "Yes. At least for a while. But if you read a copy of the Treaty of Vereeniging, you'll find a little clause saying that the Dutch language may be taught in public schools. I don't really understand why the Brits let that one get by them. It's an open statement that the Boer fully intends to cling to his nationality and to his customs, that he has no intention of letting himself be Anglicized." He grinned. "Don't be surprised to find, in the future, that the union of all the colonies in South Africa is a Boer union."

"You're saying that the Boer will accomplish by political means what he failed to do with his rifle?"

"Actually," Dirk said, "losing the war has served to arouse a new consciousness of nationality among the Afrikaner peoples. Some of the burghers are already establishing private schools to teach in High Dutch, ignoring English completely. There's also a movement to promote Afrikaans to a position of official recognition. Some publishers in the Cape Colony and in Natal are already turning out books of history and poetry in Afrikaans." He smiled. "The Boer is a hardheaded fellow, you know."

"Well, I say go to it, so long as I don't have to fight you
gain," Slone said.

"In that I concur," Dirk said. He had the glasses in his
and when Sianna and Anna appeared.

"Have you two solved all the problems of the world, then?"
nna asked.

"Most of them," Dirk said.

"You have just time for another before the meal is ready,"
nna said.

"If you don't mind, Uncle Dirk," Sianna said, "I'll have
ne as well."

Dirk looked at her darkly. "And since when, missy, do you
artake of alcohol?"

"It's British decadence," Sianna said smilingly. "My
icked husband allows it, and I have come rather to enjoy it."

Later, at a table laden with the plenty gathered from the
elds of the De Hartog farm, Slone leaned back in repletion,
atted his stomach, and sighed. "Anna, please tell your
aughter that she must not emulate you in meal preparation."

"Ah?" Anna asked, flushing, thinking for a moment that
ae meal was being criticized.

"For if she does," Slone said, "I will soon weigh a ton."

Anna smiled. Australians were an odd lot. Once another
ustralian had told her that in his country everything was
eculiar, with giant birds that never flew, rivers that petered
ut into nothing in the desert, and animals that hopped in-
ead of walking while others sat around placidly munching
n trees. That man, too, had sometimes given her oblique
ompliments. But that was long ago, and although she had
ever loved again, she felt no real regret, except for the
nowledge that Slone Shannon would soon be taking her
aughter away with him again, home to that odd country far
cross the Indian Ocean.

As if to confirm her fears, Sianna began to talk about Aus-
alia, eager to share what she had learned since becoming the
ife of an Australian. "You'll have to learn almost a new

language when you come to visit us," Sianna said. "There ar
bimbils and billabongs and bandicoots and barramundis an
coolabahs and all sorts of other wondrous animals an
things."

Anna laughed, but inside, her heart seemed to want to sto
beating. It might be years before she saw her daughter agai
if ever. It was especially ironic, because through a convolute
tale of family trouble going back more than two decades, sh
had only recently been able to acknowledge her daughter a
her own.

For the first twenty years of Sianna's life she had had t
content herself with being her daughter's "Aunt Anna,
When Anna's youthful sweetheart, Jon Mason, had deserte
her and returned to Australia, twenty or more years ago, sh
had, in her pain, given herself to a local Boer farmer. Th
resulting child was the Boer's, but she had told Dirk it wa
Jon's. To avoid scandal, Dirk had sent Anna away to have th
child in secret. With her he sent his young bride. Upon th
two women's return with the baby, the child was presented t
the world as the issue of Dirk and his wife. Sianna had grow
up in ignorance of this, calling her uncle Father and he
mother Aunt.

The truth had come out two years ago, when Sianna ha
returned from the war engaged to Slone, who was Jon Ma
son's half brother. It was hard enough telling Sianna tha
Anna had borne her out of wedlock. But a harder truth als
had to be revealed: Since Dirk believed that Sianna would b
marrying kin if she married Slone, Anna had to clear the wa
for her daughter's happiness by telling her brother about th
nameless Boer farmer who was the child's real father. In d
ing so, she had suffered a profound shame, but she had r
ceived in return a consolation. For the first time Anna ha
been able to put her arms around Sianna and say, *"Oh, m
daughter, my daughter."* And now her heart was saying
again: *Oh, my daughter.*

Sianna, sensing Anna's mood, looked at her mother wit
her blue eyes wide. "Come with us, Mother."

Anna's eyes filled. "So you're going soon."

"I fear so," Slone said. "I have resigned my commission. However, it seems a good chance that I won't be leaving government service. Probably due to my new, exalted status—" He paused. He had not yet become accustomed to being a part of the British peerage and was not sure that he liked it. Being the heir to an earldom was not exactly fair dinkum. "I've been asked to meet with Mr. Alfred Deakin when we get back to Sydney, with the object of taking a position with the government."

"I shall be a grand lady and wear fantastically daring gowns at public functions," Sianna said.

"You will remember your upbringing," Anna said automatically, then smiled.

"Yes, I will," Sianna promised. "Mother, I said come with us. Did you hear?"

"I heard."

"And?"

"And what would your uncle Dirk do without a woman to manage his house and keep him on the straight and narrow?"

"Go, Anna, if it pleases you and if Slone will allow it," Dirk said. "Perhaps I would find myself a plump young widow. God knows the war made enough of them."

"A strange woman in my house?" Anna asked, not smiling until she looked back at Sianna. "No, my darling. A newly married couple does not need a doting mother tagging along, and I don't think I'd like being in a country where everything is so strange."

"But you'll come to visit one day, won't you?" Sianna asked pleadingly, looking at Dirk. "You'll bring her to see us?"

"Perhaps, little one," Dirk said. "But whatever happens, God brought you together, and he has commanded that the wife's place is with her husband. We will be sad to see you go, both of you; but distance will not diminish our love, and God willing, we will see each other again."

Chapter VI

THE GASCOYNE, WESTERN Australia's longest river, has its headwaters inland in the range of mountains named for the Earl of Carnarvon and meets the sea at the town of the same name. For most of the year the river, which points almost straight west from the mountains, is dry. In the wet season it becomes a roaring torrent.

In the early 1900s Carnarvon had already become the dominant center of the northwest coast. Its inhabitants were almost belligerently insistent in claiming their area as that part of Australia first known to white men. The Dutch had made a landing on an offshore island in 1616.

Carnarvon town owed its existence largely to the abundance of salt at nearby Lake McLeod. Tons of salt left Carnarvon aboard ships, including those of the Mason Line, and a Mason agent worked and lived in town. Extending outward from the town toward the interior were scattered cattle stations. And then there was the Gibson Desert.

Tolo and Java Mason arrived in Carnarvon aboard a small chartered vessel, arousing several kinds of comment. First of all, men noted the little sheila. Secondly, and with some amazement, they saw that the sun-darkened, impressively large young man had actually brought a mob of boongs with him from the south, as if there weren't enough Abos in the northwest.

Tolo got Java settled in the hotel and then had some trouble finding a place for his Abos. One simply did not hire rooms for blackfellows in Carnarvon—or in any other town or city in Australia, for that matter. Ganba settled the matter by insisting that he could take care of himself and his little group if only the boss would give him a little money.

Actually, Ganba did not need money, for he had access to the huge stores of food that Tolo had purchased in Perth, but with cash in his hand he could assure himself that it would not become tiresome waiting for the white man to get ready to go into the never-never. Most establishments that sold alcohol had little windows at the back, called dog windows, where blackfellows were served. Even before Ganba had found a good campsite on the outskirts of Carnarvon, he had found a dog window and purchased a large bottle of rum.

After seeing to his crew, Tolo retrieved Java from the hotel. Freshened by a real bath in a real tub, wearing clean, if somewhat wrinkled, clothing, she was radiantly beautiful as she and Tolo entered the office of the local Mason agent.

The agent, startled by the imposing couple, came to his feet instantly. "I heard you'd arrived in town, sir," he said after the Masons had introduced themselves. "G'day to you and your wife. Won't you sit down and tell me what I can do for you?"

As Tolo outlined his needs, which included a number of horses, the agent listened in amazement.

"Let me get this straight," he said. "You're going into the Gibson on horseback, and you plan to take this pretty little bird with you?"

"Tweet-tweet," Java said impishly, for she had been exposed to the Australian male's superior attitudes all her life, and now that she was grown up, she sometimes liked to twit the fair dinkum types.

"Beg your pardon, miss," the agent said. "But, 'strewth, you're both troppo if you think you can cross the Gibson with horses."

Tolo smiled. He had already encountered in Perth the

Western Australian way of calling a man crazy—troppo, driven mad by the tropics. He did not take the comment as an insult.

In fact, Tolo felt quite at ease with the agent, who was typical of the straightforward, blunt-spoken men who had settled the continent's wild, desolate places. He respected such men for what they were. He felt as safe walking into a plank-sided pub full of bushrangers as he felt entering Bina Tyrell's plush restaurant in Sydney. Now and again Tolo might have to use his fists, if for no other reason than to give some strapping fellow a chance to try his skill against a man of Tolo's immense size. But Tolo did not mind the rough-and-tumble of such encounters, and men like the agent certainly did not offend him with their words. In fact, the agent seemed seriously concerned, for his face wore an earnest expression.

"Twice troppo," the agent commented, shaking his head. "Horses. And you're taking the bir—the lady with you."

"If not horses, what?" Java asked.

"Camels. For sure."

"Camels?" Tolo repeated.

"Camels." The agent nodded.

"And where do we get camels?" Tolo asked, after a silent period of waiting for the agent to volunteer information.

"Very little call for camels, you know."

"But?"

"Oh, they run the outback wild. Prospectors and blokes like that brought 'em in the 1850s to explore the dry country, but there's little call for 'em anymore. The bush is full of 'em, but I guess you wouldn't want to take the time to round up a few and tame 'em."

"Not really," Tolo said.

"Goodonyer," the agent said. "The camel bull can be dangerous as bloody hell in the winter when he's rutting. Best thing, I guess, if you're damned fool enough to go through with this, is to go to old Jonas Mayhew out Yinnietharra way. He might or he might not sell you some tame camels, depending on his mood at the time."

"Thank you," Tolo said.

"How are you situated for tucker?"

"We have a few things to pick up here in Carnarvon. Mostly we stocked up in Perth."

"If there is anything I can do, just yell."

"Perhaps," Tolo said, "you know of someone who is familiar with the country inland, the Gibson in particular."

"Can't say as I do," the agent said. "Most Carnarvon boys are smart enough to stay out of the desert. Best bet, I'd say, is to find yourself a dependable blackfellow and keep him well fed so he won't be tempted to eat you if things get rough out in the desert."

"You've been a great help," Tolo said, sneaking a wink at Java. "How do I get to Yinnietharra?"

"Only one road goes east," the agent said. "Follow it. You'll pass a couple of cattle stations. They can point you to old Jonas's place." He looked at Tolo for a long moment, his head cocked in speculation. "You're not really going out there just to see how a mob of boongs live in the wild?"

"Yes, I am," Tolo said.

"Truly?" The agent winked. "You're not going looking for gold?"

"Stone the crows," Java said, "he's found us out, Tolo."

"Hush," Tolo said, trying to keep from laughing.

The agent leaned toward them eagerly. " 'Strewth, I knew it. And a man like Mr. Thomas Mason wouldn't be going off on a wild dingo hunt neither. You've had men out there prospecting, haven't you?"

"We're going to study the Aboriginal peoples in their natural habitat," Tolo said.

"I've always said that all the gold can't have been found already," the agent said, his eyes burning. "I've always known that the good Lord didn't make the outback for nothing. There's too bloody much of it, thousands of square miles. He wouldn't have made it just to be an empty nothing."

"I think we should tell him, Tolo," Java said.

Tolo rolled his eyes and, with a shrug, gave up.

"Lassiter's gold," Java whispered.

"Oh, God," the agent said, and then his face went stern. "From this end? If you were going for Lassiter's gold, you'd start from Alice Springs in the Northern Territory, not from the west coast."

"Or so it's always been thought," Java replied.

The agent's interest was revived. "Makes sense, come to think of it. Poor bloke perished in the sandhills over near Ayers Rock. Found him holding a nose peg, a camel's nose peg. Figured his animals bolted for some reason, leaving him to die of thirst. You believe, then, that he had been farther west than anyone guessed at the time? You think Lassiter's mine is in the Gibson?"

"We really don't care to say what we think," Java responded. Then, to cut off further questions: "This is confidential Mason business, by the way."

The agent pulled himself up. "Of course. I know how to keep my mouth shut."

"Billions," Java said in a whisper. "In one huge outcropping. Poor Lassiter. They say he died a billionaire and his secret died with him."

"Mr. Mason," the agent said, "I've been thinking about what you said about needing a man who knows the Gibson. Now I haven't traveled all of her, but I've been around the edges, and that's better than nothing."

Tolo squeezed Java's hand to keep her quiet. "You'll be much more valuable to us here in Carnarvon," he said. "We need a secure base line behind us, a man here to send needed supplies and equipment when we call for them."

"You can count on me," the agent assured him.

Tolo took Java's arm and guided her to the door.

"By the by," the agent said, "want me to notify your home office, your mother, anybody?"

"Thank you, no," Java said. "We can handle our own communications."

"Pretty hard to communicate from the Gibson," the agent

said, determined to have the last word. "How long should I wait to notify the home office that you ain't back?"

Tolo shrugged off the agent's pessimism. "Use your own judgment," he replied.

Safely away from the agent's office, Tolo made a pretense of spanking Java. She pulled away and skipped off, laughing. "You'll have the poor fellow dreaming dreams of gold," he complained.

"It will put some excitement into his life," she said.

"But we don't want every bushranger in Western Australia following us, thinking that we really do have a lead to Lassiter's gold."

Java sobered. "I hadn't thought of that," she said. "But surely the man didn't believe me?"

The station belonging to Jonas Mayhew slumbered in the sun near the dry bed of the Gascoyne, on an arid plain that extended outward to a distant, heat-distorted horizon. A small stone house with a rusting metal roof sat amid crumbling outbuildings, and weeds and desert grasses grew in the open areas nearby. From his front stoop Mayhew could look down to the apparently dry riverbed and the water holes where his camels drank. The Gascoyne only looked dry, for under its sandy bed the pure, sweet water still flowed, a soak hundreds of miles long.

The Aborigines had known the secret of the underground waters for as long as they had existed in Western Australia. Cattle and sheep drovers, whose needs for water were more demanding, found the Gascoyne to be a source of more frustration than water during the dry season, but the river met the needs of Jonas and his camels.

Jonas had few visitors to his remote station. When the mangy dingoes that belonged to the Abo family living on his place pointed their muzzles restlessly toward the west, he knew that something was coming—maybe nothing more than a stray kangaroo. Then, when a little caravan topped the far ridge—a white man and a white woman riding horses, accompanied by packhorses and a mob of blackfellows—he went into his house and used a snaggletoothed comb to tidy up his hair and beard. He even washed his face. He would have put on clean clothing if he had owned a change, but he did not, so his flannel shirt and homespun trousers had to do, dusty though they were. At least he had had the blackfellow women wash them only last week.

Jonas was waiting on the porch when Tolo and Java Mason pulled their horses to a halt in the front yard, which was nothing more than bare sand with a few tufts of tough desert grass showing here and there.

"Come up and rest yourselves," Jonas said hospitably as his visitors dismounted.

Java walked up the stone steps first, and Jonas offered her a waterskin. She accepted and drank expertly. The water was warm and a little sandy.

"Figure on taking them horses any farther?" Jonas asked as Tolo came up and took the waterskin.

"We thought we might trade them to you," Tolo said, turning the skin up and letting water trickle into his mouth.

"Humph!" Jonas exclaimed, scratching his snow white beard. "Little use I'd have for such fragile animals."

"You could sell them to the cattle station we passed a few miles back," Tolo said.

"Got it all figured out, have you?" Jonas was a wizened, bony antique of a man with a full head of white hair that fell uncut to his shoulders, pale blue eyes, and a nose permanently reddened by years of the ravaging sun.

"We want to go into the Gibson, Mr. Mayhew. I understand that horses can't make it."

"Not very far," Jonas agreed.

"We were told that you might teach us how to handle camels and sell us animals for riding and for carrying our supplies."

Jonas squinted at Tolo. "Who told you that?"

"We'd be ever so grateful," Java said, speaking for the first time.

"*We,* is it?" Jonas turned to look at her, his lips showing a smile through his white beard. "Where this young fool goes, you go, is that it?"

"Yes," she said, answering his smile.

"Like the desert, do you?"

"Well," she said, "it's . . . interesting."

"My Annie hated it, too," Jonas said, having read the guarded expression on Java's face. "But she stayed with me. Kept up with me on the longest treks. Had more of an eye for ore-bearing rock than I did, but we didn't find gold. Found this place instead. Water, some grazing. Plenty of camels running wild. Annie was a good hand with animals. She could cool down a rutting bull camel with a few words and a stroke of her hand. We'd tame 'em and then sell 'em to other fools who wanted to go off prospecting the desert." He stared at Java incredulously for a moment longer. "You *really* want to go out there?"

"Yes, I do," she said. "Will you help us, please?"

"Never could resist the smile of a pretty woman, especially when she says 'please,'" Jonas said. "And when you fall off a camel and break a bone or two, you'll find that old Jonas is a pretty good medic. Been treating animals all my life and even a human or two. Set bones good as new."

"That's reassuring to know," Java said.

"Camel's not native to Australia," he said.

"I know."

"But then neither are we," Jonas said. "Not even the black-fellow, if the educated types are right in saying that he came over on a land bridge or something from somewhere else. Brought the dingo with him, but it took white men to bring in the camel, back in the fifties. Brought Afghani camel men with 'em and used 'em to build the telegraph and the rail-roads. So the camel helped build the very things that made him obsolete. The white man shipped the Afghans home and turned the camels loose. The bush is full of 'em. It's camel heaven, just the kind of country they love. You can use them horses to catch as many of 'em as you need."

"Well, we don't really want to take that much time," Tolo said. "And since we know nothing about training camels, we had hoped to buy tame ones from you."

"Come, then," Jonas said.

He led the way to a barn built of rough-sawn boards. Inside, two camels stood placidly chewing their cuds.

"The first thing you need to know about camels is that they're smart," Jonas said. "They're smarter than the average Abo and almost as smart as a good dog or a woman. Beggin' your pardon, little lady. Hardheaded, they are. Sometimes you have to bully 'em, sometimes baby 'em. Trick is in knowing which to do when."

One of the camels turned its comical head toward Java, its soft, velvety nostrils twitching.

"Just stand still," Jonas said. "Let her get the smell of you."

The camel's muzzle came close, and with a retching sound the beast regurgitated a slimy green mess onto the front of Java's shirtwaist. She leapt back with an expression of disgust.

"Won't hurt you," Jonas said, laughing. "Sally was just telling you that you'd invaded her turf. Camel's like a human being that way. You know how you get a little uncomfortable if someone stands too close to you, maybe puts his face right up to yours when he's talking? Well, the camel feels the same way. He'll let you come close for a reason, like putting on a saddle or maybe a nose peg, but if you're just there to socialize, stand back about ten feet, or Mr. Camel will share his cud with you."

"Well, I think she could have socialized in a less messy way," Java replied, looking down in dismay at her dress.

"Another thing to remember about camels," Jonas continued, "is that they can kick you in any direction. Anytime you're within six feet of one of the beasts, he can get you. He can strike out with his front legs, and he can kick forward, backward, and sideways with his hind legs."

"Charming," Tolo commented.

In the next few days both Tolo and Java learned more

about camels than they really cared to know. They learned how to fit the oddly shaped saddles in place on riding camels, how to balance and secure loads on the pack animals, how to hobble the camels at night so that they could forage without being able to wander too far.

Tolo spent many hours with old Jonas, deciding what to take and what to leave behind from the large amount of gear and stores that had been packed out to Mayhew Station on horseback. Aside from Java's and Tolo's mounts, two camels would carry water, four barrels each, each barrel weighing fifty pounds. Two more animals would carry provisions.

"Only six in all?" Tolo protested.

"That's enough," replied Jonas. "More'n that and you'll have a caravan so big that you and the little lady won't be able to handle the beasts."

"We can get Ganba and his people to help."

The old man shook his head. "Blackfellows are not good with animals."

Tolo had to try. He summoned Ganba, noted with satisfaction that the Aborigine was fully sober, having drunk up all of the spirits he had hoarded in Carnarvon, and quickly learned that Jonas was right. Ganba, in protest, told Tolo that he was not afraid of the camels, that he just did not like them. Ganba's dislike was returned doubly by the camels, so that he could not get within ten feet of one without risking a kick or a bite.

"Well, Jonas, you're right as usual," Tolo concluded.

"Now that we've wasted that time," the old man said, not unkindly, "let's get on with it."

The food was packed in carpetbags. Other bags held leather and tools for repairing the camel gear, camping equipment, including mosquito netting and oil lamps, spare rope, extra hobbles for the camels, Tolo's map case, and no fewer than three compasses.

Loading all of the gear and supplies onto the camels was a lengthy job, a task that was practiced endlessly before Jonas was satisfied. Over a period of days Tolo and Java learned to position the load of each camel so the beasts' relatively tender skin would not be chafed by an off-balance cargo. In the end they got the loading time down to forty-five minutes.

"It'll get easier each day," Jonas assured them. "You'll be using up some of the food all of the time. Just remember, as you make some sacks lighter, distribute the load from the full sacks."

Java's first camel ride would stay in her memory for as long as she lived. The camel—Sally, the one that had greeted her so charmingly that first day—groaned piteously as she obeyed Jonas's order to rise from her kneeling position. Java was pitched backward, then forward as the animal got first her rear legs and then her front legs under her. It was not too bad after Java got over the initial fear of falling from her high perch on the uncomfortable riding saddle. There was still the real danger of developing motion sickness, since the camel's gait produced many of the motions of a round-bottomed vessel in a storm at sea. But soon Java had the knack of it and was saying "whoosh-whoosh" like a veteran when she wanted the camel to kneel down.

When Tolo gave the word that the party would be moving out toward the desert, some of Ganba's little group of blackfellows grumbled. They had been very comfortable camped beside the riverbed, eating from Tolo's large store of provisions and roasting an occasional sheep stolen from the grazing areas of a station closer to the coast.

Tolo and Java had noticed that the farther away from the coast they had traveled, the skimpier had become the clothing of the Aborigines. Now, at Mayhew Station, Ganba and the other males wore only loincloths. Bildana, Ganba's wife, had made for herself a small triangular patch of cloth attached to a string that she tied around her waist. The patch barely covered her genitals. Her small, pointed breasts were exposed but supported underneath by a breast girdle—a string of rolled cloth supported by a vee of string around her neck. The two younger women wore only the loin patch, their tiny breasts entirely bare. Every inch of exposed skin was covered with grease rendered from the kidneys and flesh of the stolen sheep, so that even when one of the Abos approached quietly, one knew of his presence unless there was a strong wind to blow the smell away.

Shortly after the group left Mayhew Station, the land began to change. To people who had grown up in Australia's fertile coastal belt, amid greenery, soaring trees, and the tailored gardens of the cities, the first impression of the western Gibson's clay pans and sand dunes was one of vastness. A feeling of new freedom welled up in Java and Tolo; now, in retrospect, the tree-covered coastal areas seemed a kind of prison for the spirit. In the desert one's eye could use its maximum capacity for distance, to measure the purple line of hills that rested low on the unbroken horizon.

The soft, padded feet of the camels made little plopping sounds on the clay pans and splayed out on the sand to provide secure footing for the beasts. Strong tufts of spinifex grass were the most common growth. Now and then an erosion gully would break the monotony of flatness, and there would be tidbits of greenery for the camels to eat.

After consulting with Ganba, Tolo had set his course almost due east, their route paralleling the dry river. Ganba said that blackfellows would be near the river, to drink from its soaks and to hunt the game that, like the Aborigines, had known since the time of the Dreaming how to dig in the bed of the Gascoyne for life-giving water.

Tolo made camp early, while there was still sun, for unloading the camels and setting up the tent was a time-consuming affair. Next day he discovered that one does not travel a beeline course in the desert. They detoured around areas of dense brush with spikes that could push through leather. Patches of flat, hard clay, covered with small, jagged rocks as close together as peas on a plate, also forced them off their course, lest the loose stones damage the soft feet of the camels. And

Java discovered burrs the size of her fist with spikes that were very painful.

The old man had warned them not to drink much liquid during the day. They took tea and water with their breakfast, rode all morning without drinking, then swallowed half a cup at midday. The sun sucked moisture from their bodies at a fierce rate; later, when they began to doubt Jonas's advice and drank more during the day, they found that they only perspired more freely and became thirstier than ever. They cut back their rations.

After only three days in the desert, their long journey barely begun, Java's every muscle was sore from the jolting, swaying pace of the camel. Her face and hands were darkening with the sun, in spite of applications of a protective cream. Her left calf ached from an encounter with one of the huge burrs. That night, after Tolo had set up her campstool, she sank down onto it gratefully to watch Bildana prepare the evening meal. At a slight distance the Abos had already settled in and were eating peaches from tins, saving the dried trail rations for last.

Dusk came suddenly, and the temperature began to fall with that startling swiftness that marks a desert night. Brush fires sprang up in the Abo camp, the smell of the smoke aromatic and rather pleasant. Before the sun returned to bring with it the day's punishing heat, the Abos would have rolled into the warm ashes of the fires to ward off the near-freezing nighttime temperature. Now and again one could see a burn on an Abo's skin where he or she had rolled onto a live ember.

At the beginning of the trek away from the coast Bildana had adopted the white mistress as her special charge, and over the weeks she had learned much. She brought Java's plate, poured tea into Java's tin cup, and squatted on her heels at a respectful distance to see if the mistress wanted anything else.

"So," Tolo said, sitting down beside Java's stool on the sand, "what is your opinion now of life in the waly?" There was so much of it that the Australian had several names for

he mostly arid wilderness that filled the heart of his conti-
ent. Waly meant "way-out bush."

"I refuse to answer, lest I sound quite unladylike," Java
eplied.

Tolo's face showed quick concern, and Java relented in-
tantly.

"It's not exactly a picnic in the park or an overnight camp-
ng trip on the strand, is it?" She smiled and touched Tolo's
houlder. "No worries, mate. Like Jonas Mayhew's wife, I'm
vith you."

Her words were meant to be light and reassuring, but to
olo they had an ominous ring. Jonas Mayhew's wife had
ied in the desert.

For two days after Terry Forrest had watched a small char-
ered vessel carry the sweetest little sheila he had ever seen
ut of his life, he had spent a lot of time in the pubs. At first a
ood glass had driven Java Mason's face from his mind, and a
it of the old slap and tickle with the barmaid at The Nugget
ade him positively mindless—for an hour or two. Whatever
e did, however, that sweet little face came back, and he
ould imagine his lips on the pink buds at the tips of Java
Mason's breasts.

Terry could make himself morose just imagining what that
weet, delicious-looking body would be like after the scaven-
ers finished with it, once her young fool of a husband had
otten her killed out in the Gibson. It fairly set his teeth on
dge, for his imagination made Java's skeleton a very trim and
retty one.

A waste of fine womanhood, he told himself. *But none of my
ffair.*

For not even extended regret at not having tasted the
harms of Java's sweet little body was sufficient reason for
erry to give up his life in Perth and journey northward. It
ook an accidental meeting with a sailor off a Mason Line ship
oasting down from Carnarvon to move Terry into action.

"You'd better believe it, mate," the sailor told Terry over a glass of dark ale in The Nugget. "He's young, this Thomas Mason, but he's no fool. Owns half of New South Wales, he does. Went out buying stations hit hard by the drought, and when it breaks, he'll be the richest man in Australia."

"So what's he bloody well going to do in the Gibson? Buy more land and pray for rain?"

"Nothin' like that," the sailor said, affronted. "It's gold young Thomas Mason is after. Heard it with me own ears. He's got the secret to Lassiter's gold. Knows exactly where the outcrop is, solid gold. Alls you have to do is take a pickax and knock off the chunks, billions of dollars' worth."

"He told me that he was going to make a bloody study of the boongs in the wild," Terry said.

"Listen, I got my information direct from the Mason agent. I heard him talkin' to a bloke in his office, speakin' in confidence and swearin' him to secrecy. The agent said he'd had it straight from Thomas Mason himself."

"Ballocks," Terry said, taking his leave.

But the notion would not give him any peace. Hell, yes, he knew the Gibson. It was one big four-hundred-mile stretch of waterless nothing studded with spinifex grass. It could be crossed, but most probably not by a Sydney poofter and his little wife with no more help than a mob of blackfellows who, if they got hungry, would not leave much of the sheila's body for the scavengers. Gold? Not bloody likely.

But still . . . it just didn't make sense for a man of Thomas Mason's stature to go walkabout in the never-never without good reason. They said that the more money a man had, the more he wanted, and maybe the Mason boy was one of those, not satisfied with—as the sailor had said—owning half of the bush country in New South Wales. Billions in gold. Yes, that would draw even a very rich man, wouldn't it?

In the end, cursing himself for having wasted an opportunity to be Mason's guide, cursing because he had wasted days, he was on board a ship moving north up the coast toward Carnarvon. He knew, however, that it would have taken Mason time to organize a mob to move toward the east from

Carnarvon. He was sure, also, that the experienced bushmen at Carnarvon would tell the greenhorn from Sydney that a man needed camels to go into the Gibson for any length of time, and there was just one place to get camels.

Terry arrived in Carnarvon in due time and learned that the Mason party, including a very pretty little bird, had left just a week previously. And, as he had guessed, they were heading for old Jonas Mayhew's station to try to buy camels.

Arriving at Mayhew Station only two days after the Mason party had pushed off into the bush, Terry took his time bargaining with the old man for a bit of tucker. Soon he was following the very clear tracks of the six Mason camels and the mob of blackfellows into the desert. He felt wonderful. It seemed quite simple to him. He would be very flexible, taking things as they came, with no push, no worries. If, indeed, Thomas Mason had the secret of Lassiter's gold, goodonim. Terry would make himself useful and satisfy himself with a cut. A minority share in billions would buy him all the luxuries he could ever use. A man can eat only so many steaks, can sleep in only one bed at a time, and the number of women he can pile into that bed is limited by his physical makeup.

In the event that the Gibson karked out the poofter, well, that would leave Terry alone with the little sheila. Terry knew that he wasn't a bad-looking bloke, at least not according to the reactions of most of the birds he had known, and it could be very romantic in the desert with those sweltering days and frigid nights that made cuddling a pleasure. Under such conditions it would not be out of the realm of possibility for a man to comfort and even to woo the new widow and, in due time, marry into riches without having to dig for gold.

From the fresh signs along the trail Terry knew he would be catching up to the Mason party in another day. He spent the early evening rehearsing a speech of greeting.

Chapter VII

JESSICA BROOME GORDON had seen enough of the world to make Marco Polo look like a local spice peddler. Before she married Sam Gordon, a clipper man, she had traveled to Hong Kong with her mother. After marrying Sam, she had lived aboard the ships he owned and captained, including the most beautiful of all, the *Cutty Sark*. She had touched ports on all the continents save one, Antarctica, and she had been near enough to that vast frozen landmass to have felt the chill and power of its polar storms. She had survived the greatest natural catastrophe of modern times, the eruption of Krakatoa. She had been lost in the jungles of Java, and she had given birth to her one child—named for the place of her birth—in a native hut in the Javanese mountains.

In her travels she had encountered peoples of all types, sizes, and colors. The Javanese hill people, primitive though they were, had saved her life and that of her baby with their native medicines and nurturing. Her husband's crews had comprised seamen of all colors—white and black and all the shades between. On board ship a mariner's seamanship and stamina, not his color, were the tests of his worth.

So Jessica, like many educated Australians, felt uneasy, at least in principle, about the generally accepted White Australia policy, and she often spoke out against the intention of the new national government to carry out that policy. It was not until she was past her forty-fifth year, a handsome, still-trim matron of established means and social position, that she discovered she was, after all, no more holy in observing the Christian commandment of "Love thy neighbor" than the average bigoted digger. This notion of loving thy brown- or black- or yellow-skinned neighbor, she realized, depended on how close the colored neighbor stood to one's own personal space.

While her far-distant daughter was discovering that the rules of personal space apply even to camels, Jessica was undergoing another trauma, not quite as severe as the shock of having her one daughter fall in love with a half-breed Kanaka, but on the same order. Her brother was beginning to inquire about Misa Mason in a more than casual way.

It was not, to be sure, an interest that developed immediately. As a bachelor and confirmed navy man Rufe did not move quickly in matters pertaining to his private feelings. And since he was on duty now with the Australian squadron and often at sea, he was only an intermittent guest at what Magdalen was calling the unround table—a new long carved-teak dining table that Sam Gordon had ordered from a local furniture maker.

When he was present, Rufe was deemed by Sam and the other regulars at the Broome table to be something of an authority on attitudes and events in the huge outside world—the world dominated by the British Empire. And indeed, Rufe *was* very well informed for a mere captain, for he was constantly in touch with superior officers of the Pacific fleet and through them with the Admiralty in London. He obliged his host and dinner companions by sharing what information he had during their wide-ranging discussions of world affairs.

Although Australia was isolated by distance, her security and future as a nation were dependent on the actions and attitudes of the old European nations, which historically had been incapable of avoiding war among themselves for any great length of time.

Many thoughtful Australians, Sam Gordon included, be-

lieved that the natural course of events in the Pacific would
bring many of the islands under Australian control. Australia
was there, for one thing. And Australia was the only civilizing
influence in the entire Pacific, if one discounted the actions of
the American, German, English, Scottish, Dutch, French,
and Russian traders who plied the islands seeking a favorable
barter; the miners who ransacked them for gold; the planters
who stole native lands for growing copra and sugar; the
blackbirders who still coerced natives to work at slave wages
in Australia; and the missionaries who were bent on solving
all problems by saving the souls of the benighted heathen.

While it was true that Australia did not have the population of great colonial powers, not even as many as tiny Hol-
land, it was evident to Australians that theirs was a nation of
destiny.

Already New Zealand had set an example of Antipodean
colonialism by annexing the Cook, Savage, and Suvorov islands. And although Great Britain did not push Australia's
interests in the Pacific with enough vigor to please Australians, it seemed evident that British New Guinea would
become Australian within the next couple of years. Such
things moved slowly. Meanwhile, Australian traders had out-
run the Union Jack among the Pacific islands, and far-seeing
men were pushing the Colonial Office in London to recognize
Australia's claim to the New Hebrides Islands.

"My feeling is," Rufe confided one night at dinner, shortly
after returning from a cruise through the western Pacific waters, "that the Australian government has gone a bit too far in
describing the New Hebrides as our 'Channel Islands' and,
therefore, vital to our defense. I would guess that the east
would be the least likely direction for a naval threat to Australia."

"Are you thinking of our German cousins?" Kelvin
Broome asked.

"There are others. To the north," Rufe said.

"Our little brown brothers, the Japanese," Sam said.

"Surely you can't consider them to be a threat to the Royal Navy?"

"Perhaps not today," Rufe said.

"We need a navy of our own," Magdalen ventured. "Not just a motley collection of obsolete gunboats that we inherited from the various states upon federation."

"Can't afford it," Kelvin said. "That's why we let the Brits dictate terms to us. That's why Mr. Deakin has just agreed to up the Australian contribution toward the Pacific fleet from one hundred twenty-six thousand pounds a year to two hundred thousand pounds, even though there is no guarantee that the ships will remain in Australian waters. Because we can't afford to build large warships, we have to buy our protection on the cheap."

"Well, consider it a bargain," Rufe said. "After all, for a mere two hundred thousand, you get me included."

"Where do we go to ask for our money back?" Jessica asked.

"I didn't expect my own sister to recognize my true worth," Rufe persisted. "A prophet without honor, and all that."

"I know this would raise a concerted howl from all rates payers," Kelvin said, "but I wonder if it wouldn't be a good idea—just a suggestion, mind you—if we paid our upper-level public servants salaries competitive with what a superior man can earn in private business."

"Good Lord," Magdalen said.

"In that way we could have, instead of the mild-mannered Mr. Deakin, a man such as Sir James Burns." They all knew Burns, head of one of the largest trading companies, Burns Philp.

"Go on, Kel," Sam said.

"Burns has said, and I can quote him, since I wrote the story for the newspaper myself, *'The natural destiny of the Pacific Islands is that they should come under the control of Australia.'* As opposed, of course, to coming under the control of krauts, frogs, Yanks, poms, and wogs of other persuasions."

"Are you ready to fight the Germans?" Jessica asked. "Or the Americans, for that matter?"

"Well, to quote Mr. Burns again," Kelvin said, *" 'The race is to the swift and the strong, and the weakly are knocked out and walked over.' "*

"Haven't we enough land as it is?" Jessica asked. "After all, even today some parts of our continent haven't yet felt the sole of a white man's boot."

"Speaking of some of our wilder areas," Sam said, speaking to Kelvin and Rufe, "we had letters yesterday from our wandering daughter and son-in-law. They came on one of Misa's ships from Carnarvon—"

"Sounds familiar, but I can't place it," Kelvin said.

"Northwest coast, south of North West Cape," Sam said. "Salt-mining town."

"Ah, yes," Kelvin said.

"In the most recent letter our little Java girl states with regal confidence that she and Tolo are off to buy some camels—"

"The camel's a mammal," Rufe intoned in a deep voice, looking wise.

"Thank you," Sam said. "To buy camels from a station owner on the western edge of the Gibson Desert."

"Oh, Sam, do hush," Jessica said. "I don't even want to think about it."

"Well, it seems to me that if you're going to cross a desert, it would be wise to have camels," Magdalen said.

Rufe chuckled.

"Something has tickled Rufe's funny bone," Jessica observed.

"Nothing, nothing," Rufe protested, still chuckling.

"You sly beggar," Sam said. "You're doing that deliberately to make us ask you what is so amusing."

"No, no, really," Rufe replied, laughing openly.

"It's one of his jokes," Magdalen said. "I know you, young man. I'm right, aren't I?"

"No. I am very serious," Rufe said, stifling his laugh. "I was just thinking about the technique of bricking a camel. It was invented in Western Australia soon after the beasts were brought over from India and Afghanistan with their drovers."

"Breaking?" Kelvin asked.

"Don't encourage him, for God's sake," Magdalen said.

"Bricking," Rufe corrected. "Actually, you see, even the Sahara has its oases and water holes. Australia offered a real challenge, for there are stretches of country in the western deserts where there is no water at all for hundreds of miles. Not even the camel could make it across those stretches of nothing without water. There was one stretch, in the Gibson Desert, as a matter of fact, where Java and Tolo are headed, that was just a few miles too far for a camel to make it across on one drink of water."

"Rufe, should Jessica and I excuse ourselves?" Magdalen asked.

"Of course not, Mother. I'm merely imparting a parcel of little-known Australian history." Rufe nodded, took a sip of wine. "So this one digger came up with a great idea. All he had to do was figure out a way for a camel to put just one extra gallon of water into his stomach—to be stored in his hump, you know—before starting the journey out into the Gibson. He found himself two bricks—"

"Jessica, I think we should leave," Magdalen said.

"Hush, Mother," Jessica said, winking at Magdalen.

"—and just when the camel was sticking its muzzle down into the water trough to drink, the digger took the two bricks, put one on each side of the animal's ballocks—"

"Good Lord," Magdalen said.

"—and smashed them together, so." Rufe demonstrated with his hands. "The camel, to say the least, was surprised and took a long, deep, shuddering breath. And there you are. An extra gallon of water went in, and the camel made it across the stretch of desert on one drink, and—"

Rufe's words were lost in the roar of Sam's and Kelvin's laughter. Jessica tittered behind her hand. After a moment of shock Magdalen threw back her head and laughed throatily.

"And that's how you brick a camel," Rufe said.

"And that is my son," Magdalen said, still laughing. "There's only one defense against a repetition of this, Jessica, and that is to see to it that there are females other than this sailor's family at our dinners. He's enough his father's son to be a gentleman when lady guests are present."

"Hear, hear," Rufe said. "I am very surprised, as a matter of fact, Mother. Here I am a few years past my majority—"

"Quite a few," Magdalen interrupted.

"—and still a bachelor. I would have thought that you and my dear sister would be throwing unmarried ladies at me constantly."

"It's because we can have pity for members of our own sex," Jessica said.

"In that case," Rufe said, "let me tell you about these two camel jumpers from Palestine who couldn't get their camel to drink. One of them decided to try suction—"

"Now we *do* leave," Magdalen said, rising. Jessica accompanied her. Behind them they heard great gusts of male laughter.

Later that evening, after Kelvin had gone home, Jessica was seated in a rocking chair on the porch, staring out over the lights of the city to the masthead lights of ships in the harbor. Rufe, a lighted cigar in his hand, found her there.

"Mind some company?" he asked.

"I welcome yours," she answered.

He pulled another rocking chair close to hers. "You don't mind the smoke?"

"No. Sam's a cigar smoker, too."

She fell silent, and after a moment Rufe spoke again. "Penny for your thoughts?"

"Overpriced at that," she declared. "Java. I think of her so often."

"She'll be right, mate," Rufe said, using the cover-all Australian expression of reassurance.

"Sometimes I wish I could get my hands on her," Jessica said forcefully. "But then I wouldn't know, really, whether to hug and kiss her or beat the bejabbers out of her." She laughed. "Being a confirmed bachelor, brother dear, may not be so bad. At least you'll be spared the pain of losing your child."

"I would venture that you haven't lost her," Rufe said. "And actually, I wouldn't mind having a couple of little diggers running about the house. Too late now, I suppose."

"Marry a young woman," Jessica said. "You have time to fill a house, if that's what you want."

"Yes," he said musingly. "I could do that, I suppose. But Lord, Jess, having to raise a wife as well as the children?"

"I suspect she'd do her share of raising *you*," Jessica countered. "After tonight's performance I'd say you could do with a little housebreaking."

Rufe guffawed. "I guess you're right at that, Jess dear." He sighed and blew a cloud of smoke that swirled in the light spilling from the windows. "Still, I've always thought that I'd take a wife someday. It's just that the right time and the right woman never seemed to coincide. But I fear my taste in women has matched my advance in years."

"Don't talk old," she said. "After all, you are my younger brother, and I'm damned well not old."

"Of course not," he said. "But if you were—God forbid— suddenly single, would you go out and let yourself be wooed by some lad of twenty-one or -two tender years?"

"What a terrible thought," she said.

"You see?"

"No house full of little sailors, then?"

"Probably not."

"So, in future, I shall keep my eyes open for women of less than tender years." Jessica smiled.

"Not matrons, but not tight little virgins either," he said.

"You *are* rather terrible, Rufe, aren't you?"

"No more than the men aboard the clippers on which you sailed for several years."

She laughed. "I try to forget some of the things I overheard."

"Like Misa Mason," Rufe said.

Jessica's laugh died. "What do you mean?"

"I mean, I wouldn't object if you'd invite Misa Mason to dinner more often. Perhaps sometime soon, with just a few of us here? You know, a small, rather intimate affair?"

She felt her heart freeze with a cold as intense as that of a South Atlantic polar gale. *No, you don't,* she thought. *Oh, no, you don't, mister. We have one half-blood in the family, the one who stole my daughter, the one who took away my most precious possession. The brown-skinned mother of that thief will not be a member of my family. I will see to that. We will have another Kanaka in the family over my own quivering, mangled, thoroughly dead body.*

"We'll see," she said aloud. "Mrs. Mason is often occupied with other things."

Chapter VIII

JOSEPH VAN BUREN'S Queensland station was one of those landholdings that caused ire and consternation among the labor socialists and other left-leaners. To such people it seemed contrary to logic that one man should have so much while so many had so little.

Since buying the small holding owned by Sabina Caldwell and her husband Lester, Joseph, like Tolo Mason in New South Wales, had been taking advantage of the long drought to buy, buy, buy. From the original acreage centered on the spacious homeplace on the Barcoo River, Joseph's purchases had expanded Van Buren land southward into more fertile districts and westward toward the arid plains until the station contained one and a quarter million acres.

During Matt Van Buren's two-year stay in South Africa he had received half a dozen letters from his father, more from his mother. Joseph wrote only when he had added significantly to the station, each letter a brief description of a plot of land not less than one thousand acres in size. Matt had never added up the acreage of the purchases, and he did not even know about some of the smaller ones, since Joseph apparently thought that a plot of only a few hundred acres was not worth sending a letter all the way across the Indian Ocean.

Although Queensland was the second largest of the Australian states, covering fully one-fifth of the continent and having within its borders some of the continent's richest and most productive lands, its capital, Brisbane, still lagged behind both Sydney and Melbourne in size, prestige, influence, and passenger ship connections. So it was that the ship carrying Matt and Kit from Cape Town passed into Sydney Harbor for Kit's introduction to Australia.

Matt and Kit said good-bye to Trev Gorel aboard ship while harbor tugs were jockeying the vessel toward its dock. As it happened, Trev would not be spending any time in Sydney, for the trading vessel that he was to take to New Guinea was scheduled to leave the very next day. Matt wished Gorel the best of luck, told him that he deserved to find a gold mine in New Guinea, and then parted from his friend with a twinge of regret, for he had grown to like the ebullient Englishman very much. Civilian life was, he had come to realize, not very different from the army, in that people came into one's purview, made a place for themselves there, and then vanished. But at least in peacetime, friends did not usually disappear through being wounded or killed; Trev would be out there somewhere, and perhaps they would meet again.

The first Australians Kit met during the layover in Sydney, while awaiting a coastal steamer to Brisbane, were Sam and Jessica Gordon. The Van Buren family was well known to the Broome household, since Matt's grandfather, Claus, had been a close friend of Red and Magdalen Broome, so the young couple received a hearty welcome from the regulars at the "unround table."

Although Matt's new bride was considerably younger than Jessica, the two hit it off immediately and spent long hours nattering happily as they exchanged life experiences and covered in depth that favorite topic of young brides, the odd vagaries of men.

Jessica and Sam insisted that Matt and Kit stay with them. There was plenty of room. Matt renewed his acquaintance with Kelvin Broome, exchanged war stories, moaned in mock pain when Kit returned heavily laden from a shopping trip with Jessica and Magdalen, and heard, one night at dinner, things about his father that he had not known.

The subject came up when Jessica asked Matt what he intended to do now that his army days were over.

"Well, my father wants me to work with him on the station," Matt said.

"I should think he'd need the help," Kelvin said, "since it's one of the largest stations in all of Australia, and when you include the big ones out in Western Australia, that's saying something."

"I knew he'd been buying land," Matt said.

"A few hundred thousand acres," Kelvin confirmed.

Kit whispered to Jessica: "Matt didn't tell me his family was rich."

"Your father is standing for Parliament," Kelvin went on. "Its an odds-on bet he'll be elected. And the conservatives in government are already thinking of ways to plug into Van Buren money and influence."

"I knew that my father would be a conservative," Matt said with a grin, "but I'm surprised that he's going into politics. He was against federation in the first place."

"I guess he figures that if you can't beat 'em, you join 'em, so you can keep an eye on 'em," Kelvin said. "He's going to be a powerful man, Matt. He'll have the support and help of every squatter on the continent."

Squatter was the term for the rich landholders, many of whom had simply taken the unsettled land in the early days and had built up large and lucrative holdings. Joseph Van Buren had come rather late to his property and fortune, but he was still of the squatter class.

"In addition," Kelvin was saying, "your father will have the support of big business and others who are interested in maintaining the status quo. He's already spoken out against just about every aid program operated or proposed by government."

"I think he's a typical old liner," Matt said. "My grandfather Claus wasn't a convict, but I think he shared with them and with their descendants their distrust of all authority. I'd say, knowing my father, that his motto will be that government's function is not to help people, but to help people help themselves."

"He'll have plenty of company in that feeling," Kelvin said. "It seems to me that public opinion, at least in New South Wales, echoes the old state government policies. Before federation, if there was unemployment, the state didn't give out charity; it gave out employment in the form of public works. When the state broke up big holdings to put families on smaller parcels, it fully expected those families to work and become self-supporting. And in business the state did not try to take the place of the entrepreneur. It didn't try to shelter its citizens from the vagaries of the marketplace but instead endeavored to stimulate the growth of private business and competitiveness."

"Add in a White Australia and you have my father's political philosophy in a nutshell," Matt said.

"It sounds quite logical to me," Kit said.

"Don't bother to comment on politics, child," Magdalen said, with a twinkle in her eye and a wink at Kit. "Because we lesser mortals, we women, don't have the vote, you see. We're too unstable to be trusted with such power."

After a pleasant week in Sydney there were more leave-takings. Matt promised to bring Kit down to Sydney often and extended invitations to all to have a holiday in the bush by visiting the Van Buren Station. More pleasant days followed aboard ship, then a night in Brisbane, and then a long train ride though the mountains, out of the fertile crescent into the bush through towns called Chinchilla and Roma and Charleville. By rail, later by stagecoach, and finally by private carriage, Matt was showing his wife Australia, a land of contrasts.

As they turned off the public road onto Van Buren land, they were still miles from the main house. Matt was startled by the devastation as the track led them through arid, drought-parched land. Now and then they saw sheep grazing near some muddy billabong, and they stopped to talk with the drovers, some of whom had been working on the station when Matt left for the army.

"It's been bad, sir," he was told. "We ain't been eating roasted black swan in wine sauce since you left. But don't you worry, she'll be right, mate."

Kit gasped when she saw the house. It sat near the river, its wrought-iron balustrades gleaming in the sun. The roof was copper, patinated to a wonderful shade of green. Small round columns under a filigreed pediment adorned the entrance to the main living floor, which was reached by a sweeping twin set of steps open to the sky.

"It's beautiful," Kit whispered.

"Yes, I guess it is," Matt said. He had never given much thought to whether or not the house was beautiful. It was home, the house that held his earliest memories. Now he looked at it with new eyes. The lawn had obviously been watered regularly, for it was smooth and green, and the plantings around the house, which had grown in the years he had been away, gave the place a cool, luxurious look.

Matt drew the carriage to a stop in front of the house, gave over care of the sweating horses to a squat, silent Abo teenager, and ordered their baggage to be brought into the house.

Mathilda Van Buren was in the parlor, and Matt stood in the arched doorway, watching her. She had not changed: She wore her usual dark, heavy dress; her hair was arranged in the same old-country style, and she was reading the same Bible—the book in which she had inscribed Matt's name when he was born, along with the names of two sons born before Matt, babies who had not survived infancy.

Seeming to sense Matt's eyes on her, Mathilda looked up, and a peaceful smile that for a moment recalled youthful beauty lit her face.

Matt did not make an unattractive picture standing there in the light coming in the windows. His sand-colored khakis were tailored to fit his trim waist. Under the khaki tunic the high, tight collar showcased his pleasant, regular face. He held his bush hat in his left hand.

"You're back," Mathilda said quietly. "The Lord be praised."

And then she was leaping to her feet and moving rather heavily to meet him, to hold him close to her. Her head came to his chin, and he tilted it to kiss her on the forehead.

"Mother," he said, "can you take a pleasant shock?"

"After your sudden appearance, without so much as a hint that you were coming home, what could be a more pleasant shock?" she asked.

He turned her, extended one hand to reach for Kit's hand. "Mrs. Van Buren," he said, "meet Mrs. Van Buren."

To Matt's surprise, tears sprang to his mother's eyes, but he quickly learned that they were tears of joy.

"Oh, my dear," Mathilda said. "How beautiful you are." She took both of Kit's hands in hers. "Yes, yes." She turned to Matt. "And you, you great hulk of a bushranger, what lies did you tell this lovely child to get her to marry you?"

"Matt told me I'd learn to love you, Mrs. Van Buren," Kit said. "I think I'm already beginning to."

Taking Kit by the hand, Mathilda led the way into the hall, where she directed servants to take luggage to the large, airy room that had been Matt's when he lived at home. She turned to her son. "You'll find your father down at the shearing shed. Run along. This child needs some rest after your journey."

Matt did as he was told, going back out into the sunlight and walking through the grounds to the outbuildings. Down by the shearing shed a dipping pit had been set up. Even before he could see, Matt could hear the frantic bleatings of sheep as shouting drovers forced them up a runway and into a chute that dropped them into the pit. Joseph Van Buren was leaning on a plank fence, one thick, heavily booted foot cocked up on the lower rail as he watched. He had rolled up the sleeves of his flannel shirt, revealing brawny arms. He wore rough, thick trousers, a dusty wide-brimmed hat, and around his neck a red kerchief.

Matt was able to walk to his father's side and place his own foot on the lower rail before Joseph looked around.

"By God," Joseph said. For long moments he just looked at Matt, and then, in a display of affection that was quite out of character, he threw his big arms around him and squeezed him briefly.

"You're looking good, boy," Joseph said, stepping back. "Look better when you get out of that monkey suit."

"Give me a few minutes, at least," Matt said, laughing.

"Good to see you," Joseph said, having to force the words. He was of the old school, not wont to display his emotions.

"And you," Matt said. "You've expanded the place a bit."

"A bit," Joseph conceded.

"They're saying in Brisbane that you're going to add a thousand more acres and then apply for statehood," Matt said with a grin.

"Not as crazy as it sounds," Joseph said. "But not statehood. Independence."

"The independent state of Van Buren?" Matt asked.

"One way to leave the bleeding-heart brigade behind," the older man said. "Son, we're in the middle of the worst drought in two decades. The wheat crop was a disaster. Unless we get rain, the number of sheep on graze will be reduced by fifty percent by the end of the year. The drought is hitting the best parts of the country, the fertile areas of Queensland and New South Wales. The whole food-producing section of this nation is facing total devastation, and all those poofters in government can think about is giving handouts to the bloody loafers."

"I understand you're going to take a direct hand in that situation," Matt said.

"It's in my mind to," Joseph said. "Depends on the good voters of this district."

"Do you have any doubt that you'll be elected?"

"I know the solid people think as I do," Joseph said. "But with every swagman and cattle duffer able to vote—"

It was good to be home, Matt thought, with the familiar

noises and smells, the feeling of spaciousness, of freedom. It was good to look out in four directions and know that everything he saw was Van Buren land. He sighed in contentment, then remembered that his father had not been told about Kit.

"Dad, are you ready to knock off for a while? There's something up at the house I think you'll be interested in seeing."

"Sure, the blokes can handle this operation," Joseph replied. He walked with the long, distance-covering strides that Matt had once had to run to keep up with, but now the son's strides matched his father's, two strong, well-conditioned men walking side by side, faces showing the family resemblance, Joseph's just a bit darker than Matt's.

"You know how I feel about surprises," Joseph growled.

"As I remember it, you don't think much of them."

"Surprises are usually on the bad side."

"Not this one, Dad." He grinned and put his arm around his father's shoulders. "You've always wanted to be a grandfather, haven't you?"

"I've given it some thought," Joseph said, a rare smile appearing over his beard. "So you've brought home a wife."

"Surprised?"

"No. It had to happen sooner or later. You're my son, after all. And no Van Buren that I've ever known, starting with the old man"—he meant his father, Claus—"was content for very long without a woman in the house." He clapped Matt on the back. "Found yourself one of those strong-backed Boer gals, like Slone Shannon, did you?" News of the Shannon family had spread throughout Queensland, for Slone's parents, Adam and Emily, now earl and countess, had lived outside Brisbane, and the regional papers had carried pictures of the entire Shannon family, including Sianna.

"No," Matt said. "Kit's father is a general in the army."

Joseph pulled away from Matt's arm and stopped in his tracks. "Which army?" he demanded. "Since we don't have many generals in the Australian forces, you're talking about the British army?"

"Yes," Matt said.

"You married a bloody pommy woman?" Joseph shouted, his face dark.

"She's English, yes," Matt said evenly.

For a long moment father and son stared at each other in silence.

To Joseph's credit, he tried mightily to contain his disappointment and anger. But he found it difficult to bend his rigid views, for he was imbued with that strong Australian character that had been in the making for more than a hundred years, ever since the first convict ships hauled into Australian waters. For Joseph—as editorialists were already portraying him—was the quintessential "new Australian." And the new Australian was a white Australian, a self-reliant Australian.

For men like Joseph the real Australia did not truly begin until one had crossed the fertile band of coastal development and entered the bush. The bushman was Australia, for it was he who had fought against all that a hostile continent could fling at him. And from the bush, men like Joseph looked out on a world made effete by the decay of the British Empire, the weakening of the British character. The piebald empire, the old queen's nigger empire, refused to stand up for Australian claims in the Pacific, giving in to German wogs, French wogs, and the bloody Yanks. The new king was no better suited than the old queen had been to insist that the Asian vermin be stomped out as if they were rabbits.

Joseph had followed the war news from South Africa, especially reports by Banjo Paterson and Kelvin Broome. He considered the fiasco of Spion Kop to be the direct result of the decay of the British character, a national malaise that permitted good troops to be misled by bad generals—old poofters who were given command simply because, somewhere back in time, an ancestor had sucked up to a king and been given a title. When that decay touched Australians and got honest blokes killed needlessly, it was time to do something.

In short, Joseph had come to despise everything English.

He was, after all, a descendant of a Javanese woman, and his mother had been an American. He owed nothing to England, and he believed that Australia should stand on her own two feet. The days of dependency, when Australia's only function was to provide meat for England's dinner tables and wool for her mills, was long past.

If Joseph could have had his way totally, he would have added a word or two to the proposed Kanaka deportation bill pending in the legislature: He would have made it a pommy deportation bill as well.

And now his son, the young man he was counting on to keep things going on the station while he was off in Sydney playing politician, had come home with an English bride. If Matt had married a Boer, Joseph would have happier, for at least a Boer woman was not the product of a nation that was currently raping a full quarter of the world.

Joseph fought his anger, telling himself that perhaps Matt's wife was an unusual English girl, but it was a losing battle.

"You married a bloody pom?" he repeated, his face red. "My God, boy, I thought I'd pounded some sense into your head while you were growing up. An English bitch as a daughter-in-law? The mother of my grandchildren?"

Matt was, at first, too shocked to speak.

"I left New Zealand, gave up a portion of my inheritance, worked my arse off to build something for my son, something that he could be proud of, something that would carry the name Van Buren into the new century and the one after that. Was it too much to ask that my son find a girl of Australia?"

"Dad, give her a chance. You'll like her," Matt said.

"I promise you," Joseph said, saddened to the point of desperation by the knowledge that his grandchildren would carry the effete blood of an Englishwoman, "that I will not like her now, nor will I ever like her."

Matt's entire body was rigid. He stared at his father uncomprehendingly. "At least come and meet her," he said, his own voice growing a bit harsh.

"Yes, I'll do that," Joseph said.

* * *

Mathilda, meeting them at the kitchen door, saw her husband's face and went pale. "Joseph—"

"Not now, Mathilda," Joseph said. "Where's the bloody pom girl?"

"Oh, my God," Mathilda said. "Not that. Not directed at your own son, Joseph."

"Are you siding with him?" Joseph roared. "Ever since the Australians began to make something of what *they* thought was a useless wilderness, ever since what *they* called the dregs of society pulled themselves up and began to carve a place for themselves in this wilderness, *they've* been trying to get it back, claim it all, and make the whole continent an extension of England. We haven't let them do that, so by God, I won't let them take back by marriage what I've carved for myself out of this wilderness."

"Joseph, you're angry," Mathilda said. "Don't say anything that you'll regret later."

"I will say this: No Englishwoman nor any half-English child will ever be master of this station!"

Matt stood, mouth open, his mind reeling. He was beginning to believe that his father was, after all, deadly serious.

Before he could speak, Kit was there, standing in the doorway to the dining room. She had slipped into a silken dressing gown. Her eyes were puffy from sleep, her sunset hair a bit mussed. Joseph, seeing her, halted his tirade and turned toward her, his face glowering.

"I can see how it could happen," he said. "She's a pretty wench."

"Dad . . ." Matt said warningly.

"Well, missy," Joseph said. "Did you hear?"

Kit, her face pale, hurried to Matt's side and took his hand. "Matt?"

"Go back upstairs, Kit," Matt said. "I'll be there in a minute."

"No," Joseph said. "Let's have it out here and now. I wasn't consulted about this wedding, so I've had no say until now. Now you've come home, boy. And I warrant you're expecting to take up where we left off before you ran away to play soldier. I had decided to forgive you that, but I can't forgive you this."

"Matt, what is it?" Kit whispered, her green eyes showing fright.

"I have told my son," Joseph said, "that no Englishwoman nor any half-English child will ever be the master of Van Buren Station. Before I let that happen, I would bequeath it to the bleeding-heart brigade in government and let them carve it up into small holdings for the loafers."

"Ah, Joseph," Mathilda said, through tears.

"Matt, I don't understand," Kit said, taking a step toward him.

"It'll be all right," Matt said, not really feeling that it would be. He took her arm and guided her back toward the door. "We'll go pack now."

He tried to explain as he led her up the stairs. "Your father rejected me because I have some Javanese blood. My father rejects you because of your English blood."

"That's—that's idiotic," she said.

"Not to him."

When Matt and Kit came down, Mathilda was at the door. Servants were loading the luggage in the carriage. Joseph was nowhere to be seen.

"Give him time, son," Mathilda begged, taking Matt's arm. "Give him some time to adjust his thinking."

"If that happens, Mother, I will hold no grudges," Matt said.

"And you, my dear," Mathilda said, taking Kit in her arms. "How I've longed for a daughter! And now that God has given me a beautiful daughter, man takes her away."

"We'll write to you, Mother," Matt said.

"Where will you go?" Mathilda asked.

"I'm not sure," Matt said. "Sydney, perhaps."

"Your uncle could find a place for you in the Van Buren company. . . ."

"I don't know, Mother. I don't like the idea of depending on Van Buren money. Not now."

"There is this," Mathilda said, giving Matt an envelope. "I've signed the necessary papers. It isn't much, but perhaps it will be a start."

Matt opened the envelope to see a draft on a Brisbane bank for several hundred pounds.

"It's not Van Buren money," she said. "It was my dowry. Joseph never touched it. It's been sitting in banks since before you were born."

"Thank you, Mother," Matt said. "You'll get back every penny of it."

"If so, fine," she said. "If not, no worries. Write to me often?"

"We will," Kit said.

They spent the night in the open, camped beside a muddy water hole. Kangaroos came in the early darkness to drink. A lonely dingo that had slipped inside the Van Buren dingo fence howled at the moon from an overlooking hill.

Matt held Kit close. The impact of the day's events had just hit her. Her own father had said, *"I have no daughter."* And now, because of her, Matt, too, had been disowned.

"It doesn't matter," Matt assured her. "Here is the only thing that matters, you and I together."

They experienced the ultimate togetherness on a blanket in the moonlight and made new vows. They both were cut off from their old, familiar worlds. They had only each other.

"Forever," Matt promised, as his passion jetted into her in still another valiant effort to give her a baby. "And ever and ever and ever. Never anyone but you."

"I can stand anything but losing you," Kit said.

"Then, no worries."

Chapter IX

JAVA AWOKE WITH the dawn, her mouth, throat, and lips dry and parched. Outside her tent she could hear Bildana moving about, getting a fire going, and soon Java could smell the smoke. Rising, she dressed quickly.

As she stepped out into the new day, leaving Tolo to snatch a few more minutes of sleep, Java was struck by the cold. More than anything else about the desert, the extremes of temperature amazed her; at this hour it was below freezing. But the desert was beautiful in the pearl-colored light of dawn —the land rolling away on all sides to the limit of the eye's ability to see, the tufts of spinifex grass looking delicate in shades of gold and pink.

Bildana had a billy boiling. She took it from the fire, and as soon as the tin cup had cooled slightly, she handed it to Java. The sharp, aromatic tea warmed Java's hands through the cup, and then she drank.

"Body shakes you warm," Bildana said as both she and Java shivered, their teeth chattering. Bildana had a disreputable-looking skin of some sort thrown around her shoulders, her only protection against the cold.

But now the sun burst up into the eastern sky, and the spinifex, vaguely attractive in the earlier light, faded to a dull gray-green. Even though the air was stirred into a breeze by the rapid warming of the sun and the seed heads of the native grass swayed in the breeze, Java felt forewarning of the oppressive heat that was soon to come.

At least the desert's rapid changes in temperature from night to day and back again provided some variety, gave the traveler something to anticipate. The desert landscape did not. Its terrible flatness seemed to go on forever, so monotonous that even the crossing of a small erosion gully was a major event in the day. To encounter an actual tree, however spindly and shadeless it might be, seemed after days of travel as significant as the climax of a millennium.

By now Tolo had emerged from the tent. As she knew from prior experience, his first concern was for the camels, and he walked out toward the hobbled animals. They came to him, following his lead rope, looking to Java like tall, misshapen creatures out of a nightmare. Certainly riding them was a nightmare, one that came with each new day and put her on a rack of torture, a hard, shifting seat of agony that stiffened her to the point that it was painful just to move.

Tolo, too, had discovered that riding a camel was more uncomfortable than sitting a horse, and he had taken to walking in order to ease the soreness of his rump. Java had followed his example. The first time she had walked, though, she felt so much relief at being off the camel—surely a beast designed by the devil—that she had overexerted herself, and the next morning her leg joints and muscles were sore enough to make her weep with pain.

For breakfast this morning they ate oatmeal topped with brown sugar, and although they had no milk, the moisture in the porridge was delightful. Bildana had cooked it to a watery consistency, and the thick, treacly soup seemed to cling to Java's dehydrated tongue and lips, so that she began to feel better quickly.

It took a full hour to load the pack camels, for balancing the loads required painstaking care. The camels roared a protest but finally accepted their burden. Ganba had left the camp during the loading stage. In his eyes loading was white man's work, though the Abo women did help a bit, Bildana especially.

Having picked three Abo men on whom he could rely to accept his authority, Ganba led them straight eastward, aiming for a shadowy rise that might hold enough vegetation to give the camels a bit of graze and—though this was more doubtful—might also shelter some form of animal that would grace the cook fires.

When they were hidden from the eyes of the white man by the slight rise that had, indeed, led them to a place of sparse graze, Ganba signaled the other men into a hunting formation, and the four crept forward into a shallow, dusty bowl. They found no game.

One of the Aborigines, Nookar, who felt that he had a right to special status in the little group because he was of the blood of Ganba's wife, stopped in the sparse shade of a spindly tree, cocked one foot up on the other leg in a restful pose, and looked at Ganba inquiringly. The other two men were at a distance, looking hopefully for animal spoor.

"There will be no meat food tonight," Nookar said.

"There will be the tins of the white man," Ganba growled No man had special status with him. In a time of hunger Bildana's blood relative would take his place on the cook fire no sooner or later than any of the others. It would all depend on the situation at the time.

"A camel would make much meat food," Nookar said. He looked slyly at Ganba. "But we would first have to eat the whitefellas." Nookar knew Ganba's reputation. He had never for one moment believed that Ganba—the man who wore murderer's slippers—had braved the trackless sea and come into the never-never merely for a few of the white man's coins

Ganba merely grunted and ordered Nookar to go back and meet the whitefellas and guide them to the camel graze. He himself found a high place, as high as was offered by the nearly flat landscape, and watched the little caravan approach. Ganba's eyes glowed, for he saw the pistol at the big

whitefella's waist, saw the good rifle in its scabbard attached
to the whitefella's camel saddle. Those guns, he knew, would
be his, and then he could reach out with the white man's
magic and bring down a full-grown kangaroo at an incredible
distance.

It was not the white man's guns alone that aroused Ganba's
passion each time he chose to think about what the spirits of
the Dreamtime had sent his way. As Nookar had said, the
camels, those unnatural beasts, would make good meat food
for many days. And then there were the warm blankets and
the weatherproof tent of the whitefellas. In the whitefellas'
towns Ganba had seen many riches, all beyond his reach, all
protected securely by the whitefellas' law. But here in the
never-never, in his land, things were different. The whitefellas'
law was far away. Approaching him now were riches that
were so nearly his he could almost feel the heft of the rifle in
his hands and could taste the warm, half-cooked meat food.

He would not kill the whitefellas himself, for the whitefella
had ways of looking into how and when murder had been
done in the past. No, he would let the desert kill them. He
only regretted how long this would take, because by the time
the whitefellas were dead, the sun would have sucked the
juices from their bodies, wizening them to the point where
their tasty flanks and buttocks would be shrunken.

He licked his lips, tasting the rancid grease that Bildana
had smeared on his face to protect it from the hungry sun. He
would have to be very careful, in gathering that meat food, to
leave the bones unmolested; if by any chance whitefellas ever
found the remains, there must be no ax marks on the bones,
no marrow-sucked bones, nothing to indicate that Ganba or
his people had availed themselves of what had been offered by
the spirits.

Ganba, indeed most of the native Australians, could not
understand the horror with which the whitefella viewed a natural and often vitally necessary action. In the past the
blackfella had learned that it was bad enough to kill a white
person, for it caused great excitement among the white tribes,

but if a blackfella also *ate* a whitefella, the excitement became a frenzied hysteria that sent the whites into the field armed with guns. Just why wasting good meat food was a terrible thing to the whitefella remained a mystery to Ganba.

He saw Nookar coming back, easily outdistancing the slow-moving camels. The big whitefella was walking, leading his riding camel and three of the pack animals. The woman led the other pack camel from her own mount. Ganba waited until the whitefellas had reached the little depression where greenish sprigs of grass immediately tempted the camels, and then he said, "Is good we make camp here."

"Yes," the whitefella replied. Though they had traveled hardly any distance that day, fatigue was written on his face.

"Tomorrow, we go there," Ganba declared, pointing directly east.

Nookar, who had crossed the Gibson, who knew it as well as Ganba, turned his head in the direction indicated by Ganba's lifted arm. East. Into the heart of the desert.

After the whitefellas had pitched their tent and were hidden away in it to escape the afternoon sun, Nookar approached Ganba. "Blackfella there?" he said, pointing northward.

It was a question, but Ganba ignored it.

"You say you take whitefella to blackfella camp," Nookar insisted. "It is good that you tell Nookar your thoughts, kinsman, for perhaps you will need help."

"Ganba needs no help from you," Ganba said, then, relenting: "Save your water and wait. This"—he kicked the dry red sand—"and that"—he pointed to the sun—"need time to work."

Nookar grinned. It was as he had thought. Ganba had not come into the never-never for money. He hoped that it would happen soon. He wrinkled his nose, almost smelling the roasting meat food.

* * *

That night the sky grumbled, and distant flashes of sheet lightning appeared in the east. Ganba worried. Rain came seldom in the never-never, but when it did, it brought almost instant life. Not only would fresh water be available for refilling the emptying barrels carried by the camels, but a surge of green, tender growth would make plentiful food for the beasts. Rain would delay the deadly work of the desert and the sun, and it would be longer before his teeth sank into meat food.

Again the next night the eastern sky was active, filled with distant fireworks, rumbling low and long. And on the third night Ganba picked his spot carefully. A dry creek bed traversed the arid desert in a series of bends and twists. In the creek bed there was driftwood for the fires and some shelter from a wind that had arisen with sundown, a wind that stung the face with finely ground rock particles and sand. Tolo and Lava went to their tent soon after dark, snug against the eddying wind, clinging together against the rapidly chilling night. Ganba did not sleep. He sat facing the east, watching the advance of the distant clouds.

"The rain comes tonight," Bildana said, moving to Ganba's side.

The other Baadu were restless. Their fires were still flaming, and only one of the women slept.

"I will tell them to move camp," Bildana said, "to get out of the creek bed."

Ganba's hand flashed out and connected with Bildana's face with a loud clap of sound. "Have I told you so?"

"No," she said, moving back out of his reach. "But when the rain comes—"

Ganba was feeling very good. An opportunity had presented itself, and he had decided to take it. Perhaps he would lose some of the wealth that belonged to the whitefella, but if that was the will of the spirits, then he would accept it. The camels were hobbled away from the creek bed. The supplies, at Ganba's suggestion, were stored on the bank of the gully.

Only the white man's rifle and pistol, some blankets, and the tent were at risk.

There was nothing to do but wait. Ganba looked at Bildana, saw the bulge of buttock, the thrust of breast. "Bring your blanket here," he ordered. She obeyed. Ganba penetrated her immediately and bucked his way to quick completion. That was the trouble with the woman-thing. It was so quickly over, the passions and energy spent on a pleasure so fleeting that no man could hold on to it for more than a moment.

He slept. He awoke when the wind changed direction, blowing out of the rising clouds in the east. There was a moist smell in the air. He moved silently among the sleeping Baadu, waking them one by one, whispering orders to move out of the creek bed. When his orders had been obeyed, he joined Bildana, who shivered in the cold wind, and built a new fire on the bank overlooking the gully where the whitefella and his woman slumbered on.

Still the rains did not come. The rain was falling to the east; Ganba could tell that from the smell. Perhaps enough rain would accumulate there to accomplish the purpose. He watched and listened, for his first warning would be a distant roar. The sound did not come. Finally he slept, clinging to Bildana for the warmth of her body.

The dawn awoke him. The clouds had retreated, and the sun would soon warm the wastes of the desert. Below, in the gully, the whitefella woman had emerged from the tent and was stretching, meeting the dawn with upturned face.

Standing beside Ganba, Bildana laughed. He looked at her with anger. When she persisted, he struck her. She whispered, "The spirits protected them, you see."

His anger became a red cloud that engulfed him. He struck Bildana with his fist and then picked up a sturdy stick and began to beat her. She tried to scurry away, but he held her by one heel and left great welts on her sandy, greasy hide with the stick.

* * *

Java saw that the Abos had moved out of the shelter of the gully and wondered why. It was a morning that promised the uncompromising sun and broiling temperatures. Stretching with a sigh, she heard a cry of pain and looked up to see Ganba beating Bildana with a stick.

"Ganba, what are you doing?" she called out. "Stop that this instant!"

The beating continued. Bildana was making small moaning sounds, and her hands were digging into the sand as she tried to crawl away.

"Stop it, I say!" Java shouted, but Ganba ignored her.

With a cry of anger and disgust Java dived back into the tent and came out with Tolo's pistol. Holding it in her right hand, she struggled up the bank, her boots sinking into the soft sand, until she stood a few feet from Ganba. With Ganba still flailing away at Bildana's bare rump and back, Java lifted the pistol and put a bullet into the sand not a foot from the black man's leg. He froze.

"Now you will bloody well stop it," Java hissed. "Turn her loose."

Ganba's hand released Bildana's foot. She crawled away, making mewling, whimpering sounds.

"Ganba, you will never, never do that again," Java said. "If you so much as strike Bildana again, I will have my husband thrash you."

Ganba stiffened, his head lifting, and snorted with contempt. No whitefella would beat him.

"All right, then," Java said, "I'll shoot you in the leg so that you will have to walk with a stick for a long time. Do you understand me?"

Now she saw him hesitate. He stared at her uncertainly, and she had no doubt that he considered her to be like females of his own race: irrational and therefore unpredictable and potentially dangerous.

"Do you understand me, Ganba?" Java repeated.

Both Java and Tolo had been working hard at picking up

the Baadu language. They had found some of the sounds to be difficult for a white man's tongue, but all in all, it was a rather simple language, with quite rigid rules of syntax. Java had asked her question twice, once in pidgin English, the next time in Baadu.

"I hear you," Ganba replied.

"Good."

Tolo came up to stand beside her. "The old man beating his wife again?"

"For the last time," Java declared.

"Well, please don't shoot him yet," Tolo said, straight-faced, for he, too, had been disturbed more than once when Ganba had struck Bildana. "We need him to find the wild Abos, don't we?"

"Be that as it may," Java said, glaring at Ganba, "I will shoot him in the leg the next time he strikes Bildana."

The hate in Ganba's dark, squinted eyes made her tremble, but only on the inside. She had learned that the only authority she could exercise over the Abos, with the exception of Bildana, came from a show of strength. She dared not let the hairy dark Ganba know that his evil stare made her uneasy.

Chapter X

AFTER LEAVING THE Van Buren cattle station with its gracious, sprawling house, Matt had rented a flat for Kit and himself in Brisbane.

Joseph Van Buren's surprising and insulting rejection of his son's chosen bride because of her English blood had left Matt suddenly without direction. He had the money that his mother had given him, enough to enable the couple to live comfortably for a few years, and he felt a growing desire to prove to his father that he did not need Van Buren money or the vast Van Buren landholdings to make his mark in the world. The question was, Where to begin?

Kit seemed to have no worries, for her confidence in her husband was total. "You'll figure something out," she told Matt. "Any decision you make will be the right one, I'm sure of it."

For the moment they both were content simply to enjoy the novelty of married life. After a trembling, frightened beginning, Kit had proven to be possessed of a pleasing sensuality and an appetite for the pleasures of the flesh that matched that of a young, vigorous man. So it was that the days became weeks and then a month, then two.

Then they both seemed to awaken suddenly from their golden haze of happiness at the same moment, and looking around, they found that the world was still there and that it expected payment for their lazy time of selfish, solitary happiness.

For a young man with limited funds the opportunities were not to be numbered in the dozens. Matt had no professional or technical training; he had quit school, in fact, to join the army and fight the Boers. Unlike his friend Slone Shannon, he was not an engineer, and his years of service in South Africa had honed only his aptitudes for getting about in the bush and leading men into danger—skills of limited marketability in the civilian world.

Matt did not have enough money to buy land—even at drought-reduced prices—in a quantity large enough to assure success at raising cattle or sheep. He knew nothing of the mercantile trades, though he felt that he could learn if the opportunity were right. The problem was that trade in Brisbane was very competitive: Wool prices were down in spite of slack supply caused by the drought, and trading in sugar was a highly specialized field best left to the experts.

Matt always had the option, of course, of taking employment for pay. He felt sure that if he chose to settle in a larger city like Sydney, he could find a position. Sam Gordon might have need for an ambitious young man in his marine endeavors. Misa Mason, whom Matt had met at the Gordon table, did business in several areas. Perhaps Mrs. Mason could use a personable young man in one of her banks.

"The decision is yours, of course," Kit said. "I did like Jessica Broome. All the people we met in Sydney were interesting and quite nice. I wouldn't mind living there, and I'm sure you could find good employment."

Matt's dislike of this showed on his face. "You've never actually worked for pay, have you?" Kit asked softly.

Matt grinned. That simple question cleared up a lot of muddy thinking. "I think you've put your finger on it," he said. "It's not that I'm afraid of work; Lord knows anyone growing up on a cattle and sheep station can't be a stranger to work. It's just that I've never had to call any man boss. Oh, I obeyed my father because I had respect for him, and I had to

salute and say 'sir' a lot in the army; but that's the army, and
that sort of thing is—well, that's just the way it is. When you
salute, you're saluting a uniform, the insignia of a higher officer, and if the man is a poofter, you can look past him to the
honorable military tradition of the English-speaking peoples.
But to get up every day knowing one must work for a man
who has control of your life, of your finances—" He shook his
head. " 'Yes, sir, boss, I will live in a house you select for me
by limiting what you pay me. Yes, sir, boss, I will wear the
clothing you require on the job. Yes, sir, boss, I will kiss your
arse because without your goodwill there will be no food on
the table for my hungry English wife and her ravaging horde
of youngsters.' "

"I get the idea," Kit said. "Can't blame you. I wouldn't like
being subservient to a boss myself. Had enough of that with
my father, God bless his hard, pointed head. But what does
that leave, my splendid knight errant?"

"New Guinea," he said suddenly, wondering where his answer originated until he remembered Trev Gorel and Trev's
enthusiastic descriptions of the wonders of the big island and
its riches, just waiting for the man who was not afraid to
pluck them.

"New Guinea?" Kit said doubtfully. "I understand it's
thoroughly unpleasant there—very hot and damp."

"Remember Trev Gorel?"

"Of course I do," she replied. "I think he knew as much
about New Guinea as we do."

"But what if he was right?" Matt asked, his eyes gleaming.
"What if we could go up there and build something worthwhile in a few years? Could you stand a bit of heat and dampness for a short while?"

"As long as I'm with you," she said simply.

Though Matt knew very little about New Guinea, other
Australians, especially Queenslanders, had been eyeing that
island greedily for decades. The descriptions of riches to be
won on the huge island were often grossly exaggerated, but

many men were finding ways to reap some profit from the
island's forests and the waters around her shores. Traders
dealt in the exotic woods of the island: ebony, cedar, and
sandalwood. The coastal palms yielded an abundance of
copra, and the seas offered pearls and also bêches-de-mer—
trepangs or sea slugs, also knows as sea cucumbers—which
when dried or boiled were considered a delicacy even by some
whites and were much in demand in China for making soups.

In 1877 gold was discovered in the area of the Mai-Kusa
River, setting off a brief gold rush, but as was usual in New
Guinea, expectations were not matched by reality.

The reality was harsh: insects, equatorial heat, and a generally hostile landscape. Along the coast New Guinea's torrential rainfall leached nutrients from the sandy, coralline soils,
making them marginal for imported agriculture. In many
places the sea carried tidal floods into vast swampy areas.
Farther inland convoluted hills and jungle-choked gorges
made it difficult to reach the higher valleys, which enjoyed
surprisingly moderate temperatures.

Still, the belief persisted that New Guinea possessed vast
riches just waiting to be discovered, that the daggerlike extension of Queensland, thrusting northward into the Torres
Strait close to New Guinea's southern shore, pointed to great
opportunity for a man with ambition and a spirit of adventure. Moreover, investment in New Guinea could be justified
and encouraged on patriotic grounds. Bismarck had pledged
to "protect" German traders among the Pacific islands, a
threat that included New Guinea and thus came very close to
home for Queenslanders. In fact, no thinking man in Australia welcomed the idea of having Germans in sole control of a
territory so near the continent.

The concern about further incursions on New Guinea by
the Germans, who were belatedly making every effort to become a colonial power, was not new. Nearly twenty years
earlier, in 1884, after an organization had been formed in
Berlin specifically to exploit the resources of New Guinea—
the Deutsche Seehandelgeschäft—Sir Thomas McIlwraith,

premier of Queensland, had announced the annexation of eastern New Guinea in the name of the British Empire. The British cabinet had disallowed his action, for Great Britain did not want New Guinea, and it mattered little to politicians in London if Queensland, or Australia as a whole, did. It took Bismarck's "protection" statement to move the politicians to declare a temporary protectorate over an undefined area of eastern New Guinea, with the Australian colonies taking the political and financial responsibility for this newest fruit of imperialism. In a decade the joint control by Australia and the mother country would cease, and Great Britain would withdraw, leaving Australia in possession. Monies to improve native agriculture, to set up land regulations, to protect native laborers, to introduce modern medicine—in short, to thrust "civilization" upon one of the more backward areas of the world—were to come primarily from Queensland, with aid from Victoria and New South Wales.

Nothing much changed when Australia became unified. In most quarters New Guinea was considered Queensland's baby —or headache, depending on one's attitude.

The offices of the British lieutenant governor, Sir George le Hunte, were in Port Moresby, the principal Australian settlement, located on the south coast. If one accepted the common notion that on the map New Guinea looked somewhat like a misshapen lizard, then Port Moresby was at the base of the lizard's tail, below the spread of the central body and just ten degrees of latitude below the equator. Behind the town the jungle was dense as it began to rise into the Owen Stanley Range.

Neither Matt nor Kit knew much of this background when they decided that New Guinea would be their next port of call. Not being wholly foolish, they began their venture with a visit to the Van Buren offices in Brisbane.

The office was run by one of Matt's cousins. He was just a bit older than Matt, and he had been named for their mutual grandfather, Claus Van Buren. There was a family resemblance between the two young men, although Claus had accumulated a bit of surplus around his middle, and each was curious about the other.

"I think I saw you once," Claus said. "Up in Wellington, when you were just a tot."

"Pardon me if I don't remember," Matt said.

"Well, Cousin, how can I help you?" Claus asked.

"Talk to me about New Guinea," Matt said.

"It's hot and damp," Claus answered, spreading his hands.

Matt laughed. He felt that he could learn to like his cousin without much effort. "Thank you," he said wryly.

"Not much help, eh?" Claus asked, matching Matt's grin.

"Do Van Buren ships do much trade in New Guinea?"

"Not as much as we'd like," Claus said. He nodded. "Why? Is Uncle Joseph thinking about going into New Guinea?"

"No, not my father," Matt said.

Claus made a show of cleaning a fingernail with a letter opener from his desk. "I had hoped that your presence here indicated that Uncle Joseph was feeling on friendlier terms with my father."

"No, I'm sorry," Matt said. Nathan Van Buren's name had been seldom mentioned in his father's house. Matt had only scant knowledge of why the brothers had fallen out so long ago. He knew only that the brothers were estranged, limiting their correspondence to business matters surrounding the management of the family enterprises in which both still shared. "Actually, Claus," Matt went on, "I was only vaguely aware that there were hard feelings between my father and yours. My dad never talked about it. I don't know why they quarreled, and to be perfectly frank, at this point I don't really care. I just need to know a little bit about New Guinea, and I thought that a large trading and shipping firm like Van Buren would be a good place to ask. I'm pleased to have met you, and as far as I'm concerned, if it's all right with you, we could be friends regardless of the problem between our fathers."

"Pardon my prying," Claus said, "but do I detect a bit of resentment toward your father?"

"Let me say only this," Matt said carefully. "I won't be managing the Van Buren Station at any time in the near future—and perhaps never."

"Ah," Claus said. "We Van Burens can be a bit hardheaded, can't we?"

"A *bit*? Bloody hell!" Matt said.

"Well, then," Claus said, rubbing his hands. "Now and again we manage to accumulate a ship's cargo, or a partial cargo, of exotic woods at Port Moresby. We always turn a good profit. The supply is sporadic, but the demand is steady. The Englishman in his castle—his home—has developed an insatiable taste for ebony, sandalwood, cedar, and the other exotic woods of the Far East. If you're thinking of going into business in New Guinea, I'd say that timbering would be a good start."

Claus invited Matt to lunch at his club, and the cousins continued their discussion over an excellent meal. Nothing more that Matt learned about New Guinea altered his initial conviction that there was opportunity there.

"I will buy raw timber," Claus said, "at a fair price, and in just about any quantity you can provide."

"Do you think that would be wise?" Matt asked.

"Because our dads don't get along?" Claus shrugged. "Does either of them have to know?"

"Claus," Matt said, after taking a sip of his after-lunch sherry, "I've come to like you very much, but after the debacle with my dad I'm not sure I want to give him any further reason to be unhappy with me. I wouldn't want him to think that I'd deserted him and made an alliance with his brother. Someday, I think, he'll try to make amends for the harsh things he's said, and I want to be ready for that time."

"So I'm to be punished by the loss of a potentially profitable relationship for the old sins of my father and my uncle?" Claus asked. "Look, I'm working for the family firm, to be sure, but I have my own ambitions, too. One of them is to make my branch of the business bigger and more profitable than my brother's branch. There's good profit in New Guinea timber. We can do business under a name that won't connect you with the company." He leaned forward. "Here's a thought. If you're concerned that your father might think that you succeeded only because of help from my father and the company, let's share the risk. Deliver timber to me on speculation. My ships will take it to Europe, and my agents will market it at the best price. We'll share in the profits. If the market falls, we'll share in the loss."

Matt hesitated. If indeed there was opportunity in New Guinea timber, he could find other buyers, other ships. There was the Mason Line, for example; he could contact its office in Brisbane easily. But he liked Claus. Claus seemed to be the kind of man Matt would want as a business partner.

"Claus, you've just about got me convinced."

"Good."

"Let me go up to New Guinea and take a look around. I've been led to understand that labor is a real problem."

"Backward people seldom take to working for wages," Claus said.

"That puts me in the category of being backward"—Matt grinned—"so I can understand. I'll see what I can do about getting timber to the coast on a regular basis, and then I'll contact you. Fair enough?"

"Fair enough," Claus agreed, extending his hand. "Maybe, over the years, we can make the old boys forget their grudges and start treating each other like brothers again."

"If Uncle Nathan is like my father, we'll need divine intervention," Matt said.

"By the way," Claus said as they left the club, preparing to part, "how are you fixed for capital?"

"What I have is adequate," Matt said. Under no circumstances would he take a loan from Claus, even if he did decide to ship timber in Van Buren bottoms.

* * *

It rained in Port Moresby. The roof of the house where Matt and Kit had taken rooms leaked, so they tried unsuccessfully to sleep with the maddening sound of raindrops thudding into a bucket at the foot of their bed.

The streets were ankle-deep in mud. Hordes of bloodsucking insects found nefarious ways to infiltrate one's clothing, to get past the screening and mosquito netting at night. The smell of the jungle, the aroma of rotting things that made up the forest floor, pervaded the air.

Matt discovered quickly that the British presence in Papua, that eastern portion of the big island that was nominally under British protection, was mainly symbolic. The British lieutenant governor, Sir George le Hunte, was a pleasant enough man who could pay splendid lip service to those colonial ideals of improving the economic life of the natives, of bringing into the New Guinea jungles the miracles of modern medicine. However, Sir George managed to give Matt the impression that the Brits were in New Guinea only to keep it from falling totally into the hands of the Germans.

"My boy," the governor said, "as far as I'm concerned, you can hew down every bloody tree within two hundred miles. Lord knows there are enough of them. Do you know that only a day's sail from here the wogs live in houses on stilts because every high tide sweeps under their shacks?" He chuckled. "Fine way to solve the sanitation problem, isn't it? Cut a little hole in the floor and the ocean flushes your dunny twice a day, right?"

The English civil servants who were Sir George's assistants were equally lackadaisical. It took more than two weeks for Matt to obtain the proper papers to become a legally registered dealer in timber, authorized to do business not only in British New Guinea but on British-held islands in the Solomon chain. He was cautioned against going too close to German-controlled areas—the northeast coast of New Guinea, as well as New Britain and other islands in the Bismarck Archipelago, and Bougainville Island to the east.

The appearance of the natives who came and went from Port Moresby did not give Matt much hope about the prospects of lining up a dependable labor force. They were small people, almost dwarfish, with thick bodies and large heads. The dress for the men and boys seemed to be limited mostly to a loincloth or nothing at all. Women, also short and thick of body, wore only ornamental necklaces above grass skirts secured at their thick waists by handwoven ropes. In the native quarters Matt was moved to pity by the filth and squalor in which these primitive people lived.

But finding laborers was not only the logical first step but also essential. It would help, Matt reasoned, if he could find someone who knew how to select the cedars, ebony, and sandalwood trees from the rest of the forest because he himself did not know a sandalwood tree from a coconut palm. By sheer good luck he found Gihi.

Gihi, a lean man at least ten inches shorter than Matt, wore the usual breechclout, and his hair was braided into small individual strands that hung to his shoulders. His forehead was adorned with strands of cheap beadwork, and he had around his neck a large pendant in the shape of a half moon. His skin was encrusted with dirt embedded in the rancid pig fat with which all of the natives anointed their skin to ward off insects and the burning sun.

As Matt approached, Gihi was squatting on his heels. Beside him on the ground was the carcass of a roasted chicken and he was picking the remaining bits of meat from the bones and placing them on a banana leaf.

"I am looking for the man Gihi," Matt said.

"Then your search is ended," Gihi replied.

"I am told that Gihi knows the forests, that he is worker."

Gihi made a sound that was somewhere between sigh and moan. "So I am found out again," he said. He wiped his greasy hands on his chest and then spread one wide. "Sit. Join me in my meal."

"Thank you, I have eaten," Matt said, watching the flies

swarm over the bits of chicken. He sat on his heels. "You speak English well."

"Because English do not speak my language well," Gihi said.

"Will Gihi talk business now, or should I return after you have eaten?"

"Talk," Gihi said, stuffing chicken into his mouth until it was filled to capacity.

"I want to go into the forest with many men," Matt said, "to cut ebony and sandalwood. I have been told that Gihi can get men, that Gihi would be good boss for tree cutters."

"This I have done," Gihi said. "I do not know if I want to do it again."

Matt was silent. Gihi continued eating quickly, as if trying to consume the bits of chicken before they were carried off by the persistent flies.

"I have thought to return to my home," Gihi said. He pointed toward the east. "There. There in the high country the days are more pleasant. Man does not sweat as he sweats here by the sea."

"Perhaps you'd like to build a nest egg—"

Gihi's forehead wrinkled in question.

"Get money," Matt said. "Buy tools, blankets, and other good things to take with you when you return to your home."

Gihi grunted and finished off the last of the pieces of chicken, leaving the greasy banana leaf where it lay. He wiped his hands on his thighs as he rose.

Matt rose with the little native.

"I will cut wood for you," Gihi said. "How many men?" He held up one hand, five fingers, raised his eyebrows. Matt lifted both hands, spread ten fingers.

"Ten men?" Matt asked.

Gihi showed ten fingers and nodded. "They will be ready."

Matt was beginning to wonder if he should have left Kit in Australia. There were no complaints from her when the heat of the day soaked her with unladylike perspiration or when the sound of the drip-drip-drip from the leaking roof became a form of torture. No complaints, Matt realized, but there were curses aplenty. She was an army brat, and when, in the middle of the night, she sat up in bed and laced into the climate of New Guinea and the genealogy of anyone who was stupid enough to come here—much less plan to stay—she would have given the most hardened old sergeant major a tough act to follow.

At first Matt was shocked. Then came a pang of guilt, for he was the one who had brought her to this steamy place, with its Chinese water torture every night. Finally, as she continued cursing in ever more creative ways, he began to chuckle.

"Damn, I'm proud of you," he told her when she was silent at last and, seemingly exhausted, fell back onto her damp pillow. "I've never heard a more competent tirade."

"Oh . . . hush," she said, trying to hide a budding grin.

"Do you feel better?" he ask, still amused.

"By God, I do," she said. "I feel very much better, and if you will lie down and be quiet, I might just be able to close my mind to the water torture and go to sleep."

He lay back, was silent for a moment. "Kit?"

"Umm."

"I've lined up ten men and a crew chief."

"Good on you," she said. Her Australianisms, delivered in her precise Oxford accent, made her all the more dear to Matt.

"I'll be going into the bush."

She sat up. " 'I'? What is this first-person-singular business?"

"I don't think you should go into the—"

"Nonsense," she said. "What do you expect me to do, stay here and listen to the drip? I've heard that the best trees grow on the higher slopes, where it's cooler."

"We'll be cutting near the coast, near water. We have no way as yet to move logs from the high slopes."

"I'll go, nevertheless."

He sighed. "All right. We'll give it a try. If it's too rough, 'll bring you back here."

She snorted.

"Or send you back to Australia."

"Damned if you will," she said, turning to cling to him in spite of the stickiness of their perspiring bodies. "Don't even. hink that."

"Maybe I should have stayed in Australia. We could still go back. No reason to return to Brisbane; I could get a job in Sydney."

"No," she said simply. "We've already discussed that, and ou know you'd hate it."

"They tell me I'm a fool to think I can make workers of men who are not yet out of the Stone Age," he said. "They ay the natives are too stupid to be good laborers."

"*They,*" Kit repeated contemptuously.

"Kit, we can't possibly stay long in these coastal swamps . . not with the fevers, the heat, and the dampness. I prom- se you that I'll get you out of this sodden place very quickly. The timber cutting is only temporary. We can do other things. Grow coffee, maybe. Even though they say—" He paused.

"They say—" she said, prompting him.

"They say that although the highlands are quite pleasant, risk at times, and ideal for coffee plants, it would be impossi- le to establish a coffee plantation. We get back to the stupid- ty and laziness of the wogs. No labor. I talked to a man who'd been in the highlands, and he says the people there are content with their lives and have no desire to work for the white man."

"Well, if you listened to *them* all the time, you'd never get ut of bed in the morning. They'd have you convinced that 's impossible for a thing shaped like a man to balance on two eet." She kissed him on the cheek. "Let's go cut some logs; hen we've made a little bit of money, let's see for ourselves bout the highlands."

"How was I ever lucky enough to convince you to marry ne?"

"You caught me in a weak moment," she said. "Will you do one of two things, please?"

"What?"

"Either make love to me or go to sleep."

"Am I limited to only one choice?"

"Well, not if you make the right choice first."

He did.

Kit accompanied Matt when he went back into the shanty town where Gihi lived. They found the native squatting in the shade of his lean-to, built of planks and corrugated iron. Seeing Matt, he rose and showed his teeth in a wide grin.

"Well, Gihi, how many men have you found for me?" Matt asked.

"This one too white," Gihi said, his eyes on Kit. "You must protect such white skin from the sun." He ducked into his lean-to and came out with a pint jar, which he handed to Kit. Her nose wrinkled at the stench of rancid fat coming from the jar. "Use on face," Gihi said. "Arms, hands."

"Thank you," Kit said. "You're very kind." She tried to hand the jar back to Gihi.

"My wife has her own, ah, grease to protect her skin from the sun," Matt said.

"Good," said Gihi, taking the jar.

"How many men?"

"No worries," Gihi said, proving that he had learned at least a part of his English from an Australian.

"How many?" Matt insisted.

"They will be ready soon," Gihi said. "I have sent small brother to tell them."

"Where did you send your small brother?" Matt said, his suspicions growing.

"There," Gihi said, pointing east. "One time the moon swells, then he will be back with many men."

Matt stood with his mouth open, his plans dashed. The native was depending on drawing men from the high country only God knew how far away. He raised both hands and let them fall.

"Is this old bandit giving you a hard time?" a familiar voice asked from behind them.

"Mr. Gorel!" Gihi said happily, leaping to his feet.

Matt turned. "Trev," he said with a wide grin.

"In the flesh," Gorel said. "What kind of drivel is this worthless old man trying to sell you?"

"He said that he could round up ten laborers," Matt said. "It's good to see you, Trev. I inquired after you. The government slugs in Sir George's office said they thought that you had gone out to the islands."

"True," Trev said. "Look, I have a thousand questions that I'm sure could best be asked over a tall, cool drink in The Southern Cross."

"Lead on," Kit said. "Before I'm forced to use the native preventative for sunburn."

The Southern Cross was a wooden building not far from the waterfront. The inside reeked of stale beer and cigars smoked long ago. The sides of the room were shutters, which could be hoisted up by ropes if it was not raining too hard. Thus open to moist outside air, the pub was a hunting ground for the various species of biting insects, but it was slightly cooler than the open street.

Trev paid for the drinks—brown Australian ale—and started his barrage of questions. Kit teased him, saying that it was all his fault, that he had sung the praises of New Guinea too loudly aboard the ship.

Trev laughed. "From the time the Portuguese first spotted this coast in 1512, everyone has been exaggerating New Guinea's resources," he said. "It hasn't taken me long to find that out."

"What have you been doing?" Matt asked.

"What I hear you plan to do. Timber. And I'm having the same problems you are. Labor."

"You mean old Gihi was lying to me about being able to get men?" Matt asked.

"Maybe, maybe not. He promised me the same thing, though, a few weeks ago."

"Bloody hell!" Matt said.

"So, my friend," Trev said, "here we are. You came just in time to catch me. I'm planning to move out to the islands as soon as the next ship arrives. At least there's some copra there, and men who are willing to harvest it for a price. I've got just about enough left to amass one shipment."

"Tell me," Matt asked, "if we had labor, could we make a profit timbering?"

"By all means," Trev said.

"If I can come up with labor, what do you think of throwing in with us?" Matt said.

"Well, as a matter of fact, the copra business is a bit too competitive, what with the Germans all over the bloody Pacific snatching every coconut that grows."

"Give me a few days, eh?"

"That I'll do," Trev said. "Where are you staying?"

Matt told him.

"Good Lord," Trev said. "And I'll wager the roof is still leaking."

"We have a two-bucket room," Kit said.

"Must be the same one I had when I first came out," Trev said. "Look, let's get over there and pack your things. You're moving in with me. I have a rather nice place, and there's plenty of room."

Kit looked at Matt, who shrugged. "Anyplace would be nicer than where we are," she said.

Trev's house sat on a rise overlooking the town. Behind it the jungle began, but when they first arrived, there was a cooling breeze from the sea. The house was built in the Caribbean style, with wide, shady porches on three sides.

"It's lovely," Kit said. "How did you manage to get it?"

"By paying an arm and a leg," Trev said. "But I had to have a decent place. Guinevere will be arriving soon, you know."

"No, I don't know," Matt said.

"Guinevere," Trev said, and the name seemed to sing its way through his lips. There was a soft look in his eyes. "My wife."

Chapter XI

AS THE GRANDSON of an earl Tolo Mason possessed enough English blood and breeding to allow what appeared to be an inherent British characteristic to surface. All British Islanders, be they Welsh, English, Irish, or Scots, seemed to hunger for desolate places—frozen wastes, deserts, jungles steaming with tropical heat. A few cynical Australians, those who took the time to ponder the British habit of claiming the far lands of various heathen races as their own, said that lack of opportunity at home, coupled with the cold climate of the islands and the native coldness of its women, sent Britain's sons into the Sahara, into the heart of India, into the African vastnesses, to the scattered islands lying from just north of Antarctica to near the Arctic Circle.

Of all the places settled by the British—with the exception of North America—Australia had offered the best possibilities for greatness. In the beginning this fact had gone unnoticed by those who saw this distant and peculiar land as nothing more than a dumping ground for English criminals. And because of her convict heritage, Australia was perhaps the one territory, among those populated chiefly by British descendants, that was most estranged from the mother country.

In major affairs of empire the commonwealth stood loyally alongside old England, but in day-to-day life the contempt Australians felt for the poms was more than evident. So if here had been someone at the western edge of the Gibson Desert to tell Tolo Mason that he was being very, very British in his delight at being so far out in the back-of-beyond, he would have disputed the point, would have denied that it was his father's English blood calling out to its own.

Each day began in the same manner. Tolo awoke with the sweet warmth of Java beside him. They were invariably cuddled together against the cold, and on many mornings, even though they could hear the Aborigines stirring in their camp at a short distance from the tent, they lingered and made the day's beginning sweet with love. And then came the glorious feeling of filling one's lungs with the dry, sweet air of the bush. Breakfast followed, with the smell of burning desert scrub from the fire. After the loading of the pack camels and a swift consultation with Ganba, who pointed ever eastward, they were off, usually before the coming of the sun and the gradually building heat, which at midday equaled—or so it seemed—the inside of an oven.

At the end of the day, as the sun set and the arid wastes gave up their heat, the evening coolness presaging the freezing night, Tolo and Java would pore over the books that they had brought, becoming more and more enamored of their country, of Australia. They both began to grasp the feelings of the rugged bushmen who populated Western Australia; they understood that their country was more than the boomerang-shaped east coast from Queensland down past Melbourne. Seventy-five percent of all the people in Australia lived in that fertile crescent, but that was not the only Australia.

Scholarly geologists divided the continent into three zones: the highlands along the east coast, including the Great Dividing Range, which was actually a series of plateaus running in a band thirty to one hundred miles wide and averaging twelve hundred feet in elevation; the central eastern lowlands, which traversed the continent from north to south without ever rising more than seven hundred feet above sea level; and the western plateau.

The west. The outback. The waly. The never-never. The

back-of-beyond. The way-out bush. It filled three-quarters of the landmass of the continent. From its beginning in the east it extended fourteen hundred miles to the shores of the Indian Ocean. It was flat, dry, and at times grotesque. Always hostile to human life, it was often fatally perilous. For Tolo it *was* Australia. It was less a geographic subdivision than a vast, challenging fact. It had been called the dead red heart of Australia, but it made Tolo feel very much alive. There in the waly his curiosity about the geology and flora of the arid Gibson found ample nourishment, and his enthusiasm was contagious. He and Java read and discussed. They collected and admired wind-polished chalcedony and translucent quartz. They skirted a plain covered with gibbers—rocks from which all hint of soil had been blown away by scouring winds. The gibbers ranged in size from pebbles to boulders, and not even the surefooted camels could negotiate such terrain.

While the weather remained dry, they saw none of those miraculous plants that appear magically and briefly after a rain, to flower, reproduce, and die quickly. Upon entering the Gibson, they had seen mulga trees, and now and again they encountered saltbush and bluebush, whose leaves absorbed the scant night moisture and provided a bit of forage for the camels. But the principal form of vegetation was the tussocky spinifex grass, which grew everywhere except in the gibber country.

From the beginning Tolo had watched his Aborigines closely. Their actions were predictable, probably because they were living in an artificial environment. The laden pack camels kept the Abos tied to the white man's caravan. Because of the food brought from Carnarvon, the Abos were not forced to resort to their native skills and ancestral knowledge of desert survival. They were still plump. And the food supply was melting away at a dismaying pace.

"Ganba," Tolo told his guide one evening, "starting tomorrow, we must begin to ration the food supplies."

Ganba did not let his displeasure show.

"If you and your people could supplement the rations by gathering your native foods," Tolo said, "that would be a great help."

Ganba nodded, but his expression was doubtful. In fact, there was little food here beyond roots and lizards.

"And, Ganba," Tolo said, "we've traveled quite a way to the east. From all I can read about the Gibson, and from the rather incomplete maps that exist, there's nothing between us and Ayers Rock but desert. Just where do you expect to find blackfellows?"

Ganba had wondered when the whitefella was going to become suspicious. "Tomorrow we go there," he said, pointing toward the northeast. "Two, three days there is water. Blackfella live there."

Alone by their fire, keeping it alive by feeding it dried grasses and stems, Java asked Tolo, "Do you suppose Ganba really knows where to find nomadic tribesmen?"

Tolo laughed. Around him the desert stretched away as far as the eye could see. "If he doesn't, I'll skin him alive for lying to us." He put his arm around Java. "No worries, love. We have plenty of food and water to get back to Yinnietharra. I'm not going to follow old Ganba blindly forever. If he doesn't show results soon, we'll make a swing back toward the north and west, in the hope of finding wild Abos in the Hamersley Range on the way back to the coast."

Java smiled at him. "I knew you would have a plan," she said, relief in her voice. "I'll admit I *have* been a bit worried to see our food and water dwindling so fast. But if you say we have enough to take us where we need to go, then everything is fine. I have complete confidence in you, and as long as I'm with you, I feel completely safe."

He beamed at her, then looked around. "Isn't this an unbloody-believable place?" he asked, awe in his voice.

The sun was a half disk on the horizon. Far away a dust storm had filled the air, and the dying rays of the sun burned red, purple, and green. The coolness of evening was fanned by a slight breeze.

"I do love it, Java," he said. "It's empty, and it's bloody useless, I suppose; but there's something about it that makes me want to ride on and on until I force it to end, until we see that great red rock rising up out of the sand and know that we've crossed it, that just over yonder there are other whitefellows."

"If you don't mind," Java said, laughing, "I'll settle for a third of the way and back."

"Winge, winge," he teased.

"I am *not* complaining," she said. "Not yet. When I decide to winge, you'll know it."

"Yes, love," he said. "You've been fair dinkum about the whole thing."

"What's with all the Strine?" she asked.

"Oh, I guess I'm feeling my nationality," he said. "I was thinking that not too many whitefellows have seen what we've seen. And I guess I let myself do some dreaming. I envision coming on a field of gold nuggets lying exposed like the rocks on a gibber plain with chunks to make the Welcome Stranger seem small." The Welcome Stranger Nugget had weighed 141 pounds.

"You get to carry it, then," Java said.

"We'll pile it up in a golden pyramid, ride back to the coast and hire a thousand men to come and cart it out."

Neither of them noticed that Ganba had approached quietly and had overheard a part of Tolo's fanciful talk. When Tolo became aware of the Abo's presence, he said, "Yes, Ganba."

"Blackfellas say no ration food," Ganba said.

Tolo stood and thought it over for a moment. "Blackfellow want to starve when food is gone?"

"Blackfella worry about starve when food is gone," Ganba said.

"Well, this whitefellow worries now, Ganba," Tolo said. "We'll go on half rations tomorrow. Sorry, but that's the way it's going to be. Tell blackfellow that if he doesn't like it, he can hunt or dig for food." He watched Ganba's impassive face for a moment. "And perhaps if Ganba gets a little hungry, he will remember better where bush blackfellows camp?"

When Ganba had gone back to his fire, Java turned to Tolo. "I don't think he liked that very much," she said.

"I think I'm beginning to understand the Abo a bit more," Tolo said. "It would be too obvious to say he's like a child, unable to look beyond instant gratification—"

"You've been reading the anthropology book again," Java said.

Tolo chuckled. "I'm afraid so. Have you read the theory regarding the Abo's invention of the Dreaming?"

"It's heavy going," Java replied.

"Stanner says that the Aborigine's Dreamtime, or Dreaming, ranks right up there with the best metaphysical thought of the European world. He says that the blackfellow has at least two things in common with civilized man: the metaphysical gift that is exhibited in imagination and the need to ask why. Why am I here? Who am I? The Abo shows great imagination in the tales of the Dreaming. He has created a reason for his being here, and he explains in his legends how he came to be here."

"Fascinating," Java said, pretending to yawn. "I'm for the kip. How about you?"

"Not just yet," Tolo said. "There's a full moon tonight. Let's have a look at it before we go in."

"My darling Tolo," Java said, "I'm sorry that I don't share your absorption in Aboriginal legends." He started to speak, but she stopped him by holding up her hand. "But I don't doubt the worth of your desire to talk to the elders of some wild tribes. I think such a work as you envision is needed, as a matter of fact."

"Thanks," Tolo said.

"The Abo tales don't make much sense when they're presented just as isolated stories," she said. "I know that I don't understand, for example, the Abo religion. I keep reading that it's totemic, but I'm not quite sure just what that means. Bildana says that if a man's totem is a dingo, then all dingoes

—man dingoes and animal dingoes—are his brothers. She does her best to explain, but I still don't understand. She says, for example, that all natural objects, living or inanimate, were created by the spirits of the Dreamtime. All people, then, are interdependent with the land itself and with the things—rocks, rivers, animals—that exist around them. The Abos are so close to some objects that if they're removed from their home area, as these people with us have been, they get confused. She says that it's like being in a strange land, where one doesn't even speak the language, and that this is one of the things that's wrong with Ganba."

"Interesting," Tolo said.

"So, if Mr. Thomas Mason can gather together the whole body of Aboriginal lore and relate all the interdependent parts, then I think he'll be doing a great service."

Tolo nodded. "It needs to be done. More and more tribes will be dispersed or assimilated as the years go by, and the elders will die off and the young ones will not have learned the lore. What has been passed down by word of mouth for centuries will be lost unless someone writes it down."

From the Abo camp there came a woman's voice. The woman led, joined at regular intervals by the voices of the others. The sounds were odd, ranging from an ear-piercing shrill to guttural sounds almost like coughing.

Tolo had translated that particular song:

> *The swallow approaches, flying through the west*
> *   wind and the rain clouds.*
> *The swallow, its feathers blown by the wind.*
> *It is always there at the wide expanse of water,*
> *Flying through the wind, close to the clouds,*
> *It flies through the wind, close to the wide*
> *   expanse of water. . . .*

Terry Forrest felt no need to push himself as he left Jonas Mayhew's station. He could not have pushed too much at any rate, for he was on horseback. The animal that he had ridden out from Carnarvon was already showing decline. The desert killed horses rapidly, even when there was water. Terry didn't worry; the horse had been doomed from the time he left Mayhew Station. With luck it would stay alive until Terry caught up with the party ahead of him. If it did, then everyone would have a good meal of meat food. If not, Terry would have to catch up on foot, carrying only some dried food and water.

The trail led due east. Day after day Terry expected it to swing to the north, for the nearest blackfellows to the east were far across the Gibson, in the sandy country near Ayers Rock. The Abo whom Mason had hired in Perth was leading him on a merry lark, one that could end only with the poofter's possessions in the hands of the Abos and the poofter and the juicy little sheila in the boongs' bellies.

Sooner than he had expected, he was very close to the Mason party. When he found camel dung that had not dried out completely in the desert heat, he knew that he must be only hours behind them. He made camp by finding a sump where he was protected by the wind, and the next morning he was up before the sun, moving swiftly.

He smelled the smoke of the spinifex and saltbush fires before he saw them, and then he was looking down from a very slight rise to see Tolo Mason and the girl loading the camels. The bloody boongs were taking their ease, the men standing with one leg cocked up on the other, their little spears thrust into the ground for balance.

"G'day," Terry yelled as he waved his hat. He kicked the exhausted horse into motion. The animal wobbled on weak legs as he neared the camp and almost fell before Terry dismounted.

Tolo Mason was standing with his hands on his hips. Terry Forrest had made it emphatically clear what he thought of Tolo's venture into the bush. "G'day," Tolo said. "I thought you were bush-wise. Don't you know horses are no good in the Gibson?"

"Couldn't help it," Terry said. He removed his hat, made a

little bow to Java, then turned and waved to the Abos, gesturing them over. Ganba, his face not showing his concern over the unexpected arrival of another whitefella, one who seemed much more formidable than his young boss, came to stand a few feet away.

"Besides, it's meat food," Terry added. Drawing his pistol and raising it with one swift motion, he dropped the spent horse with a bullet between the eyes.

Java let out a little cry of shock.

"Sorry," Terry said. "I wanted speed to catch up with you. I trust that by this time you've used up enough water and supplies to make a riding camel available for me?"

"I have to say I'm surprised," Tolo said.

" 'Strewth, mate," Terry said. "You are not the only one. There I was, comfortable in my kip down in Perth and thinking of you and the missus out here in the never-never, and I couldn't sleep. Figured that you'd end up buying camels from old Jonas." He pulled his hat down and looked at the sun. "Might as well stay here another day," he said. "Give the Abos time to eat the horse. No sense wasting it."

"I wasn't aware," Java said sharply, "that my husband had turned over the making of decisions to you."

"Nor has he," Terry conceded. "Excuse my presumption. Come to think of it, it might be best just to leave the beggars here with the horse. They'll feast for a day or two and then head back to the coast. With me along you don't need them anymore."

"I don't quite understand why you're here," Tolo said.

"Conscience, mate," Terry replied. "You came to me with an honest offer, and I turned you down, knowing all along that I was doing wrong, that you needed a bloke who knew his way around the desert."

"We've been doing quite well," Java commented.

"Sure, any fool can see that, Mrs. Mason," Terry said with oily sarcasm. "Here you are one-third of the way across the bloody Gibson, with just enough tucker left to get you across another third. I thought you were going after wild boongs."

"As a matter of fact," Tolo said, "I was about to order Ganba to turn north and west, with the intention of coming into the Abo living areas around the Hamersley Range."

"Sensible," Terry agreed. "I think I'll have a little chat with this Ganba of yours to find out why he was leading you straight east into the desert, where no boong with half a brain would be. There aren't any boongs till the dunes near Ayers Rock."

"I suspect he simply saw a way to bludge food off the whitefellows," Tolo said.

"Maybe," Terry agreed. "They all look as if they've been living well. They're all as fat arsed as an outhouse dingo. Might be, too, that they figured to come into a tent, some fine meat food in them camels, and a few trinkets like guns and your watch when the Gibson got you."

Java had been simmering all the while since she had recognized the arrogant Terry Forrest. "That's bloody insulting," she retorted. "We don't need you, Mr. Forrest. Since you've shot your horse, I've no idea how you're going to get back across to Yinnietharra, but then that's your affair, isn't it?"

"Ah, little bird," Terry said, grinning. "Am I to be thrown out then, after breaking my arse to catch up with you in order to give you a helping hand?"

Tolo laughed. Java's green eyes were beautiful when they flamed with anger, and he was pleased by her impulse to come to his defense at the very hint that Forrest doubted his ability to take care of her. "I don't think we'll run him off," Tolo said placatingly. "There's a lot about the Gibson I don't know yet, Mr. Forrest. It's obvious that I don't know how to find the range of the desert nomads. If you can, then welcome."

"Thank you, mate," Terry said. "It's going to be damned hot soon. What do you say we spread out your tent and make a sunshade that can hold all three of us?"

In the Abo camp Ganba had slit the dead horse's throat. Each member of the group, including Bildana and the other women, had enjoyed a good draft of blood, and now the men were working with axes and knives to butcher the animal while the women ranged far to gather enough burning material to cook the meat. Ganba reserved the horse's liver for himself and pulled away from the mob, his face bloody as he ate the steaming organ with great relish.

Java tried not to watch, but just as one is fascinated by a deadly snake or by forbidden activity, her eyes were drawn to the tableau around the dead horse. But when Ganba ripped out the liver and started eating it raw, she gagged and turned away.

"Charming, eh?" Terry commented.

Java's face was pasty white, and she looked ready to throw up.

"If you're going to spew chunder, old girl, please step downwind," Terry said.

Java forgot her churning stomach and turned to glare at him.

"Well, now." He shrugged. "Got you mad enough to forget about feeling sick, didn't I?"

Lying next to Tolo, Java tried to sleep. Under the tent, spread over stakes so low to the ground that one could not stand up, the temperature fell just short of baking. The Aborigines were dozing in the sun, their bellies protruding with horsemeat.

Terry Forrest had been waiting. A haunch was still roasting in the coals of the natives' fire. He sauntered over, cut off a thick pinkish slice, and began eating as he walked back toward the sunshade.

"Please," Java said, making a face as Forrest approached.

"It's just right now, luv," he said. "Not bad either. Shall I slice you a bit of it?"

"No, thank you," Java replied.

"How about you, mate?" Terry asked Tolo.

"I'll get my own," Tolo replied. He rose and headed for the fire.

"It'll be a long time before we have meat food again," Terry told Java.

As Java watched both of the men chewing contentedly on the pinkish flesh, making sounds of satisfaction, she felt hunger in spite of herself, and finally she asked for a bite, then for more. Tolo made another trip to the fire and sliced off two great chunks.

"You see," Terry commented as the three of them ate with their hands, gnawing off bites of the tender meat, "there's not much difference between them and us, is there? They just eat their food not as well done as we like ours."

It was late in the afternoon before Terry brought up a subject that was much on his mind. He approached it obliquely. "You took a route that has not been traveled before," he told Tolo. "The usual track, such as it is, runs northeast from the Gascoyne. You came almost directly east."

"It was Ganba's decision," Tolo said. "He said that the Baadu didn't need to follow the whitefellow's roads."

Later Terry remarked, "When I was moving things to stretch the tent, I picked up what seemed to be a bag of rock samples. Anything interesting?"

"Yes, quite," Tolo said, reaching for the bag. Both men crouched, and Tolo poured out onto a blanket the stones he and Java had felt were worth saving. Among them were some well-polished pieces of quartz and chalcedony. Terry fingered one or two of the pieces.

"No sign at all in the quartz," he said.

"Sign?" Tolo asked.

"Gold."

"No, I suspect not," Tolo said.

"Know anything about gold-bearing formations?" Terry asked.

"Not the slightest," Tolo answered.

"Well, I don't suppose you'd have to be a geologist to recognize old Lassiter's digs," Terry said. "The bare gold is supposed to look out at you with a glitter that burns your eyes with reflected sun."

Tolo rose to his feet abruptly. "Mr. Forrest, if you think for one minute that I came out here looking for gold—"

"No, mate," Terry said, looking up at him. "You're looking for wild boongs. Gold just makes a topic for conversation on a long, hot afternoon, doesn't it?"

In the twilight there was another fine meal of horsemeat. Terry Forrest made his kip at a distance, having borrowed two extra blankets.

Just as Java and Tolo were preparing to go into the tent, Ganba approached them.

"Who is boss now?" he asked.

Tolo didn't answer immediately.

"Mr. Mason is boss," Java replied.

"Yes," Tolo said. "But Mr. Forrest boss man, too."

"Ganba does not work for two boss man."

"Just take it easy, Ganba," Tolo said. "Mr. Forrest is going to help us find blackfellows. I'd suggest that if he asks you to do something, you do it. No worries."

But when Tolo came out of the tent at dawn, stretched, and then looked around to spot the camels, which had wandered only a small distance away, he saw no smoke from the Abo camp. The fires had been allowed to burn out early in the night, and there was no sign of Ganba and the other blackfellows.

Terry Forrest was sitting with his back against a rock, gnawing on a piece of horsemeat. "As you see, mate, the boongs vanished with the night."

"But why?" Tolo asked.

"My guess is, mate, that when I arrived, the big one gave up hope of letting the Gibson kill you. I suspect they're already a few miles back toward the Gascoyne. Good riddance, I say."

A frightening thought struck Tolo. He turned and ran to the store of food supplies and water.

"Oh, they didn't take anything," Forrest said. "I saw to that. The big one would have."

"You saw them leave and didn't stop them?" Tolo asked.
"Mate, it's a free country, isn't it?"

Ganba set a fast pace during the night. He had led his
group out of the camp shortly after the whitefellas had gone
to bed, and by morning he and his people were miles away.
Ganba maintained the pace until, at midafternoon, he called a
halt at a soak that he had noticed on the outward journey
without having called it to the whitefellas' attention.

Because of Terry Forrest, Ganba had been unable to steal
even so much as a blanket, much less a container of water. He
was angrily bitter as he knelt and dug in the powdery soil
until, little by little, the sand began to cling together moistly.
At a depth of three feet the sand was wet enough for Ganba to
fill his mouth with it and suck out a tiny amount of water
before spitting the sand aside.

Bildana, sensing her husband's mood, stayed well away
from him and used the soak last. She brought up the rear as
Ganba set out once again toward the west.

The camp that night was dry, but each of the Aborigines
had carried horsemeat, so there was food, which they cooked
over fires. Soon the little group was asleep, lying as close to
the dying fires as possible without feeling pain.

Only Bildana did not close her eyes. She lay on the sand
imagining the coming of spirit things, fearful about what she
intended to do, but more fearful of staying with Ganba. He
would surely don his murderer's slippers no later than the
evening of the next day, for many miles of dry sand and rock
lay before them, and by the end of the next day—the day after
that at the latest—Ganba would want to quench his thirst in
blood before having a repast of his favorite meat food.
Bildana, judging from Ganba's growing impatience with her
during the journey outward when she spent most of her time
attending the young missus, feared that she would be the first
meal.

In the cold of midnight, with the moon touching the arid
landscape with an eerie, lonely light, Bildana crawled slowly

and silently away from the snoring members of her tribe, moving several yards away on her belly before she dared get to her hands and knees. Only when she had crawled into a swale that hid her from the others did she stand upright and, with her heart pounding and her spirit in an agony of fear of the things of the night, begin to run for her life.

She had only a small chunk of horsemeat that she had saved from her dinner. Between her and the whitefellas, whom she intended to rejoin, there was only the one soak where they had drunk on the previous afternoon. She asked the spirits of the Dreamtime to help her find it in the dark.

Chapter XII

SPINIFEX, THE MOST common grass of the western deserts, was not called hedgehog grass idly. Each clump seemed to be all spikes, each spike tipped with tiny, sticking filaments that penetrated human skin on contact to itch and burn devilishly. As the reduced Mason expedition turned northwestward, they encountered clumps of spinifex measuring over six feet across. The clumps tended to cluster, making it difficult to wend a way among them.

The movement of the camels lifted small dust clouds. By the end of the day Java was caked with orange-colored grit. There was, of course, no water for bathing or washing. The camels, those almost mythical beasts that were supposed to be able to cross vast deserts without water, demanded a disproportionate share of the dwindling supply. To clean herself, Java first allowed all traces of the day's perspiration to evaporate—those small areas of dampness that had not been dried by the sucking, dehydrating power of the sun—and then she brushed away the dust with her hands. More than anything in the world she longed for water—not for drinking, but for splashing onto her face and down her neck; water to wallow in. If intense longing and wishing could have made it so, she would have thrown herself bodily into a huge tub of cold water to soak and splash until the last red dust mote of the Gibson Desert had been dissolved away.

Although it was obvious that Terry Forrest considered Tolo and Java helpless big-city neophytes, he oddly enough did not try to assume leadership. He left it to Tolo, checking his compass and his maps, to set a course toward the distant Hamersley Range and the bands of unspoiled Aborigines that supposedly still lived there.

Java had come to know her husband well. Although Tolo said nothing, she could see that it rankled him to be patronized as a greenhorn. He had, after all, traveled the arid bush of Queensland and New South Wales. And he had led his own party a third of the way across the Gibson before Forrest joined them.

During the day there was little conversation. By midmorning a sort of trance seemed to come over the travelers. The sun, by that time, was doing its worst. Around them the barren rocks, the sandy dunes, and the purple-pink hills writhed like things alive in the heat, as if forced by a cruel master to continue to dance long after pain had convulsed all. Java had developed a way of slumping in the saddle, her body swaying with the odd gait of her camel, and letting something near sleep come over her so that she was numb to the heat, immune to the crying out of every body cell for water.

Terry Forrest did not wait long to begin to question Tolo again. After two days of travel, when it became evident to him that Tolo was actually heading back toward the west coast, he began to be doubtful, and after the evening meal he broached the subject that was bothering him.

A fire was burning, and a hint of gold-red color still lingered on the western horizon. The cool of evening was a welcome relief from the burning day. "I just don't quite understand, mate, why you traveled so far to the east only to turn back," Terry commented. "For two days now you've shown me that you can chart a course and keep to it. Why the wasted time and travel?"

"As I said," Tolo told him, "I was depending on Ganba to

take me to a nomad camp. I felt perhaps that some small tribe camped near one of the bores—"

"You were a damned long way from the nearest bore!" Terry interrupted. Bores, the wells on which animals and man alike relied, were sparse in this region. "The route you took made it look as if you were headed directly for what the boongs call the great-red-sacred-rock."

"No, we had no intention of going that far," Tolo said. "I've seen some of the Aborigines in the Northern Territory, and I'm afraid that the Aboriginal peoples around Alice Springs and the rock have already been changed by contact with whitefellows."

"Still sticking with that story, eh?" Terry asked, somewhat testily.

"I beg your pardon?"

"By God, I'm beginning to believe that you're just simple enough to be doing exactly what you say you're doing," Terry said, rising.

Tolo came to his feet slowly. "Forrest, you've been a perfect ass ever since you joined us," he said evenly. "If you're trying to convince us that you're a splendid specimen of Australian manhood, I think we get the message. Now, quite frankly, I don't understand your problem. I don't know what *you* think we came into the desert to find, but if you don't like what I'm planning to do, then there's a camel, and Carnarvon is that way." He stood up straighter and pointed, holding the pose for a moment.

"You're a big bloke, I'll give you that," Terry said musingly. "All right, mate." His voice had assumed a hearty tone. "It's old Terry himself who's the simple one. Listening to people and their tales of gold. Have you ever even heard of Lassiter?"

Java laughed first, and then the anger left Tolo's face as he, too, understood.

"Good Lord, whoever gave you the crazy idea we cared anything for Lassiter's gold?" Tolo asked, chuckling.

Terry's echoing laugh sounded hollow. "Half the population of Carnarvon. I talked to at least half a dozen blokes who had it straight from your agent there."

"It was a joke." Java giggled. "I told him that we were after Lassiter's gold because he couldn't believe we were going out merely to study Aborigines."

"Some joke," Terry said. "One day, when we're out of the never-never, maybe I'll see something funny about it."

Next day Terry Forrest rode lead for a while, following the course set by Tolo with his compass. The camels had been given their last drink. Tolo was aiming for a bore that was well marked on his maps, there to refill the empty water drums for the trek into the Hamersley Range. Forrest had agreed with a silent nod that Tolo was smack on in his navigation.

"If the bore isn't dry," Terry mused aloud as the three of them rested at midday in the partial shadow of a dune. "If we don't miss it by a few miles."

"The map says that the bore is dependable," Java said.

"Well, the never-never is fickle," Terry explained. "The boongs will tell you that soaks come and go." He mused for a while longer. "Funny, the boongs never dug wells themselves. They say that the water moves under the earth and that when the whitefellow digs a bore, he uses magic." He chuckled. "The boongs don't know how many bores have been driven without finding water. Some places it's just as dry under the ground as it is on top. There's a mine down in the Nullarbor that goes down four thousand feet without striking a drop of water." He grinned at Tolo. "The Nullarbor. That's where you wanted to go to look for boongs, isn't it?"

And so it went for three more days, with Terry taking every opportunity to inflict verbal pinpricks on Tolo. By the bush code, his goadings were fair dinkum; the true bushman likes nothing better than a good "blue," a fine no-hard-feelings free-for-all where the Marquess of Queensberry rules are not totally ignored but perhaps bent a bit. Terry Forrest was working himself up to finding out if Tolo's size and strength were backed by a will to fight. He was developing a deep-seated need to measure his own manhood against the big, powerful young man from Sydney.

For Terry, desert travel was a pain in the arse, but nothing to winge about. Given a choice, he simply didn't come into the never-never, and he was cursing himself for letting his yen to see the little sheila again—and his stupid acceptance of the yabber of the blokes in Carnarvon about Lassiter's gold—draw him away from the comfort of his Perth home and the boozy solace of his favorite pub. Wanting a pint and not being able to get it were enough to put Terry in a fighting mood. When, in his deprivation, he was constantly rebuffed by the little sheila, the pressure inside him continued to build.

They watched the sky for signs that the rains might come before they reached the bore. In the evenings, especially, the eastern skies put on a light-and-sound extravaganza for them, proving that somewhere to the east it was raining—how far to the east it was impossible to tell.

As they stopped to make camp on the bank of a dry wash, Terry said nothing as Tolo called a halt and "whoosh-whooshed" his camel into a sitting position. He wanted to wait until the city boy started to set up camp in the dry wash for protection from the night wind so that he could laugh at Tolo's ignorance. He was chagrined when Tolo disdained the shelter of the wash and, in fact, began to unload the camels at a safe distance from the sandy, crumbling bank. He had no way of knowing that Tolo had deduced the potential danger of camping in a wash after the strange incident when Ganba moved his people to high ground in the middle of the night.

"I'm going to gather some firewood," Tolo announced. He walked down to the wash and disappeared over the side of the eroded bank. It would take him a while to collect enough of the scattered mulga sticks to make a decent fire.

"Now we are alone," Terry said, after Tolo had gone down into the wash.

"You can't imagine how that thrills me," Java said, with very obvious sarcasm.

"For a pretty little sheila you're the unfriendliest—"

"Mr. Forrest, I find it very hard to have friendly feelings toward you," Java said. "You're egotistical, overbearing, and crude."

"But sort of handsome, wouldn't you say?" he asked, laughing as he moved closer to her. "I think if you gave it a chance, you'd find that I grow on you."

"Fungus also grows on one in the wet season," she said.

He reached out to put a hand on her shoulder, and she jerked away.

"It's sort of interesting, isn't it?" he asked. "The three of us all alone in the bush with no guarantee that we'll all get back to the coast. When you think about it that way, it makes you wonder, doesn't it?"

Without another word Java turned and started walking in the direction Tolo had gone. Terry watched the play of her hips under her skirts as she waded through loose sand, then started walking after her, his long strides closing the distance between them quickly. He caught her on the bank of the wash and jerked her to a stop with his hand on her arm.

"Look, Miss High-and-Mighty," he snarled. "I am not dirt to be trampled under your feet. I think you could at least extend common courtesy."

"I was under the impression that I had," she said. "I will be courteous enough to say please when I ask you to remove your hand from my arm."

"Too good to be touched, are we?" he asked, grinning at her.

Suddenly he felt a crushing grip on his upper arm, paralyzing his muscles. He let out a yell and turned to see Tolo who had emerged silently from the wash. Terry's hand fell from Java's arm as his fist sought Tolo's face. Tolo moved easily backward and stood glaring at him. For long moments they stood facing each other, almost of a height, Terry a bit shorter and more wiry.

"That bloody well hurt, mate," Terry said. His anger told him to do it now, to get it over. His reason reminded him that he was to hell and gone in the desert, where an injured man had little chance of survival.

"Don't touch her again," Tolo said calmly. "Never, never touch her. Don't even come near her."

The challenge was too direct. No bushman could have kept quiet in the face of such a direct confrontation of overt maleness. "And what if I do?" Terry asked.

"Oh, for heaven's sake," Java said. "Let it go. It was nothing, just the male animal feeling the urgings of his gonads."

"Lady, you have a filthy mouth," Terry said, with some astonishment.

"That's not for you to say," Tolo said.

"You sound like two little boys on the playground, daring each other to step across a line," Java said. "Now let's leave it and go have some tucker." She walked toward the tent.

It seemed that the situation had been defused, but that was not to be. Terry Forrest had lost face. "Fine piece, that," he said, his eyes on Java's behind. "Don't blame you for being willing to fight for it, boy. Just don't ever let her get a taste of a real man."

Once before Terry had been impressed by the strength and quickness of this boy. Now, in a space of less than five minutes, he was impressed again. First he had felt that incredibly strong grip on his arm, so strong that the arm had gone numb for a moment. Then, with surprising quickness, he found himself seated on the sand, little spots of light forming and bursting before his eyes.

He sighed. "Well, that's twice you've coldcocked me, mate," he said, starting to get up. "I reckon that's enough."

Terry Forrest went in low, his instincts those of a pub fighter, an alley head-knocker. His fists preceded him, sinking into Tolo's torso. Tolo grunted with pain and effort as his counterblow sailed over Forrest's head.

"Stop it," Java shouted. "Stop it this instant."

Terry danced back, avoiding another sledgehammer blow

from Tolo's big right fist. His fists danced off Tolo's face, blows that would have stopped most men. Tolo's left came at him from out of nowhere and landed with a thud that made Terry gasp and wonder if he had broken ribs. He moved in immediately, sensing that he needed to put this lad down quickly lest his youthful strength and quickness be the undoing of Terry Forrest.

Tolo went down, his head banging against a rock. He moaned. His legs seemed to have deserted him. He felt a painful impact in his side and then rolled away as Forrest aimed another kick at his ribs. Forrest caught up with Tolo and landed the toe of his boot in Tolo's side.

Java screamed. She ran forward and leapt on Forrest's back. For a moment Terry was occupied with Java before he threw her off to land heavily on the sand, and that respite gave Tolo time to get to his feet, so that when the bushman went in for the kill, he met a granitelike fist that threatened to drive his stomach through his backbone. His breath whooshed out of him, and he was able to land only a grazing counterblow before another fist burst stars in his head.

Terry staggered backward and waited. From long experience he knew the overconfidence that came to men when they thought they had the opponent beaten. He kept backpedaling until his head cleared, half running from Tolo's bull-like rush, and then he jinked to one side, sent his fists hammering into the larger man's face one, two, three. Tolo was down again. Terry knew that this time he had damned well better keep him there, if he could do it without killing the lad.

When Java saw Tolo go down, with Forrest trying to kick him again, she was running toward the tent. Forrest had time to land only one more kick before she emerged from the tent with Tolo's rifle in her hands. She chambered a round quickly, and her voice contained a hint of hysteria as she cried out, "Stop it now. Don't kick him again."

Forrest turned and saw the gun. " 'Strewth," he whispered

as he lifted his foot to smash it into Tolo's face. The young man struggled to get to his feet.

The shot blasted the silence of the evening, whining away into the shadowy distances after striking a stone not three inches from Forrest's left foot. The impact of rock and sand against his boot made him wince with pain, and he leapt back from Tolo.

"Java, no!" Tolo called out, but she chambered another round. He was up, moving in, his arms closing around his distracted opponent.

They had moved close to the eroded bank of the dry wash. They struggled there, outlined against the lightning in the east, for what seemed to Java an eon before Tolo's feet crumbled the sandy edge of the wash and, locked together, the two men fell over the edge.

Java ran to look down into the wash. The fall had broken Tolo's hold on Forrest, and the two men stood face-to-face, arms heavy, fists flailing. Neither seemed to have the power to land a finishing blow.

Java lifted the rifle. She was, at that moment, fully capable of killing Forrest, for he was hurting Tolo terribly, his blows landing in Tolo's face with sickening thuds; but even in her anger and fear Java's breast swelled with pride because for every blow he received Tolo gave at least one back, and Forrest was reeling, moving backward toward the center of the dry wash.

At that point the wash was almost a hundred feet wide. Its bed was filled with weathered rocks only partially covered by red sand. When a man went down, it was painful, and both experienced the contact of knees and hands with the stones of the riverbed. Each man was panting, bloody, and each was as determined as ever to stay with it, to be standing when the other could not.

Java lifted the rifle, trying to get a clear shot at Forrest, but each time she was almost ready to fire Tolo closed in. Moreover, in the lightning, the battling figures took on the appearance of a daytime mirage, shimmering and shifting in the flickering light. She was screaming at them to stop it, to stop it. Tears flowed down her cheeks, tears of rage and fear and helplessness. Her heart beat furiously, and she heard a roaring, a sound that covered the harsh gasps for breath, the thud of new blows. The roaring became louder and louder.

A blow from Tolo's right fist jarred Forrest's head backward. A counterblow sent a spurt of blood from Tolo's already smashed nose. Tolo drew back his arm. Before him Forrest's bloody face came and went with the flashes of lightning, and it was getting lower, lower. The bushranger was sinking to his knees. Tolo, seeing a chance to finish it, aimed a blow at Forrest's chin, but the blow missed, and Tolo, exhausted, sank to his knees and knelt there, facing the similarly positioned Forrest. Forrest lifted a hand, sent a pawing left toward Tolo's face. Tolo countered with a heavy, leaden right.

Neither man saw the forward wall of the flood come roaring around a bend to the east of them.

Java, seeing it, yelled at the top of her lungs but could not hear the sound of her own voice. She looked toward the sound of the thunder that was quite near, and the panic in the pit of her stomach was acute and painful. She saw the end of all her dreams and hopes, the end of her love, roaring around the upstream bend of the dry wash, a wall of debris-filled water that glutted the wash from bank to bank, a head rise of the type that Ganba had been counting on when he moved his people out of a similar dry riverbed. She screamed again. Out there in the wash the two men were pawing at each other, on their knees, so weak that neither could stand up. Her shouts of warning were lost in the racing thunder. She fired the rifle into the air, and the sound was barely distinguishable to her own ears.

She ran to the edge of the wash and leapt down, and there, under the bank, her terror of drowning roused in her elemental instincts of survival, a primordial terror that overrode her fear for Tolo and sent her scrambling back up the bank instead of toward her husband.

Now she looked back, saw the two men turn to see death

approaching. Tolo struggled to his feet and started toward the bank, but in his condition she knew it was impossibly far away for him. He took two running steps, then glanced back to where Terry Forrest was trying to struggle to his feet.

Tolo's lips moved in shouts Java could not hear. Forrest tried to rise, but his legs would not hold him.

"No, oh, no," Java groaned as Tolo turned and went back to help Forrest. "No, Tolo, please." But Tolo was at Terry's side, trying to lift the smaller man with his hands under his arms.

She watched in helpless terror as the high wall of water—carrying with it whole uprooted bushes and deadly sharp pieces of ancient drift—smashed into the struggling men. They disappeared in the muddy, tumbling cascade. The thundering advance of the water outdistanced Java as she ran along the bank, screaming Tolo's name.

Chapter XIII

ALTHOUGH KIT VAN BUREN would have preferred to have her own house, she was not complaining about the living arrangements that had been provided by Trevor Gorel. She and Matt had lived with the constant drip of the leaky roof in their first quarters for too long, and no other suitable house was available.

Trevor's house, on the slope overlooking Port Moresby's harbor, was relatively new. The dampness of equatorial Papua had already created some mildew that resisted Kit's efforts to eradicate it, but in general the house had a fresh feel to it, an openness that allowed good ventilation. Kit and Matt's bedroom, with all windows open and mosquito nets secured around the bed, was almost comfortable. The bed itself was a high-post brass model designed especially for the sons and daughters of the British Empire assigned to tropical lands, where insects were a problem. Finely wrought folding brass wings extended out from the high headboard, to suspend the netting in a canopy that sloped down to the lower footboard. The delicate netting material, which did not touch the sleepers, closed out most insects while admitting any stray breeze from the Gulf of Papua.

While Kit was settling in, not taking long, since she and Matt had brought only hand-carried luggage to New Guinea, the men held a marathon planning and dreaming session.

Seated at a table on one of the wide verandas, a map of New Guinea and adjacent areas spread before them, they verbally felled forests with an abandon that rivaled that of America's mythical Paul Bunyan. Kit meanwhile pitched in to help the two servants clean house. The maids were Kanaka girls whose indentures had been included in the price of the house.

"Ho, Kit," Matt called after having hunted her down in the kitchen, where she was scouring the top of a malignant-looking wood-burning cookstove. "Trev and I are going down to the harbor to have a look at his boat. Care to join us?"

"Give me a few minutes," she said, pushing back the cloth she had tied around her forehead to keep perspiration from running into her eyes. She would have enjoyed a quick bath, but she knew that she would be soaked with perspiration ten minutes later. She settled for a thorough dusting with talc, a quick repair job for her hair, and the coolest dress she owned, a loose-fitting gingham.

Port Moresby was a small town, but its population was cosmopolitan. One saw a few Englishmen on the streets, mixed with Dutch, French, Japanese, Javanese, a stray American or two, and the squat black natives of Papua, their several languages creating a polyglot of voices in passing. Closer to the harbor, the ever-present smell of rank garbage and other rotting things mixed with the salt smell of the sea. Kit, Matt, and Trev spotted a sailing ship making for open water in the Coral Sea, probably for the passage down to Australia. Two small steamers were anchored in the harbor, while rickety docks at wharfside made mooring places for a variety of nondescript small boats. Among these was the *Annamese Princess,* Trev's clean-cut, well-maintained sloop.

A Javanese man leapt to his feet when he saw Trev, and he gave a brisk little salute.

"This is Kandi." Trev grinned. "Believe me, he's not half so sweet as his name sounds."

The Javanese laughed, showing clean white teeth.

"He keeps my girl in good shape for me," Trev said.

"We sail?" Kandi asked, waving toward the sea.

"Soon," Trev said. "Soon we sail to look for timber."

"That's good, boss," Kandi said. "The *Princess* needs to run hard, knock the growth off in the waves."

"Isn't it rather small?" Kit asked. The *Annamese Princess* was just under thirty feet long. She had a single mast and a low-slung cabin that put the living quarters well below the level of her teak deck. Her open cockpit at the rear would expose occupants to every whim of the weather.

"She's just the right size for navigating the reefs along the coast," Trev said. "It's more comfortable below than you might think. Plenty of room for the three of us."

"Then your man isn't going?" Kit asked.

Trev looked quickly at Matt. "Whoops," he said.

"Now, Kit," Matt protested, "you can see that the cabin of a boat this size is no place for mixed company."

"On a small boat," Trev said, "one must leave modesty ashore. I'm sure that a lady of your—"

"I'm no lady," Kit said, smiling blazingly. "I'm the wife of a partner in this enterprise. Where Matt goes, I go. That's it, gentlemen. No discussion, please."

"Kit, blast it," Matt said. He lifted his hands helplessly. "Tell her about the sanitary facilities, Trev."

"They consist of the entire ocean," Trev explained, flushing slightly. "And a bucket for inclement weather."

"When we were stationed in Cairo," Kit said, "my father bought one of the native riverboats. It was equally modern. And it wasn't always just my parents and I aboard. Once we had a general with us, and we sailed up the Nile all the way to Luxor."

"Kit . . ."

"Please," she said, and when she turned the massive candlepower of her startlingly green eyes on Matt, he threw up his hands again.

"What about it, Trev?" he asked.

"I guess if she can stand it, we can," he said. "I had just assumed—knowing what my Guinevere would say if she were asked to spend weeks aboard such a small boat—that you'd prefer to stay at home, Kit."

"Not likely," Kit said.

"Kandi put up sheet of canvas," the Java man volunteered. "Lady sit on bucket, we no see."

"Thank you, Kandi," Kit said. "At least there's one true gentleman on board."

The *Princess* hauled away from Port Moresby in time to see a glorious dawn at sea, the eastern sky blazing with an orange light that turned brazen as the day advanced. The course was southeasterly, near the shore and in sight of the mountains that rose almost immediately beyond the swampy fringes of the island. Trev had seen some likely stands of trees on the way back from his trading journey to the British Solomons.

The first stop was only a day out of Port Moresby. Trev and Kandi maneuvered the *Princess* close to the jungled shore, carefully picking a way through coral heads, Kandi standing on the bow to indicate the deeper channels with hand signals.

"Some of these beauties could take the bottom out of a boat," Matt said. He was perched on the rail, clinging to rigging. In the nearly transparent blue water the coral seemed at times to be only inches under the surface.

"Not to mention the keel," Trev said.

When at last the little sloop was safely anchored inside the coral reef and the sails were lowered, Kandi let down the dinghy and held it while Trev clambered in. Matt handed Kit into the small boat, then followed her.

"The water is so beautiful," Kit remarked. "I'm for a swim when you two have finished your work."

Trev chuckled and pointed to a sinister-looking object that was cutting the smooth surface of the lagoon. "Well, only if you'd like that fellow for company," he said. "He's just a small one—say, six feet or so. Trouble is, one never knows when his big brother is going to come along."

"I have definitely decided I will *not* go for a swim," Kit concluded.

"Oh, it isn't that bad," Trev said. "At least we can bathe a bit by leaping off the standing board at the stern. One man keeps watch for the beggars, sturdy rifle in hand to frighten them off."

"You have to admit that old Trev searches out the possibilities," Matt said.

"Old Trev is all heart," said Kit as the little boat was propelled jerkily toward the tangled mass of vegetation that swept down to a narrow dark strand.

As they entered the jungle, the heat closed down around them like a liquid blanket. Taking the lead, Trev slashed at vines with a jungle knife. "Now there's a real beauty," he said, pointing to a monarch of a tree that soared upward, proudly straight, into the jungle canopy.

"What a shame to cut down such a splendid example of God's creation," Kit commented.

"Here, now," Matt said. "No wife of a Van Buren joins the bleeding-heart brigade. Besides, I thought you wanted to be rich."

"There are plenty of others," Trev said. "No need to weep over the few that we can harvest."

"If you cut it down," Kit asked, "how are you going to get it aboard a ship?"

"That's the fun part of the job," Trev answered. "You have noticed, of course, that we are walking in mud."

"How could I not?" Kit asked. She had lifted her skirts, bundling them into bloomerlike masses, securing them above her boots, which with each step sank into the mud almost to their tops.

"The tide sweeps back into the jungle when it's high," Trev said. "Sometimes for two or three miles. Our workmen cut a pathway into the bush, where they fell the trees and trim them up. Then, when the high tide rushes into the trench and fills it, they can float the logs out. The logs are drifted past the reef, and the timber ship hoists them aboard with a deck crane. We'll cut some logs into lengths that can be stowed in the ship's hold; others can be lashed to the deck. The real problem is that before we get the ship here, we have to have our cargo ready. We can't expect a ship to lie off the reef waiting while we cut trees."

"And to have a cargo ready means that we have to have the labor," Matt said.

They spent the morning tramping around in the mud, the last couple of hours in rising water. Trev and Matt had concluded that there were enough usable trees near the strand to make up a shipload.

It was a relief to be back aboard the *Princess*. A slight breeze had come up, and although the humidity was high enough to prevent the drying of their saturated clothing, the stir of air made for an illusion of coolness. Trev and Kandi went forward and made a pretense of inspecting the rigging while Matt stood guard with a rifle, allowing Kit to slip into the bath-warm sea and wash the perspiration and mud from both her clothing and herself.

When the *Princess* was at anchor, lying almost in the shadow of the big island's rain forests, the four of them would often sleep on deck to escape the stifling heat of the tiny cabin below. At times a fine night rain would fall, cooling them, leaving them—as Kit put it—to "molder away" until the morning sun came up to dry them with its quick heat.

It became quite clear that there was no shortage of timber for the cutting. The *Princess* made her way in calm seas down the extreme southeast coast of Papua toward the end of the lizard's tail. Perhaps such an extensive survey was not necessary, but the exploration had taken on the aspects of an outing. There was always the temptation to see what was around the next bend of the coastline, until the little sloop rounded Samarai Point, and New Guinea no longer stood between the *Princess* and the island-studded South Pacific.

They turned back, rounding Samarai Point again, and then the *Princess* flew back toward Port Moresby with all sails filled. She leapt jauntily over, into, and through brisk blue waters, and the wind of her motion was cool and pleasant. Matt and Trev spent hours talking about their plans. All they needed was labor. A few oxen would be of help to drag the trees to water. Matt would send a message to his cousin Claus as soon as they had solved the labor problem.

With the harbor at Port Moresby a day's sail away the sloop began to get just a bit too sprightly in her eager leaps before the wind. Trev and Kandi shortened sail. No clouds were visible beyond the usual tropical buildup of cottony thunderheads, but the wind continued to stiffen until the *Princess* was keeping headway in growing waves with only her foresail.

Trev made light of it at first. "Really, now," he said, "you wouldn't think you had been at sea at all if you didn't have at least one little blow."

The "little blow" was coming from a line of dark clouds that appeared at the horizon and, as if chasing the sloop with malevolent intent, rushed to overtake them. By midafternoon the sky overhead was sullen, and squalls of rain came and went, cutting visibility to almost nothing.

"Can we make it into Port Moresby?" Kit asked.

"No worries, mate," Trev replied in a bad imitation of Matt's accent.

In rain that blew almost horizontally on the fierce wind, with the *Princess* driving her lee rail under in her effort to keep course to Port Moresby, Kit asked Trev, "Still no worries, mate?"

"No worries," he said. "Inconvenience, that's all." At that point he gave up trying to make it into Port Moresby before nightfall, instead shortening sail and easing the helm around until the *Princess* was running directly before the wind.

"We'll have to run past the harbor," he said. "No problem, though. We've got all of the Gulf of Papua ahead of us. We ride out the storm with a sea anchor." Even as he spoke, Kandi and Matt were rigging the drag. Kandi tossed it over and let out the rope until the sea anchor rode a hundred feet behind them. Immediately there was an easing of the *Princess*'s almost frightened leapings. "And when the blow passes, we'll just tack back down to good old Port Moresby."

Matt escorted Kit below. They got out of their soaked clothing and into something a bit less damp. Kit had discovered that on a small sailboat one was never actually dry, that there were only varying degrees of wetness. Trev came in, bringing with him a blast of the storm. He was followed closely by Kandi.

"Who's watching the store?" Kit asked.

Trev shrugged. "All sails are reefed. The *Princess* knows better how to take care of herself now than any of us."

Minutes went by as Trev and Kandi dried themselves and struggled into semidry clothing behind the privacy screen that Kandi had installed.

"Trev, you're joking about letting the boat take care of herself," Kit said.

"Not in the slightest," Trev said. "The wind is blowing us to the northwest, parallel to the coastline. The sea anchor will keep her stern into the wind. Kandi figures this storm will either blow itself out or pass by us before the night is over. There's no point in any of us getting soaked up there in the cockpit, so I suggest that we all get a little sleep."

To her great surprise Kit did sleep. Matt was on the outside of the berth to keep her from being tossed out as the *Princess* heaved with the storm waves. She buried her head under her pillow and said her prayers with more fervor than usual, and then she slept, while the wind howled through the rigging and the following waves sent cascades of white water over the sloop's stern, only to be shed off the teak deck easily. The *Princess* was a small boat, but she had been designed in a Sydney boatyard to do exactly what she was doing: to fly like a cork over the worst that the waters of the southern seas could send her way. She did know how to take care of herself and was doing quite well at it—until her keel scraped an uncharted reef fifteen miles west of the Papuan coast.

The Javanese sailor felt the sudden alteration of the sloop's motion. If was as if she had paused in mid-leap. She floated motionless for a fraction of a second as her deep keel board dug a trench through living coral, and then, freed, she darted forward again. The lurch of the release also woke Trev Gorel. He and Kandi reached the hatch at the same instant, tried to go through it at the same time, grunted with mutual frustration. Kandi held back, and Trev burst out into the cockpit.

"Bloody hell," he yelled.

Ahead of the *Princess* the sea was being whipped to a froth as the storm crests smashed down onto a coral reef. The sound of the breakers could be heard only dimly over the whine and rush of wind and the hissing of the rollers coming up under the sloop.

"Sail," Trev yelled into the wind. "Give me sail!"

Kandi rushed to obey the order. He unfurled the small sail from the mast, and it caught in the wind, billowing and snapping like a rifle shot. Trev leaned on the tiller, but the sloop was not answering.

"Cut the line to the bloody sea anchor!" Trev yelled.

Free of her drag, the *Princess* darted forward and began to make a turn, heeling under the wind to put her lee rail awash.

Matt came topside, and Trev saw his face in the dim light of dawn, a light that seemed to be nothing more than an extension of the night and the storm. "Matt, get the life jackets, will you?" Trev shouted.

Matt hesitated for only a moment before diving back into the cabin. He put a life jacket first on Kit, then on himself. He held on to Kit's arm as they stepped out into the cockpit, where the wind of the storm seized them, tugging at them and flapping their already sodden clothing against their legs.

Trev struggled into his life jacket. Kandi had made quick work of donning his. "We're going to make it," Trev screamed into the wind as the *Princess,* like true royalty of the sea, dug her keel in, leaned before the wind, and answered the bite of her tiller to run along the front of the line of white death, where the storm crests smashed down in thunder onto raw coral. "The thing is, that bloody reef's not supposed to be here."

There has never been any satisfactory explanation for the

rogue wave, that rare, awesome phenomenon that few mariners ever see. In calm seas, with a gentle swell running, the rogue can come rearing up in white foam from the unbroken blue or green. In a storm where waves are running eight to ten feet high, as they were in the Gulf of Papua while the *Princess* fought bravely to sail away from the front of an uncharted coral reef, the rogue can come hissing and muttering out of nowhere, dwarfing the storm crests, rearing up in a frightening wall of blackness and power. In the open sea, on a calm day, a small boat merely rides up the bloated front of the rogue and drops off the back side, a carnival ride that reminds the occupants of the mystery and power of the sea. But a storm rogue can be more than a stomach-dropping kiss-me-quick ride.

The occupants of the *Annamese Princess* heard the wave before they saw it. The sound began as a distant hissing, a sound in a different key, distinct from the splash and roar of the storm and the crash of the breakers on the reef. The hissing became louder, amplified itself into low, steady thunder, and then the wave came out of the pale morning light, a wall of darkness tipped in white, a threat so dreadful that Trev Gorel cried out more in awe than in fear.

The forward surge of the wave raced under the sloop's stern, lifted her, positioned her to the exact angle of slope so that she rode the wave like a Polynesian boy's surfboard. The *Princess* accelerated. The wind in her one sail was a minute force compared with the power of the wave. Her passage through the water was made with a hissing roar of power, and over her stern the curl of the wave reared itself darkly.

"Hang tight," Trev Gorel yelled, his voice lost in the hissing roar. "Hang tight!"

All of them knew that the *Princess* was going to be driven into the reef at speed. Matt reached out for Kit to hold her fast. With each second it seemed that the wave was going to engulf them, topple onto them, and pound them down against the reef with its tons of water and force, but still the *Princess* fled before the huge wave, fled for her life, crossed over coral heads that, without the depth of water being carried along by the rogue wave, would have ripped off her keel and toppled her.

When the *Princess* struck, she struck with grinding, crashing force. Slowed, she lost her race with the wave, and the ocean fell atop her. Matt, clinging to Kit with one arm and the side of the cockpit with the other, felt himself pushed down by a great force. He went flat, clinging somehow to Kit and the side of the cockpit as he heard chaos in his ears, heard the keel digging into the coral, and felt the boat coming apart under him. He was thinking only that it was too soon, too soon to lose Kit, for he had had her such a short time.

Kit saw the towering crest of the wave begin to topple, to enclose her and the brave little sloop in its watery tubelike embrace. Her first thought was to scream, and if she had obeyed that urge, she might have died. Instead, she drew as much breath into her lungs as she could and then clung to Matt and the side of the cockpit as the world became darkness and smashing, roaring water.

Was the sloop still? She had been banged hard against the side of the cockpit, and the water was racing past her with such rapidity and force that she feared she would be pulled out of Matt's grasp, feared for her own hold on the side of the cockpit. It went on forever while little white stars began to appear on the inside of her tightly closed eyes, and her lungs began to convulse in their need to empty themselves and draw fresh breath. Her mind told her to turn loose, to try to reach the surface, to go searching for air, but Matt was clinging to his hold and to her, and she fought the coming blackness until there was a blessed halt to the sea's effort to jerk her out of the cockpit. She opened her eyes to see the faint light of dawn and white bubbles, and then her face was in the air and she was gasping for breath.

Beside Kit, Matt breathed deeply twice before yelling, "Trev, Kandi!"

"I am here," Kandi said.

"Bloody hell," Trev said, coughing up salt water.

Water was draining quickly off the deck as the huge wave passed on toward the northwest. The *Princess* sat rock-steady. Spray from a breaking wave dashed across Matt's face. The waves were breaking before they reached the boat. None of them was coming onto her deck.

"We are high and dry," Kandi called out. "Stuck on the bloody reef."

"Check below, Kandi," Trev ordered.

"I'll do it," Matt said. He was nearest the cabin hatchway. He ducked in and looked. The cabin was knee-deep in water, and more was gushing in. Bare coral protruded through the sides of the *Princess* on starboard and port. Matt stuck his head out. "We're jammed between two heads," he said. "The boat is definitely done for. We'll be all right as long as we don't slip out from between the coral heads into deeper water."

Trev dived down into the cabin to take a look for himself. The water level, he saw, would even itself out at about chest depth. He started handing up provisions and blankets to those on deck. The rain had stopped, for already the storm was moving on past them, as if it had been chased away by the monster wave that had lifted them onto the reef beyond the reach of the breakers.

Sunrise. A rainbow of colors and heat. Far to the east they could see the mountains of New Guinea, low and dark on the horizon. They had food for a few days, water for less.

"Kandi, you and Matt take some canvas and rig a trough to catch rainwater," Trev said. "Kit, would you like to select a bite of something for all of us? I think it would be wise to go easy on both food and water."

"We're no more than twelve or fifteen miles offshore," Matt said.

"Might as well be fifteen hundred," Trev replied, pointing to two different shark fins.

"Ship traffic?" Matt asked.

"Sooner or later," Trev said. "We're off the lanes for anything but a coasting ship. There's not much going on on the northern shore of the gulf. Over there, to the east, is the Fly River delta. Natives live there, but not many of them come along the gulf shore here."

"Will the boat hold together?" Kit asked.

"Unless something worse than what we've had comes along," Trev said.

"Well, then," Kit said brightly, "things are not too black after all. Here we are at sea"—only the white, breaking waves offshore from their position indicated the presence of the reef —"and we don't even have to put up with the usual motion of the boat."

"My poor old girl," Trev said, patting the *Princess* tenderly. "Poor old girl."

Chapter XIV

THE DESERT NIGHT, moonless, came quickly, the eastern horizon lit by the eerie flares of sheet lightning. The initial flood that had swept away the heart of Java Mason's life had abated, although the formerly dry wash still ran full.

For endless moments Java continued to stumble along the bank in the darkness, screaming Tolo's name, heedless of her own safety. Stumbling and falling heavily, she struggled to her hands and knees and crawled on, paying no attention to the spinifex spines that embedded themselves in her hands.

From far away she heard odd sounds—throaty moans, keening cries of wordless primeval agony. The roiling, thundering sound of the flood wave had long since passed her by. She halted, sat in the sand trying to catch her breath, and only then realized that the odd sounds were coming from her own throat.

Now the sense of loss overwhelmed her, an immense weight on her shoulders crushing her into the sand, leaving her devoid of hope. Tolo was gone. No one could have survived that cascading tumult of water and debris. Exhausted as he had been from the fight with Terry Forrest, he would not have had the strength to make his way to shore. She was utterly alone: To the west more than 125 miles of waterless wastes separated her from the nearest white outpost, old Jonas Mayhew's station at Yinnietharra. To the east lay 300 miles of the Gibson Desert. To the north and south—the unknown.

She rose and stood unsteadily. Around her the desert seemed wide and empty, the sky itself hard, cold, and indifferent. Tripping over clumps of grass in the dark, she made her way back to camp. She could see the hobbled camels, mere shadows in the dark; they smelled the water, of course, but some instinct kept them away from the crumbling sandbank of the swollen wash.

There was no fire. Suddenly it seemed to Java that having a fire, some light, was the single most important thing in her life. She managed to get one going and spent the next hour ranging near the camp to gather more burning material, including dried camel dung. Then, sitting in the fire's glow, she tried to see the spinifex spikes that were stuck in her hands, plucking at them with her fingernails. She was numbed, feeling an inner chill that was more than the result of the rapidly falling temperature. A protective barrier of shock had been erected, blocking out all thought except the need to remove the irritating stickers from her hands.

She had not yet drunk the first ration of evening water, and her water-starved cells sent little messages that became a raging thirst. In despair, she realized that she could drink as much as she wanted, consume the rations of three people if she wished, and it was as if the warm mineral-filled water became intoxicatingly addictive. She drank until her stomach protruded with it, until the water inside her sloshed audibly as she moved. She put the cap back on the waterskin and peered into the darkness. Then, seeing that her fire was low, she ran to replenish it and squatted beside it. She did not have enough material to keep the fire going for long, but Tolo would get more. Tolo was the most talented gatherer of firewood.

Tolo. "Oh, Tolo," she whispered, and the protective dam of shock that had shielded her from full realization burst before a surge of emotion as devastating, in its own way, as the flood. There was no one to hear her sobs, no one to share the grief that doubled her over in agony.

In the rapidly cooling night she wrapped herself in blankets to sit beside the dying coals of the fire. At first sleep would not come, but finally her head slumped to her chest as merciful slumber blanked out grief and fear. She eventually settled onto her side in a fetal position.

The sun woke her, and she reached out for Tolo. He wasn't there. Sometimes he arose before her. She opened her eyes and saw the day and reality. She screamed.

A sound behind her brought terror. She struggled to toss off the blankets, scrambling on hands and knees to turn to face the sound. It was Bildana, standing over her, teapot in hand. Immense relief flowed through Java. Leaping to her feet, she almost caused Bildana to spill the hot tea as she threw her arms around the dark woman, heedless of the stench of rancid grease and unwashed body.

"You eat now?" Bildana asked.

"But how did you get here?" Java asked. "Ganba took you away."

"Ganba," Bildana said, spitting. To her that explained everything. "Where whitefella men?"

Bildana's response to Java's sudden flood of tears was a soft pat on the arm, a sound made by sucking her tongue, "tsk, tsk, tsk." When she finally understood Java's choked attempts to explain what had happened, she said, "Come." She took Java's hand. "The water will be gone soon."

Java's first thought was that when the flood had been swallowed by the desert, she would be able to find Tolo. Bildana was thinking along more practical lines.

To Java's surprise the wash was no longer running with water. Not far from the camp a rocky depression held a billabong, a shallow pool, but the desert had already drunk the flood, leaving the bed of the wash dry once more. Bildana rolled the water barrels to the pool and began to fill the empty ones. At first Java did nothing. She stood on the bank of the wash and looked downstream, wondering how far the flood would have carried . . . and her mind then finally accepted reality so that she used the word *body* in her thoughts.

Tolo was dead. Somewhere to the west the falling waters would have deposited his body, and the creatures of the desert would find it, carrion eaters—birds, reptiles, insects. She could not allow that to happen. Her mind was working again, and the thought of *things* gnawing and tearing at the flesh that had pressed so closely to hers in the night was a terror not to be accepted. But she resisted the urge to run down the wash alone. It wasn't that her life was so valuable without Tolo that it could not be risked by running off into the desert. It was simply that she knew she wouldn't last long without water and food, perhaps not long enough to find and bury Tolo's body.

She gathered the hobbled camels and led them down into the wash to drink at the billabong, then helped Bildana fill the remaining water containers. It took longer than usual, of course, to load the camels because Bildana would have nothing to do with the beasts, and without Tolo's help all the work fell to Java. It was nearing midday when she mounted her camel and led the little caravan west, following the dry wash.

"No, no," Bildana protested, when she saw that Java intended to go west. "Ganba there."

"I must find Tolo," Java said.

"He is dead," Bildana said. "We will be dead, too, if Ganba finds us." She pointed east. "We must go there, to place of great-red-sacred-rock. There we will find people. My people. Your people. We have water. We have food. The extra camels will make meat food for us. Ganba has no food. He cannot follow there."

Java lifted Tolo's rifle. She had put its sheath on her own saddle. "Ganba won't bother us," she said. "Did you run away from Ganba because you were afraid he would kill you?"

"If he has not already, Ganba will have meat food soon," Bildana said.

"I don't understand," Java said. "You just said he had no food." She had prodded the camel into motion, and Bildana was walking alongside.

"Ganba is tired of me," Bildana said. "Meat food me, probably, but I run to you instead. Now you follow Ganba's track.
You find Ganba, we both be meat food."

"Bildana, you can't be serious," Java said. "But don't
worry. If we should overtake Ganba and the others, I will see
to it that he does you no harm." She was in no mood to listen
to an Abo's nonsense. She had heard stories, of course, about
cannibalism among the Aborigines, but that had been long
ago; contact with the white man and the white man's laws
had, years ago, stamped out the blackfellow's practice of eating his fellows. So Java had no time for Bildana's prattle and
her insistence that they travel east. Her mind had room only
for her grief, for the acute need to find Tolo's body and bury it
so that the desert scavengers could not desecrate it.

She had not ridden more than two miles when she saw a
patch of color in a bush on the bank of the wash. Emotion
knifed into her stomach painfully. She urged the camel into a
trot, "whoosh-whooshed" him to kneel near the bush, leapt
down, and ran to find a torn piece of Tolo's shirt. Nothing
more.

At midday the temperature rose toward the 120-degree
mark, but Java did not seem to notice—not even when the
heat at its peak seared her lungs, and her body had no more
moisture left to burst out as cooling perspiration. She rode on,
her eyes searching the wash. Flies, attracted to the lingering
moisture in the wash, swarmed around her in clouds, a continual minor torment that, like the heat, was ignored.

She had passed through this particular section of desert
before, on the way east. It was poor country, even for the
Gibson—a flat, dead expanse of gypsum dust. Not even the
hardy spinifex grew here, only a salty, succulent bush that
dotted the dismal plain sporadically.

"Missy, missy," Bildana called out, pointing ahead.

Ghostly forms shimmered and faded in the heat waves.
Startled, Java pulled her camel to a halt. The pack animals
behind her began to snort and bellow as the eerie forms co-

alesced out of the shimmering distances—camels, a mob of wild beasts led by a huge battered bull.

"She'll be right," Java said, and she felt a pang of loss, for the peculiarly Australian expression had been one of Tolo's favorites. She took the rifle out of the scabbard and chambered a round.

The wild camels were approaching at a steady trot, and her own animals were becoming increasingly agitated. She fired a shot into the sand in front of the bull leading the wild mob. The sound seemed to be absorbed by the empty vastness, but the intruding animals turned and raced away to the south.

Late in the day Java saw movement in the wash. First she spotted the reflected glare of the westering sun on water, and then, beside the billabong, something living. Her heart leapt and she urged her camel into a spine-jolting trot. Hearing Bildana calling out to her, she looked back. Bildana had halted and was motioning to her frantically.

But still she could not refrain from pressing forward, the movement in the wash next to the standing pool of water giving her hope, a surge of joy . . . until as she neared, she saw the bushy hair and beard of Ganba.

The Aborigine stood beside a fire, spear in hand, stark naked, his genitals hanging lankly, his face expressionless. The others were seated, eating.

Java pulled her camel to a halt. Bildana ran to within a few yards of her. She was weeping. "I go," she said, pointing toward the east.

"You can't go alone, Bildana," Java said impatiently. She was not upset at having found Ganba and the others. She had the guns. She had white authority. The Abos would be helpful in searching for Tolo's body and in helping her get back to civilization.

"Better that I die and be food for the animal brothers of the never-never than to be meat food for *him,*" Bildana said, turning. Java slipped down from the camel and ran to catch the

Abo woman, spinning her around to face her. The effort made her gasp in the heat.

"Damn you," Java said. "I've had enough of your nonsense. Now you come with me, this instant!"

Bildana obeyed, tears making little runnels through the dust on her face.

Java walked to the bank of the wash, rifle in hand. "Ganba," she said, "Mr. Mason and Mr. Forrest were washed away by the flood. I want you and the others to look for . . . their bodies. Do you understand?"

Ganba looked puzzled.

"When the flood came last night," she explained, "the whitefellow men were in the wash and were carried away. I want you to go walkabout there"—she pointed downstream— "and find bodies. Then we shall bury them."

Ganba shrugged. "Long gone. Sand bury them, no find. Not buried by sand, brothers of the night eat them."

"Nevertheless," Java said, "you will look for them."

"Missy," Bildana hissed, tugging at Java's sleeve. "Missy count blackfellas?"

She had not. When she did, quickly, there were only six. It was a woman who was missing. "Ganba, where is the other blackfellow woman?" she asked.

Ganba didn't answer for a moment. "She fall. Die."

"She is there," Bildana said, pointing.

For the first time Java looked at the fire, a rather large one. Roasting in the coals was a portion of meat about two feet long; it was round, the size of a roasting pig, but there were no legs or head.

"She there," Bildana said. "Meat food."

The smell in the air was not unpleasant. She had smelled meat roasting on the Abo fires many times during the trip, a mixture of appetizing smell and the char of burning skin. She stepped closer and peered at the cooking meat, and her stomach churned when she recognized it for what it was, a human thigh. At one end the flesh had cooked back to expose the large bone, much like a baking ham. She lifted her rifle, her

sense of outrage so powerful that for a moment Ganba's lif
was in real danger.

"She fall, die," Ganba said. Behind him one of the othe
men was reaching for his spear.

"Missy, we go," Bildana said. "We go now."

There were, for Java, two choices. She could either obe
Bildana's intense urgings or stay and kill all of the animal
that stood or crouched in the wash below her, savages wh
feasted on the flesh of one of their own. For a moment sh
hesitated. Then she spit out the taste of acid that had floode
into her mouth and aimed the rifle directly at the face of th
man who was reaching for his spear.

"I'm not going to kill you now, Ganba," she said. "But
you follow us, if you try to interfere with us in any way, yo
will be the second one I kill—after I shoot that fellow who'
going for his spear."

The Abo jerked his hand back.

Ganba seemed unperturbed. "You will leave one camel fc
us," he said. "For meat food so that we can reach huntin
grounds without starving."

"I will do no such thing," Java said. "There are wild camel
about, and you can kill one of those."

She walked, leading the camels. It was difficult to contrc
all of them by herself, and Bildana was of no use with th
animals. Ganba and the others showed no inclination to fo
low her. A half mile down the wash she mounted and tried t
get Bildana to ride Tolo's camel. The Abo woman refusec
and since she was able to keep pace on foot, Java accepted th
situation.

The coming of darkness forced Java to call a halt, and sh
struggled to unload the camels by the light of a flickering fir
In the clear desert air the vast field of stars cast a dim glow o
the wastelands, and it was easy for Java to imagine that sh
saw motion out there among the grassy clumps. The horror c
what she had seen at Ganba's camp beside the billabong gre
with the darkness.

Bildana prepared food. Java ate, but her eyes were on th

fields of spinifex surrounding them, her hand never far from
the rifle. She tried to explain to Bildana the need to alternate
standing watch. Bildana agreed but was soon fast asleep.

Java knew that she could not stay awake forever, but she
told herself that she could go without sleep for one night and
then, with the morning, put more distance between her and
Ganba by pushing the camels hard.

She had not pitched the tent; it was just too much work for
one, and Bildana was no help. She considered her situation,
more than a hundred miles from Mayhew Station. She had
plenty of water. In fact, one water camel would suffice. One
food camel would carry the remaining rations, while her own
riding camel could carry a bag of blankets and extra clothing.
She could handle three camels, but not six. Since camels
seemed to thrive in the desert—the wild ones she'd seen had
certainly looked perky enough—she decided to turn three
camels loose and let them shift for themselves or join the wild
mobs. And then she would make time, following the wash.
Sooner or later the wash would join the Gascoyne, and she'd
simply follow the Gascoyne to Mayhew Station. If, along the
way, she found Tolo's body, she would bury it.

A thin sliver of crescent moon rose but did not add much
illumination to the starlight. Aside from an occasional sigh of
wind and movements from the hobbled camels, the night was
silent. To stay awake, Java began to sing. Quiet tears accompanied her words, for the song, "Waltzing Matilda," had been
one of Tolo's favorites—the words by Banjo Paterson, the
tune plaintive, said to be the melody of an ancient Scottish
ballad. She shivered as she sang the final lines:

> *"And his ghost may be heard as it sings in the billabong,*
> *'Who'll come a-waltzing Matilda with me?'"*

Never to have Tolo's arms around her again . . . never to
dance as they had danced at Bina Tyrell's place in Sydney.
Never to know his voice, his pride in being Australian even
when he was called half-breed. . . . He had been a student of

things Australian and had liked the Strine slang and accent, imitating it quite well. He had liked Paterson's lyrics, too, telling the story of a bold swagman who stole a squatter's sheep for his supper, then jumped in the river and drowned himself to escape the police. The swagman had thumbed his nose at authority, even at the cost of his life. Tolo had liked that, and—

She wept bitterly. There had been no bushman's bravado about Tolo's death, no cocky defiance. He had tried to help Forrest but had been swept helplessly into the torrent of water rushing down the wash, his body tossed over and over by the debris rolling on the advancing wave. A dead kangaroo had been the last thing to jostle him as he slipped from her view. . . .

She did not know when the tears stopped and sleep took her, but presently she awakened, shivering in the freezing dawn. It was time to start the day. Her first act would be to trim the size of her caravan as she had planned.

She found two of the camels dead. The haunch of one had been cut away, the animal butchered as she had slept. She shuddered. Ganba had been within fifty yards of where she slept wrapped in her two blankets.

So there was only one camel to set free.

Bildana got a fire going while Java sorted the provisions and packed one food camel, saddled her riding animal, and heaved the water barrels to their positions on the harness of the water carrier. The smell of roasting meat filled the air, for Bildana, member of a race perennially beset by a shortage of protein, had sliced off steaks from the half-butchered camel. Java felt that she could not face meat, not after what she'd seen on Ganba's fire, but when the meat was ready—or at least ready in Bildana's view, which meant seared on the outside and juicy with hot blood on the inside—Java's salivary glands began to function, and she found herself squatting beside Bildana, clasping the meat in both hands, tearing at it with her even white teeth, making appreciative sounds in re-

ply to Bildana's unspoken question. She made no objection
when Bildana cut off a great hunk of bloody meat to take with
them.

As they got under way, Java tried to shoo the free camel
away, but the animal followed at a distance. A sand dune
reared itself in her path, and she let her own camel pick its
way to the top. Bildana paused at the foot of the dune, looking back and calling out. Java turned in time to see the Abo
men leap from behind saltbushes that seemed too scraggly to
conceal a man. The camel she had freed went down, two
spears in its chest and stomach, and the men swarmed over it.

"But they can't possibly eat three camels before they spoil,"
Java said.

"It is the fresh blood," Bildana said. "Ganba would drink
blood before sweet water."

"Well, a pox on Ganba," Java said.

At the approach of dusk she camped in the shadow of a
another dune. She saw no sign of Ganba or his fellows on the
trail behind her, and she felt more sure of herself now. If
Ganba had truly intended to kill her, or if he'd had the courage to do so, he would have seized the opportunity on the
previous night, when Java had slept so soundly that he had
been able to butcher her camels not more than a hundred feet
from where she lay sprawled on the ground.

Java enjoyed another camel steak with Bildana, filled herself with water, and made her bed. She was asleep within
minutes. She knew that she had underestimated Ganba again
when she awoke and reached for the rifle. It was gone. The
revolver in its belted holster was also gone, along with the
spare ammunition box.

"Ganba," Bildana said, pointing at the tracks of a man's
bare feet that circled the place where Java had slept.

Java shuddered, thinking of Ganba standing there looking
down on her as she slept. The rifle had been directly at her
side, the pistol in its belt at the head of her kip. He could so
easily have killed her. "But why?" she asked. "What does he
want?"

"He has the tent now," Bildana said. "He has the guns. Maybe he has all that he wants and will go away."

"Fine," Java said. "We don't need guns." Then she remembered the food and water and turned quickly. The water barrels were still there, and the food bags were undisturbed. She went to fetch the camels while Bildana prepared oatmeal cooked with water for their breakfast.

Soon they were traveling west along the banks of the dry wash, Java still searching for some sign of Tolo's body. When she saw carrion birds circling at a great distance, she became weak and had to force herself to go toward the birds. The object of their attention was in the wash, covered by croaking, fluttering, competing birds. She threw a rock into the midst of the stinking, seething congregation.

The remains of a dead camel lay in the wash, bones showing where the scavengers had been at work. She silently said a prayer of thanks. She had come to the conclusion that it was God's will that Tolo's body, and Terry Forrest's as well, had been buried under the roiled sand of the wash. Seeing what the scavengers had done to the camel, she was not sure that she could handle finding Tolo in the same condition without losing her sanity.

So she had broken down another emotional barrier. She had given up her hope of finding Tolo's body. Somehow it seemed as if it had been eons since Tolo had smiled at her, although it had been only days. Her grief was not any the less for that feeling of being distanced from the tragedy, but now she was able to think of other things: getting back to Mayhew's; breaking the news to Misa Mason that her son was dead; doing something about Ganba, the cannibal, the thief, the wife beater. That last seemed to be of the most immediate importance. She still harbored a sense of violation when she thought about Ganba sneaking into her camp, standing over her as she slept, taking her private property.

"All right, Bildana," she said, turning away as the scavenger birds that had been startled by the stone she had thrown scrambled to take their places at the feast. She turned. The camel with the food bags on his pack was looking alertly toward the bush. He gave a rumbling little roar and began to pace toward the south.

"No, you don't, mate," Java muttered, running to seize his lead. He jerked his head so hard that she feared he would pull the plug out of his nose, and he coughed a call toward the bush.

"I suppose he smells his wild brothers," she said, leading him back and tying him in line behind her riding camel.

She saw the wild camel mob again two hours later. She was looking for a decent place to camp alongside the wash when the big bull that led the mob seemed to materialize from behind an impossibly small bush. Soon the rest of the mob, their shapes shifting and distorted in the heat waves, emerged from a little depression. Java shouted and waved her arms. The wild camels snorted and jerked their heads, and some of them went back into the depression that had hidden them.

"I don't think they'll bother us," Java told Bildana as she unpacked the camels. "If they come nosing around, a well-placed rock or two will discourage them."

Her own camels, however, were restless. She inspected their hobbles twice before she released them to graze on the stunted, prickly bushes near the wash.

The wild mob invaded the camp just after Bildana had started the fire. The leader bull came charging in silently, while behind him the rest were snorting and roaring. Bildana screamed and started throwing rocks, and before Java could join in, she saw a rock bounce off the leader's head. It seemed to infuriate the bull, which bellowed and attacked the food bags lying on the ground, pawing and kicking. One bag split, and its contents were scattered. The other camels milled about, the males apparently trying to get past Bildana and Java to join the three camels that Java had hobbled. When the leader decided to go, the mob followed.

Java seized Bildana's arm and drew her aside, pushing her down behind a clump of prickly grass. The camels bolted past, one of them throwing out a rear leg that almost struck

Java in the head. The tamed camels, hobbled as they were, tried to join the others in the flight, and the water camel, a strong cow, broke her hobbles and kept up with the wild mob. Java's other two lagged behind, hopping along, hindered by the hobbles but moving faster than Java could walk.

"I have to go get them," she said.

"No," Bildana objected. "The spirits of evil men are in them."

"But we haven't any other way to carry the food and water," Java said. "You stay and watch over the camp. Gather up the food that that bull scattered."

She started after the camels at a trot. The heat was already abating a bit as the sun disappeared below the horizon. She could see the cloud of dust made by the wild mob, and she could see her two hobbled camels trying to catch up with their wild brothers. She was gaining on them. She could make do with two of them, she decided, since there was very little likelihood that she'd be able to catch the one that had broken her hobbles. She called after the camels by name. One of them stopped and turned his head. The other halted, too. She was only a couple of hundred feet from them, sure that she had them, when spears flew from both sides, piercing camel flesh, causing one of the animals to scream in pain and fright.

Java ran a few steps farther, then froze in her tracks. Ganba leaned down over a struggling camel and with one swipe of his knife slit the animal's throat.

"Ganba, you bloody bastard!" she cried out.

Ganba straightened and looked at her, his fierce face blank. Her urge was to run, but reason told her that it was useless. If he wanted to catch her, he could. She straightened her shoulders and walked to stand facing Ganba and the three men of his group.

"You have left me without an animal to carry my food and water," she said. "Since you are so eager to have meat food, eat. Be strong. For *you* will carry for me."

Ganba laughed. Only his lips moved, opening slightly as the sound of his laughter came from deep in his throat. He grinned, showing his teeth, and she was reminded of the meals that those teeth had chewed in recent days.

"Ganba, I am going back to camp now," she said. "You and the others will butcher meat from these animals and bring it to camp. Do you understand?"

Ganba nodded, still showing his teeth in a grin.

Bildana had seen the happenings from a distance. She had stopped preparation of the meal and was waiting for Java with a frightened look on her face. "Now we will both die," she said.

"Ganba knows that if he kills me, the whitefellow's law will not rest until he has been hanged," Java said.

"He will not kill you," Bildana replied sadly. "He will kill *me* and the other women when the camel meat is gone. Perhaps he will even kill the men one at a time, but he will not kill you. He will let the never-never do that so that he will be blameless under the whitefella law."

Chapter XV

THE STRANDED *Annamese Princess* sat solidly, her broken ribs clasped tightly by coral heads, her shattered keel jammed deeply into the rock: Around her the blue waters of the Gulf of Papua lifted and swirled restlessly without disturbing her. The boat had come to rest miraculously upright, and her deck tilted no more than five degrees. It was as if she were anchored in an absolutely motionless sea, a sea without heave or tide. During the day the sun baked her, driving her occupants to distraction until Trev and Kandi used a spare sail to form a canopy over the teak deck. At night a breeze arose, making sleeping comfortable. There was an adequate amount of food, fish to be caught, and, after an afternoon shower on the second day after the grounding, plenty of water.

Coral heads encircled the motionless *Princess,* their jagged tops visible in the troughs of waves when a distant storm disturbance caused long, heavy swells to break on the reef. The rogue wave had lifted the *Princess* over the outer edge of the reef. Had she struck the outer rocks, she would have been ripped apart totally, and those aboard would have been killed. In her present secure position she was protected from the battering of the waves.

The coral heads around her formed an enclosed area of calm water that soon became Kit's favored swimming pool. The big cruising sharks that were often seen both outside the reef and inshore toward the distant coastline did not try to traverse the protecting dikes of living coral, but one man always stood guard with the rifle if anyone was in the water. While Kit swam, Matt dived down and looked at the coral lining the enclosed pool, marveled at the colors, and brought up beautiful shells for Kit to admire.

So for a few days being stranded was something of an adventure, akin to a holiday. They enjoyed bright sunshine, steamy evenings, tolerable nights, the swimming, and good conversation. It was during that time, when they could do nothing but wait and hope that a vessel would come coasting along in one direction or the other—preferably headed toward Port Moresby—that Trevor Gorel spoke of his past for the first time. He had begun his adventures in the Far East as a minor functionary in the British diplomatic service. He was not eager to give details and indeed seemed quite embarrassed to talk of himself, but upon insistent and caring questioning from Kit he disclosed that his first post had been in Annam, in French Indochina.

"Ah," Kit said, "now we have a hint as to why you named your boat the *Annamese Princess*."

"For my wife," Trev said, with a proud grin.

"Tell us about her," Kit coaxed.

"Well, her name is Guinevere. Her mother was the daughter of Emperor Nguyen the Third of Annam."

" 'Strewth," Matt teased, "we're in the presence of a highness by marriage."

Trev threw a lazy punch at Matt's shoulder. Matt pulled away, laughing. "Well, your wife is a princess, isn't she?"

"I'm fascinated," Kit said. The three of them had been lying on blankets in the shade of the overhead canvas. Kit leaned up on one elbow. "She must be very beautiful."

There was a gleam in Trev's eye. "Some men are of the opinion that Eurasian women, especially those who are Indochinese and French, are the most beautiful in the world."

"Your wife, Guinevere, is half French?" Kit asked.

Trev nodded. "When the French forced Nguyen the Third

to open Annam to trade in 1858, Guinevere's father was the chief French representative in the city of Hue. As is often the case, the political agreement between Nguyen and the French was cemented—at least in Nguyen's eyes—by the marriage of Nguyen's daughter to the Frenchman. She was a royal princess, of course. The Frenchman, it seems, was the black-sheep son of a French family that had once been very close to the French throne." He grinned. "So Guinevere has royal blood on both sides, from her mother and from her French father."

"Damned if I'm not impressed," Matt acknowledged. "Do we have to curtsy?"

"Bloody bushranger," Trev said, reaching out for Matt. Matt rose quickly and dived into Kit's swimming pool. Trev went in after him, and for a few minutes the two men wrestled playfully, creating mighty splashings and blowings.

Kit had to wait for another time to hear the rest of the story about Trev's royal wife, but there was time. The days dragged on with no ship in sight, and on a pleasant evening after a meal of fresh fish that Kandi had caught and cooked, Kit finally coaxed Trev into talking about his wife again.

"Well, her French father didn't take the political marriage quite as seriously as did the Annamese," he said. "When things improved enough at home for the Frenchman to go back to Paris, he left Hue, apparently without so much as a by-your-leave. The princess—Guinevere's mother—was left alone with a young child. Since the princess had been only fourteen when she was married to the Frenchman—"

"Poor child," Kit interjected.

"—it couldn't have been an easy road. Everything was in chaos. The French were in the process of conquering all of Indochina and annexing it to the French Empire. Even though things were changing for the entire country, people clung to the old ways. The princess found herself scorned by her own people, even though her father, the emperor himself, had arranged the marriage to the Frenchman. The Annamese, like the Chinese, tended to believe that all foreigners are lesser beings. In their eyes, even a princess was shamed by marriage to a Westerner. Guinevere, as a mixed-blood, was the object of hatred and scorn, in spite of her royal lineage. Fortunately, the princess and the old grandfather had the means to protect her from public opinion, but Guinevere grew up in isolation."

"If prejudices against foreigners were so strong among the Annamese, how did Guinevere come to marry you?" Matt asked.

"I've often wondered about that myself." Trev grinned.

Only two people in all the world had understood why Guinevere would marry a minor British diplomat. One of them, the royal princess, was dead. The other, Guinevere herself, was standing at the stern of a Van Buren Line steamer that had just called at the port of Gibraltar and was now en route to Cape Town, with a scheduled stop at the Cape Verde Islands.

Guinevere Gorel was wrapped in white silk, swirls of it concealing the lines of her body, a high collar clasping the lovely line of her throat. Her thick ebony hair was coiled atop her head. She was looking at the stars, thinking of the watery distances that would pass under the keel of this ship that was bringing her from England, wondering, indeed, if she had made the right decision in answering her husband's call to join him in what he described as a pleasant house in New Guinea.

If, when Trev had decided to leave the diplomatic service, he had taken his wife to France instead of to cold, damp Suffolk, things might have been different for Guinevere. She spoke French fluently. From her father—before his sudden disappearance—and from the Frenchmen who were slowly but surely making her native country a part of the French Empire, she had acquired a veneer of French sophistication and manners that were admirably suited to her exotic good looks but made her a curiosity in England. How much better she would have fared if she had been allowed to go to France she would never know. She was haunted by the thought that if Trev had taken her to Paris, she might have found a place for herself, the kind of position that she, as an Annamese princess, deserved. Frenchmen were more appreciative of feminine beauty and more tolerant of those whose skin color did not match their own.

Guinevere traced the beginnings of her troubles in life to the day on which her mother had decided to marry her off to a minor British diplomat. Now, with her mother and her grandfather dead, with her country securely under the thumb of the French, her mixed blood a handicap in the country of her birth, her choices in life were limited.

When Trevor had first talked of emigrating to New Guinea, she had seen the move as a means of getting away from the chill and dampness of England. She was still young, so she might also have seen the move as a means of coming closer to the homeland where she had been a happy child, even though her social contacts had been severely limited by the attitudes toward her mixed blood.

On the way to join Trevor in Port Moresby, she would have the opportunity to see two Australian cities, Sydney and Townsville. She was looking forward to learning more about Australia, for Trevor had told her that after he had made his fortune in New Guinea, they would most probably settle on that continent, where the climate would be more favorable than New Guinea's and there would be more civilized amenities.

To date, Guinevere's opinion of Australians was not flattering. Aboard the Van Buren Line ship, a reefer ship with a few fare-earning cabins, she had found the passengers—mostly Australians—to be wary and distant, obviously reluctant to speak on equal terms with a woman who was half Oriental.

She had already encountered hints of racial bigotry in England. For her, product of a society that had no use for mixed blood, bigotry held no pain. From the beginning, as far back as she could remember, she had sensed the disapproval of her own people, even though her position as the emperor's granddaughter had shielded her from much of that opprobrium. She had learned to disregard this kind of prejudice, never allowing herself to be hurt by the opinions of people who were not directly involved in providing for her needs and wants. She had also learned by experience that men valued her for her personal beauty regardless of her mixed blood. Sexual attraction overcame all barriers, including racial stigmas, and she was quite adept at using her appeal to men to get what she wanted.

It was a mild night. The breeze of passage was cool and soothing. The hard-edged stars had the look of diamonds. Trevor had promised her diamonds.

Trevor. In a matter of weeks she would be with her husband in New Guinea, living in Trevor Gorel's house. She would be in Trevor Gorel's arms. That last thought was not totally unpleasant; Trevor had always been so eager to please her, so quick to do her bidding in the act of love.

She pulled her silken wrap more closely about her and let her eyes lower from the stars to the horizon. Her full lips parted, her tongue caressed her lower lip thoughtfully. Her head turned. The ship was quieting for the night, all meals having been served, the night watch having taken its posts. The captain's cabin was forward and was approached by a walkway that offered some privacy.

The captain, Simon Yates, Jr., an Australian, was an older man, perhaps in his late forties. To the displeasure of other passengers, Guinevere had been among the dinner guests at his table from the first night of the voyage. While Yates might have shared his countrymen's prejudices against people of color, he still had youthful appetites, and he was ready to set aside his racial views when it came to attractive women. He had been an employee of the Van Buren firm since his early teens, when he first sailed aboard a Van Buren clipper skippered by his father. A lifetime at sea, where women were not always available, had only deepened his appreciation of feminine beauty.

So Captain Yates had invited Mrs. Trevor Gorel to his table, knowing fully that her mixed blood would displease his other guests. He had intended to honor her for the first night only, but having been impaled right away on Guinevere's dark, flashing eyes, he invited her to the captain's table on subsequent nights as well.

From her Annamese forebears Guinevere had acquired the arrogant moral code of a family whose members had wielded life-and-death power over millions. She had lived her formative years as a favorite at the court of an emperor. True, by that time Nguyen had been reduced to the status of figurehead, and he was fighting to preserve his personal fortune and a bit of his royal authority; but he was an emperor, nevertheless, and Guinevere was his granddaughter. A royal princess could simply demand what she wanted and take it.

Now, on a night when the sea was calm and vast distances of ocean separated her from the next port stop, Guinevere had no intention of spending a sleepless night in her relatively austere cabin. She walked forward. The deck was empty, save for one middle-aged couple who stood at the rail watching the formation of phosphorescence in the ship's wake. Guinevere pulled her scarf closer around her face and walked to the captain's door. There was no need to knock. He was waiting, and she entered.

Guinevere had found that older men were often good lovers. For a while, at least, she would not have to dwell on what awaited her on an island that lay just below the equator. She let her outer wrapping drop. She wore the gown of a courtesan of old Annam, a silken thinness that clung to hip, waist, and breast.

Simon Yates, who had first sampled this delicate tidbit of sheila the second night out of England, caught his breath in awe. The dusky-skinned bird's beauty never failed to surprise him. Not even pleasant memories of several splendid nights in his cabin could match the initial impact each time she came to him again.

It was aboard the stranded *Annamese Princess* that Kit knew Matt had finally succeeded in obeying the order she had given him one troubled evening in Cape Town. The time for her monthly period came and went without her notice. It was not until she was more than three weeks late that the thought came to her, while she paddled around in the pool protected by the corals, that if the curse came on suddenly, the water would be filled with blood. Blood drew sharks. She clambered aboard the *Princess* quickly. Then she began to count the days. Matt saw her lying on a blanket, her clothing still wet from her swim.

"You look like a kitten who has just lapped up an entire saucer of cream," he said, lying down beside her, giving her a light kiss. Because of the crowded conditions—another disadvantage of mixed company on a small boat—they had not been together since leaving Port Moresby. His need for her was growing with each passing day.

"I'll have my cream chilled, thank you," she said, "and over strawberries."

"Umm," he said, kissing her again.

"Stop that now," she hissed, smiling, her own need for him heightened by the knowledge that his child had taken seed inside her.

"You're very beautiful," he whispered.

"What, with my skin as brown as Kandi's and as dry as a bone?"

"Even then."

"Bushranger."

"Pommy girl."

She allowed him to kiss her full on the mouth, then pushed him away. "Matthew—"

"Whoops," he said, "what have I done now? You never call me that. Reminds me of when I was a child. Only when I'd misbehaved did my mother ever use my full name. She'd say, *'Matthew Van Buren!'* and I'd know I was in for it."

"Matt."

"Yes, luv."

"I think you'll be pleased to know that your bushranger persistence and native skills in certain arenas have borne fruit."

"I beg your pardon?"

"Literally." She smiled, her face flushing with pleasure.

"Let me see," he mused. "It's a guessing game. Now I am supposed to have certain skills that have, ah, borne fruit." He looked out toward the distant shoreline. The low green horizon wavered in tropical heat waves. "I give up," he said.

"You goose," she said. "Don't you remember an assignment that I gave you back in Cape Town?"

His face lit up with a wide smile. "No!" he said.

She nodded. "Yep."

"You're—"

"Yes. Yes. Yes."

He didn't care, then, what Trev and Kandi thought. He put his weight atop her and hugged her to him, filling her mouth with his kiss. Then, suddenly, he pulled away, his face pale. "I didn't hurt you, crush you, I mean?"

"No."

"Are you sure?"

"Sure as I can be." She frowned. The situation was, at best, a bit unusual. It was possible that her lateness was the result of the mental strain of being stranded, although she did not feel tense, just a bit concerned about when a rescue ship would come. Should she have waited to tell him, lest nature bring the color later and disappoint him? No, she decided there was no mistake. She was as regular as the Royal Mail.

"Good God," he said. "We've got to get you home."

"Should we start swimming?" she asked.

"It's no joke," he said. "We're going to have to do something, and soon."

He rose and paced the deck, ducking his head to keep from brushing the shading canvas. Kit settled back, content to lie there with her eyes closed. The heat of the day was evaporating the water from her clothing, and a sheen of perspiration was on her forehead and upper lip.

Matt halted his pacing, looked down at the face of his wife and said a silent prayer. When he turned to look back at the empty sea, he saw a tiny smudge of smoke low on the western horizon. He waited until he could be sure. Then he called, and Trev and Kandi came to stand beside him. Kit, too, stood, and together they watched the black hull of a steamer edge over the horizon.

"She'll pass well to seaward of us," Matt said. "Kandi, get ready to light the signal fire."

At what Matt deemed to be the proper time, the signal fire, oily rags in a large washbasin, was lighted. Trev was clinging to the mast of the *Princess,* waving a shirt. The course of the steamer altered until her bow was pointed directly toward them, and it was only then that Matt realized that the ship was closer than he had thought. Sizes and distances could be confusing at sea; a small vessel quite near might easily be mistaken for a larger one at a distance.

The ship approaching the *Annamese Princess* was a seagoing steam launch of perhaps fifty feet. When she began to slow as she neared the outer reef, it could be seen that her hull was scabrous with rust, her stern smeared with leaking oil, and her upper works badly in need of paint. But to those aboard the stranded sailboat she looked as beautiful as the finest luxury liner.

A figure appeared at the rail of the steam launch. A voice made hollow by a hand-held megaphone said, "This is as close as I can come."

"Can you send a boat?" Trev called back. The *Princess*'s dinghy had been lost in the tumult of the big wave.

"Are you in distress?"

Trev made a face. "The greedy bastard's thinking about salvage rights on the poor old *Princess*." He cupped his hands and called out. "We are stranded. We require aid. Please lower a boat."

A Kanaka seaman rowed a skiff across the outer reef. Five people made a good load for the small boat, but Trev said there would be no need to make two trips. Soon Matt was helping Kit descend a rope ladder to get onto the launch. He followed her, then turned to give a hand to Trev and Kandi.

The man who faced them wore faded, much-washed workingman's blues. He was barefoot, the tops of his feet burned almost black by the tropical sun. He wore a disreputable vi-sored cap perched atop a jungle of hair that was so black it seemed to have royal blue highlights. An equally black beard covered his lower face, and his large nose, laced with blue veins, betrayed the fact that its owner tippled a bit. But domi-nating the man's appearance, drawing the eyes of the four who faced him, was a set of vivid, protruding sea blue eyes.

"Who's the skipper of that little beauty?" the blue-eyed man asked.

"Trev Gorel, sir, at your service."

"You have abandoned your craft, sir."

"Aye," Trev said.

The blue-eyed man turned and yelled out orders in some chattering language. Two Kanaka seamen leapt to ready a line at the stern of the launch. One of them was climbing down in the skiff when Trev spoke.

"If it's your intention, Captain, to put a towline on the *Annamese Princess,* you had best belay those orders. Even if you manage to pull her loose from her perch on the reef with-out ripping her apart, she'll go down like a rock. Both sides are mashed."

"You're telling Blue Jack that she's worthless?" the captain of the launch asked.

"Fear so," Trev acknowledged.

The bearded man let loose a string of words in several lan-guages that could have been nothing other than profanity.

Trev grinned. "Of course, you're welcome to the mast, the sails, and any fittings you care to remove."

The black-bearded man grinned, removed his cap, and bowed toward Kit. "Welcome aboard the *Canadian Queen,*" he said. "I'm sorry that the circumstances are not more favor-able, although, I must say, you don't look the worse for wear, any of you."

"We were lucky," Matt said. "Did I hear you say your name, sir? If so, I missed it."

"Blue Jack," the man replied. "I don't know where you

thought you were going here in these godforsaken waters, but now you're headed for Port Moresby. Doesn't matter where you want to go, you're going to Moresby, 'cause I've got the mail to deliver and Blue Jack fulfills his contract with His Majesty's government."

"That's wonderful, Captain Jack," Kit said. "That's exactly where we wanted to go."

"You didn't, by any chance, leave any liquor aboard?" Blue Jack asked Trev, who shook his head sadly.

Unlike Trev, the captain of the *Canadian Queen* was more than willing to talk about himself. The *Queen* was not a speedster. As she started to steam leisurely down the coast to Port Moresby, it became evident that Blue Jack knew the waters quite well. He hugged the coast and steered the steamer through and around shallows and reefs that the others did not see until they were quite near.

Blue Jack had a contract with the British government to deliver His Majesty's mail to several isolated settlements along the New Guinea coast. "It's not that they can set their clocks by me," he said, "what with the distances, the weather, and never knowing when mail is going to come into Moresby, but they know I'll be there. Even the krautheads up on the northeast coast rely on me."

"You go into German areas?" Trev asked.

"Deutsche Seehandelgeschäft gold spends just as well as English gold," Blue Jack said. "Actually, there's not much postal traffic directed to the Germans from sources that would use the Royal Mail, but what little there is gives me an entrée into German areas. Also, I do a good little business in things like tobacco and gin. The krauts pay through the nose for good British gin."

"Is there lots of good furniture timber up north?" Trev asked.

"No shortage of it," Blue Jack answered. "That's your business, is it? Well, one way to make a pound is as good as another, I reckon, but gold beats 'em all. Back in the early nineties, before the big strike at Bonanza Creek in the Klondike, I had me a little mine. Turned out four, five thousand Canadian dollars' worth of pure nuggets a day. Kept it quiet until the old demon got the best of me."

"The demon?" Kit asked.

"Hell, I was rich. Had thousands in the bank, knew there were millions in the mine. Tried to drink the world dry of al-key-haul in all of its delicious forms." He licked his lips. "Lost the mine in a card game. Dead broke. Hustled drinks in every bar in Canada, singing and entertaining." He laughed, threw back his head, and sang in a voice that rasped nerves very much as if fingernails were being drawn across slate:

> *"Ol' Bucket Mouth McGinty, he was quite a drinkin'*
> *man,*
> *Skipper of the schooner they called the* Peter
> *Pan—"*

"We get the idea," Matt said, winking at Kit. "You, ah, entertained them until—"

"Till they set me up a drink or tossed coins." He showed his teeth in a wide grin. "Sometimes with great force." He threw back his head again.

> *"Whenever he got loaded, you could hear him*
> *loudly bawl,*
> *'Oh, save the kids and women first; then save the*
> *al-key-haul.' "*

"Sang fifty-two verses one night in Seattle," Blue Jack said. "Had to make up thirty-five of 'em on the spot. Got so drunk I had to hang on to the grass to stay on the world and like to died. Decided right then and there that it was time to try something else. Washed dishes on a cruise ship and got to Hawaii. Went ordinary seaman on freighters till I found myself out here. I reckon the good Lord was feeling merciful. I'd been off the booze for over two years when I won the *Queen*, here, in a card game. Things have a way of evening out, don't they? Lost a mine worth millions, because I couldn't handle prosperity, I guess. Won a good life."

At that juncture a petite brown-skinned woman came on deck. She wore a colorful sarong. Her dark hair was bunned neatly, and a fresh flower was thrust into the dark mass just over one ear.

"Blue Jack, you eat now," she said. "All mens and womens eat now."

"Bless you, dear heart," Blue Jack said, reaching out to pull the smiling woman to his side. "This here's my wife," he said proudly. "Told you the Lord had been good to me lately."

Over quite a good meal featuring baked fish and yams Blue Jack waxed even more expansive. His wife, whom he called Saraba, was Jack's best audience, laughing delightedly at his attempts at witticisms.

"Bought this pretty little wench in Kieta, over on Bougainville," he explained. "She didn't understand at all when I told her that she wasn't going to be a slave, but my wife."

"Understand now," Saraba said, giggling. "Wife have to work harder than slave."

Blue Jack shook his head. "That's gratitude, ain't it?" But he laughed and patted Saraba fondly on the shoulder. "Known me a woman or two here and there, but this is my first wife. Only wife, eh, chicken?"

"Better be," Saraba said, brandishing a table knife with mock menace.

"She claims to be a native of the Solomons," Blue Jack said, "but I know she's lying. She's half monkey at least."

"Monkey wife to old boar hog," Saraba retorted. She smiled at Jack, and Kit could see the obvious love in her eyes. "We get along pretty good, no?"

"Pretty damned good," Blue Jack said.

When Port Moresby came into sight, everyone was on deck. Blue Jack was at the wheel, while his Kanaka seamen stood by on deck. As Jack deftly maneuvered the vessel alongside a rickety dock, the seamen jumped ashore and secured the *Queen*'s lines. Jack shut down his engines and turned to his guests. "What kind of timber you fellows after?" he asked. "Teak?"

"Teak, cedar, and mahogany," Trev said.

"Well, there's plenty of it," Blue Jack said. He looked at Trev, then shifted his protruding blue eyes to Matt's. "Were I you, though, I'd cut it south of Moresby. Maybe around on the lower northeast coast. Stay out of the Gulf of Papua, and for sure I wouldn't venture up around Frederik Hendrik Island."

"Why do you say that, Jack?" Matt asked, for Jack's voice had a serious tone he had not used before.

"Our friends the krautheads are very damned sincere in their pretensions to colonial power," Jack said. "They see the whole of New Guinea as being rightfully theirs. First they want to drive out the Dutch and add the Dutch territory to what they've annexed; then they want all the rest."

"British Papua?" Trev snorted. "Not a chance. They wouldn't challenge the Royal Navy."

"Maybe not yet," Blue Jack said quietly.

It was good to be back onshore. The servants had kept Trev's house in good order. The bed in the airy room that had been assigned to Kit and Matt felt good. To be able to make love and then simply to lie in each other's arms felt very, very good.

Trev seemed not too disturbed over the loss of the *Annamese Princess*. "She wouldn't have been of much use to us in the lumber business," he said. "What we need is a good, powerful tugboat and a barge or two."

"And oxen," Matt said.

"Not to mention men," Kit reminded them.

That last problem was solved by Gihi, who appeared at the house early on the morning after they arrived with ten squat but powerfully thick-chested native men.

"Ready to go to work, boss," he said. "All these hillmen. Hard workers, you bet."

As they rushed to get the timbering operations going before Gihi's hillmen started looking longingly toward the east, two notable events occurred. First, Trev received a cable telling him that his wife was aboard a ship on the way from England to Cape Town. The cable had been delayed in transmission, owing to a break in the lines, so the news was already weeks old. Nevertheless, it delighted Trev.

The second event was pleasant enough, but it had less immediate significance. Matt ran into Blue Jack coming out of the governor's office. Blue Jack wrung Matt's hand, grinning happily. "Had to get the guv straightened out on a matter pertaining to the Royal Mail," Jack explained. "The bugger keeps threatening to give the mail contract to someone with a faster boat." He laughed. "I keep telling him that he's damned lucky that there's any kind of boat available for what the crown is willing to pay."

Since Matt's own business with the British offices was routine, it was handled by a lowly clerk. This official had seen Matt shake hands and speak with Blue Jack, and he looked at Matt quizzically.

"How do you come to know the stalwart carrier of the Royal Mail?" he asked, a sneer of disapproval on his lips.

"Ran into him at sea," Matt said.

"If I were you, I'd be careful about what I said to that one," the clerk said. "He's a spy for the bloody Germans, you know."

Matt tried to envision Blue Jack as being sinister. The image did not fit. He controlled his amusement. "I hardly think that I'd have any military or government secrets to tell."

"One never knows when a seemingly innocuous piece of information might fit into a larger picture," the clerk said. "This mail contract gives Blue Jack a perfect cover. I myself would like to see him investigated. His trips into the German areas to the north seem to me to be more frequent than the flow of mail demands."

* * *

Simon Yates's ship continued down the west African coast. One night in the captain's cabin, in answer to his questions, Guinevere said, "I was born in the city of Hue."

"Oddly enough, I have cargo for the frogs in Hue on board for this trip," he replied. "We hit southern India, Singapore, then up to Bangkok and around the Indochina Peninsula to Hue."

"Have you been to Hue?"

"No, first trip there."

"You will find it to be a beautiful city," she assured him, "in spite of what the French have done to it."

"Too bad I won't have a guide who knows the place," he mused. He raised himself on one elbow. "I say, you wouldn't care to take the long way around to Sydney, would you? I mean, stay on board my ship, at no extra charge? Good accommodations. Your cabin is booked out of Cape Town, so you'll have to move in with me and rough it."

"I'm afraid that's impossible," she said.

"I've a somewhat flexible schedule. I could give you a few days in Hue."

That he had her interest was evident. She rose, her dusky skin pale in the dim light, her voluptuous figure making graceful patterns of movement as she poured brandy for two, turned, and swayed back toward the bed.

It seemed to him that she had deliberately changed the subject when she asked, "Have you been to New Guinea?"

"I have."

"Port Moresby?"

"Yes."

"Tell me about it."

He sighed. "Well, those troppo towns are all pretty much alike. You know, frame bungalows with iron roofs. The roofs'll either be new, bright and shiny, or all splotched and rusted. Nothing in between. It's the heat and humidity that does it, and it rusts people as well, in my opinion."

"It is hot and humid in Hue," she said simply. "A hot climate doesn't bother me."

"But the people—oh, you'll love them!" he said, grinning sarcastically. "Backwater places like Papua don't draw the elite, luv. They're peopled by blokes who can't make it anywhere else, by misanthropes trying to get as far away from civilized mankind as possible, by the men who fancy dark meat, if you get my meaning. But for stimulating conversation you can always talk pidgin English to the wogs, who are—next to our Abos in Australia—about the sorriest specimens I've ever seen."

"You don't make it sound very attractive," she said. "My husband speaks quite differently about it."

"All I can say, luv, is that it's a waste of fine horseflesh to bury a sheila like you in Port Moresby."

She had not been in Annam in years, and she wondered how she would find it. From what she had read, the French presence there grew ever stronger. Some writers in the French newspapers that she'd been able to find now and then in England had raved about the grace and beauty of French colonial architecture in Indochina, claiming that French taste and influence were turning Hue into the Paris of the East.

She had been aware since first being taken to Trevor's home in Suffolk that she and her mother had made a bad choice in a husband for her, that Trevor Gorel had never been a rich man and showed little promise of becoming one. In Hue, with her perfect French, with her Eurasian beauty, might she not make a better match? The French newspapers hinted that fortunes were being made in the French colonies by enterprising businessmen. Being the wife of a rich Frenchman in her native land would be, she concluded, preferable to living in Port Moresby in the conditions described by her ship's captain.

If she decided to stop at Hue, she knew from experience that Trevor would accept her decision. He could not deny her anything, even if it meant sacrifice for himself. If things did not work out in Hue, she could always take ship to New

Guinea, where she would be greeted even the more fondly for having extended the length of her absence from Trevor.

"Are you considering my invitation?" Simon asked.

She sat beside him on the bed, held the snifter for him to sip brandy, then put one hand softly, heatedly, onto a particularly sensitive male area. "Must I wait until Cape Town to move into this very pleasant cabin? Mine is so . . . ordinary."

From Cape Town she sent a cablegram to Trevor: OPPORTUNITY VISIT HUE LETTER FOLLOWS. The letter, which she composed at her leisure as the ship steamed along the African coast, was mailed from Durban, where the ship called before sailing north and east across the Indian Ocean.

In the days that followed, Guinevere, with ample time on her hands, took an interest in the ship's menu for its passengers, giving imperious orders to the cooks and accepting compliments from her captain as pleasantly exotic dishes appeared at table. She would not, she decided, want to spend the rest of her life living in a floating hotel; but it was a pleasant change, and she had engendered such a need in the captain for the silken softness of her body that he was boyishly eager to please her.

Neither she nor the captain cared a whit that their open cohabitation shocked the English passengers aboard ship.

Chapter XVI

JAVA AND BILDANA'S journey with Ganba began inauspiciously. The water barrels, it seemed, would have to be left behind. They had no camels, and there was no way for a man to carry even one of the barrels.

Ganba and his followers, three men and two women, drank water until it seemed to Java that it would be impossible for any of them to hold any more. She and Bildana drank their fill during the evening, and Java allowed herself the luxury of a good wash. During the night, when the water she had consumed caused her to awaken and seek relief, she saw that the Abos had also hit the food quite heavily, with considerable waste. Ganba slept wrapped in two of Tolo's blankets. The muzzle of the rifle protruded near his face. But recovering the weapon without waking him would be impossible.

With the morning Java set about consolidating the food, dividing what remained—rice, lentils, tea and sugar, oatmeal, and flour—into equal loads. Ganba had filled the waterskins, leaving the emptied barrels lying on their sides in the red dust. The Abo had also dressed himself in a pair of Tolo's trousers and a shirt. The garments were far too large for him, and he had cut off the trouser legs so that they would not drag on the ground. Another of the Abo men was hobbling around in Tolo's spare pair of boots, which flapped loosely on his feet and made him look like a child playing dress-up.

At first Java was angry to see Tolo's things thus misappropriated, but she had been intending to leave them behind in the desert. If the Abos could get some use of them, so be it.

When she instructed Ganba to have each of his people take a load of food, he shook his large head. Two of his men would be occupied carrying the tent, the extra clothing, and the blankets.

"Be reasonable, Ganba. We can't eat that bloody tent," she said.

"Very valuable. Ganba will save this expensive tent for you."

There was nothing she could do. She saw to it that Bildana had the bundle that held the tea and sugar. She overloaded Bildana and herself with rice and lentils. Bildana carried the cooking utensils. Reluctantly Java left behind her extra clothing, limiting herself to one blanket. She faced the Gibson dressed in a linen shirt tucked into jodhpurs—her riding costume. Her head and face were protected from the sun by a dusty, well-worn bush hat. She had only one small container of sun cream left. She had put one of Tolo's folding knives in her pocket along with matches in waterproof containers.

Ganba said, "It is time." He set out, walking toward the north.

"Where are you going?" Java asked, running to catch him. "Mayhew Station lies there, to the west."

"Water there," Ganba said, pointing.

"There will be good soaks in the dry wash and in the Gascoyne."

"We go there," Ganba said, pointing north.

"He won't kill you," Bildana had said. *"He will let the never-never do it."*

She fell back and walked beside Bildana. As the morning advanced, she noted that Ganba's course drifted off to the northeast.

"What's up there?" she asked Bildana.

"I don't know," Bildana said. "I have never traveled there."

Java knew that the maps showed the Hamersley Range to the northwest, the Macdonnells due east. To the north and northeast the Gibson simply continued, becoming the Great Sandy Desert. Ganba's route, if followed, would take them deeper into Australia's vast red heart. It was only a hundred plus miles back to Yinnietharra. In every other direction, especially the one in which they were traveling, the distance to a white settlement or town was multiplied.

Bildana lagged behind. Java slowed her pace, allowing the Abo woman to catch up. "He is leading you into the never-never to die," Bildana stated again with simple conviction.

Ganba had indeed taken charge. Carrying Tolo's rifle, he was leading the group and setting the course; his companions followed, carrying the tent and bedding. Java turned to Bildana. "Could you find water? Could the two of us make it back to Mayhew Station?"

Bildana nodded. "As you have said, there are soaks in the river."

"We'd be very short of food before we got there," Java commented.

"Eat bush tucker," Bildana replied. "Better to go there than to follow Ganba."

Java stopped. Once Ganba looked back, but he did not halt. Java and Bildana turned and started toward the dry wash.

They had walked no more than a hundred yards when a rifle bullet sent stinging particles of sand and shattered rock against Java's legs. The sound of the shot came from the rear. Java wheeled around to see Ganba chambering another round, and for a moment, as the Abo raised the rifle, Java thought that she was going to die. But instead, Ganba walked slowly toward her, the rifle aimed at her torso.

"Have you gone mad, Ganba?" Java demanded, forcing her voice out to prevent it from trembling.

"*You* are mad," Ganba said. "Whitefellas dead. Now Ganba take care of you. Let you die, whitefella law say my fault."

"We're going to Mayhew Station," Java replied. "You can come with us or not, as you please."

"Go to water, there," he said, pointing north.

Java turned and started walking, calling out, "Come, Bildana."

Ganba's English seemed to vary with his emotions. She had noticed before that when he wanted to emphasize something, he spoke almost perfectly. "If you persist in this foolishness," he cried out, "I will kill this one who follows you!"

Java heard the click of the rifle being cocked. She turned. The rifle was pointed at Bildana's head.

"I will not have the whitefella law after me because whitefella woman wants to die going where there is no water," Ganba said.

"All right, we will go with you," Java conceded.

As she followed Ganba, Bildana walked beside her, singing a mournful little song of death.

"Stop it," Java said harshly, with a confidence she did not feel, "I'll see to it that he doesn't harm you."

Ganba halted early, long before the sun was down. Java watched as he and the men set up the tent and spread blankets inside. When Ganba seized one of the women and pulled her inside, closing the flap behind them, that action told Java more about Ganba's true intentions than anything that had gone before. If he intended for Java to reach civilization alive, he would not have dared to seize her property so casually. It was true, then, that he wanted her dead. In all probability she could accept Bildana's opinion that Ganba would not kill him himself. But the desert was a vast place, and a white woman could die in many ways, all of them unpleasant. A deadly snake, guided by Ganba, could find a warm resting place in her bedding during the night. A rutting wild bull camel could trample her. But it was far more likely that Ganba would simply set a pace that would gradually wear her down and leave her spent and exhausted, at the mercy of the sun, and the heat, and thirst. Dying of thirst was a painful, extended agony.

She spread her blanket at some distance from the tent and the fires of the other Abos. Bildana huddled at her side as darkness came, and they ate rice and lentils boiled over the open fire.

"That one is angry," Bildana said, pointing to an Abo man who paced near the tent. "Ganba has taken his woman."

"Will there be a fight?"

"No, because Ganba is too powerful. He wears murderer's slippers and is unbeatable."

When Ganba came out of the tent, stretched, and scratched at his genitals, the angry man turned his back. Ganba spoke, and one of the women came to Java's fire. "Ganba want tea and sugar."

"Tell Ganba to go to hell," Java said.

When that message had been delivered, Ganba seized the rifle and stalked toward Java's fire. Bildana cowered behind Java. Ganba stood quite close, so close that Java could smell the rankness of his body mixed with the musky scent of sex. "Do not be selfish, Mrs. Mason," Ganba said. "Surely you will share your tea and sugar with me."

"Give it to him," Bildana whispered into Java's ear.

Ganba struck out without warning. His open palm contacted Bildana's cheek, and she was knocked sideways from her position behind Java. The follow-through of the blow sent Ganba's arm crashing into the side of Java's head so that she, too, sprawled on the sand. She leapt to her feet and lashed out with her fingernails, aiming for Ganba's eyes. He chuckled and with one push at Java's chest sat her down with a thud. Then he bent, gathered up the tea and sugar, and went back to his fire.

"I will be the first to be meat food," Bildana wailed softly.

She was wrong. The man whose wife Ganba had "borrowed" made a mistake by insisting on his share of the tea and sugar. He had not dared face Ganba to protest Ganba's free use of his wife, but being denied sweetened tea was a serious matter. He shouted out his protest, and when Ganba casually struck him in the face, he made a motion to fight back. Ganba's ax, at the ready in his other hand, slashed out, and bright arterial blood gushed from the Abo's throat. As the man fell, Ganba seized a pan and began to collect the spurting blood.

Java tried not to watch, but the chanting of the Abos, the songs, the cruel laughter as Ganba butchered the fallen man and put a haunch to roast on the fire kept drawing Java's eyes back to the scene of horror. Now there were only five in Ganba's group: two men in addition to Ganba, and two women.

The feasting went on for a long time, until after the pale small moon had risen and the night had chilled. Java told Bildana to lie down and pretend to sleep. She herself carefully gathered the food and put it in the bag, ready to travel. When at last the sated Abos slept, their fires dying, she punched Bildana awake—even in her terror Bildana had fallen asleep. They crept out of the camp, headed in the direction of the dry wash. Nature came to Java's aid. The rains that had been scattered to the east, the rains that had been threatening each night with sheet lightning and the distant rumblings of thunder, the rains that had filled the dry wash and carried away Tolo and Terry Forrest came with a suddenness that took Java's breath. A fist of wind hit her, and then, seconds later, the rain was being driven stingingly into her face.

"The spirits favor us," Bildana said, "for the rain will take our tracks so that Ganba cannot follow us. But we must not go in the direction he expects." She took Java's arm, turned her to face east, into the driving rainstorm.

"Bildana, we have so little food and even less water. We can't waste time circling around to the east."

"No waste time," Bildana said. "Go to great-red-sacred-rock. Whitefella town there."

"Bloody hell," Java said. "All the way across the Gibson?"

"With Ganba, death is sure. With the desert—" She shrugged. "The desert is cruel, but it will give us food."

"And water?"

"With the help of the spirits I will find the soaks and the ↄores," Bildana said. "If not, then the carrion eaters will feast, ↄot Ganba."

The rain continued until almost morning. Java estimated ↄhat they had walked at least five miles, perhaps more. She welcomed the sun, for it had been cold in the rain. Soon she was dry, though she became soaked again with her perspira- ↄion, until the sun sucked most of the moisture from her, and ↄer clothing dried once more. Bildana still set a fast pace, ↄaintaining it throughout the day.

When at last they made camp, toward evening, Bildana ↄaid, "No fire. He see smoke."

For three days water was no problem. Rock basins had held ↄhe rain and furnished them with water to drink, even water ↄo bathe, a luxury that Java relished to the fullest. And ↄround them a miracle happened, an event of such beauty ↄhat it left Java breathless. The desert burst into bloom. Green ↄhings appeared with amazing swiftness, turning the red, bar- ↄen waste into a continuing glory. Flowers of all colors ↄtretched into the distances.

To Java it was sheer beauty, God's miracle. To Bildana it ↄas a gift from the Dreaming, for many of the green and ↄlooming things were edible. The kunga shrubs put out ber- ↄies that were delicious, and several varieties of root added ↄest to their boiled rice and lentils. Mulga apples would also ↄe there for the eating within a few days.

During those good days they traveled hard, pushing to put ↄistance between them and Ganba. But soon, in the fierce heat ↄf the sun, the greenery withered and the flowers became ↄust. The succulent tubers became harder to find, because the ↄreen shoots that marked their location had faded away; it ↄook Bildana's experienced eye to spot the places where edible ↄoots hid beneath the soil.

Now the Gibson began to exact its toll. The two women ↄationed the water, allowing themselves only a few careful

swallows from the one waterskin that Bildana carried. Water
had to be used to cook the rice and lentils, while they lasted,
but if one was careful and did not boil away the precious fluid,
the water used in cooking could later be drunk and was not
wasted.

Once Bildana threw a rock with sufficient accuracy to kill a
rabbit, which she roasted over the fire. Even half raw, the
meat was delicious.

Java had Tolo's compass, and she had saved one map. They
were walking directly east, but they were often forced to detour around dense fields of impenetrable spinifex. The spiky
grass was more of a problem now, while they were walking,
than it had been when they were riding camels. Now and then
an expanse of gibber plain also forced deviation from the trail,
but Java always came back to an easterly heading. Ayers
Rock, she estimated, was more than three hundred miles
away. Alice Springs, with a surplus of food, water, people,
and soft beds, was only a bit farther.

But men had died in Australia's dead heart. The Gibson
had karked in the early explorer for whom it was named. To
think that she, a mere girl, could accomplish what Gibson
himself had failed to do seemed brazen arrogance. But she
kept on walking. In the morning, when the sun began to bake
her and water streamed from her body in perspiration, she
gradually fell into a sort of walking trance, her eyes fixed on
Bildana's glossy black hide, gleaming with the odoriferous fat
that she used as a protection against the sun. Java's own skin
felt baked, even through her clothing.

At the end of the day, though aching in every bone and
muscle, Java did her share of firewood gathering. Bildana insisted on doing the food preparation. And then they huddled
together against the cold of the desert nights. Soon Java lost
count of the days. Each day was the same, and the desert did
not change. There were times when, in a panic, she feared that
she was walking repeatedly over the same red sand, passing
the same red boulders—traveling in circles. At such times

her hope fading and her will to live flagging, she drew upon her deep reserves.

Her memories of Tolo seemed distant now, although he had been dead less than a month. In a conscious effort to keep them alive, she would parade the memories: how he had looked when she first met him; how his strong arm had guided her so easily when they danced at Bina's; how she had felt during the tumultuous celebration of the relief of Mafeking when, caught in the crowd, they had been pressed closely together and he had kissed her deeply and passionately. And she paraded before her all those she loved: her grandmother, her mother, her father.

When they had consumed the last of the water in the waterskin, Bildana declared, "We will have to walk at night."

The moon was full by then, and they could make fair progress. They walked into the morning, and when the sun began to bake them, Bildana called a halt and built a shelter with a blanket beside a huge red boulder. They managed to sleep.

They started walking again at sundown. Java's lips were dry, parched, and cracked. Every cell in her body protested, sending messages of desperate pain, demanding, screaming for water.

"We will reach the water before the sun comes," Bildana said.

But with the day the endless wastes stretched away on all sides. To the southeast, however, there was an irregularity on the horizon.

"There," Bildana said, pointing.

"How far?"

"We will reach it before morning," Bildana said.

Java thought of spending the day in the shade of a blanket stretched across rocks, but something told her that if she did not continue toward the distant protuberance on the horizon, she would not be able to rise from the sand again.

"We will not stop," she said.

"No, we will not," Bildana agreed.

By the time the sun was directly overhead, Java was drifting in and out of delirium. Her eyes were lying to her, showing her scenes of desperate beauty, huge lakes of crystal clear water, running streams with the sheer beauty of pure liquid running over rocks, singing the song of the brook. In her imagination Bildana was leading her directly away from all of that wonderful water. She tried to speak Bildana's name, and only a croak came out. She tried to hurry her step, to catch Bildana, to tell her that she was going the wrong way, but she could not force her legs to move faster. In despair she turned to go to the water, dropping her bag of food and her blanket in the sand. She would drink her fill, and then she would have the strength to overtake Bildana and bring her to that sparkling, babbling steam.

"Don't be a fool," her grandmother said.

She paused, looked around. The water was there, not a hundred yards away. Bildana was still moving doggedly toward the distant ridge.

The voice was in her head. *"You are not intended to die, child. Follow Bildana."*

"But there is water there."

"No, look."

The lone and level sands stretched far away, so desolate that in that direction not even the tough desert grasses grew.

"Your mother was once near death, burned by the ashes of the erupting volcano. She was carrying you in her womb. She had been battered and beaten as she was carried by the tidal wave. She, too, wanted to lie down and die, but she did not. She walked on."

"But they came to help her. The old Java man helped her."

"Follow Bildana. She will help you."

"I'm so tired, Grandmother."

"Walk. Turn your face eastward and walk."

She would never remember that afternoon, would never understand how she managed to keep on her feet and follow Bildana's footprints in the sand. Now and again she would hear voices, sometimes the voice of Magdalen, sometimes the crooning, soft words of her mother speaking as if she were a child in the cradle. And in the shadows, with the heat of the sun diminished by craggy rocks that towered over her, closing in on each side of her, she caught the most beautiful scent she could remember. Water. She staggered into a run, leaning forward, forcing her feet to move so that she wouldn't fall on her face.

The water seeped out slowly from the face of a rock and puddled sweetly in a rocky basin not more than half an inch deep. She fell to her stomach and put her lips into the life-giving liquid. Bildana had drunk and was smiling, though her large lips were still parched and cracked.

"I have found," she said. "I feared—"

Java protested as Bildana buried her fingers in her hair and lifted her head. "Drink easy, little one," Bildana said. "Take small sips and wait."

Later, as they lay beside a fire, stomachs full of both water and food, Java said her prayers of thanks aloud.

Bildana shook her head. "Your white god may be powerful, but he did not put the water here. It was left here from the Dreaming."

"Then I thank the spirits of the Dreaming as well," Java said.

She estimated that they had walked an average of twenty miles a day, sometimes more when they had to skirt impassable areas. They had covered, if her estimate was right, scarcely half of their journey toward the great-red-sacred-rock.

Chapter XVII

SIR GEORGE LE Hunte sent for Matt Van Buren on a morning when the southeast trade winds had begun to establish themselves, bringing with them Port Moresby's dry season. In the months ahead, the south coast of New Guinea would see its lowest yearly temperatures, meaning that it would be merely steaming, not boiling. The governor was not in the best of moods when Matt was admitted to his office.

"Yes, Van Buren," Sir George said grumpily. "You asked me, when you first arrived here, about the prospects of growing coffee in the Owen Stanley highlands."

"Yes, I did," Matt said.

"And what did I tell you?"

"That it would be impossible to get native labor."

"Ah," Sir George said. "So I did. Told the poms in the Colonial Office in London the same thing."

Matt had to grin to hear Sir George use the Aussie slang, for it would be difficult, even in England, to find a pom who was more pommy, in Australian eyes, than Sir George.

"And yet," Sir George said, when Matt remained silent, "you and the Gorel chap seem to have lined up labor for your timber-cutting enterprise."

"Not as many men as we'd like to have," Matt answered.

"And they're hillmen, I am told."

"Yes, sir, they are."

Sir George shuffled papers. "It seems, Van Buren, that the gentlemen in the Colonial Office have developed a taste for coffee—or at least for the profits that result in the growing and trading thereof. I have been requested to investigate the possibility of establishing coffee plantations in the Owen Stanley highlands. Now, I think that it is quite obvious that I myself have no interest in agriculture. I attended public school as a lad and then Cambridge. I determined at an early age that too much learning is bad for the gizzard, or whatever. I don't care to learn about growing coffee in New Guinea, or in Newcastle, for that matter. Do you?"

"I have a mild curiosity," Matt said. "That curiosity might become more of a desire if the Colonial Office just happened to be willing to give aid to a man who would become interested in coffee."

"That's one thing I admire in you colonials," Sir George said. "You drive directly to the core of a matter, don't you? As a matter of fact, I have been advised to invest—ah, a few pounds in such an enterprise. I had thought, Van Buren, that you might take a look-see at the highlands, with an eye to their potential as a coffee-growing area, when you go on a scouting trip for timber."

"Sir George, I don't think we're ready to try to move timber logs down from the highlands to a port."

"Hmm. No, I suppose not. No blasted railways, eh? Not even heavy drays. Bloody oxcarts, that's all, and not many of those." He mused. "Then can I induce you to leave your own activities for the time required to visit the highlands?"

Matt grinned and held out his hand palm up, rubbing his thumb on his fingers in the time-honored gesture signifying cash.

"I am authorized to pay, ah, fifty pounds for the survey," Sir George said.

"I think, sir, that you might get one of the English-speaking natives to go into the highlands for that amount," Matt said. "You see, I have no real desire to see the highlands simply to write a report for some gentleman in the Colonial Office. If I went up there, I'd want to be sure I wasn't wasting my time. I'd want a crown grant of any suitable lands that I might locate for coffee growing—and a guarantee in writing that if I should locate such lands, I would be supplied with seed stock and financing until the crops began to produce."

"Out of the question," Sir George said.

Matt rose. "G'day, sir. Trev Gorel and I are going south to cut down some trees."

"Now just a bloody minute," Sir George said. "I can give you a grant for up to a thousand acres—"

"Ten thousand," Matt said.

"Dammit, man!" Sir George burst out, "this is not bloody Australia, where the land is so worthless that you have to have ten thousand acres to feed a handful of sheep."

"No, this is bloody Papua," Matt said, "where we're not even sure yet that ten thousand acres would feed a handful of sheep—or grow one coffee bean. You're asking me to take valuable time away from a business enterprise that has just begun and is by no means guaranteed of success. I would be doing myself and my partner a disservice to desert him at this critical time unless I had assurances that I would not be embarking on a losing proposition. If you want me to go, Sir George, my terms are not negotiable."

"All right," Sir George acknowledged. "What you have said makes a certain kind of perverse, self-serving sense—"

"I have a feeling you're about to quote Seneca or Horace to me," Matt said. "Something about the virtue of serving my country without asking for anything in return. Well, don't bother. *Your* Jolly Old England isn't *my* country, Sir George. New Guinea isn't my country either, not yet."

"Ten thousand acres?"

"In as many plots as I choose, not necessarily adjoining."

The governor nodded reluctantly.

"And seedlings guaranteed. Plus as much capital as is needed to build a decent dwelling and utility buildings, to buy animals and vehicles needed for transportation, to pay for needed tools and supplies and living expenses."

"My God, man, you're asking for a blank check on the British Treasury."

"Now, Sir George"—Matt grinned, waggling a finger at the governor—"you're forgetting how badly the gentlemen in the Colonial Office want coffee plantations in New Guinea."

"Australian pirate." Sir George fumed; but a smile came across his face, and he rose, extending his hand. "When can you leave?"

"Well, let's see. I'll need a few days to sort out some grub and some bearers. It would also help to have whatever maps have been made of the highlands, so that I have some vague idea where I'm headed. I'll have to arrange with Trev to do the timbering without me. By the by, he will be my partner in the coffee-growing operation as well, if there is one. I think I might be able to get under way within the week."

"Splendid," Sir George said. "God go with you."

Matt broke the news to Trev and Kit over dinner. Trev grinned and got up to pound Matt on the back. "Crikey," he yelped, "ten thousand luvly acres."

"Of mountaintop," Matt said. "I'll get excited when I see land that would do for growing coffee."

"What does land suitable for growing coffee look like?" Kit asked.

"Damned if I know"—Matt grinned—"but I reckon I'll know it when I see it. High and well drained. Moderate temperatures."

"Old Gihi says it's quite cool and comfortable in the valley of his home village," Trev said.

"Remind me to have a long talk with Gihi," Matt said.

Kit did not speak much as the two men made their plans and dreamed their dreams. When she and Matt were in bed and she lay with her cheek in the hollow of his shoulder, she said, "Matt, it will be so pleasant to get away from this heat for a while."

"Hold on," he said. "You're not going."

"Of course, I'm going," she said. "There are several reason
why I'm going."

"But you're with child," he protested.

"That's the best reason for going, to have some relief from
this heat. I feel as if I'm melting away slowly here, being
dissolved in my own perspiration. I will not stay here while
you go off into the mountains and get cool. Then, too, Trev'
wife will be arriving. He hasn't seen her in many months.
think it would be nice for them to have the house to them
selves for their reunion. Finally, there is no way, mate, tha
you will be allowed to run off and leave me for weeks, not jus
when I am most in need of a little loving."

He kissed her lightly. "How much in need?"

"This much," she said, squeezing him with all her strength

"But just a little loving?" he teased.

She put her warm hand on his manhood. "Well, when
little loving is all a girl can get—"

Matt spent hours with Gihi, making notations on his map
which had a lot of blank area in the highlands. He asked
questions, writing down the names of the elders of Gihi's vi
lage along with directions to Gihi's valley.

"Will the men work for me?" Matt asked. "Will they culti
vate the fields and plant the coffee trees for me?"

"That is women's work," Gihi said. "Plenty womer
Women plant plenty trees."

"Would the men cut trees and help to haul them down th
mountains to the coast, if we decided that would be the thin
to do?" Matt asked.

Gihi shrugged. "Some like tea and tobacco. Good knive
and axes. Maybe some work. You go?"

"I go."

Gihi brought out his paint holder, a carved wooden bc
containing the pigments he used to paint his face for festiv
and official occasions. He dipped his finger into black an
made a stylized cross on Matt's forehead, then held up a mi
ror for Matt to inspect his work. "Put this sign on your for

head before you enter the pass that leads into the valley," he said. "This will tell my people that one of their own has sent you. It will get you close enough to them to explain that Gihi has sent you."

"What would happen if I went into the valley without this sign?" Matt said.

Gihi shrugged. "Maybe nothing. Maybe someone might be in a bad mood. Place arrow here." He tapped Matt's stomach. "Arrow poisoned."

"I shall be very careful to remember to paint my face," Matt said.

In the early 1900s there were many places in the interior highlands of New Guinea that had never been seen by white men. The southern tip of the island, with the Owen Stanley Range, was a bit better known than the regions to the northwest, where the body of the lizard thickened, but even in the south no roads into the mountains existed as yet.

Gihi had found bearers, two of them his own people, men who had come to the coast to try to earn white men's money in order to buy gleaming jungle knives and cookware for their women. The first day's going was slow. The jungle was dense and damp, and Matt and Kit stewed inside their clothing, gasping for breath in the steam bath air of midday. Then the land began to rise, and the vegetation changed in character. They could actually walk without having to hew a way through solid undergrowth.

After only two days of walking they found the climate noticeably more pleasant, the first indication of change being a delightful coolness at night and in the early morning. When they topped still another ridge and looked out over a corrugated landscape of interlocking ridges stretching into the distance, they were truly in the highlands. Kit realized that her perspiration was evaporating, leaving her a bit cooler and more comfortable.

They entered Gihi's valley by threading their way through a narrow pass. From the top of the pass they could look down on three native villages, with well-traveled paths leading to them from numerous directions. The guides took the middle path, which brought them to the center of the valley; then they walked through a cool, shadowy tunnel formed by the fronds of coconut palms that met overhead at a height of fifty feet off the ground. Near the village were groves of banana trees with healthy dark-green leaves. In clearings among the trees women tended sweet potatoes, yams, and taro. Matt knew enough about soils to see that the loam of the valley was volcanic in origin, much richer than the leached sandy soils of the coastal lowlands.

Beyond the village and the fertile groves and fields, the hills again rose gradually in tier after tier to wooded heights.

"If that's not coffee-growing country . . ." Matt said to Kit.

To enter the village proper, they had to cross a stream by wading through crystalline shallows. Looking downstream as they passed, they espied a deep blue pool in which swam a horde of small boys and girls, their voices piercing the quiet of the afternoon.

Matt had painted his forehead in the manner prescribed by Gihi. Consequently he was greeted with rather too much warmth for his taste by the village headman, because the traditional friendly greeting consisted of an embrace—made aromatic by the pig grease that the tribesmen smeared on their skin and hair—and a fondling of one's genitals. This latter custom was to become a continuing trial for Kit, for it was part of a proper greeting between members of the opposite sex as well.

Matt sat down with the headman and other elders to discuss his plans to grow coffee, including the payment that he would make to secure use of the land and workers both to cut the trees and, eventually, to tend the coffee plants. The headman made a show of bargaining, but in the end he settled for wages that Matt considered quite reasonable.

Kit meanwhile was taken in hand by one of the headman's wives, and within a half hour she was swimming in a deep clear pool in the stream with several of the younger women. The water was cold and delicious, and when she came out of the stream, the late afternoon temperature was mild and pleasant.

"Matt, here is where we will build our house," Kit said. She was seated on a rock halfway up the hill behind the village. The valley was spread before her. The fields and groves looked neat, as trim as a well-tended lawn. To the south a blue wall of mountains ended the view, and to the east the foothills fell away in green waves touched with purple shadows. On the slopes the trees rose in feathery clusters and in the airy grace of bamboo. A feeling of openness and freedom filled the air, and she could breathe easily, inhaling the perfume of bursting flowers or the delicious spicy odor exuded by the odd-looking trees.

"I could use a hydraulic ram to lift water from the stream," Matt said. A mountain rill gurgled toward the valley floor just below where they sat. "Or direct a sluiceway down from above."

"It would be a lovely place to raise a family."

"No doctors," Matt said. "You'd have to have the baby in Port Moresby—or in Sydney."

"Pooh," she said. "I'll bet there are a half dozen midwives in that little village who could deliver a baby as well as any doctor—and without the danger of infection that one faces in a hospital."

"We'll talk about it," Matt said.

"And perhaps once or twice a year we'll go down the hill and see if other people still exist," Kit said. "And take the children—"

"Children?"

"At least ten of them."

" 'Strewth," Matt said.

"To the big cities in Australia."

"Townsville."

"Or Sydney. Matt, what is required for a good life, actually?"

"Well, when my father and mother first moved into central Queensland, they didn't have any more to work with than we would have here," he said.

"We could cart in the necessary things. We'd need a cooking range and kitchen utensils, heating stoves if it gets cool here in the night, and, of course, a few items of furniture— beds, chairs, tables, oil lamps."

"It's a long way from anywhere," Matt said.

"It strikes my fancy," Kit answered . "To think of having you all to myself. Just you and I and the natives—"

He smiled at her, took her hand. "Anyone ever accuse you of being a romantic?"

"No one ever had the opportunity before," she said.

"I'm glad you are." He rose and paced off the level area on the side of the slope. "You want a house here? Then you'll have a house here."

"I'll want the kitchen windows to overlook the valley," she said. "And huge verandas like those on Trev's house in Port Moresby. I'll train one of the village girls to be a household servant. Just one, so that our privacy won't be endangered. And as soon as our son is old enough, I'll go with you into the groves and help plant trees and pick coffee beans when they're ripe, and—"

He kissed her. "Pommy girl, you never cease to surprise me."

"Bushranger," she said, "you haven't seen anything yet."

"Sir George," Matt said, "the first thing that is needed is a road into the highlands."

The governor snorted.

"And, sir, I think you'll probably have to double the official estimate of the number of indigenous people in Papua. We passed through only two valleys, but the people in the highlands say that there are many, and the population there is more concentrated than in the coastal areas. There are coconut groves in the mountain valleys, and I think the people could be coaxed into growing a surplus of yams and sweet potatoes. The upper slopes are ideal for coffee, maybe even tea, but you're not going to be able to open the highland areas without road access."

"Do you have any idea what you're asking?" Sir George demanded.

"Well, sir, it's my impression that we're here—and by 'we' I mean Australia and Great Britain—to bring civilization and progress to a backward people." He grinned. "While making a slight profit, of course. Since it seems to me that at least half the population of this country is in the highland valleys, I don't see how we're going to accomplish anything without having roads for access. Right now the valleys are so isolated and the natives so suspicious that it's dangerous for a white man to enter without knowing the sign of friendship, and that sign varies from valley to valley, from village to village."

"There is no possibility that the crown will endeavor to build a road to your granted lands, Van Buren," Sir George said. "You've squeezed the crown already to get your own terms, and it appears to me that you've laid out quite a nice holding for yourself. You'll have your seedlings, and you have your financing; but how you get to your holdings—and how you get the product out when and if you produce coffee—will be your own affair."

"I don't think we need to worry about having a road just yet," Kit said.

The three of them—Matt, Kit, and Trev—were sitting on the veranda of Trev's house. The men were drinking the British miracle medicine that had made it possible for the people of those chill islands to conquer and take as their own so many odd tropical places. Kit, who had stopped having gin when she learned that she was pregnant, contented herself with tea.

"I don't see how we can pack in materials to build a house and the utility buildings," Matt said.

"The answer to that is to pack in a small sawmill and use native materials," Trev said.

"Easy to say," Matt told him.

"Look at it this way," Trev persisted. "The sawmill will be purchased through the generosity of the crown. Perhaps the inhabitants of the valley will be willing to trade labor and produce for finished lumber. Do you think?"

"I don't know. They seem content with their thatched houses. Those structures are fairly well built, give as much protection against the weather as is needed, and if a man decides to move or if someone gets careless and burns down a house, it's quite easy to build another."

"I think we could educate them to want finished timber," Trev said. "We'd trade it for labor at first and then maybe—when we have a way to move things to the coast—agricultural products. There's always a market for copra, and you said there are plenty of coconut palms up there."

"I think it sounds exciting, Matt," Kit said. "It will be ever so rewarding, when the house is finished, to know that it was built with wood cut and finished on our own land."

"As it happens," Trev said, "I know where there is a sawmill, complete with trimmers and planers. It's steam-powered, wood-burning, and—"

"It would take only a thousand natives to cart the bloody thing up to the highlands," Matt interrupted. "It's crazy, Trev. You've gone definitely troppo."

"Just looking to the future," Trev said. "We're in the timber business. Some of those high-country hardwoods are splendid woods. We want a road to our valley. Every building that goes up here in Port Moresby uses imported timber at the moment, and that's uneconomical. How much would you be willing to wager against the governor's leaping to build us a road if we could supply him with lumber, eh?"

Reluctantly Matt went to look at the sawmill machinery. It was beginning to rust, as everything rusted in the humidity of tropical Papua, but otherwise it was in fine condition. The boiler, he determined, would present the most difficulty. It

ould take draft animals and a heavy dray to truck it up the
ills, and it would mean cutting a road through the jungles.
o get the mill to his valley, he'd have to do himself what he
ad been trying to influence Sir George to do: build a road.

"What in blue blazes does getting a sawmill into that valley
f yours have to do with growing coffee?" Sir George thun-
ered.

Matt had presented the governor with a proposition. If the
overnor would use colonial funds to collect and pay labor,
Matt would supervise the building of a road into the high-
ands, over which he would transport a sawmill which would,
ithin a very short time, begin to produce finished lumber to
e carted down to Port Moresby to assure the growth of the
own.

"No home for my wife, no coffee plantation," Matt said.
It's as simple as that. I will not have my wife—who is with
hild, by the by—living in a thatched hut."

Sir George considered the situation for long minutes as
Matt sat quietly, looking out the window toward the harbor.
oon, in addition to shipping whole logs, he and Trev would
e loading ships right there in Port Moresby with highly prof-
able cargoes of cut and finished lumber.

"I can provide fifty Kanakas," Sir George said finally.

"Sir George, unless you want the road building to go on
to the next century, we'll need triple that."

"Bloody pirate," Sir George growled. "You'll leave me with
o labor at all for harbor facility improvement."

"Why do we need a harbor if we have nothing to ship out
ut people who have given up on New Guinea?"

"A hundred and thirty," Sir George said. "That's the top
mit."

"Goodonyer," Matt said, elated.

Although it seemed to Matt that events moved with excru-
ating slowness in the ensuing weeks and months, the coming
f the rains saw the road, which was actually not much more

than a cleared lane, pushing over the last ridge to the pa
leading to the valley. Already the sawmill equipment ha
been moved to the highlands and set up, and the ox wago
that brought up supplies and tools for the Kanaka workme
carried back finely finished planks of cedar and mahogany. I
Port Moresby several new buildings were being erected wit
lumber cut by Matt and Trev.

Trev, meanwhile, had taken Gihi and his crew to the sout
coast, where they had loaded two Van Buren ships with tea
logs.

Kit, with her stomach growing nicely, had insisted on bein
with Matt in the highlands. She had taken up residence in th
village, seemingly quite at home in an airy dirt-floore
thatched hut. She had argued—and by her success prove
that she was right—that since it was the native women wh
did the agricultural work, it was logical that she, a woma
should direct their efforts at clearing the ground for the coff
trees. So for two months now the women had been workin
on the slopes near the site that Kit had picked for her hous
The brush was burned away from the rich soil, and then th
women attacked the stubs with long knives. It was a slo
process, but by the time coffee tree seedlings could be shippe
in, Kit would have a hundred acres of land ready to l
planted.

And then came the wonderful day when Kanaka workme
began to clear and level the house site. The sawmill was pos
tioned on the lower slopes, above the village. Timbering wa
an activity for men, and a sufficient number of the native me
wanted the white man's luxuries enough to work for them.

A stone foundation rose quickly, and atop it the workme
began to lay the huge, hard support timbers. Skeletal wal
went up. Day by day Kit watched the growth of two thing
very dear to her, her house and her child. It was going to be
race to see which was completed first.

Money had begun to come in nicely. The profits from th
timbering, plus the money Matt had squeezed out of S
George and the British Colonial Office, made Matt Van Bure

and Trevor Gorel important men, for financial success was rare in Papua. Trev had some work done on his own house in Port Moresby, spending most of his time there when he was not out in the coastal forests with Gihi and the timber crews, which continued to grow.

Only one thing prevented Trev from being as euphoric as Matt and Kit, as Kit's house reached completion and was topped off by cedar shingles: Guinevere Gorel had not changed ships at Cape Town, as the travel agent had planned. He had already received her telegram from Cape Town—OPPORTUNITY VISIT HUE LETTER FOLLOWS—and now, at last, the promised letter was in hand. He was struck by the fact that ironically, in this modern age, when steam vessels had cut the voyage from Europe down to mere weeks, Guinevere's journey had extended into months. And yet she had written most persuasively of her longing to see the few remaining members of her family:

> This ship which brought me to Cape Town goes from here to India, then to Malaya and Indochina. Although I long to see you, my husband, and to feel your strong, loving arms around me, I feel a terrible urge to take this chance to see those whom I will never see again, to walk once more the streets of the city of my birth. I will not tarry there long but will have the travel agents arrange passage to New Guinea at an early opportunity.

What else could he do but wait?

THE SOUND OF feminine laughter rang from the parlor of th Broome-Gordon house as Rufus Broome stepped up onto th porch. When he used the brass knocker, his sister, Jessic Broome Gordon, opened the door. She was smiling, and th smile widened as she threw open the screen and embrace Rufus.

"You're just in time for our private celebration," Jessic said.

Magdalen Broome rose from her chair when Rufus walke into the room beside Jessica and took her due, a quick hug, kiss on one papery, wrinkled cheek.

Rufe bowed to Bina Tyrell, dressed in a shocking red gow that went well with her glossy black hair, and his face flushe slightly as he repeated the courtesy to the fourth woman pres ent in the airy, pleasant room, Misa Mason.

"So what is the celebration?" Rufe asked, taking the chai indicated by Jessica.

"The great Australian male, in all his wisdom and charity has graciously extended to mere women the right to vote i federal elections," Magdalen said.

"Congratulations," Rufe said. "I think that any one of yo ladies would make an excellent premier of Australia. I assur you that if any of you is nominated, I will support you, and i you run, I will vote for you."

"Although I detect a slight hint of amusement in the man's voice," Bina said, "I approve his words."

"The man is not amused, just very pleased to be in the presence of such beauty," Rufe said, looking directly at Misa before playing his smile on the others.

"So, you see," Jessica said, "the male animal pays lip service to our victory and then very quickly puts us back into our place by speaking of feminine beauty."

"Well, only one of you is really ugly," Rufe said.

There was a chorus of protest.

"Actually," Rufe said, "it's been proven in survey after survey. One out of three people is incurably ugly. If you doubt that, look at the person on either side of you, and if you don't see ugliness, guess what?"

Jessica threw a delicately embroidered cushion at Rufe's head. He warded it off with a casual sweep of his arm. "Now, speaking of ugly," he said, "there is an officer on my ship who is not only ugly but creatively ugly—"

"Rufe . . ." Jessica said.

Misa Mason rose, drawing Rufe's eyes to her. She was wearing a splendidly fitted white business suit accented by an impressive pearl necklace. On her left hand was one blazing ruby. She said, "Perhaps if we feed the man . . ."

She served cakes on a little plate and poured tea. As she bent to hand him the tea, his eyes were drawn to the creamy brown cleavage shown by the fashionable dress. Feeling the almost tangible thrust of his gaze, her hand fluttered, and she had to resist an urge to cover her bare upper chest with her palm.

"But what's this?" Jessica asked, leaping to her feet and moving to finger the insignia of rank on Rufe's shoulder.

"I'm due a celebration myself," Rufe said.

"Mother, look," Jessica said. "He's a commodore now."

Magdalen came to stand beside her son, bent, and placed a kiss on his forehead. "I am very proud of you," she said softly.

"I might catch up with the old man yet," Rufe said, referring to his father, who had been medically retired as a rear admiral.

"Yes," Magdalen said, "I think that you will."

"But it's a larger navy now," Rufe said. "More opportunity. When Dad was serving, it took a real studhorse to reach the rank of commodore."

"Don't try to detract from your own achievement," Magdalen said. "What is your assignment?"

"Still the Pacific fleet," Rufe said. "I'll have a squadron of destroyers. We'll be based here in Sydney Harbor, and I should be seeing a lot of you, at least for a matter of a few months." Again he looked directly at Misa as he spoke.

"I do hope, brother dear, that your schedule will be regular enough so that you can let us know when you're in port. Not that I mind your dropping in unannounced—"

"You had me concerned for a moment," Rufe said, grinning.

"—but there's nothing in the house. Sam's off on business in Melbourne. I do wish they'd make up their minds just where the seat of government is going to be. They're still talking about a federal district buried somewhere off in the way-out bush and—"

"I think someone is trying to pattern Australia's capital after the Yanks' Washington, D.C.," Bina said.

"We're having dinner at Bina's tonight," Misa Mason said suddenly, surprising herself. Her eyes caught Rufe's, and his intensity held her for long moments. "If you promise not to be too arrogantly male, we'll allow you to join us."

Jessica flushed and hid it by turning away. Some months back Rufe had indicated an interest in Misa Mason by asking her to ask Misa to a small, intimate dinner at the Gordon house.

"My very great pleasure," Rufe said to Misa, with a little bow.

The intimate dinner had never taken place because Jessica had purposefully put it off, trying to avoid having Misa in the house while her brother was in port. Fortunately, Rufe's unpredictable schedule and his long absences at sea had made this conveniently easy for her.

"Ladies," Misa said, "I'm sorry to be the first to break up the celebration, but I must go."

"I'll go with you," Bina said. She and Misa had come to the house together in Bina's car.

"No, you stay," Misa replied. "I'm due at the bank. I can just walk down to the corner and hail a cab."

"May I escort you?" Rufe said, leaping to his feet.

"Would you, Rufe?" Magdalen asked. "You're not really ready to leave yet, are you, Bina?"

"Not if Misa doesn't mind getting a cab."

Bina's new Daimler was parked in front of the Gordon house. "Fine machine," Rufe said as he and Misa passed it.

"I have mixed emotions about motorcars," Misa said. "There's a certain thrill when one is riding in one, with wind tearing at one's hair and with that fantastic feeling of speed, but then, when I am *not* riding in one, which is most of the time, I wonder what would happen if something mechanical failed or the driver made an error and the contraption smashed into a tree or a stone wall."

"I believe it might be quite painful," Rufe said with a chuckle.

"I know, I know," Misa said, smiling up at him. "I'm a great coward, I suppose. And I know I'm going to have to give in and buy a car of my own sooner or later. One has to have one these days, I guess, out of necessity."

Her mouth was fantastic, lips full and soft-looking, smile lines at the corners. Her eyes were deep enough for a man to fall into and lose his way.

They walked down the slight rise side by side, commenting on the weather, which was lovely, and on the traffic in the harbor, which was ever-increasing. Misa listened apprecia-ively as Rufe pointed out his own ship moored in the broad harbor, a low gray destroyer with formidable guns protruding fore and aft. To Misa it looked quite threatening, but Rufe described it lovingly.

Rufe was tall, slim, and impeccable in his blues. The edges of his rust red hair, just visible beneath his cap, were tousled by the wind. In his presence Misa felt aware of herself as the epitome of mature, graceful femininity. She was dressed in white, her dark hair coming to her shoulders.

The handsome couple drew stares from a passing motorcar and also from pedestrians as they reached the corner, turned, and walked on toward the center of town. Oddly, the looks were not of admiration but of disapproval, disbelief, even open contempt.

Such looks were not new to Misa, though they were obviously lost on Rufe, for his eyes were focused on her alone. He had taken her hand and placed it on his arm, where she left it.

Misa had endured Australian bigotry before, when she had appeared in public with her now-dead husband, Jon Mason. She had felt it when white Australian men walked into her office on bank business to see a Kanaka seated behind the huge teak desk. The lily-white Australian attitude had long since ceased to be a major concern for her—until she saw it evidenced in the looks of passersby as she walked with the tall, handsome Royal Navy commodore. And then her anger was not for herself but for Rufe. How dare they be critical of such a man?

A hansom cab passed with a clatter of the horse's hooves. She made no attempt to hail it, nor did Rufe, for it was a pleasant day for walking. It pleased Misa to match strides with a tall, vigorous man again, to feel the compact bulk of his muscular arm under her palm.

The subjects of their conversation did not really matter; nothing they said during the long walk that ended at Misa's bank was memorable. Only the tacit communication was of importance: the flash of eyes, the blink of lovely long black lashes, a manly smile. Their awareness of each other, which caused nerves to be more sensitive and physical senses to be more acute, gave each a feeling of fantastic well-being.

"Saints above," Rufe said when he saw that they were standing at the side entrance to the bank. "Forgive me. I've walked you all the way. Should have found you a cab."

Misa, too, was surprised that time had passed so quickly, that the walk from the Gordon house had seemed so effortless.

"I'll just see you to your office," Rufe said.

Misa went up the stairs ahead of him. She was slightly self-conscious as she ascended, aware of his eyes on her, of the impression that her stylish costume and fetching derriere could make on a man. Rufe's expression as she turned to him at the head of the stairs confirmed his appreciation of her physical charms, and yet she felt no embarrassment, only the warm, pleasurable sensation of being alive.

She stood in the doorway to her office, pulling off her gloves as her secretary waited beside her desk, hands full of important notes for her employer.

"Thank you," Rufe said. "I enjoyed it." He seemed as uneasy as a schoolboy.

"You are very welcome," she replied, smiling.

"I look forward to seeing you tonight, at Bina's."

"Yes," she said.

He kissed her hand, not in the polite European fashion of stopping short of actual contact, but brushing her hand with his lips. He lingered, as if he wanted to have the taste of her, and a shiver traveled up her arm into her shoulders. He could not fail to note her reaction. He looked into her eyes for a long moment, hesitated, then turned on his heels and was gone.

She watched him go down the stairs until she saw only the cap atop his red hair and then nothing. She sighed.

"There are some rather urgent messages, Mrs. Mason," the secretary said.

"Yes, yes," Misa said, turning. She looked at the clock. Hours, long hours before closing time, before time to go home to dress in her empty house and prepare to go to Bina's.

"Is there anything from Western Australia?" she asked, reaching for the stack of mail on her desk.

"Nothing from your son, ma'am," the secretary replied. "I'm sorry."

Nothing. There had been nothing for weeks now. For at least a few minutes of motherly chagrin directed toward a thoughtless son drove thoughts of Rufus Broome from her mind. "Just wait until I get my hands on that young scoundrel," she said. "It isn't as if we didn't teach him how to write, you know."

"Well, ma'am," the secretary said, "if he's out in the waly, there just aren't any postal boxes, you know."

"You're right, of course," Misa acknowledged. "Now just what are those urgent messages?"

II

Chapter XIX

WHEN SUDDEN STORMS bring torrential rains to a desert area, such as the Gibson in Western Australia, the water pools atop the powder-dry soil. It is an odd phenomenon with which every gardener is familiar: The drier the soil, the greater the runoff of water. The arid dust forms a barrier to the penetration of moisture, so that the rains form muddy rivulets that pour into the erosion gullies and finally into ancient dry streambeds—like the wash beside which Tolo Mason had set up camp on the evening that brought the animosity between him and Terry Forrest to a head.

Desert rain is an example of too much of a good thing too quickly. The bloated clouds burst with spectacular displays of lightning, with cannonades of thunder, and the dry desert gasps with thirst; but at first the ground perversely rejects the gift of water. Thousands of rivulets drain into the wash, and a flash flood is the result. Countless tons of water fill the wash from bank to bank and rush toward the sea. The leading edge of the head rise is a shallow, roiling extension of the thundering wave, like a cowcatcher on a locomotive. Quickly behind the advance ripple comes the vertical wall of water, cresting at the top, carrying driftwood, uprooted brush and grass, even the dead bodies of unwary desert animals. The advancing flood, bearing everything in its path, moves faster than a man can run.

Terry Forrest had seen flash floods, but never from directly in front of the advancing wall of debris-filled water. He was exhausted from his long, battering fight with Tolo Mason, and his brain was numbed. When he first saw the wave, it took precious seconds for him to realize what was happening. He tried to stand, but his legs collapsed under him.

Tolo, too, had seen the onrushing water. He took a few steps toward the bank. He had just enough time to make it.

"Help me, mate," Terry Forrest called out.

Tolo hesitated but a moment, then ran back, lifted Forrest with his hands under his arms, and started dragging him toward the bank, which seemed now to be miles away. Tolo, too, drained by the bruising fight with Forrest, was not at his best, and his arms ached with the weight of the man. His lungs burned with his efforts, and the thundering water came closer, closer. When the first ripples lapped at his boots, he knew that they were not going to reach the bank. The cresting front of the flood was only feet away. He threw himself down, thinking that their best chance of survival was to let the crest of the wave fall over them and pass them by. In those few seconds he knew that if they were to be caught up in the debris that churned on the brunt of the wave, they would be ground up and broken, tossed and twisted, appearing and disappearing on the waters like the carcass of the dead kangaroo that seemed to launch itself directly at him.

The water crashed into them. Tolo had taken a deep, deep breath. He tried to cling to the bed of the wash, but the force was too great. Tumbled over, he felt the dull blows of collision with *things*.

Terry Forrest was holding on to him with the force of sheer panic, and at first that helped, for their combined weight acted as a drag, allowing the deadly crest to pass them. But then Forrest became a dangerous burden.

Tolo reached down, put his hand in the man's hair, and pulled hard. Slapping at Forrest's hands, which clutched him around the waist, he loosened Forrest's grip, then kicked upward, pulling Forrest with him. They were being swirled

downstream, carried by the force of the flood. When Tolo's
lungs began to burn, he feared that they were not going to
survive. He was kicking powerfully, dragging Forrest. And
then his head broke the surface, and he took a gasping breath
that was partially spray; he coughed it out and dragged a
rasping lungful of air through the pain of water in his lungs.

Beside him Forrest was floundering, and Tolo almost lost
his grip on the man's hair. Unable to speak because of the
inhaled water, Tolo gasped and coughed again, his inhalations
nothing but painful, choking spasms. And then, at last, he spit
out water and could breathe freely. Forrest was making odd
sounds and rolling over and over, trying to get his hands on
Tolo. As the current rushed them farther downstream, floating brush and drift smacked against them, sometimes sticking
painful spines into their flesh.

Forrest managed to turn and with one arm clasped Tolo.
Tolo knew that although the motivation was different now, he
was still in a fight with Forrest, this time a fight for their lives,
for if the man managed to get his arms around Tolo and
immobilize Tolo's arms, both of them would drown. He
sighted in a blow, gave it all he had, and cracked his fist into
Forrest's jaw just to one side of the chin. Forrest went limp
and ceased struggling. Tolo turned onto his back and began to
kick toward the bank. Forrest, now inert, floated easily as
Tolo pulled him along.

The water was cold, and it cleared Tolo's head; but having
to dodge heavy floating objects, he found his strength rapidly
giving way. Alone, he could reach the bank, but with Forrest
in tow, he wasn't so sure. And yet he clung to the man's hair,
fought the swift current, and angled slowly, slowly toward the
bank.

When he finally reached the bank, the current continued to
drag him downstream for some time until he managed to
grasp a mulga tree. He clung there for long minutes, one hand
on the plant, the other holding Forrest, until both of his arms
began to ache. Little by little he drew himself up until he was
out of the water, then hauled Forrest up and rolled him onto

his back. Forrest was not breathing. Tolo began to push rhythmically just below the man's diaphragm, and after what seemed an impossibly long time, Forrest gagged and vomited up water and began to gasp for breath.

Tolo fell onto his back and slept.

He awoke in the cold, shivering uncontrollably. Rising, he gathered material for a fire, then pulled his matches from their waterproof carrier. Soon he had a blaze going. He checked Forrest and saw that his eyes were open.

"You pulled me out," Forrest said accusingly.

Tolo turned his back and tended his fire.

"Owe you one, mate," Terry said.

With the first light of dawn Tolo was on his feet. "Can you walk?" he asked Forrest.

"Can a kangaroo hop?" the bushranger answered. But as he tried to get to his feet, he cried out in pain and fell back.

"Well, I thought I was in one piece," he said.

Tolo knelt beside Forrest and pulled up the man's pants leg carefully. The calf muscle was swollen to twice its normal size and was one huge mass of lividity.

"Looks as if something hit you quite a lick," Tolo said.

"Damn," Forrest said, fingering the bruised area gently. "What with all the spinifex spines in my hide, itching and burning, I guess I didn't feel it until I tried to put my weight on it."

"I suspect that Java will ride downstream looking for us," Tolo said.

"I hope she has enough smarts to refill the water barrels before the desert sucks it all up," Forrest said. The flood had passed, and by now only a trickle of water ran down the center of the wash, but there was still water in deeper rocky basins.

"How far do you think we were carried?" Forrest asked.

"Hard to say," Tolo said.

"I couldn't make a guess," Forrest said. "Seems I was out of it, doesn't it?"

"Yes," Tolo agreed.

"You know I don't swim, mate."

"I guessed as much," Tolo said.

"You didn't have to pull me out, did you?"

"I'm not sure you'll understand, but yes, I had to pull you out, or at least I had to try."

The sun rose, bathing the featureless plain in a red glow. They were on the opposite side of the river from where Tolo had pitched camp. Tolo helped Forrest down to the wash, where they drank deeply from a billabong and then took off their clothing to bathe and rinse the sand from their garments. The flood had half filled their pockets with the red dirt of the Gibson.

As the heat of the day came on in full force, they found a bit of shade under the bank of the wash and waited.

The fever came to Forrest with a suddenness that made Tolo fear for the man's life. One minute Terry was lying there sweating in the heat, chewing on a twig, and the next he was red-faced, burning with heat. Then a chill came and his teeth chattered.

Throughout the rest of the day and through a long, almost sleepless night Tolo did what he could, which was little. When Forrest burned with fever, he could cool his brow with water from the billabong. When the racking chills came, he could only put more driftwood on the fire. He wanted to go to Java, knew that she must be frantic with worry, but aside from that, he felt that she was safe. She had the guns. He could not understand why Java had not found them during the day, for by his wildest estimate he could not have been carried more than a few miles by the flood. But she'd show up tomorrow, and then they could dose Forrest with quinine or something.

After another day the fever abated, leaving Terry very weak. There was plenty of water, but no food. Tolo kept his eyes open for the approach of Java and the camels, but nothing moved but the dancing heat waves. As evening approached, he told Forrest, "We're going to have to go to them, you know."

"Give me a hand up," Terry replied. "Maybe we can make it to the next billabong before it gets too dark."

Walking was painful for Terry, because of both his injured leg and the residual effects of the fever. He explained that he had contracted malaria on a gold-hunting trip into the Northern Territory, and the immersion and battering in the flood had apparently triggered a recurrence.

As he assisted the bushranger, Tolo found that his attitude toward him had shifted slightly. The man had been damned cheeky, but he had pluck. And Tolo, after pulling him from the flood and nursing him through his fever, felt yoked to the man by the code of mateship in the bush. The elements had conspired to join them, for the time being at least, regardless of whether Tolo liked it or not.

It was almost dark when they reached the next water hole. "A mob of boongs made camp here," Terry observed. In the fading light he could just see the signs. Then they found the site of the fires.

"Ganba?" Tolo asked.

"Most likely. The boongs don't come into the heart of the Gibson too often."

Tolo scouted the banks and then helped Terry up when he found camel tracks on both banks leading away from the wash. Terry bent to examine the prints.

"Wild camels or ours?" Tolo asked.

"This one was carrying a load," Terry said. "See how the mark of the hoof splays out?"

"So Java came downstream looking for us and ran into Ganba?"

"Looks that way," Terry said. "No worries, mate. Ganba is a scoundrel but no fool. He'd steal the fillings out of your teeth, given the chance, but he wouldn't have the guts to harm a whitefellow woman."

Tolo was remembering that he had been warned more than once about becoming meat food for the Aborigines.

"My guess is, mate, that he'll go on just as before. He'll lead her on a merry chase around the bloody desert, hoping that the Gibson and the sun will kark her off. We'll catch up to them long before that."

They made a fire in the wash near the water hole. The water, Tolo knew, would be gone soon, evaporated by the sun or sucked into the rocky bed of the wash. In the meantime, both he and Terry would make the most of it.

"They had meat," Terry said. There was a lingering smell of it that both men caught.

"Where would they get meat?" Tolo asked.

"Rabbit. Wild camel," Terry said. The smell was quite strong. He sniffed, followed his nose, and saw a bit of white protruding from the sand of the wash. Digging around the bone, he lifted it out. It was a human thighbone. He threw it as far as he could in total disgust.

"Bloody—" He could not finish.

Tolo recovered the bone. His face flushed with fear when he recognized what it was.

"It isn't the little sheila," Terry said. "Notice the curve of the bone. Poor bastard had rickets or something."

"Surely not in this day and time," Tolo stammered. He felt his stomach twist. He buried the bone with his hands and pressed the sand down on it. "Surely they don't still—"

"Bloody hell," Terry said. "Of course, they do. Damn boongs. What we should do is hunt them off the face of the earth."

"She's with them," Tolo said. "She must have seen—"

Terry was moving around painfully. He had found a mulga stick that served him as a cane to take some of the weight off his injured leg. "She started toward the west," he said, examining the ground. "One Abo followed her. And then the tracks come back, cross the wash, and head off north. She was going to head for Mayhew's station, and Ganba talked her out of it. He's leading her off toward the north."

"Look here," Tolo said, "I'm going to have to go on ahead in the morning. I can move much faster than you. You stay here with the water, and when I catch them, I'll come back for you."

"The water here won't last another day," Terry said. "I'd better come with you. Sure, you can move faster than I can, but you won't last long on your own."

"And how would we last longer with you along?"

"Bush tucker," Terry replied. "I'll wager your boongs didn't teach you how to survive out here, since I figure old Ganba's whole purpose was to see you dead."

"I know only what I've read," Tolo admitted.

"Well, there are little things—roots of the potato family. Some of them will kill you within hours if you take one bite, but others are edible and have just enough moisture to keep you alive a little longer." He patted his injured leg. "It's already better. Sore as bloody hell, but better."

"All right, then," Tolo agreed.

They were under way with first light. The trail was easy to follow. "We have three or four days to catch up with them," Terry said. "After that—"

"What do you mean?" Tolo asked.

Terry bent, dug with his walking stick, and held up a tuber. "You can get some nourishment and about a tablespoon of water out of this, mate. If we're lucky, we'll find one or two of them a day. Two tablespoons of water. Enough to keep a man going two, maybe three days."

"I see," Tolo said. "Then we'd best move out, hadn't we?"

When they came upon the dead camels, Terry used a colorful portion of his vocabulary. "A damn waste," he said. "That's a bloody boong for you. Fill his belly and he has no concern for tomorrow." He had shooed away the carrion birds and was working on the carcass with his knife. He cut away the outside rot, the pecked and pierced areas, and ripped out a long muscle from the haunch.

"You're not going to eat that?" Tolo asked.

"No? Just stand and watch," Terry said. He built a fire and

cooked the meat in thin strips, so that it was thoroughly heated, almost burned. And with his mouth watering, Tolo ate his share, blocking out the taste, knowing only that his body was desperate for food.

"We'll catch them tomorrow," Terry said. He was leaning against a boulder, his bare feet near the fire. He was chewing on the well-cooked camel meat. "They're near. I can almost smell them."

The rain came during the night, obliterating the trail. The next morning Tolo led the way northward in desperation, moving at a punishing pace.

They heard the Abos before they saw them. From behind a low ridge the chanting voices came, indistinguishable at times from a sigh of wind that blew out of the storm clouds to the east.

It was Terry who led the way up the slope, covering the last few yards on his belly as Tolo crawled up beside him.

The Abos were camped beside a soak; a hunk of camel meat was roasting over a fire. There was no sign of Java.

Terry punched Tolo in the shoulder and pointed. Ganba was leading the dance and the chant, and as he pranced around the fire, thumping his bare feet onto the ground with audible thuds, he held Tolo's rifle in his hand.

"There are only five of them," Tolo whispered. "And Ganba's wife, Bildana, is not among them."

Aside from Ganba, there were two men and two women. The women were huddled beside a fire of their own, watching the prancing, chanting men nervously.

"First thing to do is get that rifle away from him," Terry whispered.

"But where is Java?" Tolo asked. The camels were dead. The water barrels were empty, scattered along the back trail.

"Well, mate, I reckon we'll have to ask old Ganba about that, won't we?" Terry asked. He motioned to Tolo to crawl back from the crest of the ridge. They found cover in a swale that was filled with spinifex grass, where they waited until the sun had set and the cold night was on them; then they crawled back to the top of the ridge. The Abos were feasting on camel meat and drinking water from waterskins.

It was a long, cold wait until the camp was silent, the fires burned down to embers. Ganba slept with one of the women at the far edge of the camp. Terry led the way, and the two men circled far out, then came up on the camp from the side nearest Ganba. Now and then, when Terry's foot slipped on a stone, he would grunt in pain.

"You," he whispered to Tolo when they were near the camp. He pointed, made a motion as if aiming a rifle.

Tolo crept forward on his hands and knees, making each move slow, feeling the ground to be sure he did not make a noise. As he moved closer to Ganba, who was sleeping in two of Tolo's blankets, the rifle clasped in one hand, Tolo rose to his feet, reached down slowly, grasped the rifle, and yanked. The weapon came free. Ganba, with surprising speed, jumped up out of the blankets. Swinging the rifle by reflex, Tolo caught Ganba in the chin with the butt and sent the Abo tumbling backward.

Terry had moved up. He saw Ganba fall and then roll toward the blankets. He saw Ganba's intention. The pistol was in its holster, lying beside Ganba's kip. Terry leapt, grunted in pain, fell, then grabbed the pistol just before Ganba's hand closed over it.

"Enough," Terry said, pointing the pistol at Ganba's face and thumbing back the hammer.

Tolo heard a noise behind him. He whirled just in time to see one of the Abo men launch a spear. He ducked and lifted the rifle. He pulled the trigger without thinking, and the Abo was thrust backward as the slug took him high in the chest.

A spear grazed Terry's head. He snapped off a shot with the pistol and the other Abo man was down.

A woman screamed. Ganba, dazed, had the fear of death on his face as Tolo stood over him. "Where is she?" Tolo demanded.

Ganba shrugged.

"Do I kill the bloody bastard or do you?" Terry asked.

Ganba looked from one man to the other, clearly grasping the reality of the whitefella's threat. "She left," he said quickly, pressing his hands together imploringly. "In the rain, I tell you. She and my faithless wife. I swear to you, young master, I did her no harm. I had explained to her that the nearest water was to the north—"

"He lies," Terry said.

"Ganba was protecting her, young master." The big mouth was contorted in fear, the dark eyes wide. "I did not touch her. Why she ran away I do not know."

"Did she have water?" Terry asked.

"Yes," Ganba said. "And food."

"Do you know which way she went?" Terry asked.

"I have seen no spoor," Ganba said. "But once she tried to go to the west, toward Mayhew Station."

Terry let the pistol fall. "He's probably telling the truth," he said. "If she and the boong woman did get away, they'd head for Mayhew's. We'll have some of this lad's tucker and borrow a waterskin or two and go after her in the morning."

"Ganba will help."

"Ganba can bloody well get as far away from me as possible," Tolo said. "Why in God's name did you kill all the camels?"

"We needed meat food," the Aborigine said, as if Tolo's question were utterly foolish.

"We saw what was left of some of your meat food," Terry said. He put the pistol in his belt and went to the fire, sawed off a piece of camel meat, and was taking the first bite when he heard Tolo grunt, as if in surprise. He turned quickly.

The spear that protruded from Tolo's back had been put there by one of the women. She had seen her man fall before Tolo's rifle and had waited for her opportunity. A strong woman, she had been standing close, and she had not thrown the spear but rather had thrust it into the whitefella's back on the run. Her aim had been thrown off at the last minute as Tolo moved, so that instead of striking him directly in the spine she had pierced Tolo's side low and to the left. As Terry

Forrest turned to look, Tolo put one hand behind him, clasped the spear, looked at Terry in puzzlement, and sank to his knees.

Terry hesitated only a moment before shooting the woman in the head. She crumpled lifelessly. The other woman started to run, and it took two shots to bring her down. And then he turned the pistol on Ganba.

In that split second a look of surprise crossed Ganba's face, as if he had thought that he, the proud Ganba, was invincible. Then the slug from Terry's pistol took him on the bridge of the nose and slammed into his brain.

Terry knelt beside the fallen Tolo. The spear had penetrated deeply, the entire head of it buried in flesh. Tolo was breathing. His eyes were open but glazed with shock. Terry guessed that the spear had ruined a kidney.

"Well, sport," Terry said, at a loss for words.

"I don't feel anything," Tolo replied.

"There's a bloody great spear in your back, mate."

Tolo began, then, to feel the pain. His face contorted with it.

Terry sighed. "Well, I guess we'll have to have a go at getting it out."

He spread one of the blankets that Ganba had stolen and shifted Tolo onto it. Tolo cried out in agony.

"Sorry, mate," Terry said.

He built up the fire. He found one of the things he needed, a large broad-bladed knife, on one of the dead Abo men and placed it to heat in the embers of the fire. When the fire was blazing well, he took a look at the entry point of the spear and whistled.

"Going to smart a bit, mate," he said as he sliced with his knife.

Tolo let out a startled bellow of pain and then went limp. "Goodonyer," Terry said. "Won't feel a thing now, mate."

When the spearhead came out, a gush of blood came with it. Terry shook his head. Too much blood. He positioned the large, flat blade of the Abo's knife—now white hot—over the wound and pressed it down. He heard the sizzle of heat, smelled the stench of scorched blood and flesh, but after a while the blood stopped flowing. He lifted the knife, examined the cauterized wound, and shook his head. He had done all he could do, so he covered Tolo with the other blanket and went to sleep.

When Terry awoke, Tolo was feverish. Flies had found the blood of the dead boongs, and soon this place would stink to high heaven. Terry took inventory, finding a few tins of food, some lentils and rice, and two waterskins. It might be just enough to get him back to Mayhew's alive, he thought, if it did not take Tolo too long to die.

He had a tin of fruit for breakfast and poured a bit of the juice into Tolo's mouth. Tolo swallowed convulsively. Later he took water but remained in a feverish coma. The carrion birds were working on the woman who lay furthermost from the camp.

"Look, mate," Terry said to the unconscious Tolo, "be a pal and kark it in, won't you? It's a bloody long walk back to the Gascoyne."

By evening the bodies of the Abos had swelled up with the gases of decay. Tolo had not regained consciousness.

"Come on now, mate," Terry begged. The scent of death was in his nose. The thought of spending a night there in that camp with the dead spread around him was a frightening prospect. Ganba's body lay only feet away, and even as Terry contemplated the long night ahead, gases roiled in Ganba's bloated stomach, and there came the long, sighing sound of breaking wind.

"Bloody hell," Terry said, leaping to his feet. He looked down at Tolo. "Sorry, mate," he said.

On impulse he left one of the waterskins. It was a damned foolish thing. "The least I can do," he whispered as he turned his back and fled that place of rumbling corpses and stench. He almost went back for the water. Tolo would have no need of it. Even if he regained consciousness and drank it, it would

merely hasten his death, what with one kidney ruined inside
him.

He walked as fast as his lame leg would allow, putting
distance between him and the scene of the deaths. He carried
both the rifle and the pistol as well as the remaining food.
Walking until the stars of morning were visible, he slept a few
winks and then was moving again with the dawn. Even with
his experience in the waly, there was no guarantee that he
would see Mayhew Station alive.

Chapter XX

THE SECOND WAVE of human invasion of the antipodal continent, those Caucasians who were, early in the twentieth century, developing the finishing touches on their unique national character, had borrowed a few things from those who had come to Australia before them. They had taken place-names: Toowoomba, Penong, Kalgoorlie, Meekatharra. Also the often musical sounds of Aboriginal names for animals—wallaroos and bandicoots. There were other miscellaneous words, too, like billabong and coolabah. And walkabout.

White bushmen had adopted both the term *walkabout* and the urge, but explorers and those who followed in their footsteps into the heart of the continent traveled for reasons very different from those that drove the Aborigines to walkabout. The white man went in search of gold, land, adventure, or simply to see what lay beyond the next rise of arid ground. The Aborigine, caught in the old life pattern of the hunter-gatherer, went walkabout when game became scarce or when native vegetation was consumed or burned by drought. He had been on the move for hundreds of thousands of years, and the pattern was ingrained in him. Accordingly, "tamed" Abos, earning what was for them a good life working on a cattle station, would disappear at unpredictable intervals and, upon return, would simple shrug and say, "Walkabout."

While the principal motivation for being nomadic was the

eternal quest for food, other motives could drive an Aborigine
and his tribal group from one place to another: the need, for
example, to visit some particularly sacred place—a body of
water, or a hill, or a rock that had significance from the time
of the Dreaming. There was an interrelationship between the
blackfellow and the land, for the Aborigine believed in the
oneness of things: He was of the land, and the land was of
him. He and the rocks, the waters, and the trees—all were
joined. Those mysterious beings of the ancient Dreamtime,
those undefined entities that had made the first men, were still
there in the land, embodied in things of nature—in the animals, the rain, the clouds. And the presence of one of those
powerful entities made a place sacred.

Thus it was, even before the time of the coming of the white
man's ships, that men were called to go walkabout, not only
to find new sources of food but to pay tribute to places made
sacred by the wisdom of their own tribe or another tribal
group. Before the white man's law was extended to most parts
of the continent, travel between tribal areas had been limited
and rather dangerous. But in more recent times Aborigines
could travel more freely, sometimes indeed attaching themselves to the peripatetic white man, who seemed bent on exploring all parts of the continent. Thus knowledge of the
sacred places was spread into the homelands and languages of
almost all the Aboriginal tribes, and the impulse to go
walkabout could result in a very long journey, to a place hundreds of miles away. Aborigines became like Christians on
pilgrimage to Jerusalem or Moslems traveling to Mecca. And
of all the sites sought by tribes all over the continent, the
great-red-sacred-rock, known to the whites as Ayers Rock, in
the southwest corner of the Northern Territory, held the
greatest allure.

The knowledge of this sacred rock had reached Uwa—a
man of high degree among his people—in his tribal lands near
the great western sea, in the hills called by the whitefella the
Hamersley Range. Even when Uwa had first heard of the
great-red-sacred-rock, where, it was said, one could return to

the spirit of the Dreamtime and learn from the ancients, he was not a young man. As he prepared for the greatest journey of his life, his several wives and all of his offspring wept and begged him not to go to his death in the arid stretches of the never-never. Young men could cross the burning, waterless vastness, but Uwa was old.

As it turned out, Uwa proved himself as vigorous as any man when it came to living in the never-never. As a young man, while accumulating the wisdom that would elevate him to a man of high degree, he had traveled far and wide, and now his experience served him well. Crossing the never-never, he set a pace that stretched the physical abilities of the younger ones whom he had recruited to accompany him. He conquered the Gibson Desert—although he did not use the whitefella's name for it—with no suffering to himself and without losing a single man or a woman.

In the far lands near the great-red-sacred-rock Uwa meditated and communicated with other men of high degree, men belonging to the tribes of what the whitefella called the Northern Territory. He tranced himself into seeing the entities that flocked over the huge red rock and saw his number one grandson take a wife from the Northern Territory tribes.

When, on the return trip, Uwa and his small band of half a dozen little families—babies had been born during the pilgrimage—paused to praise the spirits for the rain that had come to give them much-needed water, they had recrossed two-thirds of the never-never and could begin to think of arriving at their home territory before the next full moon.

While the women and the young ones played in the rock-bottomed billabongs left in the wash, Uwa and two of the younger men hunted. It was not the best of hunting grounds, but Uwa proved his worth by bagging a rabbit. Then he saw the tracks of a lone dingo and followed them. It was growing hot, the sun moving toward its zenith, when he first noted the soaring carrion birds at a distance. Curiosity led him onward. He hoped that perhaps some accident had befallen a wild camel and that he could steal edible meat from the scavengers before it spoiled too badly. But that hope faded when his nose caught the unmistakable stench of rotting flesh.

He topped a rise and looked down upon a place of the dead. The two young men who had been hunting apart from him now joined him, and they, too, stood watching the birds fight over the already mutilated bodies of no fewer than five people —three men and two women. Uwa gave orders, and the two young men ran down the slope, shouting and brandishing their spears. Then Uwa walked curiously among the dead. All of them, including the women, had died of gunshot wounds. He wondered what had occurred until he saw the remains of the body of a particularly big man. There was enough of the chest skin left intact for Uwa to see the ceremonial markings of a Baadu of Warrdarrgana. He shook his head. He himself had eaten human meat food, but neither he nor anyone else in his tribe was a blood drinker. Perhaps, he thought, the final fight that had left five Baadu dead had been precipitated by a Baadu attempt to secure one of their favorite meals.

A shout turned his head, and he hurried, galvanized by the urgency of the call, to a spot where his companions had found a whitefella who was very, very sick. A big whitefella, he lay on his stomach, burning with fever. A young man pointed to the cauterized wound on the whitefella's back.

"A hole to let the life out of him," the young man said.

"And yet he fights to live," Uwa replied.

A waterskin lay near the whitefella. Uwa squatted and squeezed drops of the muddy liquid onto the whitefella's lips. A swollen tongue moved, licking at the water.

"The *djugurba* will walk here tonight," said one of the young men uneasily. He spoke of the things of the desert, partly human, partly animal or reptile or bird.

The whitefella was greedily licking at the drops of water; Uwa doled them out slowly, knowing that it would not be good to give too much water at once. When Uwa stopped, the whitefella groaned and opened his eyes.

"You drink little now, little later," Uwa instructed.

"Please," the whitefella croaked.

"Will he die, Grandfather?" asked one of the young men.

"Only those of the Dreaming can say," Uwa said. "We will move him from this place."

"I welcome a leave-taking from this stink," said Uwa's number one grandson.

"Perhaps moving him will finish the job that these tried to do," Uwa said, indicating the dead blackfellas.

"Another whitefella was here," said the grandson. He pointed to the tracks that Terry Forrest had made in leaving.

"Handle this one gently," Uwa ordered.

"Would it not be kinder to leave him here to die?"

"We will give him warmth in the night with-fire. We will give him water and food," Uwa said. "If he dies, then it is the will of the Dreaming and not of our doing."

"That is true," said the grandson, lifting Tolo's feet while his companion put his hands under Tolo's arms and heaved. "This one is heavy."

Tolo made one grunting protest and then sank back into his merciful state of coma. At the campsite the women applied a poultice to his wound, as well as leaves carried all the way from their homeland, and they took turns squeezing drops of water onto his lips.

There was some grumbling when Uwa announced that they would camp here as long as the billabong held water or until the whitefella died. Uwa told them sternly to use their time profitably, to look for the edible tubers that made life possible in the never-never, to hunt *mamuru,* the long-haired rat of the spinifex plains. The whitefella would live or die in his own time. That it would be death seemed almost certain when, as a result of the water that the women rationed out to the injured man, he urinated and it was red with blood. But in the cool of evening he opened his eyes and took food.

It took three days for the sun to evaporate the last of the surface water in the wash. Uwa knew that he must move on. The whitefella was experiencing periods of semiconsciousness during which he prattled in his own language. Uwa's grandson, who spoke a little English, said that the whitefella's words did not make sense.

"He will die," the grandson said, "for he still passes blood. It would be kinder to end it for him than merely to leave him here to die alone."

"We will do neither," Uwa said. He showed them how to use the limited materials available, strong mulga sticks and a blanket, to rig a litter. The young men complained but did as they were told, and soon the mob was under way, with the whitefella riding in the litter carried by four of the men.

Water was scarce now, and the food inadequate even for those who were accustomed to meager bush tucker. Uwa saw to it that the whitefella got more than his share of the water, and he watched interestedly as the women got the man to swallow mashed-up starches from the tubers.

The grandson grumbled, "It seems that the whitefella will live all the way to our homeland." For with each day the man seemed to grow stronger. He stayed awake for longer periods, and his words were delivered in a more orderly manner. His urine no longer contained blood; but when the grandson tried to make him stand, his legs gave way weakly, and he crumpled to the ground. Then, just when it seemed that the whitefella was gaining the use of his legs, the wound began to fester. The fevers came again, and in spite of the women's efforts to scrape away the stinking dead flesh around the wound, their patient sank once more into a coma.

And still Uwa would not give up. The spirits of the Dreaming came to him in the night, in a sleeping dream, and there he saw the whitefella—he had come to think of him as *his* whitefella—strong and powerful, joining Uwa in a hunt, bringing down a great juicy kangaroo at an incredible distance with a native spear.

"The spirits of the Dreamtime have spoken to me," Uwa announced at dawn. "The whitefella will live." He insisted this day on taking his turn at one corner of the litter, and the drained face of the whitefella, his limpness, caused him almost to despair. But the spirits of the Dreamtime had spoken, and he would not allow the whitefella to die. He would keep him alive by the force of his own will.

Terry Forrest had been in some tight places before. He had done his tour in the old queen's war in South Africa, and he had seen men die—Aussies, Brits, and Boers. He'd come close to death himself a couple of times, but never as close as he came before he stumbled down to one of Jonas Mayhew's water holes in the dry bed of the Gascoyne.

Later, even after he had glutted himself with water and huge slabs of roast mutton, Mayhew's scales showed that he'd lost more than forty pounds in his trek from the camp where Ganba and the others had died. He had pushed himself to the limit each day, resting only in the torrid noontime, walking onward long after dark. He had known that his chances for survival were in direct proportion to the amount of time that he took to reach the Gascoyne with its life-giving soaks. There was a delicate balance between exertion, the time consumed, and the skin of water that he carried.

He made the walk in ten days, the last two without water. He was weak and disgusted. At first he rebuffed all of old man Mayhew's questions, but he knew that sooner or later he would have to answer to someone about Tolo Mason and his pretty little wife. He hadn't thought much about that during his dash for life across the western Gibson. Now, under the questioning stare of Jonas Mayhew, he put together the story that if necessary, he would tell to the authorities later.

"That Ganba and his bloody boongs," he told Mayhew, "wanted all of the equipment. Ganba was leading Mason on a chase, taking him into the driest parts of the waly, just waiting for him and the girl to die so that he could get his hands on the food, the guns, the camping equipment, and the money that Mason had with him."

"The boy took money into the outback?" Mayhew asked.

Terry nodded. He knew very well, to the pound, how much money Tolo had carried in his pack, for that money now was safely tucked away in Terry's own wallet. He had removed it from Tolo's possessions, rationalizing that money would be needed to send a rescue expedition to recover the remains for the boy's family off in Sydney.

He told Mayhew the rest of it, how he and Mason had been caught in the flash flood and all the events that followed up to the time that the boong woman put the spear into Mason's back. In his telling he altered the facts only slightly. He left out any mention of a fight between Mason and himself, and he said that the spear thrust killed Mason almost immediately.

The girl? "Well, I can only guess," he said. "She had one friend among the boongs, old Ganba's wife. Her name was Bildana. She must have known that sooner or later the little whitefellow lady would be tender meat food for Ganba and the others. And since Bildana had sided with the white sheila, old Ganba was down on her. When the boongs killed the camels—you know how they are, a meal in the hand is worth feasts in the future—and then ate one of their own, it must have made Mrs. Mason understand the immediate danger she was in. She and Bildana took off and got away from old Ganba in the rain. We lost her trail, too, because of the rain. We figured she would head for the station here."

"Logical thing to do, but would she have known enough to be logical?" Mayhew asked. "And wouldn't the Abos have guessed that she'd head west?"

" 'Strewth," Terry said. Bildana would have known that. And Java Mason wasn't stupid. "The sheila went east!" It hadn't occurred to him before, but the thought had a ring of truth. "Bildana would have known that Ganba would be able to overtake them if they went in the direction he expected them to go. Bildana knew how to live in the waly. Yes, by God, they went east. They're going to try to make it all the way across."

"Well, you'll never find her bones, then," Mayhew said.

"Don't bet on her dying," Terry said. "She's a tough little bird. And that Abo woman would know what to eat, where to find the soaks and the bores."

In that moment, although he was still weak, Terry made his

decision. He had not felt guilty about leaving Tolo to die, for a man with a spear through his kidney had only a short time to live. He knew that he, too, would have died if he had tried to drag Tolo along with him or if he had tried to search for Java Mason. No, guilt as such did not enter Terry's mind, only speculation that was part of a chain of reasoning. What if he hadn't had eyes for the little bird and thus raised Tolo's hackles? What if he hadn't felt compelled to find out who had the harder head, he or Tolo Mason? What if he'd paid more attention to the damned boongs when he and Tolo caught up with them?

"Mayhew, I took the boy's money off him." He shrugged. "No sense leaving it there to rot in the desert. I'm going to use that money to go out there again. First I'll find him and bury him, and then I'll find the little sheila. I owe that much to them, don't I?"

"Do you?" Mayhew asked.

The way the old man looked at him made Terry uncomfortable, for he himself was not sure of his reasons for wanting to go back out into the blasting heat and emptiness of the Gibson. Was it guilt? Or was it merely that one of his idle daydreams now had a chance, a slim chance, of coming true? After all, the husband was dead. The girl was alone in the Gibson with an Abo woman. From the time he first left Perth, he had fantasized about being alone in the desert with Java. That she was alive was, he felt, a certainty. God simply would not allow the waste of such a tasty tidbit of femininity. And the girl had guts. She'd fight the waly to a standstill and survive.

"I'll need four camels," Terry said.

"Going to go it alone, are you?" Mayhew asked.

"Are you volunteering to go with me?"

"Not on your bloody life," Mayhew retorted. "I lost a woman to this country. It'll get me in the end, it will, but when it karks me, I'll be in my bed or very close by it." He stood and went to stand at the end of his porch, looking eastward. "If I know Abos, they'll be moving very slow. They don't believe in pushing it. I think you're a damned fool for wanting to go, but there's a chance she might be alive. The Abos live in places where a white man would die of hunger and thirst, and she has one of them to guide her. She acted like a little gal with some spunk when she was here. As you say, she may be alive—if a snake hasn't crawled into the kip with her or if another mob of Abos hasn't come along to make meat food out of her and the blackfellow woman, too. *Or* if they haven't missed a soak and died of thirst. They'll be traveling from soak to soak, of course, hitting the bores, too. I'd say that if you traveled fast and direct, carrying enough water to skip a couple of the soaks, you might catch 'em in the dunes."

Terry gave himself a few days to fatten his spare body on good mutton, giving Jonas a few more pounds of Tolo's money to ease the man's complaints that he was being eaten out of house and home. The delay was not all self-indulgence, for water barrels had to be sent for, and that meant a trip to the trading station by the tame Abos on Mayhew's place. When Terry was finally ready, when the four camels were well watered and well fed, the pack animals well balanced, the riding saddle in place, Terry nodded to old Mayhew. "Well, mate, I'll drop you a postal card from Ayers Rock."

"You do that," Mayhew said.

Chapter XXI

LOUIS SABITIER, *résident supérieur* in the Annamese capital city at Hue, was more than a political appointee. He had earned his position by fighting as a field commander in the long and bitter wars of conquest in Indochina. It was generally admitted in both France and Indochina that for once the government in Paris had named the right man for the job, for through his able administration Sabitier had gained the respect, if not the love, of the Annamese against whom he had earlier fought.

Louis Sabitier had been a young platoon leader in 1873, when Francis Garnier occupied the Tonkin city of Hanoi, on the Red River. He had fought with Garnier in the terrible Red Delta campaign, during which the French faced the same sort of guerrilla tactics that would so bedevil the British in South Africa a quarter of a century later.

Tonkin, including Hanoi and the entire Red Delta, was under Annamese dominion. The Annamese were a proud people, and the ruling family still resented the fact that the French had forced open trade upon them during the reign of Guinevere Gorel's grandfather, Nguyen III. Annamese rulers used their gold to bring in Chinese mercenaries—the Black Flag Society of Yunnan—to help undermine French control. The ongoing battle ended in somewhat of a stalemate; the French leader died, but the new Annamese emperor, Tu Duc, was forced to accept French guidance of state policy and to maintain open trade between Annam and France. France assumed protectorate status over a country that still seethed with resentment.

In 1880 Tu Duc turned away from France, again enlisting the aid of China's Black Flag Society. And once again Louis Sabitier went into the field, fighting a jungle war that seemed impossible to win. Hanoi had to be retaken. Hue, royal seat of the emperor Tu Duc, came under siege, and after almost a year a new emperor, Hiep Hoa, was forced to accept French terms. Louis Sabitier, having had enough of the Nguyen family, was instrumental in naming Dong Khanh emperor of Annam. Dong Khanh was called by his own people a running dog, a willing tool of the French, but at last an uneasy peace came to French Indochina.

It was the French intention to unify all of the peninsula into one colony. Toward this end a governor-generalship was created in 1887, and in 1898 the French decreed that there would be a common budget to build roads and railways to link the territories. Only a few men, Louis Sabitier among them, warned that no social or economic links had ever existed between Annam and Tonkin and the more easily pacified Cochin China to the south.

In a report to his superiors in France, Sabitier wrote:

> *The relative ease with which we seized control of the areas of Cochin China, when contrasted with the hard-fought campaigns on the Red Delta, foretell, I believe, the inevitable dominance of the more aggressive Annamese in Indochina, if we allowed such a development as unification. We will have to be on our guard in the future lest we be faced with a united Indochina that we have not envisioned: a united country under the dominance of the Annamese.*

Louis Sabitier had just concluded participation in the regular meeting of the Conseil Supérieur de l'Indochine and was engaged in trying to catch up on his correspondence when his secretary entered his office and told him that a Mrs. Guine-vere Gorel, née Nguyen, requested an audience with the *résident supérieur*.

"Send her away," Sabitier snapped. "I have no time for tourists."

"Sir," the secretary said, after clearing his throat, "she claims to be the granddaughter of the Emperor Nguyen the Third."

Sabitier dropped the papers he had been examining and rubbed his chin. "Yes, there was a granddaughter who married an Englishman." Sabitier had always operated on the theory that knowledge of one's enemy made up for a lack of soldiers. He had made a thorough study of Annamese history. "You may send her in."

The *résident supérieur* was a man, a Frenchman, and a soldier who had spent much time in the field in the past two decades. Having seen, admired, and sampled the delights of Annamese womanhood, he was aware that Annamese women were among the world's most beautiful and that by traditions akin to customs in China, Annamese women were trained from childhood to please men. He was prepared, therefore, to see a beautiful Annamese woman. When he saw the splendid mixture of French and Annamese blood that was Guinevere Gorel, he was galvanized into action. He leapt to his feet and hurried around his desk to take Guinevere's hand and offer her a chair. His smile and his interest were quite genuine, and without even hearing Guinevere's request, he assured her that nothing would be denied her as his guest.

When, however, his questions had revealed Guinevere's method of arrival—passenger on an Australian cargo ship—and her intent—to determine if certain members of her family, especially an aunt, were still alive—his natural caution when it came to Annamese affairs of state quickly regained the upper hand.

"What you ask could be difficult," Sabitier began cautiously. "Aren't you aware that the Nguyen family no longer inhabits the emperor's palace?"

"I have heard that the upstart Dong Khanh sits on the ancient throne," Guinevere replied.

It was natural enough for her to express her harsh feelings about the new emperor, for the incumbent ruler was not a Nguyen and therefore, in her eyes, inferior. Sabitier nodded understandingly, and thought.

After decades of war the country was relatively peaceful. The last thing he wanted, or needed, with the drive for unification of all the Indochina territories moving forward at flank speed, was to have a resurgence of Annamese national pride triggered by the presence of a member of the old Nguyen family. The Annamese were just belligerent enough to rally around a Nguyen and throw the whole peninsula into chaos again.

He looked at Guinevere, who was smiling at him now from her seat opposite his desk. He had never seen a tastier-looking morsel. Like most Frenchmen, he fancied himself to be a good judge of women and a superior lover. He was torn between love and duty. His common sense told him to put this little one on a ship as quickly as possible and send her on her way to her English husband in New Guinea.

Guinevere was silent, staring at the *résident supérieur*. Whether she fully appreciated the delicacy of Sabitier's political position was doubtful, but she obviously could tell when a man was vacillating between his wishes and his responsibilities. Her next words tipped the balance. "It has been such a long time since I last saw the city of my birth," she said, her smile blazing. "Would it be too great an imposition to ask you, sir, to be my guide?"

Sabitier's decision was made even easier by the eager, pleading position she now assumed, leaning forward in her chair to show that unlike most Annamese females, she had the breasts of a mature woman, not a young girl.

The results were beyond anything Sabitier could have expected. He gave her a tour of the city, a trip marred only by a bitter remark from Guinevere about changes made by the French. But this was quickly forgotten during a superb dinner in a French restaurant that would have been counted among the best in Paris itself. Then there was moonlight on the veranda of the *résident supérieur*'s *maison*, and delicious wine that had made the long trip from the vineyards of France to Hue by diplomatic pouch.

Later, in Sabitier's bedroom, Guinevere held his head in her perfumed lap. "I have come home," she whispered, "not only to my country but to a man who knows that he is a man."

It was evident to Sabitier, who had not expected his conquest to be so easy, that the woman wanted something. He was intrigued. Possibly he might find some way of using her wishes to advance his political career? Or was he merely using that as an excuse to keep her with him, to have her scented, smooth, heated limbs entwined with his, to know her moist and lubricious softness, to make a study of the most desirable, the most sensuous, the most skillful woman he had ever known?

Guinevere went alone to Simon Yates's ship, leaving the official carriage waiting as she went aboard.

She had given Sabitier a memorable performance, and she was exultant. Her luck had never run so good. The first man she had met in Hue had turned out to be not only rich but also a man of position. From the security of his *maison* she would be able to live the kind of life that she had been missing in the chill old house in Suffolk.

She found Simon Yates on the bridge. "Simon, I have decided to stay in Hue," she said without prelude.

The Australian raised one eyebrow. "After only one night ashore?" He grinned. "I knew you were good, luv, but that's very fast work."

"I encountered an old friend," Guinevere said, not wanting to have to go into detailed explanations that were certainly none of Simon's business. She had enjoyed her cruise with Simon, but when compared with the sophistication, the polish, the amatory skills of Louis Sabitier, he came off badly. "There is a man here to gather my things."

"Time for a lingering good-bye, luv?" Simon asked.

She knew what he meant, but she had made it plain from the beginning that her relationship with Simon would be nothing more than an interlude. What had he called her? "The finest and most prolific source of the naughties that I've ever met." There was no doubt that alongside Sabitier, Yates was a vulgarian. But he was an honest chap, obviously fond of her, and she felt a twinge.

"No, I'm sorry," she said sincerely. She tiptoed to him and kissed him lightly on the mouth. "But I'll remember you."

"No message to hubby up in New Guinea?"

"Not at the moment," she said with a little smile.

It was quite grand, living in the *résident supérieur*'s official residence. The servants recognized that Guinevere was accustomed to command and accepted her without question. Louis Sabitier was both amused and pleased to see her take charge of his household. Sabitier told her that the meals were now better, and the entire place was acquiring a sheen of cleanness that had been lacking when the house was a bachelor *ménage*.

The status quo might have continued indefinitely, with Guinevere the unquestioned authority over household matters. But she soon evinced an interest in affairs outside the house. After attending a ball given for the members of the foreign diplomatic corps, with almost no Annamese present, she asked, "Where were the representatives of the emperor?"

"Oh, they were told that it was to be a dull affair with dull Brits, dull Germans, and other dull foreigners," Sabitier told her. "A routine duty affair to repay social obligations, that's all."

"And didn't they resent not being invited?"

"Not at all. They were grateful to be spared an evening of trying to understand the dull words of foreigners."

"When will I be able to speak with someone from the palace?" she asked casually. "I would like to find out about my aunt and some few other relatives."

"I can inquire for you," he said.

When, after a few weeks of pleasant living in the official residence, it became evident that Sabitier had no intention of letting her talk with anyone at the palace, Guinevere began to be a bit concerned.

In the end, suspicion, misunderstanding, the Annamese talent for intrigue and love of war, and a Frenchman's experience in a country that had led him to mistrust everything Annamese—all these contributed to Guinevere's downfall. She precipitated it by wondering why Louis Sabitier was so determined to keep her from having contact with any member of Dong Khanh's royal family or even a member of his staff. If the Frenchman was so intent on isolating her, some benefit would surely accrue to her if she managed to evade his efforts. She dreamed dreams, in which she saw herself a welcome guest at court, dressed in the royal colors, adorned with some of the crown jewels that she had once been allowed to wear while her grandfather was alive.

Guinevere's plans to contact the emperor might have succeeded if she had been more astute in her choice of a messenger. As it was, she chose the one housemaid who had reason to hate her, for Guinevere had replaced the young Annamese woman in Sabitier's bed. Instead of delivering her message to the palace as instructed, the housemaid took it directly to Louis Sabitier's office.

The note was simply a request to the emperor to put Guinevere in touch with her aunt, with details about the aunt—age, maiden name, and last known residence. But Sabitier knew that things were not always as they seemed in the Orient. An isolated pocket of armed resistance to the emperor's tax collectors had flared up in the past few days, and there were rumors that the old enemy, the Black Flag Society, was in action in one of the far northern provinces.

Sabitier could not quite figure out what a member of the

Nguyen family could gain by being in touch with Dong
Khanh, who had been chosen by the French to replace a
Nguyen emperor, but he was in no mood to waste energy
finding out. He had enough on his mind as it was. Like a
circus juggler who spins many plates on sticks and must keep
them all going at once, he had numerous important affairs
going at the same time. Like the juggler, he was being pulled
this way and that, with barely enough time to keep one plate
spinning before having to run to others to keep them from
falling.

After a splendid night, during which the deepest resources
of both Guinevere and Sabitier were called upon, Guinevere
was awakened by the same girl who had betrayed her. "You
are to get up," the girl said rudely.

"Go away," Guinevere said sleepily. "Leave me or I will
have you thrashed."

The maid walked to the door to Guinevere's bedroom and
said, "She refuses to rise."

The door was pushed open. Two Annamese gendarmes
stood in the doorway. "You will get dressed quickly," one of
them said.

"Get out of my bedroom," Guinevere said coldly.

One of the policemen nodded to the other. He walked to
the bed and threw back the covers. Guinevere was nude.
"How dare you?" she cried, reaching for the covers.

The policeman took her arm and jerked her roughly to her
feet. "You will get dressed. Or do you prefer that we carry
you wrapped in a sheet?"

Guinevere spoke to the maid by name. "Send for Monsieur
Sabitier immediately!"

The maid laughed. The policeman ripped a sheet off the bed
and advanced toward Guinevere, the sheet held up to wrap
her.

"I will get dressed," she said. "Please leave me."

"Five minutes," the policeman allowed. He turned to the
girl. "You, begin to pack her things."

No one would listen, not even when Guinevere forgot her dignity and began to scream out in protest as she was led from Sabitier's residence. In front of the house a police van waited, the horses standing placidly, heads down. "Help me," Guinevere cried out, "I am being kidnapped."

And then she saw Louis Sabitier across the street. He stood beside another Annamese policeman. He gave her a curt little bow and threw her a kiss. She was bundled into the police van, and after a rough, jolting ride she was helped out and escorted up the gangway of a ship. Her cabin was not as luxurious as Simon Yates's captain's quarters had been. The ship was Japanese, and there were no invitations to the captain's table. Her food was served in her quarters.

Shortly after the departure from Hue a letter was delivered to her.

"My most beautiful Annamese flower," Louis Sabitier had written. *"Why couldn't you have been content to rule my home without further ambitions? Sending you away has cost me dearly. I hope that you, too, will know some small feeling of loss."*

She muttered old Annamese oaths. She would have been content to rule nothing more than Sabitier's house. Had he truly believed that she was some sort of threat to the order of things as they were in Annam? If only he had spoken openly with her, she could have reassured him that she had no interest in politics or government. She felt bereft and hopeless, not for having lost the Frenchman—for he was only another man —but for having failed to achieve exactly the sort of life that she deserved.

She had the run of the deck while the ship was at sea, but in Hong Kong and Nagasaki she was confined to her cabin. She was allowed on deck at several island stops in the Bonin and Marianas Islands. The ship steamed into equatorial heat, made a stop in German New Guinea, and then she was being off-loaded, like a piece of unwanted cargo, at what was obviously a tropical hellhole, Port Moresby.

The Japanese had allowed her to send a cablegram from

Nagasaki. Trevor was waiting on the ramshackle dock, a bouquet of odd, fleshy flowers in his hand.

Guinevere was a patient woman. Fate had been against her in Indochina, but fate would bring other opportunities to find a place in life that was suitable for a princess of old Annam. Meanwhile, she felt a small thrill of need when she went into Trevor's arms, for although some of the Japanese crew members had ogled her during the voyage from Hue to Port Moresby, there hadn't been a real man aboard the ship.

"Darling, darling," she whispered, "how I've missed you. Take me to our home, quickly."

Chapter XXII

KIT VAN BUREN sat in a rocking chair that had been built to Matt's specifications from native bamboo. Matt was on the slopes, supervising the planting of more coffee trees. Below her the green stream tumbled over exposed rocks. Matt had chosen to build a viaduct of wood to bring water to the house from above, and the water was collected in a tank on the slope behind the house. The force of gravity put running water in Kit's kitchen and the bathrooms.

Although the sun was warm, the temperature was comfortable. A scent of freshness was in the air—the pungent but not unpleasant aromas of colorful crotons and aromatic grasses. A hushed aura of peace, tinged by expectancy, enclosed the house on the slope and the valley that lay between it and the mists of the distant mountains.

The expectancy was mostly in Kit's mind. That morning, shortly after she had struggled out of bed to fix Matt's breakfast, over his protests, she had experienced the first upheavals. Inside her womb the baby turned, and the motion was different from any she had felt before. And yet the contractions were not labor pains—not yet.

She had not mentioned this development to Matt. In fact, she had shamelessly lied to him, telling him that the baby was not due for at least two weeks. It was too late to take her down the mountain to the doubtful cleanliness of the infirmary in Port Moresby, but not too late to send for the missionary doctor who came to the valley occasionally. Kit had decided that she wanted to have her baby in her own home, with the aid of two wise old native women who were astute enough to listen to her.

"I know that in your village, when it is time for the child to come, you have the mother squat," Kit told the two old midwives. "That is not the way British women have children. I will be lying down on my back—"

"The spirits of the birthing will not be able to see clearly," one of the old midwives complained.

"*My* God will see, and he will know what to do," Kit persisted.

She had been working with the two women for weeks now, and she was sure that they would do as they had been taught. "All you must do," she repeated to them often, "is guide the child's shoulders. You will not pull and tug on the child. When the child's shoulders are clear, you will hold both hands under him and he will fall into your hands. At that time you will lift him and hold him by his heels. . . ."

The midwives understood, but they were still unconvinced that the spirits of the birthing would be able to pull the child from the womb with the mother lying on her back.

The two old women came trudging up the hill from the village, led by one of the household girls, who was dressed in nothing more than a short grass skirt. The two midwives were dressed more modestly, their breasts covered. But as the three native women mounted the steps and stood gazing at Kit's stomach, Kit saw that the skin of the two midwives was encrusted with dirt collected by the rancid pig fat that they used to protect their skin from the sun.

"First you will go down to the stream," Kit instructed, "where you will remove your clothing and wash yourselves thoroughly with soap."

The two women protested. "Am I not paying you well?" Kit demanded. "If you want to aid me in delivering my child, you must do as I say or I will send for women from the next village."

It was the threat of insult, of having the white woman bring in midwives from a rival village, that sent the two women down the hill to the creek.

"And don't apply the pig fat to your skin after you have washed," Kit called out as they went down the steps, grumbling to themselves.

While they were gone, their laughter and shrill cries assured Kit that once into their bath they were enjoying it, and when they came back, they smelled better. In the meantime, Kit had twice felt sharp contractions. A third came as the women returned and stood before her.

"Ah," said one of the midwives as Kit held her breath and grimaced.

"Now you will go to the kitchen," Kit said when the contraction was over. "You will remove your clothing and put on the gowns that are there. You will then wash your hands, arms, and faces thoroughly with soap, using the hot water that is in a large pan on the cookstove."

"Wash more?" one of the women asked in disbelief. "Never have I known a woman more overcome with washing."

It was not a typical first birth. The two native women, having seen many, many young brides suffer cramps and contractions for long, long hours, even days, had settled in to enjoy the limitless supply of sweet tea and little cakes when Kit summoned them with gasping urgency.

"Waa!" said the oldest, having lifted the sheet.

"You must get on your feet, mistress," said the other. "The child comes."

Kit knew that the baby's head was exposed. Her water had broken while the midwives were washing and donning the simple white gowns that she had made for the purpose. The contractions had become close and regular and increasingly strong, and pelvic dilation had proceeded with a force that made her wonder if she were being torn apart.

She felt another contraction coming and strained down. Only the crown of the baby's head was exposed.

"You must get to your feet and let the spirits of the newborn aid you," a midwife begged.

She strained and prayed. Again and again, and yet there was no change. The top of the baby's head was there, but the pelvic opening would not allow the child's shoulders to exit. Each contraction seemed to be stronger, more painful.

"To your feet," one of the women insisted. Both of them now lifted her, forcing her to stand and then squat on the bed. She felt a huge contraction coming, pushed with it, felt herself tear, screamed out once, and felt the midwife's hands. She felt a sliding sensation as the baby's shoulders, having expanded her to the maximum without attaining the freedom that nature demanded, tore her flesh and then cleared her, adding blood to the natural lubricity of the birth fluids. The baby popped into the midwife's hands.

"It is a man-child," both of the native women said at once.

Kit, near fainting, heard the first cry. It was a weak little protest that grew almost instantly into an angry wail. She fell backward onto the bed and laughed delightedly. She laughed because she had done it the native way after all—squatting as the women of the tribe had done since time immemorial—and because her son had very healthy lungs.

Now the two women were at their best as they tended the weakened Kit, one of them severing the cord with one nip of her teeth, the other cleaning away the fluids of birth. Kit was allowed to hold the squirming red-faced bundle that was still protesting loudly the transition from comfortable womb to the world. He had ten toes and ten fingers and a nose and eyes and ears all in the right places.

"He is a man," said a midwife. "Big at birth, big in manhood." She reached out and fondled the baby's tiny little penis. "Ah, the pleasure he will give to his woman. He will be a big man, and the shape of this tells me that he will be a man of fire in his desires."

Kit had ceased to be shocked by the native penchant for

touching genitals, and at that time she paid no heed to the old woman's prediction based on what to her looked like a normal-sized baby's penis.

"Send the girl to tell Mr. Van Buren," she ordered.

Her son was learning how to nurse from her milk-swollen breast when Matt slammed into the room, all man scent and perspiration. He skidded to a halt on the hardwood floor, his eyes wide. One hand leapt up to remove his hat.

"Kit?"

"Can't really tell yet," she said, "but I think he has your eyes."

"A boy?" He couldn't stop his giggling laughter. Kit looked at him, saw the love in his eyes, and joined him in laughter until he bent, kissed her on the cheek, and then peered at the puckered little face that was half buried in her breast.

"I'm going to have plenty of milk. We won't need a wet nurse."

"What?" He looked up at her, his eyes shining. "Oh, yes. Is he all right?"

"Of course. He's a beautiful, healthy baby. Why do you ask?"

"Well, he looks so . . . wrinkled. So red."

She laughed. "And so did you when you were fresh from the womb, where you floated in liquid."

"You're sure?"

"I'm sure."

They had spent many pleasant hours trying to choose a name for the baby. Kit, certain that it would be a boy, had not even considered feminine names. Matt had concentrated on both male and female names, but neither of them had come to any conclusion. And yet when Kit had first seen the boy, his name had leapt into her mind with a certainty. And that name had not even been high on her mental list until she saw her baby's face.

"He is Matthew Grant Van Buren," she said.

Matt opened his mouth to protest. He had not wanted a boy to be named after him. She held up her hand.

"He told me so," she said, smiling and nodding. "He said, 'I am Matthew because I am my father's son. I am Grant, and that is what I will be called, because my mother likes the sound of it.' "

"Well, if he says so," Matt said, grinning inanely. Now that it was decided, he seemed to savor the name as it fell from Kit's pale lips.

"And now, my darling husband, I am quite tired, and I think I will sleep for a week or two. Wake me only when my son, Grant, is hungry."

One of the native midwives took the baby, wrapped him well, and placed him, sleeping, in a carry box that Matt had made himself. He sat beside the bed as Kit allowed her heavy eyes to close. Soon she was breathing evenly and deeply.

Lord God, Matt prayed silently. *Thank you for this day. Thank you for my wife, your greatest gift to me on this earth. Thank you for allowing her to give me a son.*

He sat there until the twilight came and the sound of a baby's cry reminded him forcefully that he was now a father. The cry woke Kit.

"Run along," she said. "You must be famished."

"Not really. Can't I watch him—can't I watch Matthew Grant eat his tucker?"

"Lecherous old man," Kit teased. But she was pleased. The boy pushed his little red face into the warmth of her breast and nuzzled until his mouth found the swollen nipple. "Ouch you little bushranger," Kit said, wincing. She looked up and smiled. "And he hasn't even got teeth yet."

Chapter XXIII

TOLO MASON HAD no accurate way to estimate how long it had been since he and Terry Forrest had caught up with Ganba and the other Aborigines in the desert. For the rest of his life this would be a blank period in his memory, a time that would be forever hazy. His first memories after feeling that numbing blow to his back—after having reached back in puzzlement to have his hand close on the shaft of a spear—were of a high, rocky place with odd greenery and running water. Those were the hazy days.

It took him a long time, perhaps as long as a month, to gain enough strength to sit up for a few minutes. He suffered attacks of dizziness that made him so weak he could only fall back onto his vermin-infested blanket. His mind worked only partially; a dullness in his brain protected him from the knowledge of his loss of Java and from feeling frustration over his helpless condition. He was aware of the activity around him, hearing the voices and inhaling the pungent odors of the Aboriginal camp. Sometimes the scent of the Abos' food was as terrible as the odor of the unwashed, grease-covered bodies of the women who tended him.

Later, when his mind was becoming more alert, he tried to ward off lonely thoughts of Java by becoming a perfect pest to any of the Aborigines of Uwa's tribe who would put up with his endless efforts to learn their language. He bored all of the adults. They soon tired of playing word games with him, of giving the names of objects to which he pointed. They laughed at his attempts to communicate, for the Baadu words he had learned from Ganba's people were a foreign tongue to Uwa's tribe. He was reduced to bribing children to talk with him. He would gain their attention by making faces, and they would point and giggle and call him the crazy whitefella. He would perform little feats of magic, elementary things that he had learned long ago from his tutor, Dane de Lausenette, whose odd death was one of the reasons for his fascination with the Aboriginal peoples. De Lausenette had been "shaken with the bone" by an Aboriginal man of high degree who had worked on the Mason cattle station. The tutor had died in great agony.

One little female urchin, friendlier than the others, was won over when he plucked a pebble from her kinky, greasy hair, and she willingly sat by his kip, giving him the words of her people.

When he could understand many of the words and the others no longer ridiculed his attempts to communicate, Uwa told him that the men of the tribe had carried him through the never-never for many risings and settings of the sun, all the time thinking that the next day would be his last. The women who had been with Uwa's party told him how his water had been blood, how they had fed him as if he were a baby and trickled drops of water into his mouth. He thanked them with solemn sincerity.

He made silent promises. One was to Terry Forrest, for his last memory before the time of blackness was of Forrest squatting beside him, taking the money from his pack and leaving him to die alone.

Another promise was to Uwa and his people, a promise to use whatever portion of Mason money and influence it took to better the living conditions of the people of the Hamersley Range.

The Abos measured time by the seasons and phases of the moon. Two full moons had come and gone before Tolo could

stand with the aid of a cane that the women had cut for him.
His long illness had wasted his body, and though lacking a
scale, he knew that he had lost at least forty pounds. There
had been no fat on his large frame to begin with, so his ribs
now stuck out gauntly, and his hipbones were sharp enough
to do serious injury. His face —he could see it reflected in a
pool of water that collected below a drip from the face of a
rocky ridge—was drawn, cheekbones prominent and eyes
sunken into his skull.

The wound in his back, which he could not see, was still
raw and tender. The women kept it covered with leaves
soaked in a vile-smelling substance. When he probed the spot
gently with his fingers, he felt a sunken hole, still not healed
completely at the center. It was a fearful reminder of his mor-
tality. The women told him that the demons of death had
entered the wound, causing it to fester and stink; that chanting to the entities of good, while they scraped away the oozing
death, had kept him alive only because the spirits of the
Dreaming were not finished with him. He nodded in agreement. God, fate, the spirits of the Dreaming, whatever—he
was not finished with life, not until he found Java and then
Terry Forrest.

He did not know exactly where he was. He could guess,
from Uwa's description of their travels while he was in a
coma, that they were somewhere in the Hamersleys. He decided that when he was strong enough to make the trek, he
could travel to the southwest and reach the coast somewhere
in the vicinity of the North West Cape, for the Abos spoke of
the never-ending-waters to the west. For the moment he was
content with walks that at first concluded after no more than
five or six steps. He concentrated on adding a step or two
daily.

When a man has been near death and his body is fighting to
regain lost strength, nature often aids the process of restora-
tion by easing mental strain. It is as if the brain is made less
active by some soothing drug, and the urgencies of life seem
less acute. Tolo's existence was narrowed to the necessity of

stoking his body with food when it was available, of resting when his stringy muscles quivered with fatigue, of long hours of sleep, sleep that came on him several times during the day. He knew that with a proper diet that included fruits and vegetables he would have recovered faster, but he was grateful to Uwa's people for the occasional half-cooked kanga meat, for the special treat of his share of a stolen sheep. He ate anything and everything that was offered to him. Maku became one of his favorites—not that eating the large white grubs was anything new to him; any Australian worthy of the name had tried that wormy treat so prized by the Aborigines. It seemed more bizarre to him to eat the lizards and snakes that were the favorite game of the young boys of the camp.

As he began slowly to regain weight, as his ribs became less prominent and he could walk as far as a hundred feet before his legs gave out, he joined the Abos around the fire at night. It came to him that he was, after all, fulfilling at least a portion of his intent, although he had no pen, no paper to record the words of the tribe's elders.

"Moon and Spotted Possum were once men," old Uwa was saying, "but they had anger between them, and Possum picked up a sharp wooden yam stick and knocked Moon down. After a while Moon got up and grabbed the same yam stick and stabbed Possum. As he was dying, Possum said, 'All the people who come after me, all of the people of the time to come, when they die, they will die forever.' And Moon laughed and said, 'You should have let me speak first, for I will not die forever. I will die only for a few days, and then I will come back into the sky in the shape of a new moon.' "

A general sigh arose from those listening to the explanation of how death came to the world.

"Yes," Uwa said, "we humans die forever because Possum spoke first and it became truth. Death came there where Possum lay dying beside a sandy creek under the high rocks."

It was the young women who giggled as they dressed the healing wound in Tolo's back who told him of the *mamus,* the malignant spirits of the desert. "Some say they look like us," he was told, "but they can take the shape of the *ngeni* bird as well. They are as tall as the trees that line the edge of the never-ending-waters, and their teeth are long and bloody from biting and eating human beings after clawing them with their long nails. They carry long clubs and attack the man who travels alone, taking him to their caves, which are littered with human bones."

Tolo wished for writing material. The *mamu,* he thought, was nothing more than Ganba, man, an Aborigine with a club who fed on his fellows. From earliest times man had created monsters in his mind, while all the time the most frightening ogre of all sat at his own fires, for man was more monster to himself than any spirit or wild animal.

"One afternoon," Uwa chanted in the flickering light of the night's fires, "a *mamu,* an old man *mamu,* came to a water hole where a man, an elder, sat in meditation. The *mamu* joined him, and after a time they began to talk of the Dreamtime and to draw the routes between water holes in the sand at their feet. The *mamu* told long, boring stories of the Dreaming, and the man went to sleep. For this the *mamu* had been waiting. He took a stone knife from his anus and cut a line across the man's eyes from cheekbone to cheekbone. Then he killed the man and cooked him and ate him, and that is why all men who live in the desert have the lines at the corners of their eyes."

Because the hunting was good and meat was usually available in the camp, the Abos felt no need to move. Thus the filth piled up, and dingoes chewed on rotting bones. Children and dingoes relieved themselves when and where the urge took them. The stench of rotting scraps of food filled the air. Ashes from the campfires, ignited night after night, spread over the campsite, and eventually everyone was a dusky gray color, for in the chill of the night the Abos rolled into the warm ashes, which became part of their semipermanent coating of dirt and rancid grease.

When he was able, Tolo removed his ragged clothing and washed it, bathing himself as best he could. He also washed his tattered blanket and picked the bugs out of it. At bedtime he moved his kip away from the tribal fires, to avoid the places where the people congregated closely in sleep. But in the early evenings he still joined the others, sitting by the elders at the campfires to hear their stories.

He had known, of course, that the traditions of the Aboriginals were strictly oral, passed down from generation to generation by word of mouth, but he had not realized how much repetition that required. Night after night he heard the old ones talk, talk, talk, and the stories came to have a sameness. Many stories depicted that mythical time when the animals had been men, possessed of all the traits of men. And many of the stories had to do with food, the lack of it, and man's selfishness with regard to it. The young deprived their father of food, or they ate the choicest parts of a kill, the heart and the liver, leaving only flesh for the father. Their punishments explained some of man's present misery, just as Possum's dying explained why death came to all men.

There were tales of Bomaboma, the trickster, whose drive was erotic and whose desire was to seduce women who were forbidden to him, such as his father's sister's daughter's daughter; thus did young boys and girls learn the laws of the tribe regarding marriage and sexual activity. But there was no hint of the sorts of powers that had been possessed by old Colbee, father of the girl who had been killed by Dane de Lausenette when Tolo was a teenager. When he questioned Uwa, or some of the others, about being "sung" by the snake, the shaking of the bone, or about men like Bennelong, another Abo from Tolo's youth, who had fashioned the murderer's slippers of feathers and blood that would leave no track, he was met with blank stares and silence.

Gradually the strength came back to Tolo's limbs as his body filled out. One day he hunted with Uwa and his grand-

son and, to his own surprise, brought down a kangaroo from a
great distance with a skillful throw of a spear. Uwa nodded.
The vision that had been sent to him from the time of the
Dreaming had come to pass. He was content.

Tolo sat by the fire with Uwa that night, and before the old
man could begin the nightly entertainment and educational
program, the telling of stories of the Dreamtime, he said,
"Uwa, if you will be so good as to allow me to carry some of
the meat from the kangaroo that I killed today, if you will
allow me the use of one kangaroo waterskin, I will go with the
morning sun."

"It is time, then?" the old man asked.

"It is time."

"And now you will look for the woman in the never-
never?"

Tolo, feeling the usual weight of sadness at the thought of
Java, shook his head in negation.

"That is good," Uwa said, "for either she is dead or she has
gone far away where you will not find her so easy."

"I will seek word of her along the coast, and then I will
send messages to the land of the great-red-sacred-rock to inquire for her," Tolo said.

"I have seen you in a vision from the Dreaming," Uwa
said. "You will come back."

"Perhaps," Tolo said. But he no longer felt any desire to
live among these curious childlike people. He had come in
search of mysteries, but he had left all mystery behind him
with his childhood on the Mason cattle station. While it was
true that he had seen Bennelong, in murderer's slippers, stalk
de Lausenette, and he had seen old Colbee shake the bone at
the tutor, he could no longer be sure that it was Colbee's bone
shaking that had caused de Lausenette to fade and die painfully. It seemed more likely, in view of his new knowledge of
Aboriginal lore, that de Lausenette's death had been coinci-
dence, the result of one of the several tropical maladies that
were still deadly now and again in parts of the country.

"I say this," Tolo told Uwa. "Do not move from this camp
for"—he calculated—"for two full moons, and men will come
to you, men that I will send with gifts for Uwa and all of his
people."

"That is agreed," Uwa said. "The game is plentiful. The
water is good."

Tolo left the next morning with several young men and two
young women who had the walkabout urge. Traveling southwest, he found to his great relief that Uwa's homeland was
only a few days' march from the coast. It took him one week
to walk to Carnarvon. There the Abos from Uwa's group left
him, and he walked down Carnarvon's main street by himself
a lone, dusty figure, his clothing in tatters, his dusky skin
burned to a saddle brown.

His appearance in the office of the Mason agent caused a
sensation, no one quite believing he could still be alive. He
had to speak harshly to have his questions answered.

Indeed, there had been no word from any member of his
party, not until the minute Tolo walked into the office tattered
and torn as a scarecrow. He drew money, purchased clothing,
secured a room in the hotel, and then spent an hour in the
bath trying to scrub the dirt from all of his pores and creases.

He dispatched hasty telegrams to Sydney. First a simple
inquiry: HAVE RETURNED CARNARVON AFTER TROUBLE
ANY WORD JAVA?

The return wire deprived him of his last hope, for he was
certain that if Java were alive, she would by that time have
reached a point of civilization in the Northern Territory.

He sent off another wire to his mother, this one rather more
detailed to reply to her urgent query for more information.
Then he also left instructions with his agent to send blankets
and tobacco to Uwa's tribe. After having lived with them, he
knew that it would be useless to send cooking utensils, clothing, or other practical articles from white civilization, for they
would go unused. The tribe would savor the tobacco, and the

would wear the blankets until the urge to walk unfettered came to them, at which point they would simply toss the blankets away. But they would know that he kept his word, and they would remember him.

He paid a visit to the one doctor in Carnarvon, submitting himself to the man's punchings and probings and answering his questions.

"Well, Mr. Mason," the doctor exclaimed, "I'd say you're a horse of a man. From what you tell me, the spear certainly nicked a kidney. The blood loss should have killed you. The infection should have killed you. The boong women's digging around on the wound to cut off the dying tissue should have killed you. If I were a religious man, I'd say that maybe the Lord's not through with you yet."

That was the second time he had heard that sentiment. First from an Abo and now from a doctor. He was in no state of mind to disagree. Nor did he wish to speculate on the future.

Four days after his arrival in Carnarvon Tolo was aboard a ship, one of his own, traveling down the coastline toward Perth. He left behind him nodding heads as men said, "I told you so." He also left behind a legend, for he had not been overly eager to explain fully what had happened out there in the waly. He had left a written statement with the local constabulary, in which he reported the deaths of a number of Aborigines, the disappearance of his wife and an Abo woman, and the fact that Terry Forrest had left him for dead in the desert.

After Tolo had left Carnarvon, a constable, curious and unable to accept the notion that a man of Forrest's bush experience could not make it back from the Gibson, rode out to old Jonas Mayhew's station at Yinnietharra. He found the place abandoned. The tame Abos who had worked for Mayhew had apparently gone walkabout. The camels Mayhew kept were no longer in evidence, and the constable figured that either the boongs had eaten them or they had been turned loose to join their wild cousins.

The Gibson had at last claimed Jonas Mayhew. The constable found a grave, obviously dug by the Abos before they left. It was marked by a wooden cross; the name on it, most probably drawn in Mayhew's own hand as he lay dying, was already fading. And with Jonas Mayhew had died the knowledge that Terry Forrest had indeed come back from the Gibson only to enter it again, riding one of Jonas Mayhew's camels and leading three others.

From Perth Tolo Mason sent off a flurry of telegrams while he waited for a ship to take him around the southern coast to Adelaide and then Melbourne. One telegram, of course, went to his mother.

From Adelaide another storm of inquiries went out. Clive Taylor, once chief constable at Cloncurry and now a business associate of Bina Tyrell in Sydney, was called upon for his knowledge of bush country. Clive sent off some cables of his own, and soon every constabulary in the area had been queried, with negative results.

By the time Tolo reached Melbourne the results of the search of the lands around Ayers Rock were in.

Misa's wire tried to let him down gently: MY DEAR SON I THINK WE MUST SADLY ADMIT THAT OUR JAVA IS DEAD. HURRY HOME PLEASE.

But he could not give her up. He tried; all reason told him that his mother was right. Every point of civilization in Western Australia, the Northern Territory, and South Australia had been alerted to be on the lookout for a white woman coming out of the Gibson, and no such person had been found.

Now Tolo knew how long he had been dazed by his illness, and when he added that time to the time of his slow recovery in the Abo camp, and the time of travel, logic said, *She is truly dead.*

He could not face his mother and the others whom he knew in Sydney. He went to his homeplace, the station north of

Melbourne. If a half-breed Kanaka could have roots, they were there in the bush of New South Wales. There he was closest to the first happy months of marriage to Java and to the days long before that, his childhood, and his father.

Finding the station in poor repair, he turned out the man in whose care he had left it when Java and he had departed for Western Australia on their last journey together. He set an army of men to work refurbishing and redecorating the house. He took long rides into the bush alone to see Mason sheep and cattle waxing fat and valuable. Some of his workers, at least, were doing their jobs. But none of it meant anything to him without Java.

Terry Forrest came into the dunes to the west of Ayers Rock feeling more dead than alive, thinned, half starved, his eyes burning with the purpose that had kept him going through four hundred miles of baking hell. He camped at good water after crossing the dunes and talked with the local boongs. No one had seen or heard of a white woman and an Abo woman coming out of the Gibson. It was the opinion of all that no white woman could survive such a crossing.

He continued on to Alice Springs, where he sold the camels and settled in to soak up some tall brown ones until his thirst was at last satisfied. He told himself that he would never again travel more than a few hours away from that most civilized spot in all civilization—the pub.

So there he was in the Northern Territory, a long way from home in Perth. He had some of Tolo Mason's money left, but it was not enough to keep him in drink for the rest of what he hoped would be a long life. He fell in with some blokes who were going up north to do a bit of croc duffing. Since crocodile hides were bringing a pretty penny and he'd never been all the way north, he bought in with the outfit. They left the Alice on good horses with hearty, fair dinkum laughter and high hopes.

North of Barrow Creek was still another desert to be

crossed to reach the tropical swamps of Arnhem Land and Palmerston on the far northern coast. Terry's party was headed for these wetlands. They would pack their croc skins into Palmerston after a season's hunting.

Chapter XXIV

WHEN MISA MASON received the first telegram from her son, she experienced vast relief. It had been months since there had been any word from Tolo and Java. She glanced first to the bottom of the message, saw the name, Thomas Mason, and sent heavenward a fervent "thank God."

And then she read the curious question: ANY WORD JAVA?

A coldness swept over her, a sense of wrong that approached shame. It was evident that something had happened, that Tolo and Java had been separated. There had been trouble. The odd awareness that something was awry, something that was more than the tragedy of loss, deeper than the sorrow she would feel if Java were dead was, she realized, the product of disillusionment. She had felt total confidence in her son. While others, particularly Java's family, had expressed concern over the two young people going alone into Western Australia's deserts, she had felt that Tolo could handle himself anywhere and that he was quite man enough to take care of Java as well.

Now something had gone wrong, and the years of knowing that she was considered by most to be less than a human being predisposed her to be devastated by her son's failure. It was as if his losing his wife on a trip that had been nothing more than folly were sufficient proof that others were right:

that Tolo—and she—were inferior because of their Samoan
blood.

She allowed herself to wallow in regret for only a few moments.   She tasted the bitterness of doubt and self-hatred and
found it to be not to her liking. Then she dispelled it.

She had received the wire in her office. She summoned her
secretary and asked her to see if Daniel Moore was available.
Moore, the manager of her bank in Sydney, had been recommended to her by Sam Gordon and had proven to be most
competent. He was taking on more and more of the load
generated by the extended Mason business holdings, in addition to helping to make the Merchantman's and Marine Bank
a force in New South Wales. Price Vermillion, the man upon
whom Misa had depended for advice and support from the
time of her husband's death, was now in semiretirement, living comfortably in a fine and airy house built by the firm of
Tyrell and Taylor to overlook the sea near Sydney.

When Moore reached her office and they had exchanged
greetings, Misa handed him the wire. He read it and looked
up, his face showing concern. She said, "Not very informa-
tive, is it?"

"I do hope that I've taken a wrong impression," Moore
said.

"There's that possibility." She mused for a moment. "How
long would it take to get to Western Australia?"

"I'll just have someone check shipping schedules."

"No, no. Let's wait just a bit." She called in the secretary
and dictated a wire asking for clarification of Tolo's message.
Moore waited in a chair, legs crossed. "I'm wondering," she
said, "whether or not to get in touch with the Gordons at the
moment or wait until we know a bit more about what's happening."

"I would say that it might be a good idea to avoid what
could be useless worry for them," Moore suggested.

"Yes," she said. She was thinking of Rufe. He was at sea
and the date of his return was indefinite. Had he been here
she would have told him, for he was the most practical

minded man she'd known since Jon Mason was killed on a London street. Rufe would know exactly how to handle the situation with Sam and Jessica Gordon and with her very dear friend Magdalen Broome.

As it was, she waited. It was not until she learned the particulars of Java's disappearance, the words leaping out at her from Tolo's second cable, that she asked the secretary to telephone the Gordon home and request an appointment as soon as possible with Jessica and Sam. Then she ordered her Daimler brought around. It was a recent acquisition, Misa having finally given in to the necessity of owning a car. The chauffeur, a feisty little Irishman, was a skillful driver, though he often bordered on sass in his communications with the boss lady, covering his impudence with contagious good humor.

Jessica Gordon admitted Misa. "How nice to see you," she said, her smile one of politeness. "I do hope you'll stay for dinner. Actually, it's almost ready and the guests will be arriving—"

"I regret the inconvenience," Misa said, understanding that Jessica was telling her that she was intruding, that she was interfering with Jessica's schedule. Her smile, too, was nothing more than politeness, for she could sense that there was no warmth in Jessica Gordon's attitude toward her. "Sam is here?"

"Yes, yes," Jessica said with some impatience. "Come in, please."

Sam was in the parlor. As Misa entered, he put down a newspaper and rose to take her hand. His smile was genuine and his greeting warm. Misa sat down and put her hands in her lap.

"I have heard from Tolo," she began.

"Splendid," Sam said. "And how are the adventurers?"

Misa opened her purse, took out the two wires from Tolo, and handed them to Sam without comment. He used his forefinger to push his reading glasses up and lowered his head.

"Oh, my God," he whispered.

"What?" Jessica asked in a frightened tone. "What is it?"

Sam told her, his voice low and calm. She put her hand to her mouth and screamed. He rose and took her by the shoulders. "It's all simply a mixup," he said. "I'm sure that she's fine. Let's not think bad things—not just yet."

Jessica drew her shoulders up, shrugged out from under Sam's hands, and looked at Misa. "Damn you," she said, her voice shaking.

"Jess!" Sam said.

"Damn you to hell, and your half-breed son with you," Jessica said.

"I'll not have that, Jess," Sam protested.

"And damn you as well," Jessica said, whirling on him. "You could have stopped it. You were supposed to be the man of the family. I told you what was happening. I told you that she was spending too much time with that—with that—"

Misa rose, her face red with her effort to remain silent. "Sam," she said, "I'll inform you the minute I hear anything more."

"Misa, forgive us," Sam said. He followed her out of the room, down the hall, out onto the porch. The brightness of the day, the blue of the sky, the gentle touch of a sea breeze on his face seemed almost an insult to the grief that he felt inside.

"She's not herself, Misa," he offered.

"No worries, mate," Misa said, with fine irony that was not lost on Sam.

When it became clear that Java could have attempted to cross the Gibson Desert, possibly to emerge into the Northern Territory in the vicinity of Ayers Rock, Misa put the resources of the Mason business empire to work. She knew that the task would take many days, possibly weeks. Her determination and endurance were strengthened by another message from Tolo, this one from Perth.

Misa's contact with the Gordon family now was mainly through Magdalen, who had come to Misa's office the morning after Jessica's tirade to put her arms around her and beg forgiveness for the entire family.

"I have come to love you, you know," Magdalen said. "And I love Tolo as I would my own grandson."

"I know," Misa said. She could not, however, state the simple truth that she returned the affection. There had always been a barrier between her and White Australia, and in spite of Magdalen's kindness, in spite of Misa's regard for her, Magdalen was a part of White Australia.

"I like to think," Magdalen went on, "that you and I are friends, that the three of us, you and I and Bina, are truly the Terrific Threesome."

Misa let her guard down enough to kiss the older woman on the cheek. "We are. You can be sure of it."

"And the three of us will see this thing through," Magdalen said. "My granddaughter has Broome blood in her. She's a fighter. If all that is required of her is to cross a few hundred miles of desert, she'll do that. Soon, one day soon, we'll get word from some godforsaken village in the outback, and then she'll be coming back to us."

"I pray so," Misa said.

In the meantime, the inquiries went out and the negative replies came back. The weeks passed. By this time, Misa knew, Tolo had passed through Adelaide and gone on to Melbourne. There he had fallen out of touch. Queries sent to her office in Melbourne confirmed her suspicions that her son had gone home to the station, where the Masons had lived as a close-knit family while Jon was alive and where Tolo had taken his bride after the elopement. It angered her until she began to look at it from his viewpoint. He had lost the woman he loved. He had been out there in the desert, knew the conditions, and he seemed to be convinced that Java was dead. And like a sick animal, he had crawled back to his den to heal.

At the end of a long day, with fatigue and a devilish headache making the world seem not quite real, Misa left her office just as the dimness of twilight was acting as a signal for the

streetlights to go on. The bank guard let her out and locked
the door behind her. The Irishman had parked her Daimler
directly in front of the bank.

The western sky was glowing. Out there somewhere, she
was thinking, out there where the sun had gone . . . She
pictured a scattered scavenger-chewed pile of bones . . .
small, feminine bones. She shook her head to dispel the image,
but she could not clear her mind. She could only imagine the
distances involved. It was merely days by train or road or ship
to Melbourne. Tolo had come back to Melbourne from the far
side of the continent, where one measured the distances of the
deserts in weeks and months. Not many years earlier, men
had begun to explore the interior of Australia, looking for a
fabled huge freshwater lake in the heart of the land. Some had
died. Others had found not a freshwater lake but the formidable, waterless wastes of the red heartland. And now Java was
there.

How odd, she thought.

Around her lay the modern world, a world of mechanical
miracles and constant change, moving on its swift day-to-day
pace. Motorcars and steamships, electric lights and the telephone, magical boxes that kept meat frozen and messages sent
almost instantly by wire over incredible distances; and over in
America two brothers had just built a frail machine with wire
and fabric atop bicycle tires, and they had flown. Ah, but if
she could borrow that magical machine and soar over the
deserts! But the modern world seemed incapable of extending
itself into the far-out bush. There were areas in the interior
where white men had yet to walk.

The leather of the car seat, retaining the heat of the sun,
comforted her in the chill of the evening. She closed her eyes
as the driver went around to the front of the car to crank the
engine into life. She caught the scent of the gases being exhausted by the chugging motor and reached up to squeeze the
bridge of her nose.

"Dinner first, boss lady?" the driver asked, coming back to
her side of the car.

"No, I think not," Misa replied.

"Too bad," the Irishman countered. "I'm a bit hungry meself, and Miss Bina's place does set a good table."

"The trouble with you, Irish," said a deep male voice, "is that Mrs. Mason has spoiled you."

"Here now," the driver said, turning quickly to face the newcomer; but Misa's eyes had flown open, and in spite of her headache, her lips were parting in a smile.

"Give a sailor a ride?" asked Rufe Broome. He stood beside the car, tall and distinguished in whites.

"It's my patriotic duty," Misa said emphatically.

The driver opened the door for him, and Rufe climbed in beside her. He reached for her hand and kissed it. "I just heard you turn down one invitation to dinner—"

"The problem with that one was that I would have had to pay. *And* listen to the complaints of the kitchen staff when this Irishman tried to eat them out of everything—"

"Unfair," the Irishman said, clambering into the driver's seat. "They like me there, they really do."

"Bina's, then?" Rufe said. "I'd have phoned, but we just got into harbor an hour or so ago, and I decided to take a chance on catching you here." He grinned at her. "You're going to have to stop working such long hours, luv. Gives you frown lines . . . here." He touched the extreme corner of her full lips with the tip of one finger.

For Misa it was as if she'd been brushed with a live electrical wire. She shivered in spite of herself, and her lips softened.

He had never kissed her. They had been together only in company, at the Gordon house, at a table at Bina's. The dusk of evening was closing around them quickly. He reached up and drew down the curtain between the backseat of the auto and the driver's compartment. She, sensing his intentions, knew that she should speak, that she should stop him, but she did not. When he moved his head toward hers, she was drawn to him, her lips parting to receive his.

"Is it Bina's, then?" the driver asked from behind the curtain.

There was no answer. He moved the car away from the curb and shifted it up to running speed. He began to whistle, looking forward not only to the good food at the employees' table in the kitchen but to seeing the sassy little bird who was the assistant pastry cook.

Never had life seemed so unfair as it did to Misa Mason with Rufe's kiss stirring her as she had not been moved in years. She had never considered herself unfortunate, not until that pleasant Sydney night when she was in the arms of the tall naval officer, with the Daimler moving smoothly through the twilight streets. She had counted herself one of the blessed, as a matter of fact, for she had had the years of happiness with Jon Mason, she had had her son, and even though God had taken Jon from her terribly early, while she was still a relatively young woman, she had not been bitter, only saddened, for the love she had enjoyed with Jon had shone with a gladness that was enough to last her the rest of her life.

At first, as Rufe kissed her breathless, and the kisses continued, she did not think in terms of being at odds with the world. She accepted. She took. She gave. But in the back of her mind was . . . Java.

Java.

He had come directly from his ship. He had been at sea. He did not know about Java. And that was the unfairness, the ultimate unfairness, for just as she found another love, a love that roused her emotionally and physically as Jon Mason's love had done, she had to tell Rufe that his niece was feared to be dead. He would have to go to Jessica, for he was, after all, her brother.

She allowed heaven to continue for a few minutes more, until the auto came to a stop and the driver was saying, "Bina's, Mrs. Mason."

Rufe broke away from her, grinned, and took her arm. "Given a choice, I'd rather continue the ride."

"Yes," she whispered.

"I say, driver—"

"No," she said, clutching his hand.

He raised an eyebrow, bent to kiss her lightly on the cheek. "Shall we go in?"

"Rufe, no," she said, holding on to his hand.

She told him then, and his reaction surprised her. He held her close and whispered, "Oh my God, poor Java. Poor Tolo."

That his first thought was for his niece and her son, not Java's parents, was puzzling to her. "Don't you think you should go to see them?"

"Jessica and Sam?" he asked. "Yes. Yes. Of course, I'll go to see them." He opened the door. "But not just now, Misa. Since the news came while I was at sea, and time has passed, I think the urgency has probably diminished. Just now I have a duty to a lady, to see that she is properly wined and dined, and we sailors know how to set priorities, you know."

This, too, made her wonder. Was he so indifferent to the sadness of his own sister?

Bina herself greeted them and invited them to sit at her table. But Rufe winked at her and said, "Tonight we have things to discuss, luv." So Bina directed them to a semiprivate table, separated from the main room by hangings and lush green plants in huge pots.

"Poor old Jess," Rufe said, after they had been seated. "I imagine she's taking it hard."

"Quite," Misa said.

"Tough on Sam, too. He doted on that little Java girl. Is there no possibility, then, that she's not dead?"

"There was one old constable up in the Northern Territory who answered that question. He said there are two possibilities: vague and nonexistent."

"Well, Mother will steady them up," Rufe said. "Would you come with me after we've had dinner?"

She felt her face flush. It was not up to her to tell him that she was not welcome in the Gordon house. "I think not. I think it's best that you have some time alone with your sister."

"You're right, I'm sure," he said. He looked up, said, "Damn, damn, damn," in a soft voice. He looked at her and grinned. "And the evening started off so well, didn't it?"

"I don't hear anyone complaining," she said with a little smile.

"You know, I've wanted to do that from that first night at Sam's table, the first time I met you."

"And I thought that night that you had eyes only for Bina."

"Only because, when I looked at you, I felt that you could read my thoughts."

She laughed. "Were they so terrible?"

"Let me say that they were rather heated." He reached across the table and took her hand between his. "Are we so selfish, Misa, to be thinking of ourselves?"

She was silent. Her face went blank.

"Say, I didn't intend the question to be *that* serious," he said.

"But it is," she said. "There's the uncertainty of it all. Tolo thinks she's dead. He hasn't said as much, but I'm sure he does. I would so much like to try to give him some comfort, but he's down in Victoria, at the home station. I've asked him to come to me. . . ."

She looked at Rufe with the realization that she was more alone than she'd been since the death of Jon. She had always had Tolo with her, and now he was no longer an intimate part of her life. He had started to pull away—as the young do inevitably—even before he began his land-buying activities in the bush, when she had sent him north to assess the Mason plantations that she had wanted to sell, and then he had obeyed the biblical injunction to cleave to his wife, leaving home and mother. And even now, in his grief, when logic said that they should be together, he was not with her.

She promised herself then that she would move heaven and earth to hang on to this man who looked at her with adoring eyes, this tall, mature, witty, handsome man who had come into her life like a gift from God. She had never considered herself unfortunate, but now she feared that she was, for to lose Rufe, just when she had found him, would be the greatest misfortune. If it came to a fight, then she would fight. If Jessica Gordon wanted to oppose her relationship with Rufe, then it would be Jessica Gordon against whom she would fight with all the weapons at her disposal.

Chapter XXV

GUINEVERE GOREL FINISHED a light breakfast of fruit and ordered the Kanaka servant to clear the table. She was seated on her west veranda, which overlooked Port Moresby. Night mist clung to the quiet waters of the bay. No air stirred. She felt stale, damp, sticky, although she had had a basin bath after rising, standing nude in the bedroom she shared with Trevor, to swab the perspiration of the night from her long legs, her flat stomach, her full breasts.

She wore a flowing silk dressing gown with a high Chinese-style collar. On the pale yellow silk were embroidered hundreds of pastel butterflies. When she crossed her legs, the silk clung sensuously.

Although the morning was not far advanced, the lack of wind and the high humidity foretold that the heat would be intense as the sun climbed higher. It would be a day like all the others she had lived through since arriving in Papua New Guinea. Port Moresby was more frontier outpost than town. The only people she would see today were the two Kanaka girls whom Trevor had hired for her, and one's conversation with servants was limited to the giving of orders. She would not see her husband, for he was in the forests of the southern coast with his native timbering crew.

It had quickly become apparent that her social life in Port Moresby would be nonexistent. Her only outings had been visits to the general merchandise store near the waterfront, and after making a few unpleasant trips through the muddy streets, she had given up and sent servants whenever something was needed. A few English and Australian women lived in the town, but when she encountered them on the streets, they had looked sweaty and dowdy and quite common. It was ironically amusing to her when they looked askance at the golden-skinned Eurasian woman. They and their opinions were beneath her contempt. She had no desire to know any of them, and that left her to fill her own days, days that stretched into eons of boredom.

For exercise she walked the grounds of the house in the evenings and early mornings. Arising at daybreak was a new experience for her, but once the sun came up, it was impossible to sleep. If she tried to stay in bed, she was soon wallowing in her own perspiration, with the sheets clinging stickily to her.

Oddly enough, she felt no particular malice toward Trevor for having brought her to such a backwater. She had long since resigned herself to the knowledge that her mother had made a terrible mistake in marrying her to the Englishman, but that was done, and the past was past. She didn't hate Trevor. She didn't even dislike him. He was an amiable man, considerate of her needs to the best of his ability. That he couldn't meet those needs was not his fault. He, too, was a victim of fate. He had been born to a family of small merchants, and she had been born with mixed blood in a dying dynasty. She had been given a taste of power and luxury for just long enough to give her a sure knowledge of what she wanted in life. As she sat on the balcony of the house overlooking Port Moresby, she felt that the gods had made her a princess out of spite, merely to make her suffer the more when they expelled her from paradise.

Trevor kept promising her that their stay in New Guinea would be limited to a few years at most, but she was not far from her quarter century mark. She knew, even as she stood before her mirror in the mornings, that the beauty of the finest flower fades. Each day she spent in this tropical hell was a total loss, but she had not yet lost hope. One way or the other, she would escape her tropical prison. When opportunity came, she would do whatever was necessary. If it meant personal sacrifice, so be it. Better to be a courtesan in Hue or perhaps in Paris than to swelter her life away in Port Moresby.

She came from a long-lived family, at least on her mother's side, and the beauty of an Annamese woman remained undiminished into middle age—if one's face and skin had the proper unguents and care. Of course, most Annamese women didn't have to suffer the sweating heat of Port Moresby. The perfumes and oils that she had accumulated while she was living with Louis Sabitier in Hue would be gone in a short time, and she had no way of replacing them. The store near the waterfront had only powders that became pink mud in the heat and paints that prevented the skin from breathing naturally.

She was lingering over her second cup of morning tea when she saw a man walking up the drive. Dressed in tropical whites, he looked fresh and clean. He walked with a youthful vigor, and when he looked up toward the porch, evidently without noticing her there, she saw that his face was handsome, even-featured, and bronzed by the sun. She waited until one of the Kanaka girls came and said, with a little bow, "Missy, Mr. Matthew Van Buren is at the door."

She rose, tested the set of her hair with a smoothing palm, and licked her full red lips. She had not yet met her husband's business partner, but she had heard much about him from Trevor. She motioned the girl away, swayed her way around the corner of the porch, and examined Matt Van Buren closely before he sensed her presence and turned to face her.

Matt saw her for the first time at a distance of about ten feet. His eyes were drawn to her face, to her dark-lashed almond-shaped eyes. His lips pursed, and an almost audible whistle came before he realized what he was doing. He swept the straw hat from his head and nodded politely. His heart had skipped, pounding rapidly as the woman approached, a smile parting her full, sensual lips.

Now he felt the total impact of her, the thrust of bosom against silk, the small tents made by nipples showing darkly through the yellow silk, the way the long, loose garment both concealed and revealed waist and hips with movements that outlined one full thigh after the other as she walked proudly toward him. He had never seen such a garment outside his wife's bedroom, but on Guinevere Gorel it seemed appropriate. He felt none of the embarrassment he would have known had he surprised a British woman in such a revealing garment, only a heated longing that left him speechless.

"You are Mr. Van Buren," Guinevere said, extending her hand.

Matt took the hand, and as his fingers touched the soft, heated flesh, there came an electric shock that caused the woman's eyes to widen momentarily.

"He said you were beautiful," Matt said. "For once old Trev didn't use an adjective with enough power."

"Thank you," she said. "I'm having tea on the veranda. Please join me."

"I just came by to see if you'd heard anything from Trev," he said, but he followed her. He felt a great need to look at her more closely, to have the opportunity to study her face because in fleeting glances, while she was in movement, he couldn't get enough of her features in his eyes, could not pin down what it was about her that had reached out to him so powerfully.

He stared at her while the Kanaka girl brought a cup and saucer, poured tea, and placed sugar in front of him. She didn't seem to be bothered by his close inspection. She stared back at him, a small smile of amusement parting her lips, her eyes holding his.

"My God," Matt said softly.

"You have just come down from the hills?" she asked.

"What?" He shook his head to clear away a feeling of

something approaching intoxication. "Oh, yes. Just last night, as a matter of fact. Spent the night in the hotel."

"I'm sorry you did," she said. "Trevor has told me that when you are in Port Moresby, you are to have your old room here."

"Well . . ." His thoughts ran wild. Trev away. The room he had shared with Kit only two doors away from Trev's bedroom.

"If you're to be here tonight, you must let me send one of the servants to the hotel for your things."

"Kind of you," Matt said. "I don't know exactly how long I'll be in town. There's a ship due from Sydney with some tools we need. The agent says it's two days behind schedule already."

"Perhaps the fates will be kind and delay it longer," Guinevere said, favoring Matt with a smile that brought a flush to his face. "You see, when Trevor is away, I have no one to talk with."

. He could not speak. Her eyes were saying yes, yes. She crossed her legs, and the silken skirts opened to reveal a long, well-shaped lower leg. His eyes were drawn to the flash of golden flesh, and she was quite slow in pulling the parted fabric edges together.

"You must tell me all about Australia," Guinevere said. "Trevor has told me that you own a very large, how do you say it, cattle place?"

"Cattle station," Matt corrected gently. "And I don't own it. My father does." He smiled ruefully, relieved that the conversation had taken a turn and yet still aware of the message being sent by the woman's eyes. "I'm not in my father's good graces at the moment, I'm afraid."

"So you are here in this . . . place to show your father that you can make it on your own?"

He laughed. "Well, it was either crawl to him, starve, or find some form of honest work. It hurts my knees to crawl, and Kit objected to starving."

"You met Trevor on the boat when he first came out, I am told."

"He sang the praises of New Guinea, and when I was at a loss as to where to begin a career, I remembered some of the things he'd said." He spread his hands. "And here I am."

"I'm pleased," she said simply. "It's wonderful to know that Trevor has such a distinguished and capable partner. I'm sure that both of you are going to be very rich."

He laughed again. "We're bloody well going to give it a very good effort." He peered at her over his teacup. There was not a single blemish on her porcelain skin, not even an enlarged pore. A sheen of perspiration on her upper lip seemed to emphasize the delightful upturn. Her hair was black silk, a heavy mass of it bunned to expose the long golden column of her neck.

"But you could, at any time, crawl—as you say—to your father and go back to the family, ah, station?"

"I suppose so," he said.

"And it will all be yours when your father dies?"

He shrugged. "He's threatened to leave it to the government, to be divided among the poor."

"Ah, but a father would not do that to his only son," she said, her lilting inflection making it a question.

"No, I suppose not." He laughed. "I hope not, actually. We have a son now, you know, and—"

"No, I didn't know," she said, and he sensed a bit of disapproval in her tone. It made him feel guilty without reason. He was unaware that he had become mesmerized by her beauty, by the musky appeal that seemed to radiate from her. He did not want to do or say anything to displease her.

"Yes," he said, "and I'm hoping that having a grandson will bring the old boy around."

A frown crossed Guinevere's face, and again he sensed that talk of children made her uncomfortable. But then she smiled, and he forgot everything else. He had been in the woman's presence for only a few minutes, but he felt an intimacy that could have been the product of months of association. He had never wanted to kiss anyone so badly in his life.

Because he had grown up on a bush cattle station, Matt's experience with women had been limited. The nearest white neighbor had lived miles away, and the children on that station had been boys. His schooling had come from his mother and from tutors brought onto the station by his father. He was enough his father's son to disdain the method used by many young Australian boys to learn about the birds and the bees—the simple expedient of consorting with young Aboriginal girls, who grew up in a culture that did not condemn childhood sex play and indeed only vaguely associated copulation with conception. But he had not been a virgin when he married Kit, for in Cape Town he had been with women of a professional nature who took money for, and pride in, meeting the needs of soldiers of the crown.

And then Kit had come into his life. In their youthful reachings, pantings, graspings, lovings, gigglings, they had become sexually adult together.

That was the sum of Matt's experience. His ideal of womanhood had been, and still was to a great extent, his mother. A woman was patient, caring, and skilled in treating the small and large injuries that came to a workingman in the bush. A woman cooked or oversaw the servants who cooked for her. A woman made a house a home and kept it clear and as free as possible of crawling and flying things that bit. A woman was not a slave, but she was subservient to her husband in matters pertaining to politics, social intercourse, and money, including the way her husband chose to earn his livelihood. If a man was fortunate, his woman was lover, friend, and companion—as Kit was to him.

With those opinions, based on limited experience, Matt was totally unprepared for the deliberate blandishments of a woman who had as her weapons centuries of scholarly and practical knowledge of the ways of the courtesan. . . .

* * *

Once Guinevere Gorel had decided, on the basis of what
Trevor had told her about Matt's wealthy family, that Matthew Van Buren just might be her passage out of New Guinea,
she swiftly made up her mind. She had been conditioned from
childhood to think that when a royal princess wanted something, she had only to indicate her desires. She wanted Matt
Van Buren. She wanted him immediately, for the days were
long and boring, and Trevor, in his eagerness to be rich, was
away from the house in Port Moresby for weeks at a time.

In addition to using Matt to answer her temporary physical
needs, she wanted Matt long enough to have him take her to
Australia, where together they would pacify the father so that
Matt could get his hands on the family money. Then it would
be easy for her to get enough money to travel to France.

Guinevere would have been puzzled if, by some miracle,
someone with the magic to penetrate her thoughts had asked,
"But what about the wife? What about the new child?" Because to Guinevere, Kit Van Buren and the child did not exist.
Only she existed. All else, including the people whom she
allowed into her life—Trevor, for example—was real only
when related directly to her.

That was what made her frown when Matt had mentioned
his son. Having a child had never been in her own plans.
Three times, twice with Trevor and once with Louis Sabitier
in Hue, her body had betrayed her, but potential disaster had
been averted each time by the skillful use of a long, slim
carved-ivory tool that had once been her mother's. The technique had been handed down in her mother's family for generations. Her mother, in teaching it to Guinevere when the
girl proved her fertility immediately after becoming Trevor's
wife, had laughingly told her that the magic of the ivory quill
was practiced by two sorts of women: the ladies of rich houses
and women whose profession or bonded duty was to give
pleasure to men.

Guinevere was a totally self-oriented person. Only *she*
could know significant pain; the pain of others was as nebu-

lous to her as the mist that hung over the bay on still mornings. Only her needs were to be considered. She hungered,
and it was her God-given right to feed, just as the female lion
of the South African High Veld feeds, heedless of the spilled
blood of her victim.

Matt made one real attempt to break the spell that was
closing around him with directed skill and amazing swiftness.
"Well," he said, rising, "I have some business in town. You
say that you haven't heard from old Trev?"

"No," she said, rising to face him, moving just inside that
normal range of polite distance that is maintained between a
man and a woman who have not been intimate. "Will your
business take long?"

"If I can hire a boat, I think I'd better go down the coast
and see Trev," he said, backing away a bit in an effort to clear
his head of her scent.

"Ah," she said, reaching up to straighten his collar. "I had
so hoped that we could get to know each other better, become
friends." Her smile was a wondrous thing. She had tilted her
head just a bit to look into his eyes, and that position exhibited her flawless, graceful throat. He could see her life pulsing
there in delicate lines of blue under the porcelain skin. "Postpone leaving at least until I can give you one good dinner."

He swallowed.

"Here," she said. "Tonight. You will come?"

"If I can," he said.

He departed quickly and then walked back toward the
main part of town in a sensuous daze. He could remember the
aura of her, the texture of her skin, the smell of her perfume,
but he could not picture her face. He knew only that he had
seen perfection, and he wanted more than anything in the
world to accept her invitation to return that evening. At the
moment just being with her was as far as his imagination
reached; he wished only to sit across a table from her and be
allowed to stare at her until he could commit that perfect face

to memory. Far back in his mind desire stirred, a lurking force awaiting its opportunity.

As he approached the waterfront, he shook his head in an attempt to dispel her image. As he lifted his eyes, he saw the familiar shape of Blue Jack's steam launch and, reminded of reality, walked to stand beside the gangplank. Saraba, Jack's dusky wife, came to the rail, recognized Matt, and gave him a gleaming smile.

"Is the master aboard?" he asked.

"Sorry, no," Saraba said. "You want him, you find him at the governor's office."

"No trouble, I hope?"

The dark little woman shrugged. "Always problems," she said.

Matt walked over to the tin-roofed building that housed the government offices. The sun was beating down with relentless ferocity, and it was a relief to step up onto the veranda of the large building. He stood there for a time, hands behind his back. A few people came and went. If Blue Jack were in the governor's office, he would have to pass Matt on the way out.

Guinevere Gorel's face dominated his thoughts. Not far away Kanaka workmen were building a wood-frame house, and for a moment he knew a sense of pride, for it was lumber that had been cut in his valley, on his sawmill, that they were using. By association his thoughts went from the sawmill to his home and, of course, to Kit. His son was growing rapidly, a very sturdy baby. And Kit. Ah, Kit. Her beauty had been heightened, not diminished, by childbirth. Her active life had quickly taken off the pounds she'd put on during her time of carrying little Grant.

Kit. Nothing could take her place in his life.

He thrust thoughts of Guinevere out of his mind. He would not go to the Gorel house for dinner. He would not see her again unless Trev was at home.

He snorted. How odd that he was thinking such foolishness. He was an adult, a man in control of himself. He had seen a beautiful woman, and he had felt a natural male reaction to her. No need to go troppo about it.

He heard footsteps and looked up to see a familiar, if unexpected, face. Slone Shannon stepped out onto the porch, glanced at Matt, nodded, looked away, and jerked his head back.

"Slone Shannon!" Matt exclaimed at the same instant that Slone said, " 'Strewth, it's Matt Van Buren!"

"Well, what in bloody hell are you doing in New Guinea?" Matt asked, after the ritual of shoulder pounding and handshaking was finished.

"Might ask the same of you," Slone said.

"Here to make my fortune, mate," Matt said.

"You look prosperous."

"She'll be right," Matt said. "Little bit of timbering. Little bit of growing coffee. No worries."

"Goodonyer," Slone said.

"You still haven't told me what a peer of the bloody realm is doing in troppo land."

Slone shrugged. "Not a peer yet," he said. "And I hope not for many years. Just the bleedin' heir, son." He grinned. "The bleedin' heir to the title doing his duty to king and country. Count your blessings that it didn't happen to you, or you wouldn't be here having a thundering good time doing exactly what you please, free as a bloody bird."

"Not all that free," Matt said. "Wife and son now, you know."

"No," Slone said with a big smile. "No, I didn't know. That's grand, Matt, just grand. Name the little bushranger after yourself, did you?"

"Well, Kit insisted," Matt said.

"Kit?" There was an odd look in Slone's eyes.

"But you wouldn't have heard, I guess. Kit Streeter. Yes." He wondered if there was any residual emotion regarding Kit left in Shannon and felt a little twinge of jealousy.

Slone smiled and clapped him on the back. "You got a wonderful girl, mate."

"You don't have to tell me that."

Slone pulled out his watch and glanced at it. "Listen, mate, I have just an hour before I have to be on board ship." He pointed out to the harbor where a Royal Navy destroyer of the Australian squadron lay at anchor. "I'm just a diplomatic messenger boy, and his nibs the captain would be apoplectic if I delayed his scheduled departure by one minute . . . but there's time for a tall one at the pub."

Matt said, "Well, I was waiting for someone. He's supposed to be with the governor."

"Disreputable-looking fellow with an odd name?" Slone asked.

"Blue Jack."

"Yes. I imagine he'll be along shortly, then." He held out his hand. "Good to see you, Queensland."

"Nice to see you, too, Queensland," Matt said. He grinned, hesitated, then spoke again. "Hell, I can always catch up with Jack. Let's go have that tall one."

They strolled to the waterfront pub and took seats next to the long opening made by a raised shutter. Over good Australian ale, Slone spoke glowingly of his wife, Sianna, who was back in Melbourne. He listened with great interest and asked questions as Matt told him about his timbering and coffee enterprises.

"So here we are," Slone said, "bloody imperialists. Ever since the first convicts were dumped onto the Australian coast, we've been complaining, and here we are doing the same thing mucking about in another fellow's country."

"Oh, we're here to bring the wretched heathens to the light," Matt said.

"While lining our pockets." Slone grinned. "Well, better Australia than the bloody Germans, I suppose."

"Hear, hear," replied Matt.

Slone checked his watch again. "Well, Queensland, I'm off—"

"Have a good trip home," Matt said. He waved off the coins Slone pulled from his pocket to pay for the ale.

"Thanks, mate," Slone said, repocketing the change. "First leg coming up—Brisbane. Then on to Melbourne, London, and the Continent. My new assignment will be at our mission in Vienna."

"La-di-da," Matt said. "May I haf dis valze, mine herr?"

Slone laughed. "Sianna's in heaven. She'll be able to use her excellent German. Good Boer girl that she is, she feels that at last she'll be in true civilization."

Matt stood up with Slone. There was more back pounding, an exchange of good wishes, and then Matt watched his friend go.

Just as Slone reached the door, Blue Jack stepped in, squinting to see in the dimness. "Well, Captain," he said to Slone, "are you leaving us?"

Slone cast a quick look at Matt, did not answer, and hurried out the door.

Blue Jack joined Matt at the battered table.

"You know Slone Shannon?" Matt asked.

"Know him?" Blue Jack looked away and shouted at the bartender to bring him a glass. When he looked back, his eyes caught Matt's. "Wouldn't say that I *know* the captain," Blue Jack said. "Know that he's an Aussie working with the bloody pom intelligence services."

"Old Slone's a spy?" Matt asked lightly.

Blue Jack examined Matt's face before answering. "Spy master would be a more accurate term," he said.

"Really," Matt said. "How do you know that?"

Blue Jack laughed. "Takes one to know one, mate," he said. "Haven't you heard that I'm a bloody spy for the bloody Germans up north?"

Blue Jack's glass of dark ale was delivered, and he emptied half of it in a draft. He licked his lips and wiped them with the back of his hand. "So how's the coffee growing?"

"Very slowly," Matt said. "Look, Jack, I'd like to go down south and see how Trev's coming with the timbering. I have things under control in the hills, and I thought old Trev might need some encouragement and help. Are you free to run me down there today?"

Blue Jack emptied the rest of his glass before answering. "Sorry, mate," he said. "I've some engine work going on, and as soon as that's done, I have to make a mail run up north."

"Know of anyone else who could take me?"

Blue Jack gave Matt a name, told him where to locate the boat. Matt found the boat's owner and was told that the boat could get under way first thing the next morning.

"I wanted to get started right away," Matt said. "We could be halfway there before dark tonight."

"Can't do it," the boat owner said, shaking his head firmly. "It's my daughter's wedding this afternoon."

Later in life he would be able to tell himself that he had tried. He checked around the harbor and was unable to find any boatman willing to leave that afternoon for the south. He went to his hotel room, bathed, changed clothes, and went to the dining room.

He had gone so far as to take his seat and order a cup of coffee before the meal when, with a sigh, he rose, left money on the table to cover the cost of the coffee, and started walking toward Trevor Gorel's pleasant house on the rise. Ascending the drive, he saw the lights on, making a cozy glow through the windows. As he mounted the steps to the veranda, he saw Guinevere Gorel, in white, standing in the shadows.

"I knew you would be here," she said, taking his hand. "Come, we will enjoy the cool of the evening."

She led him to a sitting area on the side of the house that was exposed to a balmy breeze from the bay. She sat next to him in a porch swing. The soft warmth of her was against his haunch.

"I am so glad you came," she said. "I get so lonely when Trevor is away." She had half turned to face him, and in the dim light of the moon he could just see the smooth planes of her face, the dark shape of her almond eyes. She had changed her scent. Now she smelled of odd jungle flowers, pungent and compelling.

He would never know how his lips found hers, how that first kiss began, but time and time again he would remember, with his flesh burning in desire, the feel of her waist between his hands, the sound of contentment she made when his tongue found hers.

A servant interrupted with the muted statement that dinner was served. She answered the girl but made no effort to disentangle herself from his arms.

"Hang the dinner," Matt said, careless of the presence of the Kanaka girl, wanting only to keep that wonder in his arms, to delve deeper into the honeyed mouth, to feel the curves and softnesses under his hands.

Guinevere laughed. "Come, we must eat," she whispered. "There is time. There is all the time in the world."

Matt picked at his food. The two Kanaka girls waited table, leaping to do Guinevere's bidding, often without Guinevere's having spoken. A look, a motion with one long, lovely finger, and the girls obeyed. Her eyes were for Matt alone. In the white silk sheath that she wore she was woman incarnate, desire distilled into one human form. He thought the meal would never end.

She ate as if she enjoyed every bite, politely but without wasted time or motions. Matt would not have been able to name one item of the menu. And then, after the service of hot Oriental tea, Guinevere said to the Kanakas, "That is all. You may go to your quarters."

They were alone.

She guided him without his knowing that he was being guided. It was at her chosen time that she was in his arms again, and it was her timing that found them in the large bedroom that she shared with Trevor Gorel and then in Trevor's bed with the silken, long, heated lines of her pressed to him.

His trembling need exploded swiftly. She laughed, low and sensuously, coaxing him with whispered words and knowing touches. Again and again the process was repeated until he was mindless, a compression of passion, of need, of blind desire. To have her, to possess her, was all that mattered, and if he lived to be a hundred, he could never get enough of her.

He awoke with the sun, sweat dampening his body. He was in the large bed alone. A feeling of shame and guilt assaulted him. He could not understand what in hell had overcome him to put him into another woman's bed, and especially in the bed of the wife of his best friend and business partner. And Kit. *Ah, Kit, forgive me.* His lips formed the words silently. *It will not happen again.*

He rose, reaching for the clothing that he had strewn carelessly in the hasty night.

"Ah, the man wakes at last," Guinevere Gorel said.

She had been standing in shadows beside the windows overlooking the bay, and now she stepped into the beam of the morning sun, nude, the light gleaming on her flawless golden skin. She swayed toward him. "Are you in a hurry?" she asked, pressing herself into his arms.

In a sudden fit of self-disgust he thrust her away and reached for his shirt.

"Here, what's this?" she asked, smiling at him, moving so that one full breast brushed his arm.

He looked at her, formed the words to tell her that what they had done was terribly wrong, but the words stuck in his throat. She put her hand on his shoulder, let it tingle down, down, to his chest and to the flat plane of his stomach.

"Come with Guinevere," she whispered, leading him toward the bed.

Chapter XXVI

SLONE SHANNON STOPPED off at Brisbane when he returned from New Guinea. There he hired a horse to ride the familiar roads to the home he had left to go to the South African War. Adam Vincent Shannon, the Earl of Cheviot, was in residence with his lady, having only recently returned from England.

Slone found the place in chaos. An army of workmen was hammering, sawing, painting, and milling around doing God only knew what else. He embraced his father, hugged his mother and kissed her thoroughly on cheeks and forehead and then stood back, arms spread in question.

"I'm beginning to think," Adam Shannon said, "that I would have been as well off to stay in England." He winked at his son. "This woman is determined to rip the whole place apart and put it back together again in a larger form. Here we are, two aging creatures who don't need more than a cup of milk and a warm fireplace, and soon we'll be rattling around in a house big enough for a dozen guests."

Emily laughed. "I'm only thinking of the time when Slone and Sianna will visit with their family." She looked at Slone inquiringly. "There *will* be a family, I pray."

"Occasionally, Mother, we apply ourselves to that problem," Slone said dryly. "I assure you that we're as eager to make you a grandmother as you are to be one."

"Well," Emily replied, "if you stayed at home, where you

belong—or, better still, brought that lovely girl here, where you both belong—"

"Now, Emily," Adam demurred.

Adam had insisted on preserving one cove of quiet in the house. While Emily rushed off to check on various gangs of workmen, he and Slone retired to the earl's study. Dark paneling and richly polished furniture made the room seem quiet and cozy, and Maori artifacts decorated one wall. Slone sank down into a well-worn leather chair, accepted a cigar, and took pleasure in using the silver tool he had given to his father as a Christmas present to clip the ends of the cigar. Adam leaned down to light it for him.

"They seem to be keeping you on the run," Adam said, taking his own chair. "How do you find conditions in New Guinea?"

"To tell you the truth, sir," Slone said, "I was in and out so quickly that I couldn't venture an opinion. I gathered from the governor that development is slow, the problems being manifold. There are no roads, and the labor force has to be imported, for the most part. The funds available from the Colonial Office in London are almost nonexistent, and I fear that the small amount budgeted by our own government will not accomplish much for the indigenous population. We've made little impact on the natives, except where they've come into contact with the white man and have acquired a taste for his spirits and tobacco."

"There are people, both in the government and out, who decry any expenditure in what they call an imperialist venture," Adam commented.

"Yes, I suppose the limited funds we allocate to New Guinea could be used elsewhere," Slone said wryly. "Perhaps in building defenses to combat a future German push across the Torres Strait, after the Germans have consolidated their hold over all of New Guinea."

"Odd state of affairs in London," Adam said, "at least when we were there. One group of influential people is very much concerned with German intentions, but they are in the minority. The majority of people in authority seems to think that those who worry about the Germans are crying wolf."

"I've encountered both types," Slone said. "Most think that it's foolish even to imagine that Germany can ever challenge the Royal Navy. In reality, British supremacy of the seas comes under challenge quite often. The Germans push here, probe there, looking for a weak spot. So far they've always pulled back, even when they find weakness. Occasionally, as in the Persian Gulf, they pull back only after a very determined action on our part. When Lord Lansdowne said that Britain would resist the establishment of a naval base in the Persian Gulf, he meant exactly that. The foreign secretary was warning Kaiser Wilhelm that Great Britain would go to war with Germany on that issue."

Adam puffed reflectively on his cigar. "You know, when we're out here, so many miles from the old countries, their eternal squabbles all seem so damned ridiculous. On the other hand, I think we're right to worry. I wonder if Malthus wasn't right to a certain extent. One or two generations of peace in Europe would see an enormous increase in population and cause all sorts of problems of adjustment."

They sat for a time in comfortable silence. A veil of cigar smoke hung over their heads. The scent of a very good brandy mingled with the pleasant odor of the tobacco. Slone smiled to himself. In England there was a huge stone pile of a house, the seat of the earldom, with furnishings that would bring a fortune on the antiques market, with carefully tended acres, a forest for hunting, a stream for fishing, and willing servants to meet any need of the earl and his household. And yet Adam Shannon preferred the more rustic comfort of his station in Queensland.

"Something amusing?" Adam asked idly.

"I was just thinking. If you're not going to work at it, you might as well sell the earldom, you know."

"Can't do that," Adam said. "It's hereditary. Might step out and leave it to you early."

"Thank you very much," Slone replied, "but I'm not sure that's allowed either."

"Your son may actually want it and value it," Adam said. "How does Sianna feel about it?"

"Oh, she's still a bit awed by it all," Slone said. "She enjoys having money to spend. When we move to Vienna, it will cost a fortune just to ship her wardrobe."

"Vienna, is it?"

"Sorry," Slone said, "I didn't mean to make it seem that I was withholding the news. I haven't mentioned my new orders because I want to ask your opinion on a couple of things."

"Ask away."

"Well," Slone said, "the problem is, Where to start?" He shook ashes from his cigar and looked at the ceiling. "I went to New Guinea with instructions for an eccentric old man who carries the mail into the German areas of New Guinea. He draws pay from at least three sources, only one of which is open and aboveboard. He's paid for carrying the mail, but he also draws unknown amounts from certain agencies of both the British and German governments."

Adam, interested, nodded. "I think I detect in this the fine hand of Lord Kitchener," he said.

"Kitchener recommended me to certain people," Slone said. "Do you think I did right in accepting their offers?"

"In the past, fighting men haven't had much respect for spies," Adam said. "You know how it is: 'The man who is an informer in my eyes is a traitor to someone else.' However, the world is a more complicated place now. The South African War proved that. It wasn't just a matter of putting a couple of hundred thousand men in the field, letting them face the enemy in a fair fight, winner take all. No, the war was settled by other means than battles. It involved the civilian population, for one thing. The sufferings of women and children determined the outcome as much as did the battles." He shook his head sadly. "War is changing. For one thing, it used to take weeks and months to get armies into position for the

climactic battles. Now we can move men quickly by rail an
by steamer, and battles can take place in unexpected places
Then there's the fact that under certain conditions guerrill
tactics, such as the Boers developed, are most effective. Ther
are also the new weapons that were so deadly in South Afric;
plus God knows what other sorts of weapons that are on th
drawing boards of the various powers."

He paused to refill their glasses. "If you ask me, I'd say tha
warfare in the future will be quite unlike anything we've eve
known. A war between European powers might not be limite
to the old battlefields but could well be fought on a worldwid
scale. So you see, I'm going a long way around to say that ye
intelligence is vital in this day and time. Take your odd littl
man in New Guinea. He is the spy; you are the spy maste
Am I not right?"

"I wouldn't put it exactly that way, but yes, that's the e:
sence of it."

"I would think it vital that we have some way to keep a
eye on the Germans in New Guinea, and wherever else the
try to expand German colonial holdings. Your mention of th
crisis in the Persian Gulf indicates that war could break out i
some isolated place far from Berlin and London. To answe
your question finally, I will say that if you are, indeed, servin
well in intelligence operations, I think you can be proud."

"Thank you," Slone said. "There's a bit more to it tha
that, however. You see, they want Sianna to become a part «
it."

"Ah," Adam said.

"She's a Boer. She speaks German well. As you knov
there were some odd concessions in the peace treaty. Th
Boer republics became crown colonies, but the treaty le
them the right to teach their own languages in schools and,
fear, did more to make the Boers conscious of their nationa
ity than I personally think was advisable. As one might su
pect, the Boers harbor a great deal of resentment and hatre
for all things British. There's hardly a Boer family that didn
lose a relative either in the war or in one of the concentratic

camps. So my superiors want Sianna and me to stop off in South Africa and take a look at conditions there, using Sianna's nationality and her language to try to get a feeling about the depth of Boer hostility toward the empire."

"What does she think?" Adam asked.

"Oh, she's intrigued." He made a face. "She says that it's not *really* being a traitor to one's own people just to talk to them to find out how they feel."

"I see. Mixed emotions, eh?"

"Quite. And not only for her."

"Which way are you leaning?" Adam asked.

"Dad, I don't want to see men marching into the muzzles of pom-pom and Maxim guns again," Slone said with great emphasis. "And as a nurse Sianna saw at close hand what modern weapons do to the human body. She feels the same way."

Adam spread his hands. "Quite a just cause, isn't it?"

Slone nodded.

"I would not condone putting her into the slightest danger, however," Adam said.

"No, of course not."

Ironically, it was a German ship that took Slone and Sianna to South Africa. No fewer than half a dozen German ships were engaged in the traffic between northern Europe and the Far East, but these were generally not of the best quality, since Germany, like Britain and France, reserved her finest vessels for the lucrative North Atlantic run to America. Thus it was not always possible to travel in comfort from Australia to the old countries. But by a stroke of luck, the *Bremen* was returning from a rare trip to the Far East, with a detour to Durban in Natal, so the viscount and his lady were able to travel in great style.

After a happy reunion with Dirk and Anna De Hartog at the De Hartog place outside Pietermaritzburg, the handsome young couple was off on a tour of the former Boer-republics.

Johannesburg, on the surface, had become very British.

The mines of the Rand were in full operation, and the scars of war were mostly healed, thanks to the work of the industrious Boers.

In Pretoria they were received by the high commissioner and governor of the crown colonies, Sir Alfred Milner. Milner talked convincingly about peace and union in South Africa, pointing out that the crown had expended ten million pounds to rehabilitate the Boers who had suffered in the war. The prisoner of war camps and the concentration camps had long since been emptied, and the Boers who were returning to their lands had been supplied with food, livestock, seeds, and tools.

"We're moving toward unification," Milner told them. "Our first step was the establishment of the South African Customs Union. And the railways of the Transvaal have been joined with those in the Orange River Colony—the former Free State. So I like to think we have the support and the backing of the Boer population. I am firm in my belief that the thinking people among the Boers know that they are better off under the crown."

Slone also called on the Boer general Louis Botha, and in an amiable chat he learned that Botha agreed with Milner, at least conditionally. Botha had no official position in the colonial government, but no one, not even Milner, underestimated the general's influence with the Boer people. It was to Botha and to Jan Smuts that the Boers turned when problems arose, and the majority of the Boer population followed their lead.

"There are some, like General De Wet, who are not convinced that the war is over," Botha said. "But you and I know that it is, do we not, my dear Viscount? We Boers know that we must learn to live with the British."

"Your goodwill is evident everywhere, sir," Slone replied. "With you and Jan Smuts in favor of uniting the former Boer nations and the British colonies into one union, I think we can look forward to some vast and important changes in South Africa in the future."

"Well, I think, if union comes, most of the credit will go to Smuts," Botha acknowledged.

"I understand, however, that it is you who are the most effective in convincing the English-speaking peoples that union would not be some sort of plot to allow the Afrikaners to dominate South Africa."

Botha smiled ruefully. "I have spoken of this, much to the anger of gentlemen like our old friend De Wet."

"I've never met General De Wet," Slone said. "Now and then I may have met some of his soldiers in the field, but never the general himself."

"Well, we must remedy that," Botha said. "You seem to be an eminently reasonable man, and the fact that you're married to a good Boer might just convince the general that you are not the typical Britisher. You see, I take every opportunity to try to convince Christiaan De Wet that the divisions and blood of the past should be forgotten. If you can help in any way . . ."

General Christiaan De Wet looked as rugged and hard as he must have when he led the last Boer army in the field against the overwhelming odds of the British—odds that had finally forced even De Wet to surrender.

Lanky, gray of hair, his long beard unkempt, De Wet looked to Slone like some dissolute artist's conception of a biblical prophet. And in his talk he showed no inclination to be cautious with regard to his conviction that the struggle for Boer independence was not over.

"It took odds of one hundred to one for you to beat us," De Wet told his Australian visitor, his lips smiling grimly over his stringy beard. "And then just barely. Give me modern arms, good horses, three generals like Koos De La Rey or your father-in-law, Dirk De Hartog, and I'd raise twenty thousand commandos and push you into the ocean!"

Slone could see that words of reason were not going to change this hard old man's opinions. There had been too much blood shed, and too many good men had died. A man like De Wet, whose beliefs were rooted deep in the bedrock of the Old Testament, could never live comfortably and peaceably side by side with the British—with people who, in his opinion, were amoral sons of the devil. So Slone turned the conversation to war stories and listened with great interest as the old general told tales of the campaigns that had swept back and forth across the High Veld.

Sianna, meanwhile, was with the women of the De Wet household. The talk was in Afrikaans, the conversation friendly and lively after the initial awkwardness had been overcome by means of good, strong coffee and freshly baked cakes swimming with butter.

Trinka De Wet Du Tout, the general's daughter, was acting as hostess. A few of the other women were nieces and the wives of nephews of the general, but some seemed to be merely visitors. The De Wet house was large and sprawling; through the open windows came the sounds of children at play. Now and then one of the young mothers would go to a window to check on the brood.

Trinka was a buxom, motherly woman with astute gray eyes and a warm smile. She smelled pleasantly of the cooking she had been doing, of vanilla flavoring and brown sugar. She put cakes on Sianna's plate, and Sianna ate until she gasped in repletion, rubbed her stomach, and declared for the fourth time how delicious the cakes were.

The talk arose at first from the curiosity of the younger women. Sianna answered questions about her husband, about her travels, about Australia. When they were all more relaxed, she asked questions of her own, and then she slowly brought the subject around to the war. After that the conversation needed no priming. All the women knew of Dirk De Hartog.

"Ja," said one smiling young mother, "Colonel De Hartog. A hero of the war. He killed many British. When we fight again, he will be a general, no?"

"I pray not," Sianna said. "What I mean is that I pray there will not be another war. General Botha says—"

"Bah," said Trinka Du Tout. "Louis Botha. Was he born British?"

"I think General Botha is a very wise man," Sianna said. "He advises that Boer and Britisher live together. He wants one nation in South Africa."

"With this I agree," Trinka said. "One *Boer* nation."

"But there's little hope for that," Sianna said.

"Your views are colored by your having married a Britisher," Trinka said. She blushed, realizing that she'd verged on insult. "Not that we condemn you for that, you understand."

"I hope not," Sianna replied. She was disturbed. The bitterness was in the women, lying just below the surface, ready to erupt. If the women were resentful, if the women thought in terms of Boer dominance and further war, those views had to come from men. The Boer woman was subservient to the man in all ways, so his thoughts on affairs of importance were usually hers.

"Being married to a British officer who is highly placed in the government might be of advantage at some time in the future," Trinka Du Tout said, "*if* you are truly a Boer at heart."

Sianna felt that such talk had gone far enough. She drew herself up stiffly. "Mrs. Du Tout, I am a guest in your house. My purpose here is social, and I don't think it wise to continue our discussion along the lines—" She broke off and rose abruptly. "If you will just send someone to tell my husband that I am ready to leave . . ."

The younger women gasped. A wife did not tell her husband when to break off a conference.

"Please," Trinka Du Tout said placatingly, "I meant no offense. Like my father, I am often too prone to speak bluntly." She rose and bowed to Sianna. "Come, we will find a place where we can talk quietly, and I will try to make up for my rudeness."

Sianna followed the older woman to a very feminine sitting room. Trinka sat facing her. "As I have said," she began, "I know only one way to speak. I believe in getting to the point, and I don't know how to talk in diplomatic terms, sidling up to a subject in fits and starts."

"Of what do you wish to speak?" Sianna asked.

"Of you, born Sianna De Hartog to a good Boer father."

Sianna wondered if Trinka's opinion would be different if she were told that Dirk De Hartog was not her father, that she did not know her real father or even his name. She remained silent, interested now in what was making Trinka Du Tout so solemn and serious.

"You served as a nurse during the war. You saw what the British did to our young men."

"And what our young men did to the British," Sianna said. "The blood of Boer and Britisher was equally red."

"But you served your country."

"I did."

"And now you are married to an Englishman."

"Not actually," Sianna said. "Slone was born in Australia."

"The same. British. Now the question is, Sianna De Hartog, is this still your country?"

"Well, of course," Sianna said. "I was born in Natal. Just where are you leading with such questions?"

"There will be war, you know," Trinka said. "Not as before. Next time the British will face a stronger enemy. Next time they will not be able to concentrate their entire efforts on South Africa, for they will face Germany at home and in many other battlefields around the world. And when this happens, where will your loyalties lie, Sianna De Hartog?"

"My name, *mevreau,* is Sianna Shannon."

"So, you avoid answering the question, do you?" The Boer woman smiled. "And yet you were born Boer, and you fought in your own way as a Boer woman. I think that when the time comes, you will remember your country. As the wife of a British diplomat you will be in a position where you could offer valuable help to your country, and I think you will do it."

Sianna flushed. "Are you saying that I am to be a spy

against my husband's country, against the country that I adopted when I became his wife?"

Trinka spread her hands. "Only that you may at some time have access to information that would make it easier for all of us to achieve the goal of which we dream, a Boer nation under God's blessings that will encompass all of South Africa."

"I will go now," Sianna said, standing up abruptly.

"I will give you some names," Trinka persisted. "Remember them. My father, of course, and myself. But in the event that you can't reach either of us, remember Steyn, Hertzog, and Beyers. You know of these men."

Sianna turned and swept from the room. She knew the names. Steyn, Hertzog, Beyers. They could not forget the past, and they opposed Louis Botha's efforts to live peacefully with the British.

Slone had finished his talk with the old general, and Sianna joined him in their carriage. On the ride back to their hotel he told Sianna that De Wet would never be a friend of Great Britain, and she reported in a general way on her talks with the women of the De Wet household.

"The women fought, too," Sianna said. "And they didn't surrender. It was the men who surrendered."

"We're not fighting the battle of the sexes," Slone teased.

"They expressed the feelings that I suspect are shared by the men," Sianna said, "for a good Boer woman reflects the beliefs of her man. They resent Sir Alfred Milner; they call him the man who made the war. They say he could have averted the war at the Bloemfontein conference back in '99, when he refused to extend the Transvaal franchise."

"Well, that can be viewed in two ways," Slone said. "You could say that Paul Kruger made the war when he refused to compromise with Milner at Bloemfontein."

"Are we to argue the issues ourselves?" Sianna asked. "Or do you want to know what is in the minds of the Boers today?"

"Sorry," he said.

"They call Milner's staff, the young men who are helping

Milner push for South African unification, the kindergarten. They resent Milner's having suspended the Cape constitution in 1902." She paused and looked at Slone. "Now listen to this, for I think, as an Australian, you'll understand. What they seem to resent most is Milner's policy of bringing Chinese workers to the Witwatersrand gold mines."

"As well they might." Slone nodded thoughtfully. "I'll be damned. Remind me to emphasize that in my report. It would be an excellent place to begin working to gain the confidence of the Boer population."

"As for the big question," Sianna went on, "would the Boers of the former Boer republics be loyal to the crown in the event of a war between Great Britain and Germany? The answer is ambivalent. Some would. Personally, on the basis of the few people with whom I have talked, I think that there would be a mighty underground of sympathy for Germany, and if the Germans should be able to move troops into South Africa from their African colonies, they would have the support of most of the Boers who fought in the war."

"Do you really think it has gone that far?"

"I fear so," she said thoughtfully. "But after all, I'm a mere woman, and I was talking to other mere women."

"You are very definitely not mere," Slone said, reaching for her, smothering her playful protest in his kisses. She squealed and reminded him that the world could see them in the open carriage, and perhaps that was why—the sweet distraction— she did not mention the private talk she had had with Trinka De Wet Du Tout.

They left the north and traveled by rail to Cape Town, where they boarded a ship headed for England. She still had not told him about Trinka's smug confidence that Sianna, being a good Boer girl, would side against Great Britain if it were for the good of a potential Boer nation in South Africa. Sianna told herself that the likelihood of war, after all, was small and that if it did come, she would, of course, be loyal to her husband. She reasoned that to tell Slone about the conversation with Trinka would serve only to color his opinion of the Boer people. After all, Trinka was only a woman. General Louis Botha was more representative of the Boers than General De Wet and his embittered daughter.

She lay next to Slone in their cabin, her blond hair tickling his chest, her head on his shoulder. "Will we have a grand house in Vienna?"

"I doubt it. I'm only a small cog in the wheel, you know."

"If they don't give us a grand house, I will protest to the Foreign Office myself," she said idly. "I will tell them, 'Look, you, I will not spy for you unless you give me a grand house so that I can entertain people worth spying on.'"

"Goodonyer," Slone said. "And then you can go to the Austrian emperor and say, 'Look here, Franz Josef, you've got to convince your friend Kaiser Willie that his mucking about with the world has got to stop.'"

"I would do it, too. Why should a few stupid old men be able to cause war?"

"Honey, come up with the answer to that one, and you'll be the first president of the world."

It was not a house, but an apartment in a beautiful old building not far from the government complexes. It was quite grand, with dark old pictures painted by gloomy visionaries and brooding romantics. Thick hangings on the walls helped keep out the icy winter winds, and the rooms were furnished with heavy Germanic pieces.

They spent pleasant evenings exploring the city, confirmed that it was, indeed, the city of the waltz, and gained pounds eating the delicious pastries that seemed to be available in at least one shop in every block.

Slone was given a small office near the British Embassy, where, nominally, he was directly responsible to the man in charge of the Australian mission. His orders came, however, from another small office in the British Embassy itself.

For months it seemed that his duties consisted merely of being present at various social functions, the token British peer, the viscount. He met so many dukes, princes, and barons that it was difficult to keep them straight. He and his wife were very popular, for Sianna spoke the language beautifully, and with her help Slone was learning rapidly.

There was some talk in the Austrian court of the possibility of war between Great Britain and Russia, a consummation much to be desired from the Austrian and German viewpoints, but Slone and Sianna learned nothing worth reporting. The Anglo-Japanese Alliance of 1902 had served the purpose for which its British makers had intended it, allowing Britain to put a check on Russian activities in the Far East without having to deploy British force there.

"Why is it, my dear Viscount," asked a minor German diplomat, speaking to Slone at table in the house of a powerful man in the Austrian court, "that every action by your country is aimed directly at Germany?"

"Oh, I suppose it's just a little bad blood between members of the family," Slone said lightly. "Shouldn't we leave such things up to the relatives? Uncle Edward and Nephew Bill?"

After a moment the German laughed. It was well known in German intelligence circles that Slone Shannon served no useful purpose to either the British or the Australian government. He was simply the token British peer in Vienna, and one could expect such inane comments from that sort of man.

Chapter XXVII

WHEN JAVA SAW the pool of water lying in shadow at the base of a sheer wall of red rock, she forgot her exhaustion. Her leaden feet became light once more as she raced down a rocky incline with a haste that risked a painful fall. She managed to keep her feet, although she stumbled in the sand as she neared the water. In her imagination she could taste it, feel it trickling down her throat to cut away the long days of thirst and dust, could feel it splashing onto her face, could dream of leaping into it—although the water hole was only a few feet in diameter and the water shallow.

With a groan of dismay she jerked to a halt. Sodden, dead vegetation clogged the water hole. A green scum covered the small open areas, and at one end the bloated, stinking body of a dead dingo lay half in, half out of the water. Flies buzzed over the carcass.

Bildana, who had followed at a walk, came to stand beside Java. She shook her head when Java began to sob with frustration.

For Java life had become a progression of identical days, days of sun and thirst and hunger and endless miles of red, dry landscape studded with desert bushes and grasses. Life was, after all, not a complicated thing. Life was simply a search for the edible tubers of the potato family that hid themselves cunningly in the desert, with little evidence above-

ground of their existence. Life was making the water in the
waterskin last days beyond the crying need of the body. When
life depended upon the one or two tubers that could be found
as one walked eternally toward the east, when life was sus-
tained only by one's licking morning moisture from a slick
stone, there could be no embellishments in the form of
dreams, plans, or musings.

She had lost weight rapidly during the first weeks and was
now gaunt and stringy; but the human body is tremendously
adaptable, and after a while her weight loss had leveled off.
Her body had made its adjustment, compensating for the first
effects of starvation by reducing the amount of active tissue,
thus lessening the need for fuel. And she had fallen into a
morbid lethargy that made it a supreme effort to keep moving,
to follow Bildana up rises and down rises, through fields of
dense spinifex that continued the gradual ruin of her clothing
and left her skin with small, festering wounds. Her entire
being was dominated by the need for food.

For a time water, scant as it was, was not the main problem. There was moisture in the roots and tubers that Java was
learning to find almost as adroitly as Bildana, and some few
soaks still contained water. It was hunger that presented the
most terrifying challenge. The capture of a desert lizard was
an event to make that day stand out from all others, and after
weeks of shuffling slowly toward the east Java did not always
wait long enough for Bildana to build a fire and roast the tiny
morsels of meat.

Into that haze of hunger, lethargy, and exhaustion came
stray thoughts of a blackness that at times numbed her. Tolo
was dead. She had loved him for such a short time, had been
able to hold him and be held for such a pitifully brief interlude. Why fight the desire to lie down in the shade of a red
boulder and close her eyes and let the weariness triumph?

More than anything else the memories of one person kept
her on her feet. Her grandmother's face appeared to her often,
and in the heat of the day, when she was feverish and each

step was torment, she seemed to hear Magdalen's voice urging her on, telling her that she didn't dare give up.

She had long since lost the compass, and she depended upon Bildana to lead the way, although keeping on course was simple. They merely shuffled toward the red glare of the morning sun and kept the afternoon sun on their backs.

A few days ago Bildana had warned that they were entering a stretch of absolute waterlessness. They had left a dripping source of water with a full waterskin, rationing themselves to three swallows a day. Then the water had given out, and they struggled through a day and a night without a drop to drink, only to find that the next water hole was fouled by trash and the dead dingo.

It was too much. For the first time Java wept. She fell to her knees and sobbed, the water drying on her cheeks almost instantly. Then she saw that Bildana was kneeling at the water hole on the end away from the dead dingo, bending, brushing back the scum, and—oh, God—drinking.

Java's gorge rose. She gagged dryly, but she was crawling toward Bildana even as revulsion sickened her. "Get the dead animal out?" she gasped.

"No stir up bad," Bildana said with an economy of words.

Java lifted water in cupped hands. It stank, but it was water. It soothed her parched tongue, and she had difficulty swallowing. She drank sparingly and felt her stomach rebel. Turning away from the water hole, she heaved up the muddy water, but as soon as the retching had ceased, she drank again. When a rabbit came down to the water hole, Bildana killed it with a skillful throw of a small stone, and they feasted on half-cooked meat for the first time in many days. With their stomachs distended by water and the meat, they slept.

Java awoke suddenly, cold, and saw that a full moon had risen, lighting the desert. She used precious energy to gather dead grasses and twigs to rekindle the fire. The bones of the rabbit were hanging on the spit, and she nibbled the last tidbits of meat off a leg bone. Bildana sat up and came to join her, chewing at the bones and crunching one with her back teeth to suck the marrow.

"Blackfella not here," Bildana said.

"No one has been here for a long time," Java agreed.

"Blackfella here, he keep water hole clean."

It took a long time for the meaning of Bildana's words to soak through the protective layers of lassitude. "Are you saying that we've entered the range of blackfellows?"

"Soon reach big, rolling hills of sand," Bildana said.

"Oh, God," Java breathed. Could it be? Could it really be true that they had crossed the worst of the desert? Many times she'd asked Bildana to describe the country toward which they walked eternally, and in her mind she had envisioned it, the dunes, and then the rocks and canyons, and finally the bulk of Ayers Rock rising from the flatness. "Bildana, talk to me," she said as Bildana sank back to lie on the barren sand.

"Good water two days," Bildana declared. "Sandhills. You see."

They found good, clean water, rich in minerals, lying in pools not a full day's walk apart. The water had turned the dune grasses green, and rabbits were more plentiful. And so they slowed their progress in order to hunt and kill, twice or three times a day. Their stomachs protruded as if they were in the early stages of pregnancy, and in Java's benumbed mind the dreadful lethargy began to be penetrated by hope.

The day that Bildana caught and killed a sheep by pounding its head with a rock was a day that Java would never forget. They had no tools, but they managed to skin a portion of the animal with sharp stones, teeth, and ripping fingers. Bildana made sounds of contentment as she gobbled raw liver, and she offered Java a piece. Java's mouth was watering with hunger; she accepted the raw meat and found it to be tangy, delightfully wet, the blood trickling down her throat soothingly. And when roasted, it was a feast.

Now the flies came, drawn by the blood, millions of them, a biblical plague. After a while Java found it too much effort, a

waste of precious energy, to brush them from her eyes, and
for the first time she understood why the Aborigines did not
seem to notice the flies that crawled to the edge of the eye in
search of moisture.

A measure of strength had come back to her. It still required great determination to think of anything beyond the
next few feet, the next feature of landscape toward which she
aimed her footsteps. Her feet were painfully sore, for she had
worn through her boots.

The diet of meat, tubers, berries, and the occasional fruits
of bushes told her more eloquently than anything else that
they had left the most arid areas behind them. Such bush
tucker would not return her to perfect health, but it would
stave off starvation and would at least begin the slow rebuild-
ing of muscle tissue. Much more time, and the addition of
balancing agents to her diet, would be needed before she
achieved complete mental health. She was feeling—and would
feel for some time—the residual effects of her ordeal, and it
would be a long while before her body resumed its youthful
functioning, before the protective numbness of mind was entirely dispelled.

One lasting effect of her physical and mental deprivation
was that her thoughts had become changed. Notions that
once had been clear to her, a simplicity of black and white,
were now a montage of shadings, a confusing network of limitless choices. For the first few days of her trek she had
wanted only to reach civilization and get back to Sydney as
quickly as possible. She had yearned for the comforting presence of family, especially of her grandmother. But after weeks
of malnutrition approaching starvation, of her body's constantly crying out for food and water, odd notions had begun
to dominate—when, indeed, she bothered to think of anything
other than the desert universe in which she was imprisoned.
While it was true that her grandmother's voice had been her
primary motivation for continuing on, it occurred to her that
it was her mother's fault that Tolo was dead and that Magda-
en had not, after all, fought very hard to make Jessica under-

stand how Java felt. It became very logical for Java to con
sider Jessica Gordon her husband's murderer, for Jessica
after all, had intended to take her away from Tolo, away t
England. That was the trip that had sparked the elopement
now seemingly so long ago. To a lesser extent her father, too
was under indictment for murder, for he had been party to th
trip as well. After the long days of agony and unvarying hun
ger, she had reached the conclusion that it would be unneces
sary—indeed, undesirable—to see her parents again.

Perhaps, one day, she would contact her grandmother. Sh
would, someday, write to Misa Mason, to tell her how he
parents had murdered Tolo.

Tolo. In those last feverish, anguished, dehydrated days be
fore they entered the lands of good water it was Tolo wh
took Magdalen's place in Java's heated imaginings. It wa
Tolo who urged her on, telling her that life was worth con
tinuing, that she had a mission. They had begun the penetra
tion of the Gibson Desert agreed on an aim: to document th
oral myths of the Aborigines. The reminder of Tolo's idealis
tic goal gave her thoughts a new direction. As adequate wate
and the intake of meat food in the form of rabbits and a stra
sheep returned some strength to her, she began to realize tha
she was alive because of Bildana. She owed her life to th
small black woman. With her mind still stunned by the effect
of near starvation, it was an easy task of transferral to includ
all Aborigines in the scope of her indebtedness.

*"I think that most of the things wrong with the Abos can b
attributed directly to their contact with the white man,"* Tol
had said.

So Java hated her mother and her father because their re
fusal of Tolo had driven him into the western desert—or s
said the workings of her wounded mind—and she felt an al
most maudlin gratitude toward Bildana. Revived by plenty o
water and meat, she set herself a sacred task. Without Tolo
her life would be empty, a burden, crying out either to be she
or to be filled. Of course, she would never have room in he
heart for another man, so what could be more logical than t

devote her life to her late husband's cause, the betterment of
the much-abused native Australians?

Tolo, having known they would face danger during their
excursion into the outback, had made suitable arrangements
before leaving Melbourne. In the event of his death—a ridicu-
lously remote possibility, it seemed at the time—Java would
be able to tap substantial funds without waiting for the execu-
tion of Tolo's will and without having to go to Misa Mason.
Those funds would be used, Java determined as Bildana and
she moved on toward Ayers Rock, to bring education and
modern medicine to the Aborigines, first those of Bildana's
tribal unit, then later to others.

Thus, with her clothing hanging in tattered rags, with her
hair a rat's nest that gave shelter to two varieties of bloodsucking insects, Java pulled Bildana down behind rocks when
they sighted a mounted white man at a distance. She did not
want contact with white men, not yet.

"That man can take you to your people," Bildana objected.

"My people deserted me when I needed them most," Java
said simply. It seemed too taxing and complicated, in her
hazy state of mind, to explain that because of family disapproval of Tolo's brown blood, she and Tolo had been forced to
flee comfort and happiness to struggle and die in the wilderness.

"What will you do?" Bildana asked.

She could not explain that either. She knew that sooner or
later she would have to go into a town. She needed supplies
and clothing, and to buy them, she would have to draw on the
account Tolo had made accessible to her in a Melbourne
bank. She suspected that if she appeared in Alice Springs, she
would be immediately scooped up by the authorities and
shipped back to Sydney and her family. She would not coun-
tenance such an event.

It was she who sighted the low dark hump in the distance.
The rock. Ayers Rock, the great-red-sacred-rock. When she
pointed it out to Bildana, Bildana nodded, halted, sat down,

and chanted, bowing her head toward the looming form in the distance.

They came near the huge outcrop of red stone in the evening. Bildana led the way as they climbed onto one of its lower nodes. There she communicated with her spirits of the Dreamtime and was inspired, for she, too, had been considering her future.

Bildana did not know that Ganba was dead. He was a vindictive man, and she had threatened his manhood in many ways, first by aligning herself with the whitefella woman, then by deserting him entirely. Sooner or later he would come looking for her, and if he ever found her, she would be meat food crinkling and smoking on Ganba's fire.

"Missy, it is time for you to find your people," Bildana said when, in the morning, they sat in a little clump of trees, in blessed shade, and shared a rabbit.

"And you," Java said. "How will you find your people?"

"They are here," she said.

"Here?"

Bildana made a motion with her hands that indicated a large area. "Here, there." She pointed toward the north. "We came from there. I will go there. I will find them."

"I will go with you," Java said.

Bildana made a sound of disbelief.

"We will find blackfellows in the mountains, in the Macdonnell Ranges."

"Yes."

"Your people?"

"Maybe," Bildana said.

"Is there a town there?" Java asked, pointing toward the north.

"Barrow Creek."

"We will go there," Java said, "before or after we find your people. There I will go to a whitefellow bank and draw much money."

"Ah," Bildana said. "Then perhaps you will buy Bildana a nice dress?"

Java laughed, and it was the first time she'd heard *that* sound in a long, long time. "Two," she said. "And then we will use the money to make things better for your people."

"You will buy all of the women dresses?" Bildana asked, awed by the concept.

"No. Maybe not just dresses. We will buy the things that we will need to teach the blackfellow to live better. To teach him how to read and write so that he can live better with the whitefellow, who is sure to come. We will help the blackfellow learn to live with the whitefellow and to have some of the things that the whitefellow enjoys."

Bildana made a sound of derision.

"I want to go with you, Bildana," Java insisted. "I can't go home. Not now. It would all seem so frivolous, so futile. I know now what you and your people have to go through all the time—hunger, thirst, being cold, being hot. Please help me. I want to help you and your people. It's what Tolo would have wanted."

"Man dead, hurt here," Bildana said, thumping her heart.

"Hurt here. Much," Java said, placing her hand on her breast. "Oh, yes, I do hurt, and to do what I say will make the hurt better."

Bildana could accept that, although she still thought the missy had been crazed by the sun of the never-never.

Staying well away from Alice Springs, they reached the low hills of the Macdonnells, where they encountered a small family group of Bildana's tribe. One woman had needle and thread, which Java borrowed to make emergency repairs on her clothing. She cut off the legs of her jodhpurs, leaving her legs bare from the knees down, and stitched the rotting shirt into a semblance of covering for her torso. She told the leader of the group, an old man named Jajjala, who eyed her with great suspicion, that she needed to go north to Barrow Creek.

"There, three days," old Jajjala said. "Go."

"Come with me," Java said. "I go to the town to get money."

"Why not go Alice Springs? Alice closer."

"I prefer Barrow Creek," Java said without further explanation.

Jajjala was silent for a moment. "I will go," he said at last. "You buy Jajjala gin."

"No," Java said, "but I will buy you warm clothing, and I will buy books so that I can teach your children how to read the whitefellow's words."

"Why?" Jajjala asked.

"So that in the future they can take their place in the whitefellow's world."

"This is our world."

"I know," she said, "but one day the whitefellow will come here, too, and he will want your land and he will take it. Then what will you do?"

Jajjala laughed. "Whitefella cannot live here."

"This whitefellow lived in the Gibson," Java declared.

"Only because of Bildana. If you want to go to town, I will go, but only if you will buy gin."

Well, there was time. She could not, she knew, expect an instant acceptance of her hopes for the Aborigines. "I will buy you gin."

Later, as she wrapped herself in a ragged blanket, scratching at fly bites, she preached patience to herself. These people knew nothing but their natural way of life—squalid, uncomfortable, filthy, and savage. Things would look better when she reached Barrow Creek, bought some new clothes, had a bath with soap, and had her hair cut to a manageable shortness. Then she would begin the long, slow process of changing Jajjala's way of life.

Chapter XXVIII

TERRY FORREST HAD come to the conclusion that crocs were bloody well fond of their hides, if one were to judge by the various ways the beasts resisted parting with them. They were elusive and sly, as treacherous as a riled taipan. With crocs one never knew who was hunting whom. Getting a high-velocity copper-coated bullet into a kill point was no easy task; the croc's brain, for example, was so small that often the bullet missed or was deflected by the incredibly tough hide. Even when the croc was done for, one might not be able to put a rope on the beggar and haul him out for skinning.

Terry didn't mind the risk. He figured he had to be just a little bit smarter than a reptile with a brain the size of a walnut. What he minded most was the skinning once he'd bagged an animal. It was difficult to pierce the hide with the sharpest knife. The job was begun with an ax and completed in near apoplexy.

After a few weeks of it, living in the wet country amid mobs of flying, crawling, swarming, buzzing carnivorous insects, Terry had had enough. He sold his share to the others for a fraction of the price that the accumulating hides would bring in Palmerston, saddled his horse, and headed south, taking a tucker-bag full of smoked croc tail, which tasted like a cross between chicken and frogs' legs.

His decision as to which direction to travel had been a toss-up, except that memories of troopship rides to and from South Africa turned him away from the coast. He did not like ocean travel. On those long voyages he had spent as much time as possible on deck because under metal decks, enclosed in stifling, crowded areas, he had felt a total loss of control over his own safety. Sleeping in a tiny cabin aboard a ship that could at any minute strike something and go plunging to the bottom was not to his liking. Better to be in the outback, free to plan one's day around the water supply and the hunting of fresh meat.

He headed south, leaving the green belt of the northern wetlands and wandering through a vast and vacant land. The Tanami Desert was not the Gibson, or even the Great Sandy, but it could kill a bloke. The Northern Territory showed on the maps as a large brown void. The little settlement of Barrow Creek was the one spot of white civilization between Alice Springs and the greenery of the far north. When he reached that town, Terry was ready for a few tall mugs of ale to wash away the taste of red dust.

The little pub he found there was exactly the sort of place in which he felt most comfortable: board walls, dirt floor, hard stools, and hard men. The kitchen served a beefsteak that wasn't all bad, and the ale was all good.

It took Terry a few days of eating, drinking, sleeping—and soaking in a bathtub too small for him—to get the dust of the desert off his hide and out of his throat. Then he began to think about where he'd go from Barrow Creek. He had no intention of mucking around in the Gibson Desert to get back to the west coast. He'd crossed the Gibson once; that was enough. His solo feat made for some interesting talk at the pub, where the prospectors, especially, listened to him with great interest and asked questions about the lay of the land, the location of water, and the color of the rocks, but he didn't want to do it again.

There wasn't much going on in the Territory. Over in Queensland were cattle and sheep stations where a mate could find employment, but he wasn't really ready to go to work for some squatter, not as long as Tolo Mason's money lasted. He hadn't seen the east coast. Perhaps in Brisbane or Sydney, or farther south in Melbourne, there might be some sights to see, some sheilas to meet. If he rode east to the coast, he would have covered quite a bloody bit of Australia in his walkabouts. He'd seen a lot of the west, from the Nullarbor in the south to the Great Sandy in the northwest and Arnhem Land near the north-central coast. Hell, he might just pop into Adelaide so that he could say that he'd been in every state and territory in the country.

He was thinking seriously of moving on when, upon leaving the pub early one afternoon, he saw an old Abo woman in cast-off rags holding out her hand. She had a blank, challenging look on her face. He tossed her a coin and said, "Get out of the way, mother."

The old woman looked at the coin with apparent disgust. "Whitefella kind," she said. "But not enough to buy food." She held out her hand again. Terry snorted and stepped around her.

"And it isn't enough to buy you a bottle of gin either," he said.

"Give me enough to buy food, and I will tell you of the whitefella woman who walked with the *mamu* in the never-never," the old woman said.

That got Terry's attention. "What did you say?" he demanded.

"Good tale," the old woman said. "Give me money for food."

Terry grinned at himself as he gave the old woman a full pound. He was being conned royally by the old crone. "Now, what's this about a white woman in the never-never?"

"She walked with the *mamu*," the old woman said. "For tucker she ate the magic food of the Dreaming, and the *mamu* guided her. She crossed the never-never with a blackfella woman, and the spirits of the Dreaming brought them to the great-red-sacred-rock and there rewarded them for their courage. You can see them, the whitefella woman and the other, dancing atop the great-red-sacred-rock in the dark time."

"Where did you hear about a white woman in the desert?" Terry asked.

The old woman shrugged. "All blackfellas know."

He seized the old woman's arm and squeezed until she winced in pain. His reason told him that she was simply telling another of the myth tales that the Aborigines loved so much, but he couldn't pass it off so easily. "Where did you hear about a white woman in the never-never? Did you make up this tale?"

"I do you no harm," the old woman protested, trying to pull her arm from his grasp.

"Did you hear that the whitefellows are looking for a white woman coming out of the never-never, and did you make up this tale?" he asked again, his mouth twisted, his eyes squinting.

"I hear this from blackfella on walkabout. He come from there." She pointed vaguely southward.

Terry released the old woman. His momentary hope faded. He had heard, of course, that the Mason family in Sydney had put out an alert for Java Mason. The old woman must have heard talk of it, too, for it had been discussed in the pub, where the opinion of the desert rats was that a white woman couldn't last a week alone in the never-never. The old Abo woman had made up the tale to use as a tool in her begging.

For some reason that he himself could not have explained, Terry lingered in Barrow Creek. An old prospector talked to him drunkenly about the lost gold of the long-dead Lassiter, claiming that he had been so close once that he could see the gleam of the exposed lode, only to be driven away and lost in a sudden sandstorm. The man paid for his food and drinks with gold dust, and that interested Terry. He left Barrow Creek, heading northeast in the company of this half-crazed old bushranger.

In Terry's opinion prospecting was only marginally better than being struck repeatedly in the eye with a sharp stick. He had done a bit of it before, out west, and after a few days of digging around with the bushranger he began to question his sanity. But there was a trace of color in the sand of a water hole where the old man had made his camp, and by working hard all day, one could pan just about enough to buy a glass or two of ale.

Terry's prospecting ended when he awoke one morning to find the old man still in his kip. The bushranger was an early riser, so Terry walked over and scratched the man's belly to see what was wrong. It was, for the old man, the ultimate wrong. He had died quietly in his sleep.

"Bloody hell," Terry muttered, kneeling to place his finger on the old duffer's throat in an effort to find a pulse. The skin was cool and papery to the touch, and Terry found no hint of pulse. "Well," Terry said, "it wasn't a bad way to go, old-timer, was it?"

Barrow Creek existed because men had strung wires across the outback so that business could be conducted over long distances via telegraph. The town, built around the telegraph repeater station, was constructed in 1872 beside a spring that was not only vital to the existence of the area's Aborigines but sacred to their beliefs. The men who maintained the station—and the few settlers and prospectors who gravitated to the town as if generated from the vacuum of the desert—fenced off this sacred spring, the only good water for miles around. In retaliation the Aborigines attacked the station, killing two of the station staff. One of them, Postmaster James Stapleton, exchanged telegraph messages with his wife in Adelaide as he lay dying, and that poignant event led to a campaign of revenge, a massacre of blackfellows at a nearby site that was forever after known as Skull Creek.

There had been no big strikes of gold in the Territory, but persistent prospectors brought in handfuls of dust or even nuggets now and then, enough to warrant a small bank in a side room of the trading post near the repeater station. And in that modern age the miracle of telegraph communications linked the bank with the bank in Melbourne where Tolo Mason had arranged withdrawal rights for his wife.

At first the banker, who was also the storekeeper, could not believe his eyes when an emaciated young white woman dressed in rags stood before him. She was browned by the sun, almost to the point of being as dark as the Abo woman who had entered the store with her. And when he heard her state her purpose, well . . .

"I would like to arrange a transferral of considerable funds from my account in the Bank of Melbourne," Java Gordon Mason said with the perfect diction and accent of an educated woman.

Dumbfounded, the banker let his mouth go slack for a moment, then recovered. "Ah, yes." He frowned. "Yes, such a thing is possible. Highly irregular." It was quite irregular for the Bank of Barrow Creek, for that institution had never been called upon to do much more than pay cash for the small amounts of gold brought in by the local diggers.

"My name . . ."

The banker tried to hide his gasp. Inquiries for Java Gordon Mason had been wired into the station weeks past.

"Bloody hell," he blurted. "You came across the Gibson?"

"Yes," Java said. "There is an arranged code for my identification with the Bank of Melbourne. You will ask for the transfer of, ah, a thousand pounds—"

" 'Strewth," the man gasped.

"And include with my name the words *Kanaka Kash,* the second word spelled with a *K.*" She waited until the banker had written it all down. "And if you would be so kind as to advance me a few pounds, I would like to buy some clothing and find a room where I can have a bath."

The banker cleared his throat. "Ah, well, hadn't we better wait until we hear from the Bank of Melbourne?" After all, he had nothing but the word of a very odd-looking person that there was money available to her in Melbourne. And it would take a devilishly long time for the transfer to actually be made.

"Oh, for heaven's sake," Java said in exasperation, "do I look like someone who would try to steal from you?" Suddenly she laughed, looked down at her truncated jodhpurs, ragged and filthy, and considered the state of her underthings and shirt, her face and hair. "I bloody well do, don't I?" she added.

"Let us say, ma'am, that you are not, at the moment, dressed in the height of fashion." But the way she had been able to laugh at herself helped him make his decision. "Twenty pounds enough?" He opened a drawer and started counting. "It's enough to buy any items of clothing I have in the store, sure enough, with enough left over to hire the widow Stuart's spare room."

"That will do nicely," Java said.

The banker sent the wire, including the code words and an inquiry whether Mrs. Tolo Mason's account would bear a withdrawal of one thousand pounds. He whistled when the reply came: ADVANCE MRS. MASON ANY AMOUNT SHE REQUIRES. ASK SHE CONTACT THIS BANK.

The message from the Bank of Melbourne said *any* amount. That covered a lot of ground.

Java, meanwhile, had soaked in a tub in a weathered frame house near the station, had dressed herself in the men's shirt and trousers purchased at the store—women's skirts were a bloody handicap in the bush—and had gorged herself on good hot food cooked in real pots. When she checked back with the banker and found him eager to push money on to her, she accepted a few pounds and bought a pretty red dress for Bildana and, reluctantly, a bit of gin for Jajjala. She ignored the request to contact the Bank of Melbourne. She was not yet ready to make contact with anyone.

Some writing materials—paper and pencils—were available in Barrow Creek, but not in the large quantities she desired. She bought up the storekeeper-banker's entire stock and then asked him to order more, adding to the order a gross of first

primers. And then she was gone. But her appearance in Barrow Creek and the contact with the Bank of Melbourne had
already set events and people in motion.

Elbert Hays, the young vice-president of the Bank of Melbourne who had handled the transaction from the bush bank
in Barrow Creek, could scarcely contain his excitement. As it
happened, Misa Mason's Sydney bank was at that very moment preparing to purchase the controlling interest in the
Bank of Melbourne. The bargaining had been going on for
months, so that the Mason name had been mentioned frequently, not only in connection with the impending purchase
but regarding the return of the young Thomas Mason after
having lost his wife in the western desert. Although Tolo had
not sought publicity, of course, several newspaper stories had
been printed, with most of the information coming second-
hand to Melbourne from papers in Sydney, where the Mason
interests were conducting a nationwide inquiry for the missing woman.

Hays saw his knowledge that Java Mason was alive as an
advantage to be pushed with Thomas Mason, who was in
residence at the Mason cattle station north of the city. He
presented the information to the bank manager, suggesting
that it would be good form if he rode with all haste to the
Mason station, to give the good news to the man who was the
son of the woman who owned the majority share of the bank's
stocks.

With the manager's blessing, Hays rode as fast as his stamina and his courage allowed. But the hard riding sobered him,
and he did some serious thinking. What if some unscrupulous
person had somehow obtained the code words that had identified Java Mason? What if, in his excitement, Hays was riding
to deliver false news and it turned out *not* to be Java Mason
up in Barrow Creek?

The solitary months in the house where he had grown up
had had a healing effect on Tolo. He had long since overcome

the lingering disability caused by his wound and the time spent with old Uwa's tribe. He rode daily, working with the white foremen and the Abo stockmen to gather up the scattered cattle in preparation for the annual sale of beef animals. He was lean and fit, and his work in the open kept his skin as dark as it had been during his long trek in the Gibson Desert. The whites of his eyes had the opalescent gleam of perfect health.

Elbert Hays found the master of the station leaning on the rails of a cattle pen, watching the Abo stockmen make steers of young bulls. He introduced himself. Tolo looked at him silently, leaving it up to Hays to open the conversation.

"Mr. Mason," Hays said, "there has been a certain development that we felt should be brought to your attention."

"If it's banking business," Tolo said, "refer it to my mother in Sydney."

"Yes, well," Hays said, "as a matter of fact it has to do with banking, ah, at least indirectly, you see. Ah, it seems that there's been a withdrawal on one of your personal accounts made by wire from Barrow Creek."

Tolo felt as if he had been hit in the stomach with a sledgehammer. He could not speak.

"That's in the Northern Territory, you know, north of Alice Springs."

Tolo could barely move his lips. His voice was weak. "Tell me, damn you. Who made this withdrawal?"

"Well," Hays said carefully, "we cannot say for *sure,* can we?"

Tolo seized Hays by the front of his shirt and lifted him to his tiptoes, thrusting his face into the face of the banker. "Who?"

"The person used the code words assigned as identification to Mrs. Thomas Mason," Hays gasped.

Tolo released his grip. Hays stumbled and almost fell.

"When?" Tolo demanded.

"Just this morning, as a matter of fact."

"And the bank in Barrow Creek said that Mrs. Thomas Mason made the withdrawal?"

"She did have the code, after all," Hays said. "Of course, there is always the possibility that the code was obtained by someone else. I pray not—"

"The code words were never written," Tolo said. He had helped Java commit them to memory. He felt as if he were on fire. He *had* to move, to be on his way. He left Hays standing beside the cattle pen and ran to the house, pausing on the way to give orders to have his fastest horse saddled. He threw a few things into a bag. His horse was ready. He went pounding down the approach lane at a run, leaving Elbert Hays behind him in the dust.

In Melbourne Tolo sent wires to his mother and to the Gordons. Like Hays before him, he had come to entertain doubts. It seemed too good to be true. He worded the telegrams to limit the hope that they would give to his mother and to Java's parents, but it was necessary to tell them something. He asked for immediate replies with word if Java had contacted Sydney. The answers were negative.

Though the telegraph had crossed the continent, linking Melbourne in the south to Barrow Creek and points north, no rail connection existed. The trip to the Northern Territory would therefore be roundabout. The first leg, the train trip to Sydney, seemed to take forever. Tolo, impatient, decided to remain in Sydney only long enough to book ship passage to Brisbane and to wire ahead to the Mason office there, with orders to find the quickest way to get from Brisbane to Alice Springs.

Even so, Tolo had to be in town overnight, time enough for visits with all who were concerned with Java's welfare. Misa embraced her son and prayed mightily that Java was alive, that the miracle had happened. Jessica Gordon greeted Tolo coolly, not letting him see that she, too, was filled with hope. Sam Gordon shook his hand and said, "I wish I could go with you."

Magdalen gave him a hug, a kiss on the cheek. "Of course, it's Java," she said. "I have said all along that if all it took for her to survive was crossing a bit of a desert, she would do it."

But Tolo had been torturing himself with questions. If indeed the person who had asked for one thousand pounds to be transferred to a bush bank in the Northern Territory was Java, why had she not contacted her parents? That was the one thing that concerned him most. He knew Java. She had been saddened by her parents' disapproval of their marriage; but she loved her mother and father, and one of her first thoughts would have been to contact them. It was understandable, on the other hand, that she had not tried to get into contact with him. The last time she had seen him he was being washed away by a flash flood in the desert. She would have thought him dead.

The next morning he boarded the ship for Brisbane, and by noon the vessel was leaving Sydney Harbor, heading toward the Pacific. Tolo was restless. The ship would take too damned long to reach Brisbane. It would take too long to travel to the end of the Queensland rail lines and too long to cover the distance to Alice Springs by stage or horse. And then he still would have to cross dry bush country to reach Barrow Creek. Why hadn't Java gone to Alice Springs, a larger town? He paced the deck, weighing this question, and then grunted in surprise when he came face-to-face with Magdalen Broome.

"Grandmother Broome," he said. "What on earth—"

"I know it's Java," Magdalen said. "I feel in my heart that it is Java. But there's something wrong, Tolo. Don't you feel it?"

"I'm afraid so," he replied. "You're wondering why she hasn't contacted you."

"Exactly. She's ill, or she's in trouble, or someone forced her to send for that money. Whatever, I'm going to be there when you find her. I have a feeling she's going to need me, Tolo, so don't make noises about leaving me in Brisbane or sending me home. I'm going to Barrow Creek in your company or alone."

He smiled. He had always been fond of Java's grandmother, and she was a tough old bird. Her presence would slow him down a bit, but if, as she suspected, Java was in some kind of trouble, then it would be good to have someone she loved and trusted with him. "I think," he said, "that I've just acquired company for my long journey."

"You have indeed," Magdalen said.

Alone in the never-never, Terry Forrest buried the old prospector, took the meager supply of gold dust, maybe two ounces, and rode back to Barrow Creek. He reported the death to the man who doubled as constable and head man at the repeater station, and in return he heard the unlikely story of a white woman who had appeared in the general merchandise store all baked and dried by the sun, wearing precious little clothing that exposed her lower legs and discolored underwear through slits and rips. She had stated that she was Java Gordon Mason and soon was drawing out money from the bank to buy the bloody Abos books to read.

It didn't take Terry long to confirm the story from the storekeeper-banker himself.

" 'Strewth," Terry whispered. "She made it. The little bird made it after all."

The Abos who had come into town with the woman had been identified as members of old Jajjala's tribe, usually hunting down in the Macdonnell Ranges.

"I tried to get her to stay in town," the banker said. "But she wouldn't even answer the Melbourne bank's request to contact them by wire."

"Might I find this Jajjala if I went into the Macdonnells?" Terry asked.

"Hard to say. It's a big country. But there are only a few good water holes. I'd guess you'd find Jajjala's tribe near one of 'em. You don't have to go out there, though. The bird's

going to come back in a few weeks to pick up the bloody
books she's ordered for the bloody boongs. Why don't you
wait?"

"No, thanks, mate."

Chapter XXIX

WHEN KIT VAN Buren looked out over her valley, she was so content that it frightened her. Was she too happy? Was she tempting fate by being so smugly euphoric? Or was it merely the contrast between her present serenity and the past few years that made her wonder if her life had turned too sweet to be real?

Before marrying Matt, she had known tragedy, anger, frustration, all compressed into a relatively brief period of time. The death of her mother was still a raw spot in her emotions, and the bitter parting with her father was a wound that was newly scabbed over; but she felt, on those balmy mornings when she arose with the sun and took young Matthew Grant Van Buren onto the veranda for his breakfast and a bit of air, that all things would come to a good end—that, for example, the letters she wrote regularly to her father and sent off down the hill with Matt when he went away on his frequent business trips would convince Roland Streeter that she had made a good match, that he could be proud of his son-in-law. She *knew* that if she mended her ways just a little, if she became more pious, read the Bible a bit more often, erased from her vocabulary some of the words that she had picked up while being raised on army posts at odd spots around the empire, she would be reunited with her mother one day.

She did not let a morning pass without sending up silen

thanks for her good fortune, for having a man to love and be loved by, and for Grant, who was a husky little chap with a bone structure indicating that he would be a big fellow, perhaps taller than Matt, taking after the men on the Streeter side of the family, who tended to be above average in height. She thanked God for health and for the prosperity that was coming to the Matt Van Buren family with pleasing swiftness. The coffee plantation was not bearing yet, but the timbering operations being conducted under the supervision of Trevor Gorel were profitable—so much so, in fact, that Trev worried.

On one of the Gorels' rare visits to the lovely, airy house on the side of the ridge overlooking the sweet and fertile valley, Trevor had said, "Matt, one of these days someone is going to start adding figures, and they'll see stars and rockets when they realize how much we net from a shipload of mahogany. And the big-money fellows will start moving in here in droves."

"The thing to do, then," Guinevere Gorel had commented, "is to milk the cow dry as swiftly as possible, and when the big money moves in, move out."

Guinevere's statement had startled Kit, for it relegated to unimportance the work being done on the coffee plantation and advised abandonment of an enterprise that had the potential of becoming as profitable as timbering.

Kit had tried, but she had not been able to penetrate the aura of aloofness about Guinevere. Of course, with Guinevere living in Port Moresby and Kit living on the hill overlooking her valley, the two women had not been together often. Kit had not been down the hill since Grant was born. Guinevere had come visiting with Trev only twice.

Kit was often alone, but she didn't mind. She had become quite close to a few of the women of the village, particularly to the midwives who had attended her at Grant's birth and to the younger women of their families. The women were members of the clan of the patriarch Foja, a dictatorial white-haired tyrant who controlled his family and the village with a fist made iron-hard by the traditions that were in his keeping.

The men of the village continued to disdain work among the growing coffee trees, but old Foja always sent a sufficient number of women and young girls whenever Kit notified him that the trees needed tending. With the plantings in the ground the work consisted mainly of keeping native vegetation from overwhelming the alien trees. Kit enjoyed the workdays. The women sang and laughed, and now and then the nearly nude young girls would break out into a playful chase among the trees.

Foja had become very protective of the little white mistress who lived in the wooden house on the hill, and when she became pregnant again, confiding the glad news to her female friends, Foja heard of it immediately. He made an official visit, sending two young warriors ahead of him in formal paint and headdress to inform Kit that the *luluai* was coming to visit the Little Mistress, thus giving Kit time to have the teapot ready, cakes and sugar in place on a little table on the veranda. She greeted Foja with formality and genuine respect. He sat at the table and waited for her to pour tea and dip four spoonfuls of sugar into his cup. He drank, smacking his lips in polite appreciation.

The baby was in a carry box beside Kit. Foja leaned over and tickled the child's cheek with the tip of one finger. "Soon it is *ozaha neta*," Foja said.

Kit knew. It was the talk of the village. *Ozaha neta* came once in a generation, so that only the older people remembered the last time "the old men's thing" had been performed in dance, song, and ritual. The purpose of *ozaha neta* was to assure the fertility of humans *and* pigs. Pigs, being one of the few sources of protein for the natives, were almost as important as people; they were valued on a par with members of other tribes, who occasionally shared a use in common with pigs.

"At the time of *ozaha neta*," Foja said, still tickling the baby, eliciting coos and giggles of pleasure, "we show our young boys to the gods." He looked at Kit for a long moment and pointed to Grant. "It is his time."

"Foja," Kit said carefully, hoping that she was choosing the right words, "I have already shown my child to his God, to the one God. I thank you for your concern, but my God, as you know from having listened to the missionary, is a jealous God and would not approve of showing the little one to other gods."

"Here are our gods," Foja said, sweeping his arm wide to take in their surroundings.

At one end of the valley the mountains met in a closed wall of purple. At the other end the hills fell away toward the coast, rolling down into blue distances as far as the eye could see. The valley floor was level and well kept, studded with feathery patches of bamboo and the graceful shapes of trees. Below the house the mountain stream sparkled and muttered as it sang its way over its rocky bed.

It was not the first time that Foja had reminded Kit that her son had not yet been shown to the gods. She knew, however, that if she gave in on this matter, there would come a time when Foja, as self-appointed protector of the Little Mistress, would expect her to hand Grant over to the village men for the initiation rites, including circumcision with an unsterilized knife. While it was true that she had come to respect Foja's people and to understand many of their beliefs, it was also glaringly obvious that they were barbarous primitives. She could persuade the women who came to her house to work and help tend Grant to wash themselves and wear clean clothing. She could not, as yet, influence the rest of the villagers, whose casual attitudes toward sanitation she found shocking. She had seen mothers clean their children's runny noses with their fingers and wipe the mucus on their bare thighs. Spitting was a habit shared by man, woman, and child, and it continued incessantly even in the dirt-floored huts.

She did not want to snub Foja. She explained again about the Son of God who came to earth to shoulder the sins of mankind, and when Foja brought up the point that the white man spoke of one God and three gods in the same breath, she smiled and put four spoons of sugar in Foja's fresh cup.

"Foja," she said, "you have your beliefs; I have mine. Can we not live with respect for each other, leaving each to his own ways?"

Foja let Grant hold his forefinger and look at it with crossed eyes. "It is danger for the boy, but I bow to your beliefs." Grant released his finger, and Foja pointed it directly toward Kit's nose. "But you will learn someday, Little Mistress, to listen to Foja. You do not hear when I say that the gods want to see this boy. You do not hear when I speak of the snake under the skin of the woman with the long eyes—"

Foja was speaking of Guinevere Gorel. He had taken an almost immediate dislike to her. On Trevor and Guinevere's first visit, Matt, out of politeness, had presented them to the villagers and the village headman. After their second visit Foja had come to Kit with a warning.

"She pretends kinship, that one," Foja had said. "But in those eyes is the cold look of the snake at the moment before it strikes."

"But she is our friend," Kit had insisted, "and the wife of my husband's best friend. She is the daughter of a princess from a land far away. Her manner is not like ours." By that time she did not think it was odd to express the fact that she and Foja, a man whose tribe was not far removed from the Stone Age, had things in common.

"You have the good heart," Foja had told her. "Beware lest it lead you into pain because of that one."

Kit took Grant in his carry box to watch the beginning of the once-in-a-generation festival. Women and young girls crowded around her to see the baby, and there was much touching. Distant relatives from other villages were arriving, and each arrival brought on a spate of native greetings in which both males and females embraced and fondled one another's genitals.

Kit had taken a place among the women. The warriors, their naked bodies decorated in bizarre patterns of red and yellow, were doing a dance that illustrated strength, which in their minds meant more than mere physical power or stamina. Strength, to them, belonged to the man who killed his enemy from ambush as much as to the man who killed face-to-face. Strength was pride and hair-trigger temper. This idea of strength, to an outsider such as Kit, was an almost amusing sort of swaggering.

Around her, women often reached out to another's thigh. Young girls stood with arms entwined. A young mother leaned to kiss a child's lips and to nuzzle the baby's tiny penis with her nose before planting a smacking kiss on a plump rump.

Pigs were roasting over fires, and in the coals yams and sweet potatoes were baking. Ears of corn, cooked in their green husks, had a fresh, delicious taste. A soft breeze stirred the tops of the casuarina trees, but it did not carry off the dust kicked up by the dancers' feet. It had not rained for days, and Kit was reminded that if the rain did not come soon, she would have to put the women to work watering the coffee trees.

As the evening progressed, the men's dancing became wilder. Many of them showed signs of advanced intoxication from imbibing the fermented banana liquor that the women had brewed. Kit began to feel slightly uncomfortable, although she considered herself to be among friends. Many of the women were also drinking the homemade liquor, and the celebration was becoming quite noisy. She would have felt better if Matt had been with her.

She stifled the disloyal thought that Matt should be there, for he was doing his best to make a future for her and their children. It would be totally unfair for him to leave all of the responsibility for the timbering operations to Trev. Besides, it was Matt who had made the financial arrangements with his cousin Claus Van Buren, and Matt had a better business head than Trev. So it was natural for him to be away from home often. No worries.

Some people might have criticized both Matt and Kit for trusting primitive savages like Foja's people, savages who reg-

ularly warred on their neighbors, but in truth Kit had become
an honorary member of the tribe and was as safe as the
women of the village. In her own home she was also safe
because Foja's young warriors guarded the approaches to the
valley.

She told herself that her uneasiness stemmed from the
strangeness of the ceremonial dancing and singing. Nevertheless, she motioned to Guma, third wife of Foja. Guma came,
touching her on the arm affectionately.

"Guma," Kit said, "I must go home now."

"You will miss the feast," Guma objected.

"The young one needs his bath and his supper. Will you
walk with me?"

"I will walk with you," Guma agreed, sighing.

The spear that suddenly appeared between the elongated
hanging nipples of Guma's bare breasts had been thrown with
enough force to sink a full four inches into her torso, punching its barbed head through Guma's diaphragm into her
heart. She made no sound at all. Kit heard only the thud of
the spear striking Guma, a sound like that of a ripe melon
dropped onto stone. Then Guma sank to the ground like a
marionette with the strings cut.

Kit heard a scream and the enraged shouts of the warriors.
Whirling to face the dance area, she saw chaos as the warriors
milled around and dived for their weapons, as they dodged
arrows and spears that all too often found targets in their red
and yellow painted hides.

A woman grabbed Kit's arm, pulling her down hard. Kit
reached for Grant's carry box and dragged it to her. Keeping
her head down, she turned slightly to see old Foja release a
spear that impaled a ghostly white-painted shape just within
the light of the flickering fires. By now the warriors were
organized, armed with axes, spears, and bows, and they
moved rapidly into the darkness.

Kit heard shouts of anger and fear from the darkness and
an occasional cry of agony. Then all was quiet. The women
who had been lying flat on the ground or who had crawled

away into the darkness emerged into the firelight and began to identify the dead and give comfort to the wounded. Four men and Foja's third wife had died, and six others were wounded.

Some of the warriors began to come back, the whole ones supporting the injured. Foja was not among them, and others were missing as well, including two of the strongest men of the village.

"Foja will not return until he has caught and punished the enemy," said Asema, second wife to Foja. "You will sleep here tonight, Little Mistress."

"No," Kit said. Gathering up the carry box, she left the village, for she knew what was going to happen. The enemy dead had been gathered, three of them, and lay naked beside the fires. The women were gathering their butchering instruments even as she walked alone into the darkness with her son. She could not change the ancient customs of the Geheto people.

"You have to admit, Kit," Matt had told her once, half-jokingly, "that it's quite practical. New Guinea does not have many animals to be hunted. There are only the pigs to provide meat protein. When an enemy is killed, isn't it a terrible waste to leave him for the vultures or to bury him?"

Knowing that your friends and nearest neighbors were cannibals was one thing. Seeing the hunger and eagerness in the faces of the women as they got ready to prepare human meat for cooking was another.

Arriving at the cottage, Kit lit only one lamp and prepared for bed, laying Grant in the bed with her and giving him her breast so that he went contentedly back to sleep. She lay there with her son, a warm and precious presence by her side, until long after the pale sliver of a moon had started to sink down into the western sky. She knew enough about Foja's people to understand that an old war had been revived with the raid during the once-in-a-generation ceremonies, when the tribe's collective guard was down. Now more raids and counterraids would follow, until one side or the other was decimated. The native tribes tended to keep their feuds among themselves, but she would not feel safe in her own house while the tribal war raged.

"Matt," she whispered, "I think you should be here."

Matt Van Buren had sailed the new company boat down the coast. It was a trim little ketch, easily handled by a crew of two, and Matt had with him the Kanaka boy whom he and Trev had hired to look after the ship and keep it seaworthy.

They reached the point where Trev and Gihi's crew of mountain men were felling huge trees and snaking them through the swamps with oxen, the beasts wading in water up to their bellies. A huge raft of logs had been collected by the time Matt arrived at the site, and he stayed until a Van Buren ship sailed in, to use its hefty deck winches to lift the logs into her hold and onto her deck.

Matt left only when Trev loaded Gihi's crew onto the workboat and moved to a new location where the trees nearest the water still soared toward the sky. He was uncomfortable with guilt when he was around Trev, and he felt guilty in another way when he stayed away from the logging operation too long. Before Trev set out on the workboat for a new site, Matt said, "Look, partner, I stopped by to see Guinevere, and the lady is complaining—with some justice, I think—that she never sees you. Why don't you take the ketch and go home to see your wife for a few days? I can stay with Gihi and the men."

"No, my friend," Trev replied. "You have not only a wife but a child, and you spend far too much time away from them. Sometimes I wonder if you come down here just to see my handsome face or if you want to check up on me."

Matt forced a laugh. He knew, and Guinevere knew, that he used the trips to the lumbering sites as an excuse to pass through Port Moresby and Trevor Gorel's bedroom, where Trevor Gorel's wife was always eager to apply her ancient wisdom in the art of love to the man she hoped was going to take her away from Papua.

As far as Matt knew, the Bible did not record the first act of adultery, only the first murder. In a way that was strange, since killing and committing adultery were equally forbidden by the Ten Commandments. Matt experienced moments when he would willingly have exchanged his crime of betrayal of his wife and best friend for a simple act of murder. At least if he murdered someone, the modern legal penalty would be swift and clear. If he killed in cold blood, the law would kill him in turn. An eye for an eye. Simple enough. But how do you take an eye for an eye when adultery and betrayal are the crimes?

The punishment for adultery is not death, unless the betrayed husband turns violent. He wondered if that would happen if Trev found out, although it was unlikely that he would. On the two occasions that the four of them, Trev and Guinevere, Kit and Matt, had been together recently, Guinevere's aplomb had astounded him. She had given every indication of being a loving wife, of doting on Trev, in fact. Her attentions to Matt conveyed mere politeness, courtesy to her husband's friend and business partner. Matt, on the other hand, felt as if his relationship with Guinevere were emblazoned on his forehead. He made it a policy not to look at her too often, to speak to her only in the natural context of the conversation, yet he was sure that anyone who looked at him could see the heat that grew in his blood when he was in Guinevere's presence, that Kit could not fail to see lust in his eyes.

To be around Trev was to be in an agony of guilt. To be with Kit was a bittersweet awkwardness. He had no doubt that he still loved Kit. When he was with her in the house on the side of the ridge, the two of them playing with little Grant, he could forget the warm, pungent eagerness that awaited him at the end of the short ride into Port Moresby. But when he held Kit in his arms at night and did the little things that made love good for her, when he heard her sigh in completion, and when he pumped his own seed into her, he closed his eyes and pretended, God help him, that Kit was Guinevere. And afterward his guilt was almost too heavy to bear, for he told himself that his imagining Kit out of existence was the vilest betrayal of all.

Each time he visited the Gorel house in Port Moresby he promised himself upon leaving that he would never go there again in Trevor's absence. And each time that promise faded quickly as he remembered the fullness of Guinevere's mouth under his, the honeyed textures and the lubricity of her.

Macbeth murdered sleep. Matt Van Buren murdered peace of mind by succumbing repeatedly to his overwhelming ache to be with Guinevere.

Aboard the ketch once more, Matt willed it to move faster, willed the wind to rise to a near gale to rush the boat back toward Port Moresby. Desire pushed guilt and regret back into a dark corner of his mind and closed a door that would not be opened again until, once more, he was replete with her.

At Port Moresby's wharf he left the Kanaka to tie up the boat, took only his travel bag, and hurried to the Gorel house. One of her Kanaka girls told him that Guinevere was in her bath. It was late evening. He knew her habits: She bathed before the evening meal. She would emerge from her bath dressed in one of those pagan silk creations that was worn without underclothes, and she would be perfumed, trailing a faint scent of soap and exotic perfumes. He told the Kanaka girl to leave the bedroom. It had bothered him, at first, to realize that both of Guinevere's servants could not help knowing that he was sharing the mistress's bed, but Guinevere had told him not to worry.

He waited in the bedroom. Behind the bamboo screen that separated the room from the bath she was singing a song in her native language, a plaintive, atonal whining that fired his blood. When she called out to her servant, he grinned.

"Come quickly," Guinevere said impatiently. "I am ready to be rinsed."

He stood behind her and lifted a bucket of clear water, poured it carefully onto her rounded, soft shoulders, onto the padded, soft planes of her back. She made sounds of delight. She stood, still unaware that he had taken the place of the servant. "My towel," she said harshly.

He pulled the towel off its rack and spread it over her

shoulders, his hands savoring the shape of her through the material. She turned her head sharply.

"Matthew!" she whispered, completing the turn to thrust her wet self into his arms, heedless of his clothing. "Ah, I am so glad you're back. I've missed you so."

He lifted her and carried her to the bed. She protested playfully. "I'm wet," she said. "We'll dampen the bed."

"It will dry," he said.

He placed her on the bed and began to undress. She took his hands. "Matt, wait," she said. "There is something "

He leaned down to kiss her and she turned her face away. "No, be fair," she whispered. "Give me a chance to say the thing I feel I must say before—before you turn my foolish head as you always do."

He saw that she was serious. He sat on the edge of the bed. She pulled the sheet up over her breasts and stared at him with her huge almond eyes. "Matt, I do love you, so very much, but—"

He felt the beginning of panic. He promised himself regularly that he was going to stop the affair, but now, when he wanted her, having the taste of her lips in his mouth and the smell of her fresh from the bath in his nostrils, the idea of losing her was too dreadful to contemplate.

"—I feel so guilty," she said.

He sighed in relief. They had spoken about guilt before. "What can we do?" he asked.

"That is just it," she said. "We must do something, my darling. I am only a weak woman, and I can't go on knowing that we are betraying the man who has been so kind to me and the woman who loves you so much."

"What are we to do, then, stop seeing each other?"

Huge tears sprang from her eyes, rolled down her smooth cheeks. He put his hands on her shoulders and kissed the tears away.

"I would die if I could not see you," she whispered.

"Guinevere, we've talked about this before. Didn't we agree that you couldn't stand to hurt Trev? Didn't I tell you that honor ties me to my wife? What can we do?" *You keep asking her that,* he thought. *Do you really want her to tell you what you can do?*

This time she did. She had played his emotions for months now, knew him well, knew his guilts and his passions. She knew him physically, too, knew exactly how to give him the maximum pleasure, how to lift him to new passion once he was spent.

"We must go away," she said. She closed her mouth with her hand as if trying to take back the words, and her eyes were wide.

"Guinevere—" She had said it. He had no immediate answer.

"But don't you see, my darling," she said, "that it would be kinder for both of them, for Trevor and for your wife, if we made a clean break? Do you like pretending with her? Does she wonder why she is not getting all of you, the way she once did?"

"I don't know," he said.

"She knows. A woman knows when love dies."

But his love for Kit was not dead. He started to protest, then realized that such an admission would be totally in contradiction with his actions.

"We must leave quietly and quickly," she said. "Leave the timber and the coffee for . . . *them.*"

He felt a pang of loss. He'd worked damned hard to get the coffee planted. The timbering operation was just beginning to pay off well.

"We will go to your home," she said. "You will beg your father's forgiveness."

How could he tell her that if Joseph Van Buren had been angry when he brought home a pommy wife, there would be no bounds to his rage if Matt appeared with a brown-skinned woman, however royal, however beautiful?

He knew that what she suggested was impossible. His financial future was in Papua, and it was tied closely to Trevor Gorel. Away from the plantation and the lumber business, he would be penniless, and a man did not keep a woman like Guinevere long without money.

"I can't leave. Not just now."

"When?" she persisted.

"That I can't say." He reached for her, and with a sigh she came to him.

Later, when she brought up the subject again, he was silent.

"I really can't stand it much longer," she said. "Every time Trevor comes home, I cringe with guilt. I feel an overwhelming urge to tell him all and to beg his forgiveness."

Panic brought Matt wide-awake. "You can't tell him!"

"I know, I know," she said. She clung to him. "Oh, Matthew, please take me away. Take me away from this place of biting insects and sodden heat. Take me to one of your cities. I don't care which one. Take me to a place where we can sleep in a bed without getting the sheets wet with our perspiration. Show me your home. I know that it must be beautiful."

"I can't."

She raised herself on one elbow and looked him in the eye. "Tell me why you can't."

It came out before he could think clearly. "Kit's pregnant again."

She pulled away from him, gave him her shapely back. When he touched her, she jerked her shoulder away.

"Guinevere?"

"You say that you love me, and now this."

"She is my wife, after all."

"But you profess to love me."

"I do, God help me, I do."

"Well, then." She turned to face him. She had made a decision. It was obvious to her that he would not leave Kit now, not while she was carrying his child. She would simply have to find some other way to set Matt free. Once that was accomplished, Trevor Gorel would be no problem.

Chapter XXX

AMID THE GORGES and tors of the Macdonnells, frilly palm trees towered high over a cool gully, shading a permanent spring of clear mineral-rich water. The beauty of the natural parkland was marred by a tangled mat of dead palm fronds that had accumulated over the years. The decaying vegetable matter offered shelter to several forms of life, both mammalian and reptilian. Although Jajjala's tribal group had been coming to this green oasis for generations and claimed it as its own, no one had ever made any attempt to clean up the debris, to make the beautiful spot even more beautiful. The water was sweet and plentiful. Life was good, and easy. The hunting produced results most of the time. Young boys of the group swarmed over the palm debris, chasing desert rats, for these small animals were a steady—and surprisingly tasty—staple of the Aboriginal diet when the group was in residence at the oasis.

When not hunting rats or stirring up the water hole with their wading and splashing, the boys climbed the walls of the gorge, explored caves, played games of war, and politely but steadfastly resisted all efforts on the part of the self-appointed schoolmistress to teach them about the odd scratches the whitefella woman loved to make on paper.

In the beginning, when Java Mason first began her campaign to interest young Abos in learning, the boys caught the idea of the marks on paper and showed her where men of the Dreaming had made similar marks on smooth vertical surfaces of the red rock. Seeing the work of early Aborigines reminded Java forcefully of Tolo. The pictures and designs scratched into stone were the sole permanent mark left on the land by untold generations of blackfellows, and to Tolo they had been significant. One of his goals had been to make copies of as many of these artworks on stone as possible.

So Java dutifully made copies of the designs and drawings near the oasis, using up most of the small supply of paper she had bought in Barrow Creek, rationalizing that the teaching of the young would have to wait until she had paper and pencils for all of the boys and girls, as well as the primers she had ordered.

It was green in the main gorge away from the oasis. She often walked alone, thinking of Tolo, thinking of her grandmother and her parents, fighting the growing doubts that burdened her. The most insignificant things confused her determination to do something significant with regard to making life better for Jajjala's mob and, by transference, for all of the remnant of Australia's original people. In Barrow Creek she had eaten well-seasoned leg of lamb and—ah, heavenly dried apple cobbler. The cobbler came back to haunt her time and again. She dreamed of filling a soup bowl with a high, rounded serving of apple cobbler and eating and eating and eating until her stomach protruded.

She told herself that her longing for that delicacy was juvenile. That she was still very young, not long past being a juvenile, did not occur to her. Nor did she suspect that her ordeal in the desert, the malnutrition that still had lingering effects on her body, also affected the workings of her mind. To her it seemed absolutely logical that she would be able to teach the wild youth of the group the importance of the white man's written words. Without consulting the Aborigines themselves, she had concluded that what she desired for them they would want also. She had acquired the cast of mind that had sent thousands of well-meaning souls traveling outward

from the British Isles to bring the wretched heathen to the
light. But she did not preach God to the Aborigines; she
preached learning. She dwelt on ambition and goals. She tried
to instill *need* in the young ones of the group, the need for
things. The need for warm clothing, iron tools, and cooking
utensils. The need for a roof over one's head and a steady job
that produced income to make one a part of civilization.

Bildana spoke for her to the others, not in her presence.
"She has not been the same since watching the death of her
husband. The sun of the never-never has baked her brains, but
she has pure heart."

As in all primitive societies there was among the Aborigines a tolerance for the one driven mad by the spirits. Because
Java was bright, cheerful, smiling, and considerate, many
kindnesses were done for her in return, but her efforts at conducting school failed totally.

More and more she sought solitude. She took long, explor-
atory walks through the green gorge, lay in the heath watching cloud galleons sail the faultless sky. It was the season for
the ground orchids to bloom, the underground plants sprout-
ing their tiny flowers on the surface, minute spots of beauty in
a monotonous landscape. She lay on her stomach admiring a
particularly fruitful bloom, heard the faraway snort of an animal, ignored it, then recognized the scrape of a shod hoof on
rock.

The rider was coming directly up the gorge toward where
she lay examining the ground orchid. He was a tall man in
typical bush clothing, the inevitable wide-brimmed bush hat
pulled low over his eyes. As he approached, she saw something familiar in the way he sat his horse. She remained still.
He would pass no more than a hundred feet away, but the tall
grass concealed her position from him.

She felt suddenly faint as she recognized him. She leapt to
her feet, her mind in a turmoil. She had seen two men disappear into the roiling, debris-filled thunder of the head rise. If
this one was alive, then Tolo—

"Terry Forrest!" she called.

The man jerked his mount to a halt and swiveled his head. Then he turned and rode slowly toward her, his horse picking its way carefully among the rocks.

Terry Forrest had been riding the gorges of the Macdonnells for over two weeks without seeing so much as one single boong, and now here she was, the little sheila, alive and pretty as a fresh new pound note. Reining in, he slipped from his saddle and faced her with a broad smile.

"By God, you made it," he said.

"Tolo . . . ?" she gasped.

Terry removed his hat. "Saved my hide, he did. Pulled me out of the bloody water."

"He didn't drown?" Her heart was pounding.

"He didn't drown," Terry repeated. "We went looking for you, Java. Found Ganba and the boongs. One of them put a spear into him."

He stared at her. She was very thin; her perfect skin, bronzed and baked by the sun, looked dry and leathery. She was dressed in a man's clothing that showed the narrowness of her waist, the bulge of her breasts, the womanly spread of hip.

"I'm sorry, little girl," Terry said. "I did my best to save him."

She did not weep. She made a little sound, but stared back at him dry-eyed.

"Did he . . ."

"He didn't suffer," Terry lied. "It was quick and painless."

"No, I didn't mean that. Did he *say* anything?"

"Just your name," Terry lied again. "Said it twice."

"Oh, God!" She sat down suddenly, her head dropping.

Terry went to her, reached down, and took one hand. "Come," he said. "I'm going to take you home."

"Leave me alone," she said, pulling her hand away.

He stood there awkwardly. "You made it across the bloody Gibson," he said, awed. "You'll have a story to tell."

"What did you do with—what did you do with . . . his body?" she asked in a small voice.

"Buried him," he said. "Built a cairn of stones over it. Didn't have anything to carve his name on, though."

"Thank you," she said. "And you came across looking for me?"

"That I did. Gave up on you. Didn't hear the tales from the Abos about you until a month ago. Came looking for you. I can't figure out, if you made it into Barrow Creek, why you've come back out here with the boongs."

"That's not your concern," she said.

"I'm curious, nevertheless."

She was silent. He couldn't read her expression; it was vacant, as if she were somewhere else. "I am going to continue my husband's work," she said dully.

"Well, goodonyer," Terry replied. "But I would have thought you'd have had plenty of time to study the bloody boongs, having crossed the desert with one. That Bildana still alive?"

"She is."

"Boongs don't make the best house servants, but you might take her back to Sydney with you."

"I'm not going back to Sydney," she said.

"I see." He squatted, sat on his heels, put his face even with hers. "What are you going to do then, live with the boongs? You must have traveled with this mob of them from the rock, eh?"

"Not all the way."

She wasn't herself, Terry decided. "Look," he said, "I don't think you should be out here. I mean, a doctor—"

"I appreciate your concern for me," she said, cutting him short. "Thank you for coming across the desert to look for me, but I don't need to be rescued. Bildana and I took care of ourselves. I am perfectly at home with Jajjala's people, and intend to stay with them. So I'm sorry you've gone to so much trouble. If you're in need of funds to get back to your home, I'll be happy—"

Terry snorted. He'd come a long way. He was put out to think that she considered him no more than a hired hand to be paid off, but he wasn't going to let that drive him away.

"I've got a few bob," he offered. "So you're going to stay with the boongs?"

"Yes."

"Then I reckon I'll do a bit of Abo study myself, if you don't mind."

"It's a free country," she said.

Terry took one look, one sniff of the Abos' campsite and put out his kip at a distance. He cleared away the rotting palm fronds from under a tree on the other side of the water and opened a tin of bully beef. He could see Java over there with the Abos, talking their jabber, making her talk more expressive with hand motions. She had gone as troppo as an outhouse mouse. Not only was it in his own interest to stay with her, but it was the human thing to do. It was not that he worried about doing the right thing, but of late he'd been having dreams about Tolo Mason. They had started when he'd been all alone, just he and the camels, in the waly. He kept seeing Tolo lying there on the ground, his eyes open, his mind fully functional. And he kept walking away, afraid to look back to see the look on Tolo's face, a look of unbelief, of total condemnation. He told himself that if he'd freighted himself down with a wounded man, they both would have died in the Gibson. But that didn't help.

In a peculiar way his decision to stay with Java was a tribute to Tolo's memory. At least he could save Tolo's little sheila from herself, from her delusions of duty to a dead man. She'd soon get enough living like an animal, and then he'd take her to the Alice and on home to Sydney. What happened after that was to be determined.

Several possibilities existed. One was that he could so ingratiate himself with Java during the long journey that she would marry him. He knew that Tolo Mason had been quite well off, the son of one of Australia's richest women. Not a bad job, being husband to another of the country's wealthy ones. If that didn't turn out, then at worst he would be offered, and he would accept, quite a nice reward for having brought the little bird out of the bush. And the man who had found and rescued Java Mason just might be offered a post of some importance with the firm of the Mason woman.

He felt that he couldn't lose, and if, on the way, he sampled the merchandise, well, who was to know? He wouldn't rape the sheila, but if she gave in to his blandishments in some pleasant camp beneath a lover's moon on the way to the coast, she certainly wouldn't go around bragging about it once they reached Sydney.

He had enough tucker to last for a while. He could supplement it by hunting. He settled in, and now and again, when Java went walking, he joined her, not intruding, speaking only when he was spoken to.

When it became apparent that Terry Forrest was not going to try to force her to leave the oasis, Java came to accept his presence. She would never have invited him to stay, not after the advances he had made toward her in the Gibson, but his coming across the desert after Tolo had been killed was one point in his favor. And it was a relief to have someone to talk to in English. She had learned a combination of three different Aboriginal tongues and could communicate well with Jajjala and the others; but the Aborigines' languages were rudimentary, often requiring a combination of several words to express one descriptive adjective, and she could not use their speech to render the subtler shades of her feelings.

She was still recovering from the shock occasioned by Terry's arrival and the news he brought. It was as if Tolo had died twice—resurrected from the flood, only to be killed again. It eased her grief to speak about this to Terry. She told him, too, about her personal fight against the desert.

Terry, in turn, told her of his own experiences coming across and talked laughingly about the rigors and unpleasantness of being a croc hunter up north. He complimented her, telling her that she had learned more about living in the bush than most men knew; indeed, she could teach him some tricks.

After the renewed shock of learning the exact manner of Tolo's death had passed, she asked Terry to tell her in detail about the encounter with the Aborigines, and she felt a dull but fierce satisfaction in knowing that the evil Ganba had died.

Finally she carried her dirty blankets to Terry's camp. He made no untoward move. If anything, he became more polite, more considerate. He shared his tins of food with her, and she readily expressed her gratitude, for she was growing just a bit tired of eating roots, berries, and half-cooked meat. He accepted her thanks for his generosity with a laugh, saying lightly that he wanted to put a bit more meat on her bones.

With game becoming scarce because of the pressure of hunting, Jajjala announced that the mob would go walkabout. Java gathered her belongings, few as they were, and tied them into a pack. She did not protest when Terry offered to carry the bundle on his horse. When the group set out, the men and boys first, women following, she walked with Bildana.

They walked for days, the march taking them south out of the Macdonnells. Jajjala had set a course that was leading them past Ayers Rock, toward other mountain ranges, where the Abos could find sufficient meat to settle for a time. Along the way they found enough small game to sustain them, the Abo men eagerly stalking their prey.

One strong young hunter, more skillful than most, had taken an interest in Bildana. His courtship consisted mainly of vain struttings and demands. As a widow Bildana no longer could command a bride price.

Java remonstrated with her. "You are not offal tossed aside to be claimed by any man who wants you, Bildana. You are a valuable human being. Have some pride. Tell that young jack-ass to leave you alone."

"But he is strong," Bildana said. "He is a good hunter, and he has no wife."

In the end Bildana moved to the young man's side and for the next few nights shamelessly gave herself to her new husband. It was not the Abo way to seek privacy for the sex act, and Java, sickened, feeling childishly betrayed, left the Abo camp once again to spread her blankets close to Terry's fire.

Next day she walked with Terry and made no objection when he lagged far behind the others to make the most of a pool of clean, clear water. First he asked Java either to go for a walk or turn her head. She chose to walk, and before she was out of earshot, she could hear him splashing and blowing in the water. When she returned, he was dressed, his hair wet and slicked back.

"Your turn," he said. "I was careful. Didn't stir it up too much. There's a mite of soap in the dish."

She hesitated. "No worries," he said, grinning. "I fancy a bit of a walk myself."

It was pleasant to lave her body with soap, to feel squeaky clean as she waded out of the pool, one hand covering her pubic mound, the other crossed over her breasts. Terry was nowhere in sight, so she let the sun dry her.

He came back after she was dressed, smiling when he saw that she had been trying to make something of her hair. It was still damp. She had pulled it back and plaited it into two ropes of braids.

"Very becoming," he said. "Makes you look young."

He had killed a rabbit. After building up the fire, he cleaned and spitted the animal, and soon the aroma of roasting meat was a reminder that she was hungry. They ate sitting side by side in the shade cast by the wall of the gorge. Terry told her about his first attempt at skinning a croc, and she found herself laughing with him.

He had washed his clothing while bathing, and he had a crisp, clean smell about him. His eyes had laugh lines at the corners, and his teeth were white and even. He was a big man, almost as large as Tolo had been. Without knowing it, she was staring at him. He turned and caught her at it, and she felt herself blushing, though it could not be visible through her tan. She turned her head away quickly, aware of a new feeling, a visceral knowledge that physically, at least, she had become attracted to Terry.

A week of good food had begun to have an effect on Java. She felt refreshed upon awakening in the morning, eager to start the new day. She had begun to think about how good it would feel to have a bath in a real tub, to have the softness of nice underthings against her skin, to wear a new gown in high fashion. She was discovering, as had thousands of exiles before her, that it is the little things that one misses. Fresh butter on newly baked bread. The scent of a perfumed bar of soap. A pillow, soft, deep, feathery, and smelling of the laundry. Crisp, ironed sheets.

"Never seen Sydney," Terry said that evening as they made a dinner of bully beef and some particularly delicious berries Java had gathered. "Nice place?"

"Yes, it is," she said. "There's a wonderful view of the harbor from our—from my parents' front porch."

"I fancy your folks are concerned about you."

She nodded. She had been thinking about that of late. She suspected that news of her bank transaction had made its way to Sydney, if indeed the storekeeper-banker in Barrow Creek had not notified her family directly. "I think they know by now that I'm alive."

"Wouldn't stop them worrying."

"Are you saying that it's time for me to go home?"

"Not at all, luv. It's a free country, as you told me once. You want to live with the boongs, that's your canoe and you can paddle it."

"Then you're leaving?" Java asked, feeling a touch of panic. It had been pleasant having him around, being able to talk in her own language with someone who was a product of her own culture. There were differences between her and Terry, of course, for he'd grown up in the bush, but they had more in common than she had with Bildana and the other Abos.

"Well, it seems to be a profitless project, this. I mean, here we are following old Jajjala on walkabout, wandering wherever he chooses, seeing nothing but red rock and sand and dust devils. Get a little tired of that."

"It's a cruel country," she said.

"Java, do you ever think that you could help them more by going home, settling your affairs, getting your hands on your husband's money, and then setting them up with a bit of land and stock and maybe a couple of men to teach them how to grow beef and mutton?"

"But that would be so remote," she said. "Here I can—"

"Honey, I've seen you try to get the young bucks interested in reading and writing. You're farting in the wind—" He stopped, looking nonplussed. Java tried to smother a laugh.

"Sorry," he said. "Things like that come out now and again. Result of living in the bush all my life."

"It is a very descriptive expression. I've had that feeling at times, but—"

"But you owe it to Tolo to muddle on?" He snorted. "Look, it's time you realized that Tolo Mason is dead. Now I don't know whether there's really a heaven or not. If there isn't, then whatever you do matters not a whit to him. If there is, then he's up there playing his harp and singing hallelujah and knowing that whatever you do is just a temporary thing and of passing significance and won't mean a damn thing when you join him up there."

"Why, Terry," she teased, "I've never known you to be quite so philosophical." She sobered. "Yes, I know he's dead. I've accepted that. And I'm beginning to think that maybe I am farting in the wind"— she blushed—"trying to be school-marm to the Abos."

"Then let's go to Sydney, luv."

She turned her head away. "Let me think about it," she said.

Bildana was totally involved with her new husband. The tales that the old ones were telling around the Abo campfires had become a sameness. But it was a lovely night, cool, clear. The stars were cold, and steady, and distant; the moon was so brilliant and full that one had only to look and see the hint of roundness to understand that it was not a flat coin in the sky but a globe, a ball.

She walked away from the fire and stood in the darkness, looking up at the indifferent stars. Tolo was dead. She would die and become dust, and those same stars would look down on the same red emptiness in the heart of Australia; it would not matter to them if the Abos became a lost race, and it would not matter to them in the slightest if all of their rather silly legends died with them.

She started, whirled to face the sound, and saw the easily recognizable bulk of Terry.

"Didn't know how far you'd walked," he said.

"Far enough, Terry, I think," she said.

He came closer. There was a purposeful directness in the way he approached her, and sensing his intent, she was frozen, unable to move. One part of her protested when he took her into his arms, for he lifted her from her feet, as Tolo had done, and covered her mouth with his.

She accepted him only once. She allowed him to lead her back to the campsite, place her gently on his blankets, and remove the men's clothing. She accepted him because she was tormented by guilt, for she had decided to give up the quest, to go home. She accepted him because she had been alone for so long without the companionship of her kind. She took him and used him for her own pleasure, giving and taking with swift, hungry upward thrustings because it was an affirmation of her own resurrection. And when it was over, she went alone to the water hole, bathed, and slept peacefully through the night.

With the morning she said, "I'm going home, Terry."

"Goodonyer."

"I'm going back up north, to Alice Springs."

"I'll come with you."

"All right, if you want to."

"Well, of course I want to, luv." He moved close. She ducked out from under his hand when he tried to place it on her shoulder.

"I don't want you to touch me," she said.

"Hey," he said teasingly. "Was I that bad?"

"You were very good, as a matter of fact," she said.

"Then what's the problem?" There was a touch of anger in his voice.

"That was just something that happened," she said, "because we were together, because there was a moon, and because I was lonely. It won't happen again."

"I see," he said.

He let it go at that, and Java was relieved. Even a man like Terry Forrest could understand that her conscience might be hurting her.

Java found that it was good to be on the move, her mind settled on a definite destination. She felt as if she had been wandering the wild, desolate places of Australia for eons. Previously, while with Jajjala's group on walkabout, she had been content with the varying rates of progress they had made each day, accepting the Abos' casualness about their ultimate destination, their seemingly aimless drift toward the new mountain ranges and hunting grounds in the south. Now, traveling on her own, with only Terry as company, she was eager to move more quickly.

But they could not go in a straight line. They still had to find water, and this required many detours. To Terry's surprise, Java found the watering places and at the same time kept them headed generally north—the right direction—all without Terry's help. Now and again she accepted his offer to rest a bit and ride his horse, but most of the time she walked.

When they camped at night, she kept her distance from him. Terry respected her wish to be left alone. He remembered that she had responded to him once, and he was confident that when she had worked her way clear of her guilty conscience, she would respond to him again. It was a long trek to the Alice and then a much longer journey to the coast. There was time; she was no ordinary sheila, and he was playing for high stakes.

Chapter XXXI

ASEMA, SECOND WIFE to Foja, had a son working with
Trevor Gorel's timbering crew. The son, Zaho, was a powerfully built young man, a warrior who had proven his strength
in battle. He was dutiful to his mother, a character trait of
some rarity among the Papuan natives. On his visits to his
home he brought Asema gifts from the white man's store in
Port Moresby—beautiful beads to adorn her and delicious
sweets to please her palate. He also brought a story that held
her attention through a long, detailed telling, a story about
the wife of the timber-cutting boss man and the young master
of the house on the hill of the coffee trees.

Asema listened with rapt attention. Zaho had seen the master of the house on the hill enter the house of the timber boss
man and emerge after the passage of a night. And the women
who worked in the fine house for the timber boss man's beautiful wife had told the women who collected the waste from
the fine house that only one bed was in use when the master of
the house on the hill was in the house of the timber boss man.

Because many young men who had been away working in
the timber were now at home, the flutes played that night, and
the keen voices of the women wailed the ritual songs. The
quavering, deeper voices of the men broke out now and again
into basso shouts, heavy drumbeats of sound that exploded

from fully expanded chests. Because the celebration went on far into the night, Asema slept late next morning.

When she awoke, Zaho was squatted outside her hut, shredding meat from the carcass of a small pig and putting the succulent bits on a large banana leaf. Loving son that he was, he smiled at Asema and indicated that she should sit and eat with him.

Zaho wore only a loincloth and a large half-moon-shaped pendant hanging on a metal chain around his neck. His tightly braided hair hung down in small locks and was held in place by a beaded headband. He was now one of the rich men of the village, having brought up the hill metal axes and knives purchased with his earnings in the timber. Asema expressed appreciation for the food and praised Zaho for his participation in the celebration.

"You danced well, my son," she said.

"I had gladness in my heart," he replied. "It is good to be home."

"Will you stay, then?"

"In the white man's store there are guns," Zaho said. "I would own one of the long guns. It would make the punishment of our enemies swift and sure."

"So. You will go again to the sea to work for the white man?"

Zaho nodded. "We will load one ship and then another, then I will return with the long gun, and I will take a wife."

Asema smiled. The thought of having grandchildren pleased her. And thinking of children, she was reminded of the Little Mistress on the hill and her boy child. "I would ask one thing of you, my son," she said. "It is an evil thing for a woman to steal another's husband, as the beautiful foreign woman does in the white man's town. I would have you relate to the Little Mistress what you have seen and heard."

Zaho looked uncomfortable. "Would not your retelling of what I have seen and heard serve the purpose?"

"Perhaps the Little Mistress will desire to have a strong warrior to tend to her interests," Asema said. "To perform such a service for her would be a great thing and would bring much reward."

Zaho's eyes squinted in thought; then he nodded. "I will speak with her."

"Little Mistress, this is my son, Zaho."

Kit nodded gravely at the strapping youth who stood beside Asema on the veranda of her house. It was late in the day, and the sun was perched atop the western mountains. Kit invited them both to drink tea, and she watched and waited while the two natives squatted and drank the beverage, heavy with sugar, from the delicate china cups.

When Asema spoke again, her manner was grave and ceremonial. "My son, Little Mistress, works with the white boss man of the timber cutting."

"Mr. Gorel," Kit said. "Yes. He is a friend of my husband's. What about him?"

"When the logs are cut and floating in the raft, waiting for the ships to come and carry them away, my son and the others are taken to the white man's town, where they are allowed to buy food and the white man's beer. It was during such a time that my son saw a thing that you must know, Little Mistress."

"Speak then, Zaho," Kit said, not suspecting that the smiling thick-chested little black man was going to shatter the foundations of her world.

Zaho recited the tale simply, staring into Kit's eyes as he spoke. That he did not falter, telling his story as if he had rehearsed it, only made it seem all the more evil. Finally Kit could bear it no longer.

"No, Zaho," she said, cutting him off. "You are wrong. The Kanaka servants have been lying to you. They are making a fool of you." Kit leapt to her feet and stalked to stand a few feet away, her back to Zaho and Asema.

"Little Mistress," Asema said calmly, "it is an evil thing, this. It is a natural thing that you are angry. There is but one way to end that anger and punish the woman who steals your

man. My son is strong. He will kill the foreign woman if
you—"

"Be quiet, Asema!" Kit said angrily, whirling to face the
two natives. Then she saw the stricken look on the face of the
woman who had become her friend, and she went to put a
hand on Asema's shoulder. "Forgive me. Yes, I am upset to
think that anyone could believe that Matt would do such a
thing. I know that you and your son mean well, Asema, but
you are involving yourselves in matters that you don't understand. Yes, my husband does spend the night in the home of
Mr. Gorel when he is in Port Moresby. But I assure you that
any hint of wrongdoing coming from the Kanaka servants is a
fabric of lies."

"As you say, Little Mistress," Asema acquiesced.

Zaho stood and spoke. "What I have said is true. You have
been a friend to my mother, so I will be your warrior in this
matter."

"Thank you, Zaho," Kit said. "But I really don't need a
warrior."

"Are you, then, tired of your man and wish him to be
stolen by the foreign woman?"

Kit was herself again. She had controlled the hurt, anger,
and fear that had swept over her when she heard Zaho's claim
that Matt was being untrue to her. Loyalty to Matt had won
at least a temporary victory. "Zaho, you are a brave warrior,
and if I ever need someone to be my champion, I will come to
you humbly. I thank you for coming to me. That you and
Asema value me enough to be concerned for me pleases me,
and that concern will not go unrewarded."

"I seek no reward for things not done," Zaho said. "Tell me
to kill the foreign woman who steals your man, and then we
will speak of reward."

His gaze met Kit's, and she could see that he was absolutely convinced he was right. For an unguarded moment an
agony of doubt filled Kit, but she smiled. "Will you have
more tea, Zaho, Asema?"

"We will go now, Little Mistress," Asema said.

* * *

Alone with Grant, Kit sat in a rocking chair looking out over her valley. The baby crawled vigorously around the veranda, secured from falling down the steps by a harness and leash that Matt had made for him. Nausea roiled in her stomach. She had not been bothered by morning sickness while she was carrying Grant, but this new one rode a bit more uneasily. There was no one to see. She went to the rail of the veranda and vomited up a small amount of greenish viscous fluid.

She carried Grant to the kitchen, where she toasted a bun and ate it with a cup of tea. Her stomach felt better. Her heart was another matter. Although she *knew* that Zaho's story had come as the result of misunderstanding, because of gossip among Kanaka servants and native workmen, although she was positive that Matt loved her and would not be faithless, the mere thought of it was an ache that filled her bosom. And somewhere, deep down in her mind, there was a reminder that she had given up her only family, had alienated her father, in order to marry Matt. After that, God simply would not permit Matt to hurt her so much. So much for the emotional level of it.

On a more practical level, whatever would become of her and Grant and the unborn child if what Zaho had said were true? While she was able to manage the plantation alone much of the time, supervising the work of the women and seeing to it that the trees were watered in times of temporary drought, she knew almost nothing about how to harvest the coffee beans when the trees started to bear. And she knew nothing about the arrangements that Matt had been working on to market the coffee. Oh, God, she was so far from home! The house was wonderful, a jewel of a house, clean, fresh, and comfortable; but it sat on a slope in the high mountains of southern New Guinea, and the nearest white face was two days' travel away in Port Moresby. The nearest point of familiarity for her was oceanic leagues away.

What would become of her? She had no home other than

this airy house. She and Matt had lived in Australia for a few months, but she would be a stranger there. Cape Town? She did not even know if her father was still there, for her letters had not been answered.

Her stomach convulsed, and for a moment she was almost overwhelmed with self-pity; but when her eyes filled with tears, she sniffed angrily, wiped the tears away, and said to the crawling Grant, "Hear me, young man, and remember what I say. We simply will not allow any disruption of our lives, will we? We are the Van Buren family, and you are the firstborn, the heir. We are a family, and if anyone—*anyone*—tries to diminish our happiness in the slightest degree, we will—"

Will what?

Zaho had offered to be her warrior. He had spoken so casually of killing the "foreign" woman. Death was a familiar thing to the Geheto people of the high valley.

"—we will ask Zaho to be our warrior," she continued. "And . . ."

Matt came home two days later. She went into his arms, accepting his kiss, which was warm and deep. She watched him as he lofted little Grant, who giggled and cried out in pleasure when Matt pretended to eat the lad's stomach, his lips and teeth tickling playfully to make the baby laugh heartily.

She found herself watching Matt ever so closely during the next few days, and she forgot to concentrate on her own pleasure when they were in bed, because she was so interested in observing his actions and reactions.

She had heard it said that when a woman's husband is unfaithful, the woman can always tell. If that bit of folklore was true, Kit decided, then Matt was assuredly blameless, for his love for both her and the boy was unstinting. It was just that he found an excuse to go down the hill again so quickly, more quickly this time than on previous occasions.

Alone again with her child, the servants, and the people of the village, she found that it was difficult to keep the ugly pictures out of her mind. Matt and Guinevere in carnal embrace. Matt and Guinevere talking softly in the low voices of lovers.

Zaho and Asema had, indeed, planted the seeds of evil suspicion in her, and she prayed daily for the wisdom and the maturity to put her doubts to rest forever.

At the time Trevor Gorel was killed, Matt Van Buren was in bed with Trev's wife. For the first time he was making love to Guinevere by the light of day. He had arrived in Port Moresby after a hurried trip from the valley and had gone directly to the Gorel house. He was a man bewitched, totally obsessed with his desire to experience once more the delicate textures of her skin, her silky touch.

He had thought that he knew all there was to know about the woman who had come to possess his soul, but on this hot, humid afternoon Guinevere showed him the complete range of her amatory skills, tying him closer to her, making him a slave to his lust. When he thought that he was spent, her magic, her knowledge of male anatomy and emotions, a combination of words and touches and soft applications of her silken lips, brought arousal again and again until the sinful bed was sodden with their perspiration and Matt was totally used up, wanting only to cling to her and sleep.

Today was the first time she had unleashed all of her art on him. She lay with her head on his shoulder, her eyes half closed. He was still exhausted, breathing hard. His heart pounded against the cage of his chest.

"Matthew . . ."

"Umm?"

"Please, can we talk?"

He groaned. "Not now."

She laughed. Her hand began to do things to him, and her tongue traced a pattern on his sweat-filmed chest.

"Guinevere . . ." He groaned.

"Matt, it is not enough, these moments we steal."

"Umm."

"Are you listening to me?"

"Yes," he said.

"My days are empty when you are not here. I want you to be with me always."

He opened his eyes.

"I know what you will say. You will say 'Trevor' and you will say 'Kit.' But I have reached the point where I think that Guinevere and Matt are at least as worthy of concern as Trevor and Kit. We think always of *them,* how they would be hurt, but we do not think of how I am hurt when you have to leave me here, when I go for weeks without seeing you. We do not think of how you hurt—" She lifted herself onto one elbow and looked down at him. Her dark eyes filled with tears. "Or do you lie to me, telling me how much you want and love me, then leaving me without a thought to go back to your wife?"

"You know that I do not lie to you," he protested.

"Do I? Then the time has come when I must ask you to prove you love me, because I will not go on living an incomplete life. It is as if I am balanced on the edge of a sharp blade; if I fall off on one side, there is no Matt, and I will weep forever. And if I fall to the other side, there you are swimming in the tears of your wife, and I find myself drowning there—"

"Hush, hush now," he said, kissing away the tears.

"So you must decide, Matt. I do love you, but I will not go on living with just a fraction of your love, being only a sideshow in your life."

Matt was undergoing agonies of indecision. When he was with Guinevere, Kit faded into the back of his mind, but she was still there, pale and beautiful, her face set in lines of hurt and disapproval. How could he destroy the woman who had been his first love, the woman who was the mother of his son, the woman whom he still loved in a way that he knew he could never love Guinevere Gorel? His love for Kit was a soft thing, a beautiful portrait of *wife* in pastels. Guinevere was a splash of crimson, a demand, a fire. On that muggy, heated afternoon, having been drained of all lust by a woman so skilled in love that he had not suspected that he was being used, he was incapable of imagining life without either Kit or Guinevere.

As if reading his thoughts, Guinevere said, "Matthew, no longer can you have both."

He pushed her away and rose from the bed. "Leave it, can't you?" he asked, his voice harsh.

"I can," she said. "But can you?"

"Guinevere, this is not the time," he said. "Look, the timbering operations are going well. Trev and I are partners."

"You are concerned that if you tell Trevor that we are in love, that I am going to marry you—"

"Marry?"

"—that your income from the timber will cease."

"Well, by God, it is a consideration," he said. "It'll be a couple of years at best before the coffee begins to produce income. Look, this house isn't furnished free, you know. The foodstuffs you buy in such quantity come from Australia or from England, and they are not given away either. You want to leave New Guinea, but that would take money, much more money than I have. If I broke up the partnership now, it would cost both Trev and me thousands in the long run."

"Is money, then, your first concern?"

He grinned at her. "Well, we could go into the hills and build us a grass shack and live on coconuts and grubs."

She snorted. "There is your father."

Unreasoning anger was Matt's response to the pressure. He stomped out of the room, slamming the door. One of the Kanaka servants, passing in the hall and seeing him nude, gasped and covered her mouth with her hand. He flung open the door and stalked back in to dress hurriedly, not speaking to Guinevere, trying to keep his eyes away from the perfection of her body.

Fleeing the house, he went to the waterfront, where he rousted out his Kanaka boatman and set off in the ketch. They met the workboat coming north as they sailed southward toward the area where Trev had been cutting cedar. In the calm sea they were able to bring the ketch alongside the workboat. But Gihi was shouting to them even before they could get close enough to toss a line to the larger vessel.

"Boss man dead! Bad accident!"

Matt felt a cold chill. Gihi's face was set in grave lines. The other workmen and the entire crew, also looking subdued, were arrayed on the deck of the workboat.

When the ketch was pulled close to the workboat, Matt leapt over, landed on the gunwale, and stepped lightly down onto the deck. "What happened?" he asked Gihi.

"Tree go wrong way," Gihi said, making motions. "Boss man yell, 'Timber!' and run like hell, but run wrong way. Tree bend this way, fall that way." He made motions again.

"Where is he?" Matt asked. He felt numb inside. Old Trev dead. It was impossible. No more of Trev's good-natured joshings. No more of Trev's ancient jokes. No more business partner with whom to share the triumphs of early success.

But on the other hand, there would be no more guilt, at least not on Trev's behalf—except, of course, for the fact that Trev had died at about the same time that Matt was expending himself with Trev's wife. For that Matt would always feel the burn of guilt. And yet his time in Guinevere's bed had not caused Trev's death. That had been a stupid accident, no one's fault. Trev had felled enough trees to know what he was doing, but this one had been old and out of balance and deceptive. It had killed Trev, and there was no help for it.

It had not been an easy death. When Matt was led to the scene, he saw that the tree had fallen across Trev's back, and he had lain there, mashed into the muddy ground, with the tide coming in to soak him. The thing that had killed him was a protruding stump, the stump of a sapling that had been slashed off six inches above the ground when the workmen were clearing a path for the ox teams. The weight of the tree had pushed Trev down onto the jagged stump, thus driving six inches of three-inch-thick wood into his stomach. He had died slowly, painfully, even while yelling instructions to the men who were working diligently to cut the huge tree into movable sections so that it might be lifted from his broken back.

Trev's expression was calm. Matt looked at the pale, waxen face, reached out, and brushed back a lock of hair.

"I am so sorry, Trev," he whispered, and he was not sure whether he was saying he was sorry because Trev was dead or because of his own betrayal.

An Anglican missionary from Birmingham conducted the funeral ceremonies, which took place almost immediately, as the climate necessitated. Matt was a bit surprised when Guinevere put on a convincing display of grief, dressed in black, her face hidden behind a dark veil. Blue Jack and his little wife attended the funeral, and other members of the Anglo community came as a courtesy, simply because the white population of Port Moresby was small, and it was a sad event when one of their few members died. Kit was not present because there was no time to send for her, nor would Matt have wanted her to make the journey now that she was pregnant again.

Usually it was fever that killed a white person. Being broken almost in two by a falling tree was a unique way to go, and it was the subject of several animated, if hushed, conversations as the funeral party broke up and the gravediggers were shoveling the soggy soil into the gaping cavity in the earth.

Matt invited Blue Jack and his Saraba to come to the Gorel home, perhaps because he was not yet ready to face Guinevere's surprising grief and her inevitable desire to speak about their future, now that Trev was dead. Guinevere seemed pleased to have guests, but she excused herself quickly. Little Saraba followed her from the room, asking if there was anything she could do.

"Losing a good friend is a sad thing," Blue Jack said when he and Matt were alone.

"I'm going to miss old Trev," Matt said, meaning it.

"Understand you had a good thing going."

"Yes, we did."

"Going to keep up the timbering operations?"

Matt nodded. "Have to, for a while, at least. The coffee plantation is for the future. If I stop timbering, the income stops."

"Ah," Jack said. "Word around town is that you and Trevor are already rich. People say Trevor's widow shouldn't want for anything. That right?"

"Not rich," Matt said. "We've been putting a lot of the profits back into the operation. The ketch, the workboat, and new machinery for the sawmill."

"I suspect, if a man wanted to chuck it, he could find a number of eager buyers for a going proposition like yours."

"Yes, I suppose so," Matt acknowledged.

"Might be a good time to sell and get out of Papua," Blue Jack said.

"Why do you say that?"

"What if this little dispute between the Russians and the Japanese spreads?" Jack asked, spreading his hands.

"I have to confess that I have been out of touch with the outside world," Matt said.

"Well, I won't try to explain everything that led up to it," Jack said. "Same old story of the European powers trying to divide China among themselves, with the Japs building an army and a navy just as fast as they could so that they, too, could bite off a chunk of China—or Korea, for a start. But I reckon the Russians got too greedy at the expense of Japan, and the long and short of it is that the Jap Navy kicked hell out of the whole Russian fleet near the South Korean coast at Pusan."

"Good Lord," Matt said.

"Yep. Reckon that'll send shivers up and down a few backs down in Australia?"

"The little brown fellows from Japan whipping the navy of a major Western power?" Matt whistled. "The yells of pain and surprise will be heard all the way to the Colonial Office and Buckingham Palace."

"Might just be the thing that sets Australia to building her own navy, eh?"

"It just might," Matt said. "What were the Russian losses?"

"About two thirds of the fleet sunk, and it was a big one. Six ships were captured. Just four ships reached their intended destination at Vladivostok. Six took shelter in neutral ports. And the Japs have also been kicking the hell out of the czar's army on land."

"Hard to believe."

"Well, the Japs are talking, and talking real loud, my boy," Jack said. "They're saying, 'You jokers insisted that we come out of our centuries-long snooze, and now here's the result.' Maybe we all should have applied Napoleon's advice about China to Japan. Wasn't he the one who said we should let China sleep, for her awakening would shake the foundations of the world? Well, the Yanks in particular refused to let Japan sleep, and so now here she is, a threat to us all. The thunder of her naval guns was heard all the way across the Pacific and across the United States, in Theodore Roosevelt's office in Washington. The Yanks are offering to mediate a peace treaty between Russia and Japan, and since there's no way the Russians can regain control of the seas in the Far East, they're eager to talk."

It had occurred to Matt on previous occasions that Blue Jack seemed to be profoundly well informed and articulate about world affairs. "Jack," he asked, "where do you get your information?"

Blue Jack laughed. "Well, let me say only that I just got back from up north, and my friends in German New Guinea keep up with what's happening."

"Everyone says you're a bloody German spy," Matt said, grinning.

"Sure," Blue Jack said, also grinning. "Everybody knows that."

* * *

"Now you cannot leave me," Guinevere whispered.

With Trevor in his grave for mere hours, she lay atop Matt in her bed, silken loins pressed tightly to him, her hips moving, questing, until, with a sigh, she found the object of her search and engulfed it in heated, honeyed softness.

She made no further attempt to discuss the future. The tropical night was perfumed by her scent. In the morning she dressed in black and awaited Matt at the breakfast table.

"You cannot leave me," she repeated.

"I have much to do," he said. "I have to talk with the timber crew. We don't want them just to drift back into the hills because I might never be able to assemble so good a gang again. That's the first order of business. I'll be spending more time with Gihi and the men from now on." He did not say it, but he was thinking that he might have to move Kit down from the valley to Port Moresby. The coffee trees, barring severe drought, could take care of themselves for a time, with a bit of judicious cultivation to keep them from being overgrown by native vines.

"I am free," Guinevere said. "All that is necessary is for you to make yourself free, and then we will be married and leave this place far behind."

"It isn't going to be that easy," he said. But in his mind he was imagining having her near constantly, being able to quench his burning desire for her without guilt and without having to travel miles of jungle trail to reach her bed. It was as if Kit had ceased to exist for a few moments, but then she was back in his mind along with his son.

"Is it not true that I own half of the business now?" Guinevere asked.

"Yes. Trev told me he had made out a will to that effect."

"Then, as your partner, I vote to sell the timbering operation and the coffee plantation. There will be enough money for you to provide for your little wife. There will be enough money for us to go to a civilized place, to London, or to Paris."

"Dammit, Guinevere—"

"I will not be left alone."

He had to find Gihi quickly. He had to get the crew work-ing again. Everything that he had struggled for, hoped for, was at risk in the next few hours. "I will not leave you alone," he said. "But I have to go now."

Finding Gihi at the waterfront, Matt learned that three of the workers who had returned to Port Moresby were already heading up a well-marked trail to their home valley. Matt followed and overtook the men, gave each of them a bonus, bought them all an extra ration of smoked ham, plied them with dark, strong beer, and saw them stagger and crawl aboard the workboat. They would sleep there safely for a few hours.

Now he badly needed a boss man, a good white man to act as pusher for the native crew as they cut timber in various locations. He knew of one possibility, a young Irishman named Thomas Carrol who worked in the general merchan-dise store. He was inexperienced, but he seemed to have confi-dence. He was, indeed, interested in bettering himself. He agreed to work for Matt on salary, with the possibility—if things worked out—of becoming part owner at a later date.

"Just let Gihi tell the boys what to do until you get the hang of it," Matt advised him as he sent him off with the native employees to fell trees in the hills.

Matt hurried back to the Gorel house, where he found Guinevere waiting for him. "Now we will talk about what we must do," she said.

"Listen to me," Matt said in a harsh voice. "I will not sell the business, not just now. We will not leave New Guinea, not just now. I will not hurt Kit, not while she's carrying my child. Do I make myself clear?"

"Quite clear," Guinevere said. "Are you going back to the valley now, back to her?"

"I am."

"Then I will go with you. I told you that I will not be left alone in this sodden, barbarian place. I will go with you to this wonderful valley, and I will see this wonderful wife o' yours again so that I might better understand why you fee free to hurt me, whom you say you love, but refuse to tell he that you no longer love her."

"I don't think that's a good idea," Matt said. How on eart could he keep his emotions hidden, with both of them to gether in the same house? And how would he find the oppor tunity to make love with Guinevere in Kit's house with Ki and his son present?

"The matter is not open for discussion," Guinevere said.

"Bloody hell, woman," Matt thundered. "Just who do yo think you are? You can't tell me what to do. I've told you will not have Kit hurt while she's carrying my child. That's it Period. End of discussion. Stay here or be damned. If you fee that you must get out of New Guinea, I will advance yo what ready cash we have on hand, as payment against you share of future profits. Then you can leave, set up in Austra lia, or go all the way to your own country or Europe or wher ever the hell you want to go."

Guinevere wept quietly, tears of anger, not grief. But sh made no further demonstration as Matt packed and left he going off to his wife and his valley.

Keeping her indignation from Matt was the hardest thin she had ever done, but she was too close to her goal to spo her chances now. If all that stood between her and Matt– with the entire net worth of the business converted into cas —was a fetus being carried by Kit Van Buren, that was a stat of affairs that could be altered.

She gave Matt one day's start and then followed hin guided by two natives, who looked at times as if they wer hungry enough to cook her and eat her. She did not enjoy th journey, hating the smell and the dampness of the jungle trai She detested having to climb the steep slopes, getting he clothing wet with perspiration, and being caught in the rai By the time she reached the valley and was directed to th Van Buren house on the slope, she was more determined tha ever that she would leave all primitive places behind her as soon as possible.

"I'm terribly sorry to burst in on you like this," she told a surprised Kit Van Buren, who met her on the veranda with an embrace and muttered condolences, "but I couldn't stay alone for another minute in the house where we were so happy."

Guinevere was thoroughly convincing as the mourning widow. She saw Kit hesitate for an instant, a shadow—the hint of a question or a doubt?—crossing her face. But Kit's words conveyed only concern that sounded genuine.

"Oh, my dear," she said, "I do know how you must feel. You did right to come to us. In fact, I told Matt that he should have insisted you come with him. I'll give you the big guest room. It's bright and airy, and you stay just as long as you wish. Our home will be yours until you're ready to return to Port Moresby. It'll be nice having company when Matt has to go down the hill again."

"You're very kind," Guinevere replied. "I will be grateful to you forever."

While Kit went inside to make the arrangements, Guinevere remained on the veranda. She looked out over the valley, already making her plans. It was cooler up here, and less humid, but she was surrounded by sinister jungle growth and squat, savage people. She had no desire to make Kit Van Buren's home her own. All she wanted from Kit was her husband, and she had determined her course of action even before leaving Port Moresby.

Kit, busying herself in the guest room, pushed from her mind what Asema and Zaho had told her.

Chapter XXXII

THE ROLE OF women in the Geheto tribe, as in most primitive societies, was that of servant, agricultural worker, tender of children, and receptacle of man's passions—be they aggressive or amatory. As second wife of the headman of the village, Asema ranked lower than any newly initiated young warrior, but she held a position of respect among the women.

She still had the small, taut breasts of a girl. Her customary dress was a grass skirt that came to her knees. The skirt, secured at her thick hips by a braided rope made of vines, hung below her navel; the skin between skirt and navel was covered by a decorative black belt made of leather. Her left wrist carried half a dozen bone and tortoiseshell bracelets, gifts from her son, Zaho. She disdained the usual corn-row style of tiny hair braids, so her hair remained a dense ebony mass on top of her head, tapering into two large, neat braids that hung down in front of her shoulders. Her eyebrows were heavy, making her natural expression an unblinking, dark-eyed, sometimes flirtatious glower.

She was years younger than Foja's first wife, and being gifted with just a bit more imagination than others, she had always been more impressionable. She was a serious student of all the Geheto myths, and while she could not have articulated her religious beliefs precisely, she was aware that man was not alone in the world, that he shared the valley with others. These were not gods—there were no gods as such in the Geheto religion—but rather demons, or bogeymen. The demons, assuming the shapes of frighteningly deformed men, appeared when one was alone and unprotected.

What Asema feared most—perhaps because as second wife of an old man she had had quite limited sexual experience—were those evil spirits that enticed women away from the safety of the group and seduced them with clever words and slick ways. Death was the inevitable result of such an encounter, and the victim knew that she was going to die when, after the seduction, the spirit revealed his malevolence by spitting in her face.

Not long after the foreign woman came to live with the Little Mistress, Asema began to wish that one of the spirits of the recent dead would lure Guinevere away, ravish her, spit in her face, and leave her to expire in total agony.

Since assisting at the birth of Grant Van Buren, Asema had been allowed the run of the house on the hill. She had come to feel that three cups of very sweet tea each day was her rightful due, for did she not see to it that the Little Mistress's house was aired each morning, that it was swept clean by the young girls using their grass besoms, that the night jar was emptied and rinsed? The Little Mistress herself had said, *"Asema, you are a true friend."*

Asema's introduction to Guinevere Gorel had come on the morning after Guinevere's arrival, after Matt Van Buren went back down the hill to attend to his timbering business. Asema had been in the kitchen, making her first cup of morning tea, adding the fifth spoonful of sugar.

"Get out of here, you horrible creature!" Guinevere screamed at her.

Fortunately, Guinevere, in her surprise at finding a native in the kitchen, had spoken in French. Asema did not know the words, but she understood the tone. She lowered her head, looked at Guinevere unblinkingly from beneath her dark brows, and wondered who this new white woman was.

"She is the wife of the dead timber boss," she was told.

"The one who steals the Little Mistress's husband for her own use?" she asked.

"The same," said her son, who had run away from the timber gang now that the old boss was dead and the crew was being directed by a strange young white man who was not familiar with the Papuan jungles.

"I will watch her," Asema promised.

"I don't see how you can stand those animals in the house," Guinevere said, speaking of Asema and the two girls she supplied as household servants.

"They're good girls," Kit answered. "Quite clean. They bathe in the stream every morning and often in the evening. Asema was one of the midwives when Grant was born."

"I couldn't abide one of them touching me," Guinevere said, shivering in disgust.

First one and then the other girl was driven away by Guinevere's dislike, which turned to open hate when Kit was not present. The second girl left, telling Asema that she would not go back as long as the she-demon was in the house. Guinevere had taken a leather strop to the girl's bare back for having spilled a bit of sugar on the kitchen table.

"Little Mistress," Asema confided to Kit, "the tan-skinned one has a disposition like that of a wasp seeking water in the dry time. The others who have worked for you will not come back."

"That's ridiculous, Asema," Kit replied. "The other girls are probably simply tired of working. Now, really, does Guinevere's presence make for that much more work for you? She's quite a good cook, and I've noticed that none of you turn away when there's food left on the table after she has prepared a meal. She tidies up after herself, so you don't have to pick up after her."

"It is not the work but her evil tongue," Asema said.

Kit would not have considered herself bigoted in the slightest, but Guinevere was, after all, from her world, a woman of her class. Naturally she defended Guinevere against criticism from a mere native, from a servant, even if—had she been asked—she would have said, "Why, certainly Asema is my friend."

"Little Mistress," Asema insisted, "I will not let that woman drive me away, even though that is her intent. She wants to have you to herself, alone, without your friends nearby."

"Asema," Kit said sharply, "you exceed yourself. I will not have you criticizing Mrs. Gorel in that manner."

"Then, Little Mistress, I want you to put a halter on your man when he comes home. I want you to keep him in your own garden, lest he—"

"That's enough," Kit said forcefully. "I will not hear any more of that, ever again. Do you understand?"

"It is sad that there are times when one does not know that one needs a friend," Asema said. "But I will watch, Little Mistress. I will be nearby. Perhaps you will not always see me, but I will be nearby."

The days passed quickly for Kit. It was pleasant to have another woman in the house. The two of them sat on the porch, little Grant in Kit's lap, gurgling happily while the two women nattered on. Their conversations went on for hours, for there was no man about to grin a superior grin and make remarks about women's talk. Guinevere was very solicitous of Kit, inquiring about her health often and showing sympathy at a recurrence of the morning sickness. And she played with Grant, tickling him and making him laugh.

When Matt came home unexpectedly, Kit was so pleased that she ran into his arms with a glad cry. He smelled of gin. It was not like him to drink while on the trail. He greeted her with fondness and gave Guinevere a little bow. He told them that he should not have come home just then, for he had just agreed with officials in Port Moresby to provide timber for some additional buildings going up there, and he was awaiting the return of his crew from the hills with wood intended for the buildings. But, he explained, looking at neither of the women, "I was a bit lonely. I had to see you."

Guinevere made the evening meal, and Matt was profuse in his praise. After the meal he drank. This, too, was unlike Matt. In bed he took Kit with a fierce hunger and with a display of energy that made her say, "Hush. You'll waken Guinevere."

After breakfast the next morning, he said, "I want to have a look at the coffee trees." His eyes were red, and his breath was tainted with the stale aftereffects of too much gin. "You'd better stay here, Kit. I'll take Guinevere with me for company."

"Ah," said Guinevere, "I'm to be offered a real treat, a stroll up and down a mountain." But she laughed to show that she was not serious.

"I'll come along," Kit said. "The exercise will be good for me."

"I said you will stay here," Matt said, his voice harsh. "In your condition—"

"In my condition exercise is good for me," she replied sharply. "For heaven's sake, Matt, I climb that hill half a dozen times a week. Just two days ago I walked every foot of it, checking to be sure that the ground wasn't getting too dry."

He smiled at her. "Sorry, Kits, it's just that I am concerned about you. The sickness you've had—"

"The sickness is all but over," she assured him, "and it's quite a normal condition when one is with child. Not being ill in the mornings with Grant was the thing that was abnormal, you know."

Asema saw them, the three of them, walking among the coffee trees, the two women so different, Kit in a dark, comfortable dress with an ample skirt that had been shortened so as not to sweep the top of the weeds, short enough to show her shoe tops, Guinevere in sweeping white, holding her skirt up with one hand, walking daintily, catching Matt's arm now and then for support. Asema grunted. Her glowering expression did not change.

Matt's frustration grew as the slow days passed. It was almost as if Kit suspected something and made it a point never to leave him alone with Guinevere, not even for a few minutes. Once he had a chance to lean toward Guinevere and whisper, "I want you so badly I can taste it."

"Then do something about it," she answered, then smiled broadly, for Kit had reentered the room to hear her reply.

"Do something about what?" Kit asked.

"About getting so bloody rich we can all get out of New Guinea," Guinevere said.

"I'll be sad when we leave this place," Kit said, taking a chair. "I told Asema that one day we would leave and she said, 'Little Mistress, when you go, it will be as if you have died. I will cut off my finger and cover my head with dirt, and I will burn down your house so that I will not see it every day and be reminded.'"

Opportunity came for Matt the very next day. One of the women who had worked in the house before Guinevere's arrival came to the veranda, weeping and almost incoherent. Through her tears she explained that her little girl had fallen, and the bone in her arm was protruding.

Kit gave crisp orders to Matt to get her medical bag. Being isolated as they were, they had a supply of medications—quinine, laudanum, and patent medicines for itching, diarrhea, constipation, ague, menstrual cramps—as well as bandages, disinfectants, and even catgut for stitching up wounds.

"Come with me, Guinevere," Kit ordered. "I might need your help."

"Sorry, my dear," Guinevere replied, "I'm really no good at these things. If you don't mind, I'll stay here."

Matt's blood surged.

"Then you'll have to come with me, Matt," Kit said.

He felt a great sense of loss, but he did not protest. He knew that their good relationship with the people of Foja's village was an asset to be guarded. Kit's doctoring of small and large hurts was a continual source of goodwill for them.

The child was no more than five years old. She was bleeding badly and was weak from it. Kit fought a battle with the wailing child and finally got some laudanum down her, enough, eventually, to calm her. The child screamed shrilly when Kit pulled on the broken arm, snapping the bones back into approximately the right position. Blood spurted anew, and the child fainted, giving Kit an opportunity to set the bones as best she could and begin to stanch the flow of blood.

"She will be all right?" the mother asked after Kit had splinted the arm. The girl was still comatose but resting well.

"She is very weak," Kit answered. She patted Matt on the hand. "You were a very good assistant," she told him.

He grinned. "You'll never know how close I came to losing my breakfast."

"But you didn't."

"You, lady, are very impressive." He was sincere. She had set the bone expertly, used needle and catgut to close the wound where the bone had punctured the flesh.

"I'm going to have to stay here until she wakes up," Kit said. "She's going to be in pain, and I'll want to give her something for it. Why don't you go on back to the house?"

His pulse leapt. *She* was in the house alone. For some reason about which he had not inquired, the servants made themselves scarce those days. Not even Asema stayed in the house much. "Sure you won't need me?" he asked.

"Yes, I'm sure. No point in your staying."

He had to make a conscious effort to keep from appearing to hurry up the slope. Guinevere was sitting on the veranda as he approached the house. He ran up the steps.

"Where's Asema?" he asked.

"I sent her away," Guinevere said.

"Goodonyer," Matt said, taking her hand, lifting her from the chair, and leading her into the house to her bedroom. He could not wait. He took her in a tangled heap of clothing, his trousers around his ankles, her skirts and underthings bunched.

It was not Asema, then, who watched the house but her son, Zaho. He saw Matt jerk the foreign woman from the chair and lead her into the house. After a while he moved silently down through the green coffee trees and stood underneath a window to hear the grunts of completion of a man in rut, the high, piercing, mindless wail of a woman lost in fruition. He waited until it all began again, and then, shaking his head, he left to go down into the village, where the Little Mistress was talking soothingly to a whimpering little girl with a broken arm.

It was torture for Matt to stay at the house. He and Guinevere had narrowly missed being discovered when Kit came home from her errand of mercy. He had simply lost himself in glorious dissipation, losing track of the time. He had barely gotten his clothes back on when he heard the click-clack of Kit's heels on the porch. He ran from Guinevere's room, tidying himself, feeling that all Kit had to do was look at him to know what had happened. Behind him Guinevere calmly went to her washstand and began to clean herself.

"How's the child?" Matt asked, coming onto the veranda.

"If we can keep her clean, keep the arm from becoming infected, she'll be all right. Where's Guinevere?"

"She said she needed a nap."

"Good day for it," Kit said. The hurried walk to the village, the strain of setting the arm, and the walk back up the hill had left her exhausted. "Do you mind if I follow Guinevere's example?"

"Not at all," he said.

Guinevere joined him on the veranda after Kit had gone off to her room. "Had you stayed with me a bit longer," she said, "our problems would be over."

He shuddered. It had been a near thing, and he could not stop thinking about what Kit would have felt had she come home a few minutes earlier to catch him in Guinevere's bed. He didn't like the thought, but neither could he abide the thought of never having Guinevere again.

He was a man in torment, and by no means the first to postpone the solution to his torment by running from it. He told Kit that he'd been truant from responsibility long enough, and then he was off and away. He made just one attempt to change the situation. He suggested, as he was leaving, that Guinevere might be tired of living in someone else's house, that she might be ready to go back to her own home.

"Oh, no," Kit said. "Why, we're not talked out yet."

"If you want me, Kit," Guinevere said sweetly, "I'd like very much to stay—just a bit longer."

Returning to the lowlands, Matt found that Thomas Carrol and his crew had arrived with lumber cut and ready for the buildings in Port Moresby.

Carrol was taking hold nicely as foreman. Gihi's crew was shorthanded; but Matt had talked with some of the men in the village, and he had been promised that several young men would make themselves available for work. He would go with them, he decided, when it came time to return to the south coast for more timber cutting there.

No fewer than four buildings were going up in Port Moresby, constructed entirely of the lumber cut by Matt's crew and finished at his sawmill, the same mill that had prepared the wood for his own house. And the trail from the town to the high valley, once obscure and very difficult to follow, was gradually being cleared; it was becoming a thoroughfare for oxcarts carrying lumber to and from the mill. The firm's bank balance was growing at a pleasing rate.

A representative from the Colonial Office was visiting in Port Moresby, and when Matt was introduced to him, the official asked searching questions about the condition of Matt's coffee plantation. The government was quite eager for production to get under way.

"How quickly could you expand the plantings?" he asked Matt.

"Just about as fast as the plants could be shipped in," Matt said. "Depending, of course, on weather and the willingness of the women in the valley to work."

"Van Buren," the official said, "in London and in Melbourne, too, we are quite eager to see this territory become an asset rather than a liability. You and Mr. Gorel have proven that timbering can be a profitable business, and I'm sure that there'll be others coming out here to enter that field. If you can prove that it is also feasible and profitable to grow coffee on the mountain slopes, you'll be able to tell your grandchildren that you were personally responsible for the opening of Papua to the benefits of civilization."

Kit encountered Asema and Zaho as she was walking by herself along a row of healthy coffee trees. Guinevere, not fond of outdoor exercise, had declined to walk with her.

Having been free of morning sickness for more than a week, Kit felt wonderful. Her skin glowed with health, and she carried a parasol to protect it from the brilliant sun of the high elevations. The air was clear and sweet, and she had been singing happily when she saw the two natives climbing toward her, weaving in and out of the trees.

"Good morning, Asema, Zaho," she said cheerily.

"Greetings, Little Mistress," Asema said.

"Do you seek me out, or are you, too, simply enjoying this glorious day?"

"I have sought you out," Asema said, "to tell you of a serpent that lives within your walls."

"Oh, Asema, not that again." Kit sighed. "It's too pretty a day to spoil it with unpleasantness."

"My son, Zaho, saw it and heard it." Asema nodded to the warrior.

"It was when you went to straighten and mend the arm of the girl," Zaho said. "He plucked her from the chair in which she sat like a ripe fruit, taking her by the hand—"

"Zaho, I do not want to hear this," Kit said; but her heart was pounding, and she felt quite weak.

"And then I went down . . . there," he continued, point-ing, "making my way unseen through the trees. I stood be-neath the window of the room in which the foreign woman sleeps, and I heard two pigs breeding, the squeals and the grunts—"

"Shut up, shut up, shut up!" she screamed, putting her hands over her ears.

Asema was shorter and thicker of body. She had to reach up to seize Kit's hands and pull them forcefully away from her ears.

"Please leave me alone," Kit said weakly. She had tried to put out of her mind the things that Asema and Zaho had told her previously, but she had not been successful. During the early days of Guinevere's stay in her house, when they talked and talked, finding things that made them both giggle like girls, she had felt confident that the natives had been mis-taken, that Guinevere was truly her friend, that even if Matt did desire her, she would not yield to him. But then she had seen the little changes in Matt, the way she would catch him staring at Guinevere, the way he tried to get her to stay in the house when he suggested that Guinevere and he inspect the plantation. And in the village, after she had mended the bro-ken arm, the old Matt, the man she had loved and married, would not have left her, not even at her insistence.

Zaho's words had the ring of truth. It was his descriptive phrase regarding the mating of pigs that convinced her that what he said was not to be denied, for she had sometimes teased Matt about the sounds that came from his throat dur-ing his pleasure.

"Here is Zaho," Asema said. "The woman is there, alone. You have but to give the word."

"My God, Asema, I can't just have her *killed*."

"You have only to say the word," Asema repeated, not understanding Kit's reluctance. "She steals your man in your own house. You have every right under the laws—"

"Not under the laws of the white man," Kit rejoined. She was talking to keep from weeping. She did not want to break down in front of Asema and Zaho. "I believe you, Zaho. I know that you speak truth. I wish I could say that I am grateful. I will, however, manage this affair in my own way. You are a brave warrior, but I do not need your services."

"As you will," Zaho said, turning to stalk away down the slope.

"I will go with you," Asema said to Kit.

"No, please," Kit said. "I'm fully capable of handling this myself."

Guinevere was at her toilet, seated before a dressing mirror in the guest room, applying a perfumed oil to her face, neck, and arms. She had been thinking about the day that Kit had doctored the little native girl, and she had come to a conclusion. She had proven that Matt wanted her badly enough to risk discovery in his own home. She would go back to Port Moresby now and be there when he returned from the lumbering operations. It was time that she forced him to a decision, and she did not doubt what that decision would be. She rose, donned a form-fitting robe of yellow silk, and seated herself once more before the mirror.

Kit found her thus, her beauty painfully evident, not only in face but in body. To the bitterness of betrayal, to the agony of loss, was added the ego-shattering realization for Kit that this woman, whom the natives called foreign, was indeed more beautiful than she.

With her stomach beginning to protrude once more, to mar her slim figure, with her sunset hair faded and dried by the tropical sun, Kit felt dowdy and ordinary.

"Back so soon?" Guinevere asked, looking at Kit in the mirror. Her almond eyes were so exotic, her ebony hair was so richly lustrous, and her skin so perfect.

"Yes," Kit said, her anger smoldering.

"Dear Kit," Guinevere said, "I am so grateful to you for having taken me in like some stray animal, but it is time that I returned your privacy to you. Would you be kind enough to ask some of the natives to escort me to Port Moresby?"

Kit had been thinking that the sooner the foreign woman was out of her house, the better, but she realized that if Guinevere were back in Port Moresby, there would be nothing to keep Matt from her bed.

"No," she said, on an impulse that, even as she spoke, began to seem right. "I will not. Nor will you go back to Port Moresby. I want you here, Guinevere. I want you here where I can keep my eye on you. You have bedded my husband in my own house, but don't think that you'll ever get the opportunity again, for I'm going to stick to you like glue. If you ever again try to tempt Matt, or if I catch you with him, I will kill you as quickly and as surely as I would kill a snake in the garden."

"Kit?" Guinevere played for time by pretending innocence. "Whatever are you saying?"

"Do you find it amusing that Matt grunts like a pig when he is feeling his pleasure?"

"I—I don't know what you're talking about."

"I find it only mildly amusing, rather expected, as a matter of fact, that you squeal like a pig. I might have guessed that you'd yowl like a jungle cat, but somehow squealing like a pig fits you better."

A little smile twisted Guinevere's lips. She turned to face Kit. The yellow silk robe gaped open to show her large, perfect breasts, larger and more shapely than Kit's. Kit felt a pang of sorrow. Had Matt's lips caressed those honey-colored mounds as they had touched her own creamy softness?

"Did you creep to the door like a little mouse and listen?" Guinevere asked, her voice full of coldness. "Or did you stand underneath the window? If you're so brave, Kit, why didn't you confront us? Were you afraid that Matt would choose me?" She turned back to the mirror and continued smoothing the oil onto her skin. "He will, you know. He has stayed with you only out of pity and because in your peasant fertility you carry his child again."

The ring of truth? Perhaps. It didn't matter. She would never have Matt, this foreign woman.

"You're going to notice a change around here," Kit said. "You're going to start earning your keep. For starters, find something that you don't mind soiling. It's dry, and the women are watering the trees. I think it would be very nice of you to help them."

"You're balmy," Guinevere said with a cold little smile. She picked up a brush and began to stroke her hair. Kit walked out of the room, heels going click-click. She suspected that Asema would have followed her, and sure enough, Asema was there on the veranda.

Guinevere whirled around on the stool when Kit reentered the room with Asema beside her. "Get her out of my room," Guinevere demanded.

"Asema," Kit said, "the foreign woman is going to help water the trees, but she may need some convincing. Do you think you could help her find her way to the slopes?"

Asema's blank, glowering look broke into a smile for just a moment. She moved swiftly, grabbed Guinevere by the arm, and tugged. Guinevere slipped off the stool and landed hard on her rump. She leapt up and swung wildly at Asema and was rewarded by a solid slap to the face.

Asema was short, thick, and powerful. She dragged the slender Guinevere to the floor and rolled atop her, straddled her, and slapped her face back and forth, back and forth until Guinevere was weeping and screaming in pain, anger, and frustration.

"Enough," Kit said. And to Guinevere: "Would you like to change into work clothes now?"

"I have no work clothes, damn you," Guinevere screamed.

"Then we'll have to find you some," Kit said.

Dressed in a pair of Matt's old work pants, his shirt baggy on her, Guinevere bent down to pick up a bucket of water that the native women had carried from the irrigation flume. Her back hurt, and the flaming sun burned her face. She had never exposed her skin to its rays, and she hated the woman who was making her do so. From exposure to the sun came bad skin, wrinkles, dryness.

"What are you doing to me?" she whined as she passed Kit, who was standing leaning on a walking stick.

"I'm merely trying to improve your character, dear," Kit answered.

When the watering was done and the buckets secured in a little storage shed, the women of the village left in small groups, waving their farewells. Asema had gone down to the house to begin the evening meal, knowing that after the long day in the fields the Little Mistress would need food for herself and the baby she carried. Guinevere had poured her last bucket of water on a tree that clung to the steepest portion of the slope. Below the last terrace the hillside fell away, through uncleared brush, to a precipitous drop to the streambed a hundred feet below.

"My hands," Guinevere moaned, looking at her reddened palms. "Look what you've done to my hands!"

"Why, Guinevere, I thought your whole intent was to become the wife of a coffee plantation owner. Matt would expect you to pull your share of the load, you know. You're quite sure that he's going to choose you, aren't you?"

"When he returns, you'll see," Guinevere said.

"If so, you'll thank me later for having taught you the things you'll have to know. You see, he can't be here to take care of the trees all the time, so that would become your duty."

Guinevere's face burned. She lifted one aching hand and touched her reddened skin with her fingertips. "Peasant!" she spat at Kit.

"Now, be nice," Kit said. "Come. Let's go down to the house."

Kit stepped past Guinevere on the downhill side, walking on top of the mound of the dirt terrace. With a strangled cry of hate Guinevere threw herself at Kit, not caring if she, too, went off the terrace.

Kit seized a handful of hair, but it slipped through her hand as she fell. She landed with a solid, jarring thud and began to roll. She tried to stop herself, but the slope was too steep. Only the growth of brush kept her from going over the drop to fall a hundred feet to the rocky streambed. Her skirts became entangled in the wiry brush, and she was jerked to a stop only feet from the edge of the overgrown cliff. The world was fading in and out. She thought she heard a woman laughing wildly, and then there was only a pain in her stomach and darkness.

Kit awoke, moaning, trying to push away the hands that were hurting her wrists. She opened her eyes. Zaho was trying to pull her away from the brink of the drop.

"Come, Little Mistress," he coaxed. "Try to help me."

She dug in the toes of her shoes, and soon he was pulling her to her feet. A storm of pain struck her stomach, and she bent over. She felt wetness inside her clothing. A dark stain of blood had soaked all the way through her dress.

"I can't walk, Zaho," she gasped. She sat, clasped her stomach, and with a rush of acute sorrow knew that she was losing the baby. "Get Asema," she whispered, leaning back against the slope and closing her eyes to the pain.

As if by magic Asema appeared. "The foreign woman came down alone," she explained as she fell to her knees beside Kit.

"The baby," Kit whispered.

Asema looked at Zaho, pointed down the hill toward the house. He nodded and left them. Asema was straightening Kit's skirts, lifting them.

"It is over with the baby," she said.

"Oh, God. Poor little thing."

"It did not really know. So small. Not yet formed. Now it is you that we worry about." She ripped away strips of Kit's underskirt, packing her to try to stop the bleeding. Other women came hurrying up the hill, and three of them helped Asema carry Kit to the house. Kit fainted before the trip was well begun.

When Kit was stretched out on her bed, Asema began to work frantically, heedless of the damage that the blood was doing to the sheets and the mattress. The Little Mistress had lost much blood, but at last Asema stopped the bleeding.

Kit awoke to darkness. She tried to sit up and fell back, sick with dizziness and weakness.

"Rest easy, Little Mistress," Asema said.

"The baby?"

"It is over with the baby."

"Poor thing." She had a vague memory of having heard or said something similar. There were odd noises in her ears, like the rushing of birds' wings combined with the whine of souls in pain. She opened her eyes and looked out the open window to the starred sky. A cooling breeze blew from the south. Slowly she began to sort out the odd sounds. The souls in torment were the flutes of the men of the village, sounding sometimes like the fluttering of wings. And she could just distinguish the explosive, drumlike sounds made as the men expelled breath from their lungs forcefully.

"What is the celebration for, Asema?" she asked idly.

"Nothing special," Asema answered.

"Odd," Kit said. The villagers did not simply decide to throw a party. When the flutes played and the men made drum sounds, there was a reason. Her heart sank when she recalled one of the reasons for an unscheduled round of celebration, and she started to ask if a war party had returned with some captives. But the sounds faded, and she slept. When she awoke again, it was still black and the flutes were playing a more frantic rhythm. She smelled something odd, a coppery warm smell.

"Do you wake, Little Mistress?" Asema asked.

"I feel so strange, Asema."

"You lost much blood."

"Yes, that would be—" She did not finish the sentence. Asema was standing beside the bed. In the moonlight that came through the window Kit could see that she had a kitchen utensil in her hands.

"I have something for the weakness," Asema said. "Eat."

Dutifully, in a haze of faintness, Kit opened her mouth. The taste was raw, like an uncooked slice of beef. She chewed, and it was tough, with a taste of blood. She managed to get her head over the edge of the bed and spit out the mouthful. She gagged once, twice, but the vomit did not come. She fell back, spent.

"You should eat," Asema said.

"I . . . can't."

"The blood was taken from you. This will put it back."

She felt as if Asema's words were coming to her from the stars themselves, across incredible distances. "Light a lamp, please."

She closed her eyes until she sensed the glow of light. Asema was seated in a straight chair beside her, holding the kitchen pan. She saw a red, wet, membranous mass at the bottom of the pan.

"It will put back the blood you lost," Asema said, using a knife to cut away a bite-sized bit from the red, oozing mass.

"For the heart," Asema said, "is the source of blood."

The flutes rose to a soaring height of sound and fell silent. Down in the village the cook fires would be banked, the embers just right for roasting choice cuts of meat. There would be a smell in the air, half-burned, half-delicious hide, as when, in celebration, Foja's people roasted pigs on the open fires. And now the entire tribe would be gathered, competing good-naturedly for the choice parts, but the choicest morsel of all was in the pan that sat on Asema's lap.

"Where is the foreign woman?" Kit asked, her voice barely audible.

"She is gone, Little Mistress," Asema said with one of the few smiles that Kit had ever seen on her face. "She said that she would go to the white man's town, but none of our men would travel at night, lest the spirits of the newly dead come to them. Some say that the spirits do not frighten white people, but Zahò thinks that that is wrong and that the foreign woman could, indeed, meet with a demon, and—"

Kit felt an elemental drowsiness, the demand of her body for healing sleep. One part of her mind told her to be outraged, horrified, stunned. As her eyes closed, she saw Asema pop a bit of meat into her mouth and chew heartily. And oddly, she could not be shocked or indignant.

It is said that the needs and impulses of primitive man, the survival instincts of the cave time, remain with all of us, deeply buried in that portion of the mind to which we do not have conscious access. As sleep closed about Kit, she knew only that she was glad to be alive, that she was sad because something of value had been taken from her—her baby. She was viscerally relieved to know that she would not have to confront the woman who had caused the death of her unborn child.

"Enjoy," she tried to whisper as Asema cut another chunk from the muscular, bloody mass in the pot. But she was not sure that she had spoken aloud.

Chapter XXXIII

THE EXPANDING NETWORK of rail lines made a portion of the journey from Brisbane to the midpoint of the continent's empty red heart relatively comfortable. However, not even the power of the Mason fortune and the influence of the Mason business empire could negate the reality of distance and remoteness, of dusty, rutted, bumpy bush roads that seemed to defy the logical belief that everything is finite. Magdalen knew that she was not the youthful, vibrant lass that, so long ago, had married Red Broome, but until she began to experience the sheer vastness of her country, she had not felt particularly old.

Tolo had arranged for the finest of coaches. In spite of his desperate desire to make haste, he gave consideration to Magdalen's age and limited endurance, cutting short the day's travel at times to give her a chance to rest.

In the magnificent emptiness of the Northern Territory the dusky red impressiveness of the vistas seemed to put new vigor into Magdalen, and she insisted on long days, fretting about the passage of time.

At Alice Springs, after sleeping fourteen hours in a real bed, she caught up with Tolo in the office of the constabulary and made Tolo and the chief constable repeat what had been discussed. Yes, rumors of a white woman living among the Abos had reached Alice Springs. There was, in fact, a spreading Abo legend about a white woman and an Abo companion crossing the never-never by walking with the spirits of the Dreaming.

"She dances on the rock?" Magdalen asked with a laugh. "Sounds very much like our Java, doesn't it, Tolo?"

Tolo was impatient to be under way.

"It's a big country out there," the chief constable said. "It's not an easy trek, no matter where you go. For a lady of your age, Mrs. Broome, well . . ."

Magdalen winked at the constable. "You just let me worry about my age." She turned to Tolo. "But I'll want a wide, fat horse."

"I must advise against your taking a lady into the bush," the constable told Tolo.

"Listen, young man," Magdalen said. "They tried to make me stay in Sydney. They said a woman of my age would not be able to stand the rigor of traveling into the Territory. But look, I'm here. I have a bit of dust behind my ears yet, and I'd guess I'm about four pounds lighter; but I'm here, and I intend to be with Tolo when he finds my granddaughter."

The constable sighed.

"You mentioned a particular mob of Abos," Tolo said, to get the talk back to practical matters, since Magdalen was obviously not going to budge on the question of making the journey.

"Yes, Jajjala's mob," the constable said. "They range all over. It's pretty well established that they were up around Barrow Creek at the time your wife was there, and she was with them. Jajjala, you see, hasn't really given in to the white man's vices, though he likes gin when he can get it. Mostly he still lives in the old way, and although his mob gets smaller, he still has a following. They stay in one place until the game is pretty well hunted out or scared off, and then they go walkabout, covering immense distances, though they take their time about it."

"Any idea where they are now?" Tolo asked.

"Well, Barrow Creek's at the northern end of their range,

so in the time that's passed since Mrs. Mason drew money there, I'd say they'd have come south again. In fact, I had a fellow tell me a while back that he'd seen them a long way south of here, south of Ayers Rock. They could have been heading for some mountains down there, where there's game."

"So there's a lot of ground to cover, Constable," Tolo said. "What would you recommend?"

"I'd suggest you get together a small mob of your own—say, at least half a dozen good bushmen—and explore the good watering places around Ayers Rock. Wherever Jajjala and his people are, they return to that spot sooner or later, it being sacred and all. If you work your way from water to water in that vicinity, you'll have your best chance of finding them—and Mrs. Mason."

"That makes sense," Tolo said. He had seen parts of the Northern Territory, and he knew that it was not going to be easy finding one particular group of Aborigines in an area of hundreds of square miles.

"I wish I could spare you a man or two," the chief constable said, "but we're a small force, and we're undermanned at the moment. I can suggest one bloke that would be valuable to you. His name is George Dutton. He's half Wonggumara. Usually he works the stations. Proud man for a half-breed. When his last employer tried to treat him like a boong, he told the man to get bent. He knows the country. If anyone can find old Jajjala, George Dutton can. If he hires on with you, just don't try to make him eat on the wood heap—"

"What does that mean?" Magdalen asked.

"It's a manner of speaking about how we usually treat the boongs. On a station the white stockmen eat at a table, while the blackfellows sit on the woodpile with their plates on their knees. But not George. He demands and gets pay equal to a white bush worker's, and he earns it."

Tolo found George Dutton drinking in one of the Alice's pubs, standing at the bar unchallenged by the whitefellows.

George Dutton was flash. His clothes had the look of being made to measure. Gleaming silver long-necked spurs jutted out from his well-polished boots. The inevitable bush hat was new and clean, his open-necked shirt gleaming white, starched to wrinkle-free perfection.

"Mr. Dutton?" Tolo asked, moving to stand beside him.

Dutton's face was weathered by the elements. The features were strong. He had a prominent nose more Caucasian than Aboriginal, and his bushy eyebrows were turning white, to match the hair of his luxurious sideburns and his short, well-trimmed beard and mustache. His eyes were dark. When he looked at Tolo, he squinted, one eye half closed, the other bright, alert, challenging.

"I am George Dutton." He said it proudly, defiantly. He waited for Tolo to speak, listened quietly to Tolo's proposition, and then nodded affirmatively without hesitation. He stated his price, a fair price but not Abo cheap. He asked about horses and seemed satisfied at the answer, but he raised one bushy white eyebrow when he learned that a white woman was going along. When Tolo asked him if he'd be able to find four or five others to help search for Jajjala's mob, he shook his head and said, "We won't need them. Just slow us down and complicate things."

Tolo decided immediately to trust Dutton, and the speed and efficiency with which Dutton sorted out the animals and supplies needed for the trek seemed a fair measure of his competence.

Dutton saw Magdalen Broome for the first time on the morning that the expedition was to start. He whipped his hat off his head; he had left the new, clean one in his room and was wearing his work hat, dusty, battered, with a go-to-hell flip to the brim. "Well, madam," he said, "I was not told that our female traveling companion was to be a woman who shares my maturity."

"I think I'm going to like you, Mr. Dutton," Magdalen replied. "That's a delightful way of saying that I'm an old lady."

Dutton laughed.

"But I assure you, Mr. Dutton, that I won't hold you up," Magdalen said.

"Mrs. Broome," Dutton said, with a little bow, "you and I will set a pace that will make this young one cry out for mercy."

The rains had come at last to the area south of Alice Springs, and the land was carpeted with blue, yellow, red, and white wildflowers. The track selected by George Dutton meandered around hills and over lesser rises, then dropped down into a sandy creek bed, disappearing to all but George's eyes on rocky ridges. Where there was soil, the wildflowers were thicker along the sides of the track. Magdalen examined them curiously. Tolo was leading the way at that time with George riding beside Magdalen. Just as Magdalen asked why the flowers grew more profusely along the track, Tolo's horse lifted his tail and defecated noisily.

"There's your answer," Dutton said with a little grin. "Horses, sheep, and cattle. Not much travel on this track, but enough to enrich the earth."

They camped the first few nights along a creek bed under tall gum trees and frilly acacias. The curious birds examined them—swallows, Major Mitchells, kestrels, cockatoos, and willie wagtails. Dutton gathered bush tucker for Magdalen to sample. The fruits of the rains were kunga berries, mulga apples, solanums, and that product of the eucalyptus called manna.

"In good times the desert is our garden," Dutton said.

"I think I'm beginning to understand how the Aborigines can live out here," Magdalen said.

"Yes," Dutton said, "the land provides for us—most of the time." He showed Magdalen a nearby plant and dug up its root. "This is a member of the Solanaceae family. It's a cousin to the potato and the tomato. Many varieties. Tricky little bastards. This one happens to be good, but another one that looks almost like it is deadly poison." He grinned. "Now me,

I want my bush tucker spiced up a little bit. When I'm on a station away from the cookhouse, I want a hunk of mutton or a little tin of sardines now and again and a cup of tea."

"You're a pretty amazing fellow, George Dutton," Magdalen said.

He shrugged. "Oh, I read a book now and then. Botanist fellow went walkabout with me once. Paid me double station wages to dig up and gather bush tucker for him. Taught me a lot of fancy names for the plants I've known all my life."

George had told Tolo that it would be a two-week ride to Ayers Rock because he had feared that Magdalen would not be able to take a ten-hour day in the saddle. After the first few days, however, he gradually began to lengthen the time traveled.

"For a mature whitefellow lady," he told Magdalen one evening, "you're much woman."

"You should have known me when I was Tolo's age," Magdalen said, laughing.

Tolo seemed more than content to remain outside the conversations that developed each evening over the campfire between George and Magdalen. But he listened, and he heard. At first he had been a bit contemptuous of Dutton, thinking that he tried too hard to be white and perhaps disdained his Aboriginal blood, but as he listened more and more, he realized that he had been wrong. Dutton simply insisted on being treated not as an Aborigine or a half-breed but as a human being. And because of this expectation, he received respect.

That Dutton was aware of the problems facing his mother's people became evident one night after a week on the trail. Magdalen had been asking him questions about his youth. He spoke of the "good time," when he worked various sheep and cattle stations in the "Corner," the country at the junction of New South Wales, Queensland, and South Australia. He had been horse breaker, fencer, drover, and stockman. "Took some time off and went gold hunting, too," he said with a wry grin. "Found dust and heat and dry."

He poured tea from the billy into Magdalen's cup, put the
billy back on the coals, and leaned back. "But you could see
that it was running out," he said. "Bloody rabbits. Eating up
every blade of grass. Drought. The rabbits ate the vegetation,
the sandstorms took the topsoil, and the stockmen put too
many animals on the range. The sheep began to die, and they
tried to sell them before they starved. There was less work for
the Abos. Stations became smaller, and there was no need for
Abo labor. The people left the bush and huddled around the
towns to eat the whitefellow's scraps." He sighed. "I walk the
streets of a town now and sing the old songs, and the blackfellow children don't know them. They laugh at me."

Tolo, listening to Dutton's hushed voice, felt a surge of
guilt. He had set out to do a task, a task worth doing, and
even if he had lost—or thought he had lost—his wife, he
should have continued his work. Of course, he had extensive
notes that he had written out during the time he had spent on
the home station, but he'd had to depend on memory, and
memory can be flawed when months have passed between the
hearing of an Abo story and the writing down of it. But he
could not dwell on his guilt for long. The important thing was
that Java was alive. The first priority was to find her. After
that? He could not look past simply holding her in his arms.

Magdalen found it easy to understand why the Abos
thought that Ayers Rock was a sacred place. It loomed ahead
of them, growing slowly as the leisurely pace of the horses
brought them gradually nearer.

"My granddaughter dances on the rock in the light of a full
moon," she told George.

George laughed. "As long as there are people here living in
the old way, your granddaughter will be immortal, and the
telling of her feat will be expanded with the years."

"Well, I rather fancy seeing it," Magdalen said. "If I don't
see her disembodied spirit dancing, I shall force her to dance
in person when we find her."

The sun was hot, the air parched. Heat waves made the red

mass of the rock glimmer and shift. They pushed hard, trying to reach water, but the desert night came on too quickly, and they were forced to make a dry camp about an hour short of their destination.

As Java and Terry Forrest had come north on their journey toward the Alice, the days passed and the tinned food ran out. They ate like the Aborigines. Then the big mound on the far horizon became a red presence, and the rock stood before them.

From a distance Ayers Rock looked like one smooth, huge mound. By the time they made camp at Maggie Springs, they could see the clefts and nodes of ages of erosion on the rock, the unevenness of cave openings, offshoots of the rock flattening into little plateaus.

Maggie Springs, known to the Aborigines as Mutidjula, was a cascade of clean white water falling over stone into a splendid, quiet pool. They bathed separately and then cooked rabbit.

They were still a good distance from the Alice, but even so Java felt as if she were nearing the end of an era. She had come so far through the bush, and soon the walking would end. Looking back on it, she tended to diminish the hardships and the discomforts and to emphasize the moments of inspiration and beauty. There at the rock, with good water, with her stomach full, she regretted that Tolo was not with her to experience the satisfaction of having done what few had done before them, to share the quiet evening made musical by the magical sound of the waterfall.

"Do you know the legends of the Kuniya, the carpet-snake people?" she asked Terry.

"Can't say I do."

"They lived here at the time of creation, when the heroes were doing their mighty deeds. The rock was just a big, flat sand hill then, but it turned to rock. The Kuniya were attacked by the poison-snake people, the Liru, led by the warrior Kulikudgeri."

"Bless you," Terry said, laughing.

"And in the fighting they made the features of the rock. The potholes are marks of the Liru spears. A Kuniya woman whose son had been killed by the Liru warrior Kulikudgeri hit him on the nose with a digging stick, and he died in great pain. That's his nose there, at the entrance to Mutidjula."

"Wonderful," Terry said. He rose, walked to her, and sat down beside her on the blanket. "I like your stories," he said, putting a hand on hers.

"No," she said, pulling away.

"Let's be a little reasonable about this," he said. "We've come a long way together. We have a long way to go. I, for one, like the company, Java, and I'd like to make it permanent. What do you say? When we get back to the Alice, let's have a preacher hitch us up as a team."

She looked at him with new eyes. He was the last man whom she would have suspected of having a sense of honor. Her tone was not unkind. "I'm sorry. I'm just not ready for any kind of commitment, Terry."

"Then I'll make the commitment. You need someone to take care of you, that's all."

"Funny, I thought I'd done a fair job of taking care of myself," she answered. She stood and walked away, wanting to avoid any further evidence of his emotion. He followed and jerked her around to face him. Putting his hand under her chin, he forced her head up and smeared her tightly closed lips with his.

"Blast you," he said, "you weren't cold that time back when we were on walkabout with the Abos."

"I want you to stop, Terry," she said. "I want you to release me."

"And it doesn't matter what I want, eh? Give the bloke a taste of the old naughty and then make him suffer, is that it?" He bent to force his kiss on her again. "Well, it isn't going to work that way, is it?"

She let herself go limp and passive, sagging in his arms. With a snarl he lifted her and stalked back to the blankets, put her down roughly, and loosened his belt. She rolled away and leapt to her feet and ran into the darkness.

They were camped in the shelter of an outcrop from the main bulk of the rock. She had explored near the campsite before dark, so she easily found a crevice that led upward on the rock, and she climbed slowly, trying to be silent.

"Java, come on back," Terry called from below.

She kept still for a while.

"Don't be a ninny," he yelled. "I'm bloody well not going to chase you, and it's going to get very cold and uncomfortable up there."

She climbed until she came out on top of the outcrop. She could see their fire and Terry standing beside it.

"You're being very damned foolish," he called. "I'm not going to hurt you, you know."

"If I come down, will you leave me alone?

He laughed. "I won't promise that. I *will* promise you that I won't do anything you haven't enjoyed before."

She clasped her knees. The night was cold and growing colder. After groping around to find a little hollow in the rock, she curled up in it.

She awoke hours later in the cold of the night, shivering and spent the remaining hours of darkness with her teeth chattering and her body jerking, remembering that Bildana had said that the body warmed itself by shaking.

She wished that day would come, and when it finally did he was still there in the camp below. He had rolled out of his kip and was heating a billy. She knew that she would have to go down sooner or later, so she stood where he could see her.

Looking up, he shaded his eyes. "Have a nice night?" he called.

"Lovely," she answered. "Is it tea or coffee?"

"Tea, luv," he called out. "Warm the bones, won't it?"

She climbed down the rock stiffly. She was still shivering and she accepted the cup of hot tea that he handed her. H

vaited until she had finished it and her body had almost
topped shaking with the early-morning cold.

"Still cold, are you?"

"A bit," she said.

"We can fix that."

He seized her before she could move away, and this time he
et his intentions be known by immediately beginning to pull
t her clothing.

"If I were you," he said, "I'd be cooperative. It would be a
hame if I have to rip these things off you and you have to go
nto the Alice half naked."

She wrenched herself free, the movement tearing her cloth-
1g, and stumbled back toward the rock face. She reached the
revice that led upward and climbed rapidly. This time, how-
ver, Terry followed.

Reaching the top of the huge, flat boulder, she ran to the far
dge. It was a long way down, the sides rounded and smooth.
'he crevice up which she had climbed seemed to be the only
scape route.

Terry climbed more slowly. He did not know the route, and
e was heavier and clumsier, so it took him longer to reach
1e top. When finally he straightened and stood still, looking
cross the intervening distance at Java, he felt her eyes burn
1to him. There was a grin on his face; she looked down to see
1at her shirt and underclothing had been ripped to expose
er breasts.

As he started toward her, she felt like some helpless animal,
ornered, and she darted to and fro, seeking escape.

Awakened before dawn by the cold, Tolo, Magdalen, and
corge were under way as the first glow of light in the east
ghted their path. George led the way, skirting the main bulk
f the rock, riding through thickets of small trees and around
oulders that were offshoots of the main body of the rock.

It was just past sunrise when the horses smelled water and
egan to prance and tug on the bits.

"We're coming to Maggie Springs," George said. "Blackfellows call it Mutidjula, and it is the home of the sacred serpent, a water python. If the people ever come and find Mutidjula empty, they have only to cry, 'Kuka, Kuka, Kuka. That means 'meat.' Hearing this, the sacred serpent opens its mouth and out comes water."

"Gaaa!" breathed Magdalen with distaste.

"It is never dry," George said, laughing.

They rode on rapidly. Magdalen was admiring the color of the walls against the blue sky when she saw the girl dancing atop the rock. She knew immediately that it was Java, in spite of the man's clothing, and she was jumping and moving back and forth, back and forth, an odd dance. With an eerie feeling, Magdalen called Tolo's name and pointed upward.

Tolo, riding farther out from the rock wall, looked up toward the flat-topped outcropping and could see two figures. A tall man and a smaller figure, also in man's clothing, were moving there, the silhouettes clear against the sky.

He pulled his horse to a halt and shaded his eyes. His heart pounded, for there was a feminine grace in the frantic movements of the smaller figure. He kicked his horse into motion and left the saddle on the fly as the animal neared the rock wall. He saw an indentation, a crevice that offered access to the top and swarmed up it, the rock tearing at his fingers.

"Don't be daft, girl," Terry coaxed, moving toward Java. "I have no intention of raping you."

"Then go away and leave me alone," she said. She paused in her agitated movements, needing time to catch her breath.

"Why?" he asked, spreading his hands. "I thought we were mates. You enjoyed it. Don't try to tell me you didn't."

Java moved again, this time circling toward the crevice. As Terry moved to cut her off, she leapt first to one side, to lead him away from the escape route, then changed direction, trying to run past him. But he moved too swiftly and caught her by the back of her shirt. Fabric ripped.

Java instinctively lifted her hands to cover her bare breasts just as Tolo came leaping up from the crevice, shou

ing something that was totally incomprehensible. She screamed as much from the shock of seeing Tolo alive as from the pain as Terry jerked her backward. She sat down heavily.

Terry had seen the onrushing Tolo. "Bloody hell!" he whispered. He seemed paralyzed. Tolo barreled into him, and they fell together, both of them rolling and losing skin to the rough surface of the rock. A solid blow galvanized Terry into defensive action. He managed to flip Tolo off, and both of them leapt to their feet.

At first Java could not speak. She scrambled to her hands and knees and scurried toward the struggling men. When she found her voice, she screamed, "Stop it, stop it!"

It was as if she were reliving the horrible moments in the Gibson when she had watched Tolo and Terry locked in combat with the flash flood bearing down on them. This time there was no flood, but they struggled back and forth, coming dangerously close to the sloped edge of the rock.

Java looked around for a weapon, but eons of wind and weather had swept the surface of the rock clean. She came to her feet, heedless of her seminakedness, and ran toward them, but before she could get to them, Tolo swung mightily, striking Terry, his momentum carrying both men over the edge. There was water again, but this time it was the quiet pool of Mutidjula.

Tolo felt himself falling, and he kicked away from the rock, shoving Terry at the same time. They fell separately. Tolo saw the water below, the rocks that lined the pool, and he twisted himself to go into the water feetfirst.

He hit bottom and shoved himself up, blowing and gasping for breath. Terry Forrest lay crumpled on a rounded boulder at the pool's edge. Tolo's last-minute push from the top of the rock had carried him to the water and to safety. Terry had landed headfirst. His neck was twisted.

Climbing out of the water, Tolo bent over the fallen man. Terry's legs began to twitch and jerk; then came the gravelly sound of air leaving his lungs, then nothing.

"Tolo!" Java was screaming as she started down from the top of the rock.

George Dutton and Magdalen arrived at Tolo's side. One look at the man lying on the boulder told Magdalen that he was dead. "Go to her," she told Tolo. He turned away, running as fast as he could run.

Java clambered down the rock, heedless of scrapes and bruises on her hands, and as Tolo came toward her, she flung herself down the last three feet into his arms. He went over backward, and she was on top of him, clinging, seeking his lips, trying to talk, weeping. She kissed him hungrily, clasping him tightly, stifling his half-formed words with more kisses. Then she saw that he was crying; her heart burst for love of him, and she kissed away the tears from his face, whispering his name over and over.

Magdalen, who had approached the lovers, broke the spell. "Java!" she said sternly.

Java, lifting her head, cried out in joyous disbelief.

"Get up, please," Magdalen insisted. She had removed her dust jacket, and now she handed it to her granddaughter. "Make yourself decent, girl."

Java came to her feet and threw her arms around her grandmother. "You, too? Oh, wonderful, so wonderful."

"Put this on," Magdalen ordered Java.

Looking down, Java saw her bare breasts, jerked the duster out of her grandmother's hands, and shrugged into it. "But how—" She could not find words. She turned and smiled into Tolo's face. He was still weeping. "How did you—"

And then she remembered how she had taken Terry into her arms and into her body, thinking at the time that it didn't really matter, that with Tolo dead nothing mattered, thinking that if the closeness of another human body kept her warm and reassured her that she herself was alive, then nothing else mattered. But now Tolo was alive. She put her hand over her mouth and screamed. It was a sound of pure anguish. It filled the pretty gorge of Mutidjula as once the shrieks of the dying had filled it, and she fell to her knees with sobs shaking her shoulders.

Tolo pulled Java to her feet, but she turned away. Her mouth was contorted; her sobs were wild. She jerked out of his grasp and ran a few feet away to fall to her knees, bending with her forehead almost touching the ground, the weeping jerking her body, the sounds of it deep and tearing.

Tolo looked helplessly at Magdalen, then started to go to Java.

"No, wait," Magdalen said. She went to kneel beside her granddaughter.

"You're alive," she whispered. "Tolo's alive. Whatever has happened to you, the fact that you both are alive is the only thing of importance."

Java's weeping was verging on hysteria. Magdalen seized her by the arms and tugged her to her feet at the cost of her own aching muscles and shortened breath. Java was throwing her head from side to side, wailing. Magdalen slapped her stingingly, twice, quickly, back and forth. Java's eyes widened. She caught her breath, and the sobbing stopped.

"I have killed it," she whispered.

"Whatever you're talking about," Magdalen said, "forget it for the moment. Remember who you are, Java Gordon Mason. That's your husband over there, wondering if you've gone starkers. Now you listen to me. You pull yourself together, this minute! I don't particularly want to know what's bothering you, but I think I can guess. A fate worse than death, was it? But you're alive."

Java stared at her grandmother mutely, her eyes wide, taking in her grandmother's advice as if she were a little girl again.

"Think, girl," Magdalen added forcefully. "Go to him. He's been suffering the agonies of the damned, blaming himself for everything. Now you go to him and you be a wife to him, regardless of what has happened, because to him having you back is all that matters."

She approached Tolo almost shyly. He was smiling uneasily

until she reached up, wiped away her tears, blew her nose on her fingers Abo style, and beamed at him. "Tolo?"

He shook his head. "I had forgotten just how beautiful you are."

Now her weeping was silent as he enfolded her in his arms.

George Dutton buried Terry Forrest. Magdalen spoke a few words, as many as she could remember from the rituals in the Book of Common Prayer: *"Man that is born of a woman hath but a short time to live, and is full of misery. . . . In the midst of life we are in death. . . . Earth to earth, ashes to ashes, dust to dust."*

In the night, before she slept, Magdalen could still hear the murmurous voices of the young couple but could not catch the words, only the rise and fall, the cadence, the emotions that put a sob in Java's voice. She wondered, but she would not ask. She would never ask. Her granddaughter had crossed four hundred miles of the burning Gibson Desert. Whatever she had done, whatever had been necessary for Java's survival, had been the will of God, and if Java had done anything wrong, it would be forgiven. When she did sleep, it was with the knowledge that once again all was right with her world. There wasn't too much left of it, her world, or at least there wasn't much time left for her in *this* world. She was past the average age of death for Australians. In her deep faith she knew that she was to be reunited with the man who had wooed her so many years ago, the man for whom she had patiently waited during all of his long and dreadful absences at sea. Death could not be terrible at all if it meant she would be reunited with Red Broome.

She dreamed that she was a young girl again, seeing her youthful sailor for the first time. His face was as clear to her as it had been then. His voice was so familiar, so dear, so sweet to her ears.

"Well, old girl, it has been a long and bloody lonely time, hasn't it?"

Oh, my, he was handsome, that young Red Broome. His

eyes fairly glinted with mischief, and his look made her legs weak.

"*It's all right, my love,*" he whispered, holding out his hand. "*It's time.*"

And her heart leapt, but she felt no pain, for it was joy that she felt as his hand closed on hers and she stepped up to his level and looked down. She saw the old husk with the still heart that had been strained by the long journey. It was resting now. She saw her granddaughter sleeping in her husband's arms. She did not know what Java had told Tolo in that long, hushed talk that had continued far into the night, but she knew that all was well.

"*It has been bloody lonely, you red-headed pirate,*" she told Red Broome.

"*No longer,*" he said. "*No longer, my dear love.*"

When she had been a young girl, she had always felt that to be in Red Broome's arms was heaven.

Chapter XXXIV

MATT VAN BUREN had just spent three weeks in the coastal jungle. He had waded through tidal water and struggled through clinging mud. He had been bitten by a variety of flying insects and an occasional leech, and he had narrowly missed being bitten by a snake with such poisonous venom that if he had not leapt aside in the nick of time, he would have been brought back on the workboat wrapped in canvas, like Trevor.

His presence was not required at the timber-cutting site; Thomas Carrol, an efficient foreman, had matters in hand. So he came north to Port Moresby on his sleek little ketch, but once in port he dawdled, watching the Kanaka boatman check and double-check the bow, stern, and spring lines and then, working hard under the unaccustomed supervision of the master, begin to clean the deck. Usually, upon reaching the dock in Port Moresby, Matt was in a burn to get to the Gorel house.

He had done a lot of thinking down there in the coastal jungle. He kept remembering how Kit had almost caught him in bed with Guinevere. He ran the scene through in his mind time and time again, but altering the time sequence slightly: Kit entering the house, walking normally, but with her footsteps muffled by the rugs in the entry and main room. Kit hearing odd sounds from Guinevere's room and investigating.

She would not have been rude enough simply to throw open the door but would have called out, "Guinevere, is there anything wrong?"

Or upon hearing the piercing little cry that Guinevere uttered when he did the things she had taught him to do, with her clinging to him, Kit would have opened the door to see if something horrible had happened to her houseguest. . . .

And then—ruin.

He had told himself, during his weeks in the jungle, that he was not a villain, not some piece of gutter trash. In defensive moments he rationalized that he was only human, a man, young and in his prime, with the normal measure of sexual needs. But he could not explain away the fact that he had violated not only his marriage vows but his personal commitment to Kit.

Then he tried to justify his inability to stay away from Guinevere by thinking, *I am not the first man to be caught so in a woman's web of passion.* Tales of feminine witchcraft and supernatural allure had been part of man's heritage from the beginning of time. The ancient bards had sung of Helen and the fateful beauty that bewitched Paris and brought down a kingdom. Guinevere, then, was Helen—and Sheba and Delilah, too. She was Woman incarnate, and he was no more capable of resisting her than the moth the flame.

"Ballocks," he said, as he walked up the hill toward the empty Gorel house on a muggy tropical day that promised rain.

The smell of her was in the house. He bathed in her tub and slept in her bed. He would start the trip to the high valley with the morning. Meanwhile, alone in the bed where he had tossed and struggled in amatory battle with Guinevere, he cursed himself and promised that when he reached the house, he would send Guinevere away. Her fondest desire was to be out of Papua; he would grant her that wish. There was enough money built up in the company to send her away to Sydney or even to Paris. She had spoken of Paris often, al-

ways with longing, though she had never seen the city. Well,
Paris was just about far enough away.

He had fought a war and faced death many times. He had
come to a tropical rathole at the end of nowhere, he had
carved out a holding for himself and his family, and he
had built the beginnings of prosperity. Soon he would be able
to take the proceeds of his labors and move to a kinder climate, to a more civilized setting like Brisbane or Sydney, a
place where Grant and the child that Kit was carrying could
have proper schooling and the association of others of their
kind.

He himself had spent his formative years on a cattle and
sheep station in Queensland, where his playmates had been
the sons and daughters of the Abo bush workers. But those
Abos had been at least halfway civilized, and he had also
enjoyed on occasion the company of the white sons and
daughters of other squatters. He simply could not allow his
children to live among the Papuan savages, learning only
what their mother could teach them, being imprinted with the
primitive culture of the little dark people. If his conscience in
itself was not sufficient, if his sense of duty to Kit was not
strong enough to enable him to resist the quivering need he
would feel the minute he saw Guinevere, then the future of his
children must be the determining factor in the transformation
of Matthew Van Buren.

He started the familiar trip up to the house with his mental
purpose set in concrete. He guessed that Guinevere would not
protest his decision, not when she learned that her share of
the business amounted to a small fortune. And Matt would
add to that an allowance for her, for Trevor had been not only
a partner but a friend, and Matt owed it to Trev to see that his
widow continued to receive the fruits of his work.

The new Matt Van Buren pushed himself, eager now to see
his son, to hold Kit in his arms, and to send Guinevere Gore
down the hill toward the first ship that called in Port
Moresby.

He was, of course, too late.

* * *

For days Kit had tossed in fever. Asema had been by her side, cooling her brow with a dampened cloth, changing Kit's clothing now and again when sweat and incontinence had made her sodden. It was not the loss of the child that was making Kit so ill. This Asema knew. The whites were weak against the fever that rarely troubled the People. Some said that the fever attacking the whites was the spirits' way of saying, *"This is the land of the Geheto and the Nagamidzuha and the Anupadzuha."*

When Kit opened her eyes and asked weakly for water, Asema smiled and lifted a glass to Kit's lips. Two days later, when Kit walked feebly to the front veranda and sat in her rocker, looking out over the valley, Asema brought food and coaxed until Kit nibbled a few bites. Then Kit begged to see little Grant, and Asema brought the child and placed him in Kit's lap.

"The fever will not come again, not for a long time," Asema said.

"But you're saying that it will come," Kit said with resignation. Not, perhaps, if she was more careful in taking her quinine. Malaria was the price of empire. For a few self-pitying moments she felt, *Well, to hell with empire. To hell with all of this.* She longed to be back in Cape Town, in a kind climate and in the company of civilized people. She longed to see her father, even though her last sight of him had been unpleasant. But could she endure his "I told you so"? Could she admit, even now, that she had been wrong in marrying Matt?

In a way, she could understand. Guinevere Gorel had been a woman of transcendent beauty, a princess, exotic and alluring, and Kit had contributed to the inevitable by agreeing that it was sensible for Matt to sleep in the Gorel house while in Port Moresby. After all, she had thought, Matt and Trev were business partners, and Matt loved her above all else. She had believed that Matt could never be unfaithful. They had made vows to that effect, not only in the marriage contract but repeated often at moments of love.

And so, weakened by the loss of the child and the residual effects of malaria, she felt for the first time that particular agony known only to a woman betrayed.

But he chose me! Out of all the women in the world, he chose me, and he told me that he loved me. I gave myself to him. He was the first, the only one. I gave him a child. But he preferred another woman. I am not enough for him. There is, therefore, something wrong with me. I am not beautiful enough, not sensuous enough. Not enough! There is something lacking in me!

Asema, seeing the tears start, sat at Kit's feet and patted her on the thigh. "You should eat more, Little Mistress."

"No, thank you."

Because she had failed . . . She had given her husband all she had, all of her womanhood, and it had not been enough. What had she done wrong? Where had she first started to go astray, to lose his love?

Self-pity was a delicious, debilitating, and habit-forming emotion. Some people seemed content to go through their lives wallowing in it. But Kit Streeter Van Buren had a bellyful of it within minutes. She spat out a few barracks words. There was one advantage to having been raised an army brat: One's vocabulary was always a match for the worst of times.

Perhaps Guinevere's beauty *had* surpassed her own. Just perhaps, for they were two entirely different types. That Kit had possessed a beauty of her own was indisputable. She had never lacked suitors after the age of sixteen and, prior to that, had never lacked boyish admirers.

Slone Shannon. He had loved her.

Whoops, watch that. After all, Slone chose another woman.

No, that was all right, too, for she had been the one who rejected Slone by putting him off endlessly, by listening to the call of her family duty.

She felt anger now, for it was difficult to erase the hurt, the knowledge that twice she had been spurned for another woman.

And even as she tried to sort through her thoughts and feelings, even as she tried to dull the ache of hurt in her heart,

Matt came riding up the trail from the valley. Her heart leapt. He was so handsome. He sat the saddle well. The khaki he wore was damp with his sweat. His hat was pushed back on his head to show a thatch of sweat-dampened hair.

Suddenly everything seemed so simple. Matt had erred, but after all, he was only a man. Not every man was a Joseph, strong enough to resist the seductive charms of Potiphar's wife. Joseph had been close to God. Matt was just an ordinary man working hard to build something worthwhile for his family. The fault, then, had been Guinevere's. Grievously had she offended, and grievously had she paid for her offense.

Matt came walking swiftly from the outbuildings, saw her on the veranda, waved, broke into a jogging trot, and bounced up the stairs, smiling, his arms open.

"Little Mistress sick," Asema told him.

He jerked to a halt, the yellowish cast to Kit's face plain to him, the lines of gauntness clear. "Kit?"

"Fever," Kit said. "It's past. I may have been a little careless about taking my quinine."

He knelt in front of the chair, taking her hands. "Thank God you're feeling better." He kissed her hands, one after the other.

Tears formed and rolled down Kit's cheeks, for at first she had felt warmth when his lips touched her hands, and then a shudder of revulsion, for an instant picture of him in bed with Guinevere had flashed before her.

"When you feel better, we must talk," Matt said.

"We have things to discuss now," Kit said. "We must talk about Guinevere."

He flushed. "Great minds in conjunction," he said, "for it was Guinevere I wanted to talk about. It's time she began to live her own life, Kit. I'm going to give her Trev's half of the accumulated cash. She's been wanting to get out of New Guinea ever since she arrived."

"She's gone," Kit said.

"What?"

Kit stabbed him with her eyes, watched every nuance of his

reaction as she said, "She told me that she was going to take you with her. She told me that you loved her and that there was nothing I could do about it."

"Damn her," Matt said. "She—"

"Don't lie, Matt. Don't lie to me, please. Just listen. She said that the only reason you had not left me was that I was carrying your child."

He was shaking his head, but there was a stricken look in his eyes.

"Well, I am no longer carrying the child—"

"My God, Kit—"

"Because she tried to kill me and she succeeded in killing the child."

He leapt to his feet. "What on God's earth are you saying?"

"Don't call on God. It's not becoming to you, since you've never needed him before," she said.

"Kit, what *are* you saying?"

"She said that you loved her, that you were going to take her away from Papua. What were you going to do with me, Matt? Were you just going to leave me here?"

"Kit—"

"Or were you going to do the gentlemanly thing and send me back to my father, the man who warned me against marrying you?"

"Kit, listen—"

"I am not finished," she said. "She pushed me off the hill. I lost the baby. And then the fever came. Perhaps the fever got a hold on me because I was weak from losing the child."

After a moment Matt asked, "Where is she now?"

"Gone," Asema said, spitting a spray that expressed her opinion of Guinevere.

"Gone?" Matt asked. "I didn't see her on the track. She was not in Port Moresby. There hasn't been a ship, so she could not have arrived in Port Moresby and left before I came back from the south coast."

"She gone," Asema said, waving in the general direction of the coast.

"Did someone go with her?" Matt asked. His voice rose. "Bloody hell, Asema, I'm asking you a question."

"Leave her the hell alone!" Kit hissed at him. "She was here when I would have bled to death. Where were you?"

"Kit, I'm sorry I wasn't here," Matt said. "We can sell everything. The Colonial Office can come up with a buyer, I'm sure. We won't get what it's all worth, but we can sell and go back to Australia, and I'll stay with you—"

"Bugger off," Kit said.

"I don't like your using language that would make a sergeant major blush," Matt said. In a very masculine way he was adopting an age-old technique. When one is caught in betrayal, deny everything and then get defensively angry.

Kit asked him rather politely to perform an unnatural act upon himself.

"Bloody hell, Kit!" he bellowed.

"Why are you getting angry?" she asked calmly. "I am the one who has been wronged. I am the one who should be angry. I'm not, Matt. I'm only very deeply disappointed in you. Was she good, Matt? Did she do things for you that I didn't do? Or was it mounted sideways, as in the sailor's myth about Chinese women?"

"Don't talk dirty," he said.

She smiled with her lips only. "All right, Matt. What do you suggest we do now?"

He cleared his throat. "Well, Kit, I guess what I do now is beg you for forgiveness. I came up here with the honest intention of sending Guinevere away. I swear this to you. I was going to arrange for her to live wherever she wanted to live, except in Papua. I don't know why I did it, Kit. It wasn't that I didn't love you."

She reached out and patted the bulge at his groin. "And I thought that unlike most men, your brains were located a bit higher up than that."

"Goddammit, Kit!"

"Yes, goddammit."

He turned, ran down the stairs, stopped, then looked back at her. "I do beg your forgiveness," he said.

"Where are you going?"

"I have to find Guinevere."

"Why?" she asked.

"Because—because dammit, she might be lost. What were those savages thinking about, letting her go off alone?"

"Those *savages,* many of whom are my friends, were probably thinking *good riddance.*"

"I don't blame *you.* You were ill."

Blazing, fiery anger. "Well, bless me," she said. "You really don't blame me? Isn't that generous of you!"

"I have to go find her," he said.

"Go, then," she said. "Go and be damned."

She came close to telling him then that he would not find Guinevere lost in the forests. The words were on her tongue to say that she herself had tasted the fresh blood of Guinevere's heart, but she remained silent.

Matt stood at the foot of the stairs, looking at her for a long time, unable to read the look on her face, waiting for her to speak, to ask him not to go.

But he was also thinking of the report he would have to make to the governor's office and the constabulary.

"I want to report that Mrs. Trevor Gorel has disappeared."

"How and when did she disappear, Mr. Van Buren?"

"She was a guest in my home in the Geheto Valley. While I was away, she decided to come back to Port Moresby. She traveled alone."

"Why was she so eager to strike out on her own when one or more of the villagers might have guided her?"

"She tried to kill my wife."

And then the hardest questions of all: *"Why would she want to kill your wife, Mr. Van Buren? Are you certain that there is not some mistake? Might she herself not have been the victim of foul play? If she is missing, why have you not searched for her?*

*We shall have to take a statement from Mrs. Van Buren, and
we shall send men to question the natives. . . ."*

Kit, in her turn, waited for him to speak, to say that being
with her was more important than the safety of the woman
who had tried to kill her and had succeeded in killing her
baby.

When he said nothing, she decided that he had had his
secret, so she would have hers. It was not her fault that he
and Guinevere had been so careless, so lost in passion, that
they had ignored the fact that the eyes of the servants were on
them, that they had consummated their unholy lust with
Zaho listening under the bedroom window. Although her secret was shared with many, as Guinevere herself had been
shared, the people of the village—knowing how excited the
white men got about such things—would not reveal it. Nor
would she. Let him look. Let him scour the track all the way
to Port Moresby. Let him look behind every tree, into every
gorge. Let him climb every ridge and wade every stream. Perhaps someday an anthropologist, stumbling by accident upon
the place of bones near the village, might see a femur, or a
pelvic saddle, more delicate and more shapely than those of
the Papuan natives, and wonder why the bones of a white
woman were mixed with the well-gnawed, marrow-sucked
bones of native victims of the need for meat protein in animal-
poor New Guinea. But Matt would never find Guinevere, not
even her plundered bones.

When he returned, two full weeks later, he seemed thinner.
He had festering sores from insect bites. He came to her con-
tritely and told her that he had gone all the way to Port
Moresby, making detours off the beaten track all along the
way, questioning any native he met. He told her that Guinevere had not arrived in Port Moresby. He had made his report
to the constabulary and the governor's office. There had been
many questions. He told them that Mrs. Gorel, an impatient

woman, had grown restless and had refused to wait for him to return to the valley to escort her back to her home.

"She's dead," he said finally.

"Did you weep when you realized that?" Kit asked. She was seated on the veranda, Grant in her lap.

"No, Kit."

"A part of me is dead," she said. "My baby is dead."

"We have Grant," he said, gesturing toward the child. "You can have other babies."

"Not *your* babies, Matt," she said. He looked at her with pain evident on his face. "Yes, I decided on that definitely, when you left me, still weak, not fully recovered from the fever, to go look for her."

"I've had a lot of time to think, Kit," he said. "I know now how wrong I was. What must I do to have your forgiveness? I do love you. You are my life, you know, you and Grant."

She was silent for a long time, and when she spoke, it was not in answer to his question. "With both Trevor and Guinevere dead, what about the businesses?"

"There was a written agreement between us to cover the possibility of death or deaths. It's all ours now."

"Yours," she said. "We are under Australian law. It is all yours."

"What's mine is yours, of course."

"Not unless it is in writing. I want you to sign over the plantation to me," she said.

He looked at her in surprise.

"I am the one who talked to the women, who got them to work. I am the one who supervised the planting and the one who has checked to see when the growing trees needed water. I feel that this is my house, that the coffee trees are my trees."

"All right," he said. "I will sign them over to you."

"I would like a partnership agreement between us," she said. "Not so much for myself as for Grant." She hugged the child tight. "You know that it will require more cash investment here before the coffee begins to bring a return."

"You talk as if we are not to remain married."

"I don't know about that, Matt," she said. "You, of course, may do as you please. If you want to divorce, then we'll work together to do it in a way the least scandalous and the least damaging to our joint financial interests."

"I don't want to divorce."

"But if you decide later that you do—"

"Let me see if I understand you," he said. "You want the place here in the valley in your name and you want half of the proceeds of the sawmill and the timbering operations?"

"For me and for our son."

"And we will be married in name only?"

"Yes."

"Forever?"

She chewed thoughtfully on her lower lip. "That would depend."

"Bloody hell," he said. "I am to be contrite, to crawl to you forever or until you choose to—"

She whirled and walked away, went to her bedroom, and slammed the door behind her. He went to the door and called her name, and when he heard no answer, he threw his weight against the door and smashed the fragile lock. She was seated at the side of the bed.

"You say it shall be done and I do it, is that it?" he asked angrily.

"No, you can go straight to hell if you don't want to see to the future of your son."

"I want to see to the future of my son," he said, lowering his voice. "I want to look after you as well."

"There is another choice," she said. "If I am not to be given this place, which is the result of my work, then I must have enough money put aside to buy passage to Cape Town."

"And take my son with you?"

"Should I leave him with you, so that he can be mothered by the next whore you find?"

He stomped out of the room.

* * *

They did not speak again until the next day. He had slept i
the guest room, where on a fateful day he had romped wit]
Guinevere in mutual passion.

"I will do as you wish," he said.

"Thank you."

"I take it that I will be free to come here to visit Grant an
to check to see if you're handling my part of the plantatio
sensibly."

"You may, of course, visit your son."

His voice softened, and his eyes were moist. "And can
hope, Kit, that there is a chance for reconciliation in the fu
ture?"

"I will be quite honest with you," she said. "At the momen
I wouldn't care if I never saw you again, Matt. You will neve
know how badly you hurt me. I simply do not care to pt
myself in a position to be emotionally mutilated again." Sh
paused. "There are aspects of it that you may never know."

She had been exposed to horror. She had been fed a warn
bloody piece of human heart. She had endured the flutes an
the drumlike grunts of the men and the songs of the wome
while seeing in her mind the long, once lovely legs turnin
brown, being basted in their own juices, being torn and slice
and chewed. Matt was the living, visible reminder of th
horror. The taste of bloody human flesh and the texture of
as she chewed were the culmination of his affair with Guin
vere. She had not asked to be a part of it. He and Guineve
had forced it on her with their actions.

She herself was not free of guilt. She had played the gam
of *what if* many times. What if, when Asema had first come t
her with the story of Matt's infidelity, she had confronted hir
immediately? What if, feeling about Guinevere as she had fel
she had refused to allow her to stay when she had appeare
on the doorstep of the house on the slope? Most probably sh
could have forgiven Matt his infidelity in time. Her moth
had often said that a man's weakness for the flesh was n
sufficient cause to break up a home unless the man becam

o openly arrogant about it. In all likelihood her mother had
ffered those words of wisdom because she suspected, or
new, that Roland Streeter, often oceans apart from his fam-
y, had indulged that most common of masculine weaknesses.
o she might have forgiven Matt a simple affair. But even
hough she could conceivably be said to share the blame for
lowing the situation to develop past mere sexual dalliance,
hen she could have stopped it simply by telling Matt that
e knew he was sleeping in Guinevere's bed while he was in
ort Moresby, she could not forget the terror of falling, of
nowing that her baby was dead. Nor could she forget the
ste of human flesh in her mouth.

"Then I ask only that you give me a chance to prove to you
at I love you," he said. "I ask that you let me try to heal the
ounds I have given you."

"No promises," she said.

"No promises," he agreed.

Chapter XXXI

THROUGH THOSE MODERN miracles the telephone and the telegraph, the news went out from Alice Springs that a white woman had walked across the Gibson. She was young and beautiful, if a bit thin, and she had a catchy name. Although each newspaper account was careful to include in the first paragraph that Java Mason was the wife of the heir to the Mason business empire, not many of them called her Mrs. Thomas Mason.

Because the unexplained presence of another whitefellow, one Terry Forrest, complicated the dramatic story of Mr. Mason's daring rescue of his wife, the accidental death of the Forrest bloke was a separate item that very quickly became yesterday's news. The constabulary in Alice Springs handled Terry's death almost as casually. If Mr. Thomas Mason, his wife, and a half-breed bush worker all agreed that Mr. Forrest had slipped and fallen to his death at Ayers Rock, then it was so.

Against her will Java became a national heroine, at least for a few days. And Tolo's exploits, too, were celebrated, for after the initial news reports there were follow-up accounts describing how Thomas Mason, upon reaching Alice Springs with his long-lost wife and a half-breed bush worker named George Dutton, equipped a mob to travel back to Ayers Rock, then to disinter the body of a Mrs. Magdalen Broome, widow of the late Admiral Murdoch "Red" Broome of the Royal Navy.

Thus it was that Magdalen made the return trip to Sydney in a sealed coffin that was rarely out of the sight of Mr. Thomas Mason.

To Tolo, the manner of Magdalen's death was an accusation. If he had not taken Java into the Western Australian deserts, if he had absolutely refused to let Magdalen try to make the journey into the heart of the continent, she would still be alive. Magdalen Broome was the only member of his wife's family who had taken him at face value, accepting him for what he was instead of judging him for what his mother's lineage had been. Of all the people in the world, he had loved Magdalen almost as much as Java or his mother. He was going to miss her very much.

To Java, losing her grandmother was, of course, great sadness, but God builds into us the visceral knowledge that the old ones are going to die and prepares us for the inevitable loss of the beloved mother, the honored father, the grandparents who, quite often, die before we are old enough to know the meaning of death. Java could think, *She led a full life, and now she's with Grandfather, the two of them together again.*

Java had been eating like a teenage boy. By the time they were aboard a Mason Line ship en route from Brisbane to Sydney, she had regained her youthful, feminine sleekness of figure. The strenuous outdoor life she had led for what seemed to have been ages had built long, lean muscles in her legs, making them more shapely. She radiated good health. When Tolo moped, she tried to brighten his outlook by talking of future plans: how, together, they would put down on paper all that they had learned about the Aborigines; how they could use some of Tolo's surplus money to help the more unfortunate members of the native race, starting with those who clustered around the white man's towns in their pitiful shanties. She had come to the conclusion that those like Jajjala, who had managed to avoid being caught up totally in the white man's way of life, were best left alone as long as there was free bush for them to roam, kangas to hunt, and water holes to sustain life.

Looking back, Java considered her hysteria at the rock quite childish. She had told Tolo that first night about what had happened between her and Terry Forrest, explaining her feeling that nothing mattered, her loneliness, telling him that what she had done with Terry was not even a pale imitation of their own love. She had tearfully begged his forgiveness, and she would always remember his answer.

Tolo had clasped her tightly, only he knowing the knife of pain in his heart to think of Java in Terry's arms as he said, "I must bear the responsibility because it was I who insisted on taking you to the desert. I will never blame you for anything. I feel as if I've been given a second chance. You're alive, after I thought you were dead, and that's all that matters."

As for Java, her lapse with Terry Forrest would become, oddly enough, a plus to her marriage, for having Tolo understand and forgive her so readily strengthened her regard for him. Being in Tolo's arms showed her quite clearly how vastly different from the almost accidental encounter with Terry it was to be with the man she loved. Each time she gave herself to her husband there was an importance to the act, a magnitude of significance that had been lacking with Terry. She had attained physical pleasure with Terry, true, but not the lingering, sweet, all-encompassing warmth and love that she felt for Tolo.

From Alice Springs Java had sent a long, expensive telegram to her mother and her father, informing them of Magdalen's death. The acknowledgment had come from her father: MOURN SAD NEWS. REJOICE YOUR SURVIVAL. HURRY HOME.

Her father's telegram gave no hint of how Jessica Gordon had taken her mother's death.

They wired both the Gordons and Misa Mason the date of their departure from Brisbane, the name of the ship, and the expected date of arrival. They were met at the docks by what amounted to a delegation. Jessica and Sam, of course, with Kitty Broome and Kelvin Broome; Misa and Bina Tyrell; Bina's business partner, Clive Taylor, and his new wife. There was also a gaggle of reporters.

Tolo noted immediately that his mother's party stood slightly apart from the Gordons and the Broomes. It was as he had expected. He was not sure how Sam Gordon felt about him, but Jessica Gordon's disapproval had always been glaringly evident. He knew that Jessica hated him for marrying Java against her wishes, and he knew that it was his Kanaka blood to which she objected most strongly.

In glad reunion Java and Tolo separated, Tolo to squeeze both Misa and Bina, shake hands with Clive, and bow to Clive's new bride. Java flew into her mother's arms, kissed her father on the cheek, hugged her aunt Kitty and cousin Kelvin.

A party of celebration had been arranged at Bina's restaurant, and the entire group clattered through the streets in gleaming new motorcars. Both Misa and Sam Gordon had become addicted to this modern form of transport and seemed to compete with each other in buying the newest model of Daimler.

The restaurant was not yet open for the evening meal, but the kitchen staff had outdone itself. Good smells assaulted them as they walked in. Java, the first to enter, ran ahead to see what seating arrangements had been made; frowning, she began switching place cards, for the group had been divided up as if to debate, one side against the other.

"I've mixed up the cards a bit, people," she said as the others caught up with her. Her beaming smile was so confident that not even Jessica could object. "Mother, you and Misa are here—"

She saw her mother's ill-concealed displeasure as she took the chair beside Misa. Java had placed herself between Tolo and her father because she felt that she was going to need the support of both. The coolness between Jessica and Misa Mason had not escaped her. She had not been able, yet, to talk with her mother in private, but she suspected that Jessica blamed Tolo for Magdalen's death.

There was excited chatter and many questions, and Java, taking over, said, "Listen, I'm starved. I still haven't caught up from having to eat tubers and desert lizards—"

Clive Taylor's wife made an odd sound and put a handkerchief to her mouth. Jessica made a face of distaste but said nothing.

"—so would you please be patient and let the meal be served, and after I make a glutton of myself, I'll tell the whole story?"

Sam Gordon said the blessing, speaking to the Lord God as if he knew him well. The food was, said Java, "un-bloody-believable." And soon it was time.

"I think you have the podium," Sam told Java.

She looked around, her smile fading, her face becoming serious. "Everyone I love is here in this room," she said.

"Your grandmother isn't here," Jessica said bitterly.

"I think she is," Java said. "I think she's somewhere with Grandfather, and they're both looking down on us, wondering if we're going to continue to be as bloody asinine as we've been in the past."

Jessica's lips tightened.

"You see, Mother, I know how Grandmother felt because she wrote it down for us." She took a folded letter from her bag. "This letter was in her things. It's addressed to you, Mother, but I'm going to read it aloud so that everyone can hear."

"If it is addressed to me—" Jessica said.

"Now, Jess," Sam cautioned. "I think Java knows best in this instance."

"I don't know when she wrote the letter," Tolo spoke up. "It was some time during our trip out to Alice Springs. It might have been after we reached the Alice. It might even have been during the trip from Alice Springs to Ayers Rock. Because when my head hit the kip at night, I fell asleep right away, but sometimes I awoke to see Magdalen—Mrs. Broome —sitting by the fire in deep contemplation."

"As I said, Mother," Java began, "it is addressed to you." She read in a clear voice:

"My Beloved Daughter,

"I wish that I could share with you the odd, barren, awesome beauty of the heart of our nation, but something in me tells me that I will not return from this journey of love.

"If my intuition is correct, you are not to feel guilty and tell yourself that you should have raised Old Ned to keep the old lady at home in her rocking chair. Jessica, I would not have missed this trip for the world! It was my last chance to see that area of the country which— at least according to the poets like Larson and Patterson—is the real Australia. And if I am correct in my feeling that my time is near, death would come to me in Sydney as quickly as it might come out here in the bush. If I am right in my feeling that I will not see you again, it is God's will, but I am sure that he will not call me until I am given the chance to see my granddaughter again.

"I know in my heart that Java awaits us somewhere ahead in this great red heart of the continent. I can feel her presence, and the sure and certain conviction that I will hold her in my arms before I die takes the ache out of my old bones.

"This letter will not be given to you until I am dead, Jessica, and therefore I can be blunt with you and play upon your grief for my passing. I want to speak of Java and Tolo. I've been traveling with Tolo now for a donkey's age, and I've come to know him as I never knew him before. Jessica, he's a gentle man, a loving man, quite a wonderful man."

Tolo, overcome, pushed back his chair and moved rapidly away from the table to hide the quick tears that came in spite of the fact that he had read and reread the letter many times. Java continued:

"He loves Java as my Red loved me, as your Sam loves you. Now, despite the fact that you've tried to hide it under the veneer of civilized politeness, I know that in your heart your dislike for Tolo and his mother comes from the fact that you are a product of Australia and our times. When the entire nation relegates the peoples of the Pacific islands to a labeled status—Kanakas—you, as a part of that nation, cannot help being affected.

"It is difficult, I know, to look past the skin color of people, and quite frankly, I think God intended it to be that way. We are different from the Aboriginal people. Any fool can see that. Perhaps there are some races in the world who will never 'catch up'—or apply any phrase you care to—to our status. But I don't see how, by the wildest stretch of the imagination, anyone could feel superior to Tolo Mason because he has what looks like a deep suntan. Or for that matter, how some bushranger could think himself superior to a woman like Misa Mason, who has become, most probably, the most powerful woman in Australia.

"Misa Mason has been my friend, and I am proud to say that. I have found her to be considerate, warm, loving, kind, generous, and a lovely person to be around. It is time, Jessica, that you forget the teaching of people like Henry Lawson. It is time for you to look Tolo Mason, your son-in-law, in the eye and say, 'Tolo, I beg your forgiveness.'

"That doesn't mean that I withhold permission for Sam to turn Java over his knee and wallop her good for worrying the dickens out of us. She and Tolo were wrong in running away, but then you and Sam were wrong in trying to separate them, weren't you?

"It is time that you look Misa Mason, the mother of your son-in-law, in the eye and say, 'Misa, forgive me.' This I demand as a deathbed promise from you, Jessica. Try to be worthy of having Misa as your friend, and you will find that the rewards far outweigh your old, unthinking prejudices.

"If, indeed, we find Java and bring her back to you, Jes-

sica, you will have been given a second chance. Heed my
advice and do these things for me, your mother."

Both Jessica and Misa were weeping quietly. Sam cleared
his throat. Tolo had come back to stand behind Java's chair.
Jessica wiped her eyes and swallowed hard. She looked at
Misa, then reached for her hand. Her voice was made fragile
by her emotions. "There will be a vacant chair at the table for
the Terrific Threesome," she whispered. "Might I fill it at the
next opportunity? Will you give me a chance to get to know
you?"

Misa could not speak. Her full lips were twisted as she
fought back tears. It was Bina who answered Jessica. "We'll
save Magdalen's chair for you, luv."

When Commodore Rufus Broome's squadron of destroyers
next made port at Sydney, he greeted his niece and her husband with genuine joy, although he had not known either of
them well. What pleased him most was to see Misa's face at
his side at dinner. He had been notified in Wellington of his
mother's death, and his grieving had been done in the privacy
of his shipboard cabin. He noted and approved the warmth
that obviously was shared among his sister, Java and Tolo,
and Misa Mason. He had been allowed to read Magdalen's
letter, so he understood Jessica's new attitude toward Tolo
and Misa.

On Rufe's first night at the Broome-Gordon dinner table,
the talk was typical, although now only Kitty Broome remained of the older generation. The affairs of empire were still
a concern. Rufe held forth on the aftermath of the "Dogger
Banks incident," a by-product of the Russo-Japanese War, in
which Russian warships had opened fire on neutral vessels—
unarmed British fishing boats off the Dogger Banks. The resulting tension between Russia and Great Britain persisted,
though it was fading in the face of Britain's continuing com-
petition with Germany. In central Africa, meanwhile, affairs
were barely back to normal following an uprising of the

Ekumekus, a fanatical sect in southern Nigeria; the rebellion had been put down by soldiers of the king. But the subject of greatest interest was the stunning defeat of the Imperial Russian Navy at the hands of the Japanese, for the rise of Japanese military power would affect Australia's future.

"It will affect the British Isles as well," Rufus declared. "But it's giving the navy a boost, my friends. Keels are being laid as fast as the yards can be made ready. One of them just might be my future command."

Misa looked up at him with interest.

"I'm one of several officers being considered for command of the first big-gun battleship," he said. "She's to be called the *Dreadnought*. She'll carry turrets housing ten- and twelve-inch guns."

"Because of the Japanese Navy?" Tolo asked.

"And the German Navy," Rufus said. He was still talking directly to Misa. "It'll be a long time before she's ready, but if I get command, it will mean having home port in England."

Misa felt her heart skip a beat.

"Now, if you don't mind my changing the subject," Rufus said, "I want to pose a problem to all of you and get your opinion. For a long time now, I've been asking this lady at my side to marry me."

"Hush, Rufe," Misa said, blushing furiously.

"No, I won't hush," Rufe said. His smile told the others at the table of his feeling for Misa. "This lady has been giving me various excuses. She was too busy; she was worried about her son and Java; she was under attack by the socialist press because she dared to be rich in Australia." He laughed. "I find that last to be rather amusing, don't you? She came to this country an indentured laborer. Now that she's built the businesses started by her late husband into one of the biggest conglomerates in the country, she's being damned for being one of the upper class."

"Rufe, if you don't hush . . ." Misa said, but she, too, was smiling.

"Well, now Tolo and Java are back safe and sound. Here's

Tolo to take some of the responsibilities off your shoulders. That excuse is no longer valid." He took Misa's hands in his. "Can you think of any other reason you can't marry me now?"

Misa's eyes were aswim. She would never disclose the main reasons why she had resisted the dictates of her heart for so long. She would never reveal that she had been ready to fight for Rufe, against Jessica's prejudice if need be, but that in the end pride and delicacy of feeling had won out, holding her back, for it would have been both insensitive and beneath her dignity to start a row with Jessica Gordon while her child was missing. But now . . . She looked at Rufe. "Not a single reason," she whispered.

"Hear, hear," Sam Gordon said, lifting his glass.

And to Rufe's surprise and pleasure, Jessica joined Java in a rush around the table to embrace both of them and tell them, "I order you both to be very, very happy."

Epilogue

THEOBOLD, GRAND DUKE of Saxe-Coburg, wore a military uniform because that was the chosen apparel of the man he admired most in life, his cousin Willie—William II, emperor of Germany. Since Theo, as he was called by friends, had unlimited funds at his disposal, he had a varied wardrobe that included, for formal evening wear, an elegant white outfit with vertical crimson stripes down the legs of the trousers and a well-tailored tunic, on which resided a forest of golden buttons, medals, and decorations.

In this stunning apparel Theo was now residing over the banquet he had ordered at his apartments in Vienna, immediately following his assignment there as liaison between the German General Staff and the High Command of the Austrian Empire.

The entrée and several following courses had been served at the long, heavy dining table, and as befitted the occasion, the conversation was weighty. Sir Norman Angell, who styled himself an author, held the floor, telling Theo and a sparkling assemblage of guests why there would be no European war.

"Actually," Sir Norman said, smiling broadly, "my book on the subject is almost ready for publication, so I shouldn't give away my entire rationale." He raised a very British forefinger. "However, in this distinguished company I suppose my secret thoughts will be safe. I believe war will be impossi-

ble in the twentieth century because in this modern age all of
the great nations are so financially and economically interdependent that war would simply be unprofitable. The victor
would suffer with the vanquished. Let me give you one small
example. As I'm sure our honored host, the grand duke,
knows, the German merchant marine is the second largest in
the world, second only to that of Great Britain. There are at
least half a dozen German passenger liners—and this I'm sure
our young friend from the British Embassy knows—that
travel through British Suez to service the British colonies in
the South Pacific, mainly Australia and New Zealand. And
hardly an Atlantic run by a German liner would be profitable
unless she first stopped at a British port for a steerage load of
emigrants to the New World. Those are just two small examples. This interdependence extends as well into industry and
trade on all levels." He smiled and spread his hands. "Under
these conditions, no nation would be so foolish as to start a
war."

"I shall look forward to reading your book, Sir Norman,"
Theo said, adjusting his pince-nez. Theo was proud of his
resemblance to the kaiser: the steel-steady eyes, the strong
nose, the facial bones that were the result of centuries of selec-
tive breeding, and the mustache trimmed in the style favored
by William. Theo let his gaze take in the faces at the table.
His eyes lingered for a long moment on Sianna Shannon, the
delightful Boer wife of the young viscount, Slone Shannon, of
the British Embassy. A charming girl.

As for Sir Norman's contention that a twentieth-century
war would be so commercially disastrous as to be unthink-
able, Theo had read in manuscript a book by General Frie-
drich von Bernhardi, with chapters entitled "The Right to
Make War," "The Duty to Make War," and "World Power or
Downfall." In 1871 Bernhardi had been the first German to
ride through the Arc de Triomphe when the victorious Prussian Army marched into Paris. As chief of the military history section of the German General Staff, he was recognized
as an authority on the teachings of Clausewitz, Treitschke,

and Darwin. War, Bernhardi believed, was a biological necessity, the result of the natural law upon which all other laws of nature rest, the law of the struggle for existence. Theo remembered one specific quote from the general's book: *"Nations must progress or decay; there can be no standing still. Germany must choose world power or downfall."*

"I find Sir Norman's theory to be very reassuring," said Slone Shannon.

Theo cast a glance in Slone's direction. The viscount and his lady were old hands in Vienna, favorites of the diplomatic circle, invited to every affair. Perhaps because Sianna was so pretty, Theo had cultivated their acquaintance. Sianna spoke German better than most who were German-born and -reared, and her husband's German was improving with time.

"However," Slone was saying, "wasn't it the kaiser himself who said that he feared the next war would be started by some madman in the Balkans?"

The obligatory representative of the Habsburg court, the Austrian general Joseph Buchlau, roused himself like an old, tired lion. "That may be, but Willie is often careless in his speech, is he not?"

An embarrassed silence fell.

Buchlau, like the Austrian Empire, was old and exhausted. But he had seen grand times, and he considered William II of Germany an upstart. "Three hundred dinner guests heard Willie say that Edward the Seventh of England is Satan." Buchlau chuckled. "He even repeated it, to be sure that everyone heard. He said, 'You cannot imagine what a Satan he is.'"

Theo was chagrined, but Sianna came to his rescue. She laughed gaily and said, "Well, that's family for you, my dear General. Always in families there are those little moments of anger, but they soon pass."

Her comment eased the tension. The old Habsburg general nodded and went back to semisleep. Theo changed the subject and began to describe—"for the benefit of the unmarried ladies among us"—the handsome Prince Canilo of Montenegro who would be visiting within a fortnight. "What a party we

hall give for him," he declared. "Sianna, should we have a
and that plays the waltz or, for a change, one that knows the
ld songs from the beer gardens?"

"The waltz, by all means," Sianna declared.

Theo, aristocratic and very Prussian, enjoying his role as
he perfect host, spread his smile and his comments around
he table and elicited opinions on this and that from each
uest.

After dessert, when the dinner party was breaking along
he usual gender lines, Slone Shannon felt a tug at his elbow.
General Buchlau pulled him aside into a little nook, letting
he other male guests go on into the sitting room for brandy
nd cigars.

"Shannon," Buchlau said, "we talk around the subject. We
retend that because Willie is Edward's nephew—because
host of the royal families in Europe are related in some way
–there will be no war. But if Willie doesn't want war, why
oes he persist in building a navy to rival that of England?"

"Good question, General," Slone replied.

"Bismarck told the Germans to be content with land
ower," the old general said. "And Willie knows that. He
uilds the navy to pressure England into doing nothing while
e exterminates France with his land armies. He knows that
Napoleon was beaten at Waterloo, not at Trafalgar."

The old general was not noted for being closemouthed.
lone tried to make comments on Buchlau's rash statements
n what he had come to call diplomatese, words that sounded
ood but meant absolutely nothing. He made only brief, non-
ommittal remarks on what the general was saying.

"You see," Buchlau went on, "Willie has taken the Ameri-
an president's motto and turned it around. With Germany it
 not 'Speak softly and carry a big stick,' but 'Speak loudly
nd brandish a big gun.' "

Slone laughed. He wondered where the general's rambling
lk was going. He had known the old man for two years now,

and although he gave the impression of senility, he still pos
sessed an active brain under his thinning strands of gray hair

"Shannon," the old general said, "it's no secret that th
Habsburg Empire spends less on armaments than some Bal
kan nations. We're surrounded by countries that would like t
bite off a piece of our territory, and we're like an old bull o
his last legs, stumbling around in circles, staying on his fee
through sheer willpower. Germany tolerates the Habsbur
monarchy because we act as Germany's agent in southeaster
Europe."

"General," Slone said, a little uneasily, "I think the party i
breaking up."

"I am almost finished," Buchlau said, a new crispness en
tering his voice. "You see, there are those of us who do no
want war. We feel that war would be ruinous for Austria, fo
it would mean the end of the monarchy, the end of empire
But as you know, we are bound to Germany by th
Dreikaiserbund, the pact among the three emperors of Russia
Austria, and Germany. What I want to tell you is this: Don'
be taken in by such drivel as was being spouted by Sir Nor
man tonight. At every opportunity Germany will scream
'Einkreisung!' or encirclement, but you are wise to make you
alliances, you British. You are wise to look askance at Willie'
rush to make the German Navy strong."

At this moment Sianna and Theo were in the front entry
Theo was bidding good night to his guests. When the last on
had left, with the exception of General Buchlau and the Shan
nons, Theo took Sianna's arm and said, "Since Slone and th
old man seem still to be caught up in a serious conversatio
perhaps we have time for just one glass of a very good Frenc
champagne that I bought by the gross when I was last i
Paris."

Sianna allowed herself to be escorted to an elegant sittin
room. Theo gave orders, and soon the champagne, proper
chilled, was bubbling in their glasses.

"To the beauty of the good German ladies of South Af-ca," Theo said.

"Are you so sure that all the German ladies of South Africa re good?" Sianna asked archly, lifting her glass.

Theo laughed delightedly. "Charming," he said. "But yes, m sure that being German, or at worst Dutch, they are." He aned toward her, and his face became serious. "And, my ear Sianna, when next the Boers of South Africa lift their eapons against the English, we shall wish them better suc-ss."

Sianna frowned. "Pray God there will not be a next time," e said.

"The Germanic spirit will not remain forever in bondage," heo said. "But it is an unpleasant subject. One question, fore we abandon talk of war and move on to what we can) to entertain Cousin Canilo. I have often wondered just here one's loyalties would lie in an instance such as yours— Boer girl married to an Englishman."

"To an *Australian*," Sianna corrected.

"Well, British, shall we say? You have told me that you ere a nurse during the war. If there were to be another, ould you nurse Boers or Britishers?"

"In the last war I nursed both," she said. "When I first saw one, he was a severely wounded British officer." She did not y that he had been stripped by the natives and that she was aaware of his nationality until he first began to speak.

"Ah, you are, indeed, the wife of a diplomat," he said.

"I can tell you this, Theo," she said. "If my father, who is ler, went to war against my husband, who is Australian— , to take your point, British—I would stand in the middle d scream as loudly as I could, telling them that in order to oot each other, they would have to shoot through me."

Theo laughed and adjusted his glasses. "Well said. But per-ps, my dear Sianna, it would be better to scream—rather ietly and in a ladylike manner, of course—*before* the shoot-g starts. Let me put this question to you: If it were possible the former Boer republics to gain independence from

Great Britain in a peaceful way, would you want to aid ther
in that cause?"

She mused for a moment. "I think every people deserve t
have their own chosen form of government." She held up
hand quickly as Theo started to protest. "Now I know tha
sounds as if I'm against all colonial powers. Perhaps I shou!
say that every nation *capable* of governing itself should hav
that opportunity."

"Then you would be in sympathy with a movement f
independence in the Transvaal and the Orange River Colon
and even in Natal?"

"I think the ideal situation would be a united Boer republ
from the Cape to the Transvaal."

"And if called upon, would you aid in achieving th
ideal?"

She frowned. "What are you trying to do, Theo, recruit n
as a German spy?"

He laughed again. "I would not ask you, dear lady, to d
anything that is not honorable. I am merely asking a rhetor
cal question, out of idle curiosity." He winked. "But if, som
day, I feel that you might be of help in the cause we discusse
would you not feel kindly toward the friend who helps esta!
lish a Boer republic?"

Sianna had no time to answer, for at that moment Slor
and the old general entered the room. Buchlau said his goo
byes and left. Slone apologized for being the last to go, b
Theo insisted that he join Sianna and him in a glass of chan
pagne.

"Now, what was on our friend Buchlau's mind?" The
asked when the champagne had been poured.

Slone, in his capacity as an intelligence officer, knew th
Theobold was more than a mere military liaison man. Ge
many, like all the great nations, was developing a network
agents that extended around the world. He had worked wi
one of them, the double agent Blue Jack in New Guinea. F
knew at least half a dozen German agents in Vienna by nam

and others by sight. He and Theo had sparred verbally many times in the past two years. He decided to give Theo a tidbit.

"The general says that Germany tolerates Austria only because Austria does what Germany wants done in this part of Europe."

Theo let his pince-nez fall into his hand, his eyebrows raised. "That old fool is becoming more senile every day."

"And he warned me, Theo, that the Austro-Hungarian Empire is going to take a step in the near future that could mean war."

"Oh?" Theo's eyebrows were still raised. "And what is this step?"

"He wouldn't say," Slone said. "I thought perhaps you might know and be willing to share the knowledge with me."

"Well, I would, old boy, if I could, but I have no idea what the old fool was talking about."

Slone finished his champagne and rose. Theo saw his guests to the door, shaking Slone's hand and kissing Sianna on the cheek.

At home, in their own apartment, Sianna asked Slone to undo the snaps on her gown. They stood before a dressing mirror looking at their reflections in the mirror.

"Crikey," Slone said, "if we don't still make a handsome couple." He pulled down the opened dress, exposing Sianna's nicely developed chest. "And there's another handsome pair."

She slapped his hands away and went to the bath.

"Slone," she called out.

"Yes."

"Theo tried to recruit me as a German spy tonight."

"That's nice," he said.

She stuck her head out of the door. "That's 'nice'?"

Slone laughed. "Just what did he say?"

"He intimated that there was going to be a war and that under cover of war the Boers in South Africa would have an opportunity to become independent of England. He asked me if I'd be willing to help bring this about."

"Hmm," Slone said.

"I'm afraid I didn't sound like a good British wife," she said. "I may just have left the idea in his mind that I might be open to such a proposition if it should arise."

"Yes, good, good," Slone said, deep in thought.

"So, like Blue Jack, I'm to become a double agent?"

"We won't let it go quite that far," he said.

He was still sitting on the side of the bed deep in thought when she came out smelling of soap, dressed in a soft nightgown. She lay down, looked at his profile. So handsome. Her man. Her wild bushranger.

"Slone?"

"Umm?"

"General Buchlau told you something that is making you very pensive. Was it really that Austria is going to take some action that might cause a war?"

"The Habsburg Empire is going to annex Bosnia and Herzegovina," he said.

"I'm not even sure there is such a thing as a Bosnia and whatever," she said.

He laughed. "Buchlau said that Austria couldn't afford to annex any more of the southern peoples. He said the empire had too many useless Slavs already. But it could get serious, Sianna. Both the Austrian Empire and the Ottoman Empire are tottering, old, and weak. The Balkans are stirring. Serbia has gotten away with stealing territory from the Turks, and when Austria makes this move, God knows what will happen, because it will be a direct slap in the face to Serbia. Russia has designs on the Balkan areas, you know, and the tangle of alliances is, in my opinion, a dangerous one. In the Russo-Japanese War there was some tension between Britain and Russia because Great Britain's ally Japan was kicking hell out of France's ally Russia. But now Russia is our ally as well as France's. Sometimes it's rather difficult to remember just who is allied with whom, especially if you consider the little Balkan countries. I keep remembering what the kaiser said about some madman starting the next war in the Balkans."

"I doubt seriously that war will start tonight," Sianna said. "It's very late."

She thought for a moment. "Slone, the kaiser has also said that as long as he has alliances with two of the countries that rule the world, he is secure. And he has said that if England were one of those with which he was aligned, a mouse could not stir in Europe without the permission of Germany and Great Britain. Why is there no entente between Germany and Great Britain, between Uncle Edward and Nephew William?"

"I don't exactly move in those circles," he said, "but it's no secret that the kaiser is jealous of King Edward."

"If Boer families fought among themselves the way Queen Victoria's descendants do, the war would have been over in a few days," Sianna said.

He joined her in bed and lay there with his hands under his head, eyes open. He thought about what old Buchlau had told him and the reasons for it.

"I am not betraying my country," Buchlau had said. "It was a command decision to leak advance word of our intentions to Great Britain. We do not, you see, want you to be unpleasantly surprised. Russia is your ally, not ours, and if the Russians should get excited about our little excursion into Serbian territory, perhaps, with this advance warning, you might be able to calm them short of war."

The Balkans were an odd, tangled collection of countries: old, debilitated Greece, tiny Montenegro, vigorous Serbia, enigmatic Bulgaria and Albania, and multiracial Romania, all facing the Ottoman Empire across the Strait of Bosporus, control of which was greatly desired by the czar of Russia, which shared a common border with Romania.

There were times when Slone longed for the simplicity of life in his native Australia or even for the days of war in South Africa, for at least in the war he had known the day-to-day objective. It had been merely to kill Boers and resist being killed by Boers. In Europe he and Sianna had been put down in the middle of a cat fight in an alley. Five nations were said to rule the world: Great Britain, France, Germany, Russia, and Austria-Hungary, for to a European these old countries were *the* world. The fact that Japan had sunk the Russian fleet was deemed only an aberration from the norm. True power could not reside for long outside Europe, except, perhaps, in the ever more prying United States.

And yet it was exciting to go into the code room at the embassy each day and have reports from British agents from all over the Continent waiting for his disposition. His position in Vienna was a vital one, for it was his duty to reroute the reports, to pass along the accumulating intelligence to those who could use it, to those who had a need to know. Soon Austria was going to make a potentially unsettling move in the Balkans. Slone could feel the anticipation, the tense expectancy, and all thoughts of peaceful Australia or the "good" days of the war were washed away by the feeling that he was at the heart of things, that he would be among the first to know of any major event in Europe.

The next morning he alerted his small crew of cryptographers to the possibility of a significant occurrence within the next few days. Then he sat back to wait. It was going to be an exciting winter.